SHE'LL NEVER GET OFF THE GROUND

Robert J. Serling

She'll Never Get off the Ground

1971

Doubleday & Company, Inc., Garden City, New York

The characters and events in this
book are fictitious, and any resemblance to actual persons
is purely coincidental.

For my wife, Priscilla

". . . no pilot may execute an instrument approach procedure or land under IFR at an airport if the latest U. S. Weather Bureau Report or a source approved by the Weather Bureau for that airport indicates that the visibility is less than that prescribed by the Administrator for landing at that airport."

U. S. Federal Aviation Regulation 121.651 (a)

SHE'LL NEVER GET OFF THE GROUND

CHAPTER ONE

Mr. Horace Studebaker performed his usual double ritual before opening the door of his office that bright April morning.

He made sure his tie was straight, giving it a couple of delicate tugs, and he looked with pride through his professorial rimless bifocals at the neat if rather tiny black lettering on the opaque glass.

DEPARTMENT OF NEW PERSONNEL
Mr. Studebaker, Director

It was precisely 8:30 A.M., for Horace Studebaker was a precise man who believed that a company's official work-starting time was a Rule, and Mr. Studebaker always mentally capitalized the word "rule."

"If our airplanes are supposed to leave on schedule," he was fond of admonishing tardy underlings, "the least we can do is to report to our jobs on schedule. After all, we don't have as many problems about punctuality on the ground as we do in the air."

His occasionally tardy underlings, most of whom had to buck Los Angeles freeway traffic, privately doubted the accuracy of his analogy. Also privately, they regarded Horace Studebaker as somewhat of a pompous ass while simultaneously conceding that he was pretty damned good at his job. After all, maybe it took a pompous ass to hold down a position that involved not only the hiring of new employees for Trans-Coastal Airlines but orienting them—which meant that to Mr. Studebaker went the post-employment chore of convincing every newcomer he or she was about to enter a corporate heaven where Pride, Loyalty and Diligence invariably were rewarded by Advancement, Raises and Happiness.

"The thing about Horace that gets me," a cynical colleague once commented after observing one of Studebaker's orientation lectures, "is that he believes that crap himself."

It probably would have endeared Mr. Studebaker to his subordinates if they could have heard him complain to his wife when he got home (if only after his habitual pre-dinner double martini), "Christ, I get tired of making the same stupid speech day in and day out." He probably also would have been more popular if those who worked for him were aware that Horace Studebaker was no pompous ass away from the office. He coached, albeit badly, a Little League baseball team, he was an expert at composing extremely dirty limericks, and he was an insatiable bull in bed as his wife confessed to a few close, non-airline friends.

But, as with many men, his professional demeanor was a façade erected deliberately and sturdily around his private life. It was rather typical of him that the reason no one in his office realized he could be a hell of a lot of fun at a party was because he refused to socialize with his immediate associates.

"If I get to like someone from the office away from the office, I'll start playing favorites," he told his wife after she wondered aloud why he didn't invite anyone from New Personnel over for dinner. "Dammit, that's part of the guff I hand out at orientation—this airline promotes on ability, not favoritism. It's a bunch of bull in a few departments but, by God, not in my shop."

In truth, Studebaker was bored with the orientation lecture; he far preferred the more intimate and challenging task of interviewing new employees, particularly flight crew applicants, and he loved to write business letters. Perhaps that was why, on this particular day, he felt especially cheerful. There was no orientation lecture scheduled and, as far as he knew, his agenda tentatively called merely for cleaning up a small mountain of back correspondence.

It looked like an easy day. Horace Studebaker opened the door to New Personnel, marching by the secretarial desks placed around the big room at random like square gopher holes, and chirped brightly, "Good morning. Good morning."

He received a few nods and an occasional "Good morning, Mr. Studebaker," rather patronizingly from those who had put him in the pompous ass category—and who would have been totally surprised to know that as his sparse, tall frame strode toward his private office at the rear of the room he was busy thinking up the concluding lines to a limerick that began:

> Two nymphos who doubled as teachers
> Had bodies with peculiar features . . .

He was still trying to decide what bizarre form the features should take when he reached his office and surprised his secretary, Mary Martinez, with the warmth of his greeting.

"Mornin', Mary. You look charming today."

Miss Martinez was a striking brunette whose thin legs and huge bosom gave her the appearance of a wineglass mounted on two stems. She uttered a rather stunned "Good morning, Mr. Studebaker," and looked at her usually austere boss with veiled suspicion.

"I thought we'd get to that correspondence backlog today," he announced as he lowered himself into his small swivel chair. "I assume there's nothing else that's pressing."

"You have one new pilot applicant coming in at nine," she informed him. "Preliminary hiring interview. The one you said looked like a good prospect even without any military experience."

"Who would . . . oh, I remember. That boy from Alaska. What the devil was his name?"

"I've already pulled his file," Miss Martinez said efficiently, pointing to a brown folder on his desk. "It's right there underneath your mail. His name's Devlin. Dudney Devlin."

Studebaker glanced at the folder, nodding in remembrance at the "E" he had written himself at the top of the folder. "E" for Excellence.

"I don't recall setting up an appointment for today." He frowned. "It's not on my calendar."

"I gave you a note on it a couple of days ago," his secretary remonstrated gently. "You got a letter from him saying he was arriving a day earlier than planned because he couldn't get confirmed space on our Flight 903 from Anchorage on the twenty-fourth. You told me to wire him it was okay to move the interview up a day."

"It's not on my calendar," Studebaker began in a petulant tone that changed to apologetic as he suddenly remembered something else. "Damnation, I did tell you I'd make a note of the appointment myself. I seem to have forgotten that little chore. Well, I trust he'll be punctual."

"Want to start dictating now?"

The personnel director shook his head.

"Let's wait until I see Devlin. Shouldn't take long. I recall now how we happened to pick him. That new 737 class starting next week—we lost that Navy pilot to Western and this Devlin looked very promising. We would have accepted him sooner except for his lack of any military background. I'll have to question him on that. Don't want to lose him to the service a couple of months after he starts flying for us. He was the only really good prospect we had to fill that class vacancy."

"An awful lot of flight time," Miss Martinez commented. "More than most military pilots."

"Over four thousand hours," Studebaker agreed. "Tell you what, Mary, I'll just review his file here and if you'd be good enough to bring me some coffee, we won't worry about this correspondence until after I see our Mr. Devlin. Curious name, Dudney. Wonder if it's supposed to be Dudley?"

"Dudney's correct," Miss Martinez said. "I checked it myself. I'll go for your coffee, Mr. Studebaker."

She returned with the steaming brew which the personnel director sipped slowly, grateful for its hotness but conscious of the drawbacks of coffee dispenser machines which apparently were incapable of turning out anything that tasted stronger than hot water.

He already had read the first letter of inquiry from a Dudney A. Devlin, expressing interest in becoming a pilot with Trans-Coastal and mentioning, without any details, that the writer had amassed considerable multi-engine time. His answer had been the usual form letter sent to all applicants.

TRANS-COASTAL AIRLINES, INC.

Department of New Personnel

Dear Mr. Devlin:

Thank you for your letter of inquiry regarding employment with Trans-Coastal as a copilot. These are our current qualifications:

AGE:	Minimum age 21.
HEIGHT:	5'6" minimum, 6'4" maximum.
PHYSICAL REQUIREMENTS:	Must be able to pass the FAA First Class physical with no waivers, plus company physical.
EXPERIENCE:	Our minimum requirement is 1,000 hours in multi-engine jet or heavy transport equipment.
RATINGS AND LICENSES:	FAA Commercial License. FAA Instrument Rating and Restricted Radiotelephone Permit.
EDUCATION:	Must be a high school graduate. Preference is given to college graduates with a degree in one of the physical or exact sciences, particularly aeronautical engineering.

I am enclosing an application form. Thank you for your interest in Trans-Coastal Airlines.

Sincerely yours,
Horace Studebaker
Director, Department of New Personnel

Dudney A. Devlin
16 Bennett Avenue
Anchorage, Alaska 99502

The next entry in the file was the completed application, which Studebaker now reviewed with satisfaction. This kid had one hell of a record, even with no military time. Twenty-five years old, five-eight but only 126 pounds. Must be built like a pipe cleaner but that was no drawback. Slim pilots were supposed to be healthier and less subject to heart trouble. Eyesight 20/20 without glasses. Eyes and hair brown. Marital status: single. First-class physical with no waivers or limitations.

His FAA Flight Certificates included Commercial License 9646383, instrument-rated, plus type ratings in Cessna 180, Cessna 310, Lockheed Lodestar, DC-3, DC-4, DC-6, Lockheed Electra, and Lockheed Jetstar. Qualified flight instructor both single and multi-engine types including DC-4. Degree in Aeronautical Engineering, Arizona State University. Previous employment included first officer with Air Alaska—that was a cargo carrier, Studebaker vaguely remembered—and a pilot with Alaskan Air Taxiways, Inc. He also held an ATR—the coveted Air Transport Rating that was a license to command heavy transports. Add to this his experience with Air Alaska, a small operation, Studebaker knew, probably not more than a half dozen aircraft, which explained Devlin's high log time—4,135 hours as of the date the application was mailed, 1,097 hours of this impressive total in DC-4s, 350 in DC-6s and 148 in Electras. Not even the hot shots coming to Trans-Coastal from the Navy, Marines and Air Force could match this. Studebaker wouldn't look a second time at an application listing under 3,000 hours, but even the most experienced military pilots he was processing never logged over 4,000.

This train of thought reminded him anew that he must question Devlin on how he had managed to avoid military service—there was no record of such in the application. As a matter of fact, next to the item marked "Selective Service classification" Devlin had written "none," and after "If deferred, give reason," he had simply said "Ineligible." That was a new one to Studebaker, and an omission of facts serious enough to warrant disqualification or at least further investigation. The personnel director somehow had gotten too busy to press Devlin for further details, and when the vacancy opened up in the next Boeing 737 new pilot hirees class, the Alaskan's application was so promising that Studebaker fired a telegram authorizing an interview, thinking at the time that he could press Devlin on his draft status later.

The copy of the telegram came next in the file.

DUDNEY A. DEVLIN
16 BENNETT AVENUE
ANCHORAGE, ALASKA

WE HAVE THOROUGHLY REVIEWED YOUR QUALIFICATIONS AS A
FLIGHT OFFICER WITH OUR COMPANY AND ARE HAPPY TO INFORM
YOU WE WOULD LIKE TO ARRANGE A CONVENIENT TIME FOR A
PERSONAL INTERVIEW. IF THE DATE OF APRIL 25 AT 9 A.M. IS
SATISFACTORY PLEASE WIRE THE UNDERSIGNED COLLECT AND
WE WILL FORWARD YOU A POSITIVE SPACE PASS ON A TRANS-
COASTAL FLIGHT FROM ANCHORAGE TO LOS ANGELES.

HORACE STUDEBAKER
DIRECTOR, DEPARTMENT NEW PERSONNEL

Studebaker closed the file folder and began to open his mail, a
process interrupted by Miss Martinez, who approached his desk, a
strange look on her face. It could only be described as a mixture
of hilarity and concern, blended with disbelief, all three emotions
struggling for supremacy.

"Mr. Studebaker," she started, then stopped and shook her head
almost as if in pity for the personnel director because of what she
was about to dump on his unsuspecting head.

"Well?" demanded Horace Studebaker, annoyed at Miss Martinez'
apparently sudden loss of speech faculties.

His secretary began to giggle, which annoyed Mr. Studebaker even
further. "Come on, Mary, what's wrong? What are you laughing
at?"

She managed to straighten out her features and she stopped giggling but into her eyes came a gleam of sheer glee.

"Mr. Studebaker, that pilot applicant is here."

"So? Well, I'm delighted he's punctual. Tell him to come on in.
Mary, what in the hell is wrong with you? Has this Devlin got two
heads or something?"

Miss Martinez mustered sufficient composure to answer him
quietly.

"No, sir. Mr. Studebaker . . ."

She shook her head again.

"Mr. Studebaker, Dudney Devlin is a girl."

She sat in the interviewing chair by his desk, her clear brown eyes fixed on his flushed, uneasy face. In those eyes he read defiance, challenge, pride, yet also wariness and perhaps a tinge of pleading. She was, Mr. Studebaker conceded, a damned attractive female. She wore a smart navy-blue suit which subtly hinted at the curves underneath and her legs were just about perfect. Her closely cropped brown hair reminded him of photographs he had seen of Amelia Earhart, although the resemblance stopped there. Dudney Devlin's face would have been pretty, almost beautiful, except for a some-what pug nose that came close to looking as if it had been broken at one time. Her mouth was wide, rather sensuous with full lips and just a touch of a pale lipstick. Other than the latter, she apparently wore no make-up—not even around her eyes, which were the only incongruity to the twenty-five years of age she had listed on the application. Tiny crow's-feet flanked them, giving the impression that this area on her face had somehow been transplanted from a woman in her forties.

Yet, thought Studebaker, even these paths of imperfection provided a look of calm maturity devoid of chronological aging. Her eyes were those of a pilot's, the wrinkles formed from squinting at a thou-sand skies, and they seemed to be as much a part of her as her legs and breasts and arms. They even went with her voice, low and firm, yet still soft and feminine. The personnel director had the silly idea race through his mind that she would sound great on a cabin PA, but he brushed this heresy aside hurriedly and impaled her on what he hoped was friendly but forceful disapproval.

"Miss Devlin," he began, "I don't want to sound harsh but I think you've deceived us."

"In what way, Mr. Studebaker?" Her tone was mild and he had the uncomfortable feeling he, rather than she, was on the defensive.

"Well, you certainly didn't tell us you were a girl. Nowhere in your application . . ."

"Nowhere in the application was there any question regarding my sex," she interrupted.

"That's not the point, Miss Devlin. By, uh, implication . . . uh, you led us to believe you were a man."

"I did nothing of the sort, Mr. Studebaker. Trans-Coastal didn't ask me so I didn't volunteer the information. For obvious reasons."

"That's what I mean about deception," Studebaker said hastily, leaping at what he believed was a lowering of her guard of self-righteousness. "You knew perfectly well your sex disqualified you."

"I wasn't aware that sex had anything to do with a pilot's ability. In what way does my being a woman disqualify me?"

"Well, uh, well . . . physical strength, for one thing." Mr. Studebaker was groping frantically for arguments in an area of which he really knew little.

"I assume Trans-Coastal operates aircraft with hydraulically boosted control systems," Miss Devlin said. "There's nothing a man can do in an airplane that I can't do. Now just a minute"—Mr. Studebaker had opened his mouth and left it open as she continued—"my record speaks for itself. I've flown some pretty heavy equipment. The Electra's no Piper Cub, Mr. Studebaker."

The personnel director closed his mouth long enough to regroup his debating forces. It occurred to him that maybe a legal technicality was a better tack than a biological argument. He opened up her folder with an air of importance and took out her application.

"I agree you have considerable experience. At least you seem to. May I see your ticket?"

Wordlessly, she reached into a small briefcase that she had placed on the floor beside the chair.

"My FAA commercial and ATR tickets and this little volume is my logbook, Mr. Studebaker. I think you'll find them all in order."

He examined them with a show of thoroughness that was mostly window dressing, because he already was convinced that Dudney A. Devlin was not the type to (1) alter an FAA certificate or (2) pad a logbook. He handed them back and decided, for want of any better tactics, to be Friendly.

"Your experience is indeed unusual, Miss Devlin. I noted on your application that you left Air Alaska because of, I believe you termed it inadequate salary. May I ask what the salary was?"

"In effect, zero," Miss Devlin said calmly.

"Zero? You flew for an air cargo company without pay?"

"The president and founder of Air Alaska, up to three months ago when he passed away, was Ralph Devlin. My father."

"I see," said Studebaker, without really seeing. "I'm sorry."

"My father started the company on the proverbial shoestring, Mr. Studebaker. At first he had a couple of DC-3s and a DC-4. Later he picked up two DC-6s from American and the last plane he bought was a Western Electra. But it was tough going. When he died, we were operating only one of the DC-3s and the Electra. I checked out in everything he was using because he couldn't afford to pay pilots what they really were worth, flying cargo in that part of the world. I lived at home with Dad. There wasn't any need to pay me a salary—he clothed and fed me. He wanted to pay me but there wasn't that much money available."

"And who's operating the company now?"

"There isn't any company. I sold the last two planes to pay off all the debts after Dad died. That included what we still owed the pilots and a couple of mechanics."

"On your application you said you learned to fly in Phoenix while you were going to college."

Dudney Devlin smiled, but it was the kind of smile that was more wistful than humorous. "Officially, that's where I learned to fly. That's where I got my commercial ticket. Actually, the first plane I ever flew was one of Dad's Gooney Birds—I was fourteen. He taught me how to fly long before I went to Arizona."

"Gooney Birds?" Mr. Studebaker was a good personnel man but his aeronautical background was limited.

"Gooney Bird was a wartime nickname for the DC-3." Studebaker liked the way she supplied that bit of information, with no iota of condescension. He was warming up to this girl and he was acutely conscious that he was prolonging the interview not only because he didn't know what the hell to do about Dudney Devlin but because he actually liked her.

"Well," he ventured, "I don't mean to pry but, from your apparently limited financial resources, you must have had some difficulty getting through college."

She smiled, but again it was that sad, sweet smile with no trace of happiness. "My mother died when I was ten. She left an insurance policy that Dad refused to touch—as hard up as he was. He insisted on using it for my college education."

"How did you happen to pick Arizona State? That's a long way from Anchorage."

"Dad had a flying buddy during World War II who taught aeronautical engineering there. To be truthful, Mr. Studebaker, I didn't want to go to college and I hated most of it. I felt Dad needed me. But it was the one thing he was adamant about. Said I'd be more of a help if I had some technical background. I suppose he was right."

Horace Studebaker studied her, with a gnawing, growing feeling of frustration. He knew only too well that Dudney A. Devlin was a problem to be solved by the simple process of buck-passing. He couldn't hire her, but something told him that he couldn't reject her, either. He admitted to himself that she was about as impressive a pilot applicant, disregarding her sex, as had ever walked into his office. Well, maybe—just maybe—he could discourage her. Or, better yet, offer her an attractive alternative.

He began cautiously. "Ah, Miss Devlin, quite frankly Trans-Coastal would like very much to have you in the, ah, family, so to speak. I think we can find a place for you. A very attractive post, I might add."

"As a pilot?"

Mr. Studebaker's hopes sagged slightly.

"Well now, I'm sure you understand the difficulties of our accepting you for pilot training."

"I either cut the mustard or I don't," she said quietly. "I fail to see *your* difficulties. I'll admit it won't be easy for me, Mr. Studebaker; I'm either qualified for first officer school or I'm not. If it's the latter, I'd appreciate your telling me exactly why I'm not qualified."

"Because," he snapped with a trace of anger, "you're a woman. And there's no such thing as a woman airline pilot."

"I don't mean to deliver a lecture either on commercial aviation history or the story of women's rights, Mr. Studebaker. But you're wrong. SAS hired a woman copilot in 1969. A small French airline has at least one woman copilot. Pennsylvania Central had one in the thirties. Some of the Iron Curtain airlines have a number of women pilots. El Al has a woman instructor."

"SAS is a foreign carrier for one thing, and what a U.S. airline did in the 1930s is an entirely different matter," Studebaker refuted.

"SAS has the same operating and safety standards as any American carrier," she replied with devastating calmness. "If Trans-Coastal is worried about establishing any precedent, it already has been established."

He retreated to the Friendly strategy. "As I said earlier, Miss Devlin, there are a number of positions open to women in the airline industry and, with your considerable background, I believe I can assure you of a very fine job."

"For the sake of argument, such as?"

"I'd have to check on what's available immediately, but I might suggest you consider starting out as a stewardess. You're attractive, you fulfill all of the qualifications, you—"

"I also fulfill all of the qualifications for first officer," she said. "Except sex."

"Which isn't listed among the qualifications."

"It's implied," Studebaker pressed. "Look here, Miss Devlin, I didn't say you're not qualified for pilot training. You are. Better than most of the male applicants we get. But you know damned well that the pilots themselves would never accept a female in their cockpits."

"They've never been faced with the possibility," she said sweetly. "I won't argue your point. I'm fully aware of the handicaps. I'll be ostracized, teased, kidded, ignored, hazed and even hated. I'll have to be twice as good as a man just because I'm a woman. I may never really be accepted. But I'd still like to try."

Once more he warmed to her quiet earnestness. "And just why do you want to try? When you know how difficult it's going to be?"

For the first time, she hesitated, weighing her answer on the delicate scales that pit honesty against persuasiveness.

"It's . . . it's hard to put into words," she said finally. "It's something I've always wanted. The only job in the world that ever really appealed to me. Even . . . even when I was flying for Dad I kept wishing there were passengers aboard. People who—who trusted their lives to you. I flew for an air taxi outfit for a couple of months before Dad asked me to go back with him because he had to lay off a salaried pilot. Those two months were the happiest of my life."

"Why didn't you take up where you left off, with the air taxi company?"

"Because it's more than just the idea of carrying people. It's the planes themselves. The big birds. I remember the day Dad got the Electra. The two of us took it up, just the two of us. She handled like a fighter plane, but she was all power and strength and she didn't forgive any mistakes. I couldn't go back to small aircraft after that. I knew I had to stay with the big stuff, and that meant the airlines. Are you a pilot, Mr. Studebaker?"

"No, I'm not. I suppose—"

"Then you wouldn't know what I'm talking about. The way pilots feel. The way we feel about the sky and our planes and everyone else who flies. It's not something you can put into words, any more than you can describe the color red. It's a feeling. Like maybe you feel God without ever being able to tell what God looks like. It's a way of life, and everyone who's part of it is like . . . like they're all in a kind of fraternity."

"Fraternities," he could not resist saying, "are for men."

She did not reply but her eyes narrowed in pain as if he had unexpectedly kicked her. Studebaker had a pang of guilt.

"Look, Miss Devlin, I'm sorry I said you deceived us. I know you didn't, not really. But you could have signed your application 'Miss Devlin' or something. That damned name of yours—it could be a man's, you know. That's what misled me. Where did your family come up with a handle like that?"

"Dad's closest friend was an American Airlines captain—Dudney O'Reilly. Dad flew with American a long time ago. He promised Captain O'Reilly he'd name his first son after him. When I came along instead, he and Mother decided Dudney could be a girl's name too. So I got stuck with it. Maybe I should have told you I was a woman right from the start. But I wouldn't have gotten as far as this interview, would I?"

"No, you wouldn't," Studebaker admitted. "I rather imagine I would have told you we had no immediate openings for pilots—and

I would have filed your application away so deep even the dust would have had dust. That 'A' in your name. What's it stand for?"

"Amelia. After Amelia Earhart. Dad knew her a long time ago."

"That figures," Mr. Studebaker sighed. "You an only child?"

"Yes, sir."

"No interest in becoming a stewardess?"

"No, sir."

For some reason her use of "sir" finished off his disarmament, just as he figured he was getting the upper hand. There was no subservience in the way she said it, only a natural respect and innate discipline. Ralph Devlin must have been quite a father, Studebaker thought. Well, he wasn't going to be the one who turned this kid down. Let somebody higher up figure out a way to get rid of her. He drummed his fingers on the brown manila folder marked "Devlin, Dudney A.," swung his swivel chair to the right so he was gazing at a blank wall, then swung back to face her.

"Where are you staying?"

"The Hacienda Motel. The one on Sepulveda."

"Got enough money to live on for a couple of days?"

"Yes, sir."

"I can't pass judgment on you myself, Miss Devlin. I've got to take up your case with my superiors. Hope you understand."

He liked the way she merely nodded, with no outer show of resentment and no tendency to continue arguing. "Why don't you go back to your motel and take it easy. Let's see. It's nine thirty-five. Suppose I call you no later than 1:00 P.M. By that time I'll have had a chance to talk this . . . this, uh, situation over with the higher-ups."

She rose and put out her hand in a totally feminine way. He noticed that her handshake was firm but far from masculine. He also noticed something else. In those deep brown eyes was the faintest hint, the barest glistening, of tears. It made him a trifle angry, as if even this small display of female emotionalism was out of character for her. She seemed to read his thoughts, and her voice was boulder-steady.

"I appreciate your patience and courtesy, Mr. Studebaker. I only hope I've gotten it across that I'm no crusader for women's rights. I'm a pilot who wants to work for a good airline. Period."

Mr. Studebaker showed her to the door and watched her walk

through the personnel office to an outside corridor, convoyed all the way by stares from every secretary in the place. Miss Martinez, who apparently had spread the word, could not wait to confront her boss. Before the tall figure of Dudney Devlin disappeared outside the office, Miss Martinez was figuratively climbing the walls.

"What was she like, Mr. Studebaker? What did you tell her? How are—"

"Miss Martinez," he interrupted her sternly. "Get me Jason Silvanius."

For the first and possibly only time in her tenure as Horace Studebaker's secretary, curiosity rode roughshod over professional decorum.

"Is she going to go to work for us, Mr. Studebaker?"

Mr. Studebaker was still staring at the door through which Miss Devlin had departed. He shook his head, not in negativism but in grudging respect.

"I wouldn't be surprised, Mary. I wouldn't be a bit surprised."

Officially, Jason Silvanius was listed in Trans-Coastal's hierarchy of top executives as Vice President, Public Relations. Unofficially, he was kind of father confessor and general trouble shooter for the whole airline. Anyone who had a major problem usually took it first to Silvanius before poking an uncertain head over the next rung of the top-echelon ladder. Invariably, Jason's advice was wise, mainly because his sharp mind was uncluttered by any fears of the men who outranked him. He didn't have to be afraid; everyone at Trans-Coastal, from President Tom Berlin on down, knew that Jason Silvanius had standing offers from at least four other major airlines, at higher salaries, and he stayed with Trans-Coastal mainly because he regarded loyalty as the noblest of human virtues.

He was a thoroughly contented man in his work, and it somehow provided him with a serenity cushioning him against the inevitable corporate crises so much a part of any big company. It was not that he couldn't take anything seriously; he did, but he also surrounded every problem that crossed his desk—his or someone else's—with a fence of perspective. He never got rattled, either by situations or people, not even when faced with that hectic, horror-filled ordeal dreaded by every airline PR man, namely, a crash—a nightmare populated by insistent newsmen demanding answers, explanations and solutions before the wreckage stops burning.

It was remotely possible, however, that Jason would have preferred a non-fatal accident to the predicament Horace Studebaker dumped in his lap that morning. When Studebaker called him, Silvanius was occupied with nothing more serious than supplying three stewardesses to grace the opening session of the annual Los Angeles Automobile Show, and editing a news release prepared by an assistant announcing Trans-Coastal's purchase of three additional Boeing 727s.

"Jason? This is Horace Studebaker in New Personnel. I got a problem." Studebaker was unaware that eight out of ten intracompany phone calls to Silvanius started out in precisely the same language.

"Hi, Horace. Don't tell me somebody's applied for my job. Go ahead and hire him."

"I wish," Studebaker said glumly, "somebody had applied for mine. I'm sitting on a can of worms and I'm about to throw the whole damned can upstairs to the brass department."

"Proceed," Silvanius said placidly as he deftly pried a cigarette from a freshly opened pack and lit it—all with one hand (a trick learned in his newspaper days).

"I have on my desk a very impressive application from a very highly qualified pilot who wants to start 737 school. Name is Dudney Devlin."

"So?"

"Dudney Devlin is a girl," Studebaker blurted, his tone mixing dramatic emphasis with a note of sour foreboding.

"A girl? Hell, that's no problem, Horace. We've had a couple of female pilot applicants before. Never had any trouble finding an excuse to turn 'em down. What's so special about this one?"

"This one happens to have about four thousand hours, multi-engine, including jets. She's a better prospect than four out of five male applicants. If you can come up with an alibi for saying no, you're a genius."

"Eminently qualified, huh?"

"So eminently, Jason, that she'll nail us to the cross if we reject her and she runs to the FEPC or Equal Rights Commission. We're short of new pilots and that's all the government would need."

"She give any indication she would?"

"No. On the contrary, she doesn't sound like any damned crusader. That's what impressed me, Jason. She just left my office and she really wants to be an airline pilot. And I've got a strange feeling she'll make us one hell of a pilot."

"Maybe," Silvanius said doubtfully. "But personally I wouldn't have hired Amelia Earhart. Too many problems."

"Don't laugh, but her middle name's Amelia. Her father ran a bush cargo line up in Alaska and flew for American a long ways back. Seems he knew Lady Lindy."

"She sounds like quite a prospect," Silvanius conceded. "I guess you're right, Horace. Let me kick it further upstairs. You gonna be in your office for a while?"

"Glued, chained and shackled to this desk until I hear from you."

"Get back to you as soon as I can. By the way, she taken any of the psychological tests yet? Or a physical?"

"No on both counts. That won't be a way out, Jason. I doubt if we could flunk her on a physical if we sent her through the Mayo Clinic. And I'll lay you odds she'll grade higher on the psychological tests than I would."

Silvanius pondered this unpromising judgment before coming up with another idea. "How about tossing a Stanine at her?"

"That's not fair," Studebaker protested. "We only give the Stanine test to a marginal applicant."

"What in the hell's more marginal than a dame who wants to be an airline pilot?" Silvanius chuckled. "Be a good way to get rid of her, and all perfectly legal."

"Not as legal as you think. Most airlines have dropped the Stanine for pilot applicants, and it's no secret. My God, Jason. I heard Eastern threw it out after some smart cookie gave the Stanine experimentally to about fifty senior captains and half of them flunked it. If this gal wants to make a fight of it, she won't have much trouble discrediting a bad Stanine grade. Besides, I don't think she'd get a low grade."

"Well, I'm just trying to find you a loophole," Silvanius said. "That's all we need—just a little technicality."

"When you find one, call me."

Studebaker hung up, and Jason replaced his own phone on the hook, staring at it thoughtfully in a kind of self-mesmerism as if waiting for the inanimate object to speak up suddenly with words of wisdom. He rose and walked into his outer office where his secretary was typing letters.

"I'm going down to Mr. Berlin's office," he told her. "If anyone calls, tell 'em I'm in a meeting and you don't know when I'll be back. If it sounds important, you can call Berlin's secretary."

It was indicative of Jason Silvanius' status at Trans-Coastal that he could walk into Tom Berlin's domain unannounced at any time and—unless the president was hopelessly busy—be ushered into the latter's imposing presence almost immediately. And "imposing" was the word for both Tom Berlin and his inner sanctum. The president of Trans-Coastal was a burly bear of a man, six-three with ice-blue eyes and a bristling crew cut. There was only a suggestion of a paunch on his big frame. Until one got close to him, he resembled a retired pro football player not more than ten years away from the loud smack of shoulder pads and agonized grunts of charging linemen. Proximity destroyed the illusion, for then one could see that the ice-blue eyes were a little tired and bloodshot; the strong, craggy face was lined with the twin fatigues of age and corporate responsibility, and the youthful crew cut was an incongruous white. Then he looked his sixty-four years of age, as if each too reddish vein and furrowed wrinkle recorded one of the forty-two years he had spent with the airlines, as the rings on a tree reflect its age.

He had started out as an air mail pilot and had been president since 1937. In those earlier days he knew every Trans-Coastal pilot plus about eighty per cent of the rest of the airline's employees by their first names. Now he was a bit more dignified and aloof, although he still retained the split personality that makes up the average pilot as well as the average airline—practicality blended with idealism, toughness softened by an occasional throb of sentimentality. Most of Trans-Coastal regarded him with awe rather than affection, and only a few of the veterans knew how accurate was Jason's description of Tom Berlin: "A concrete frame, erected on a steel skeleton, to cover up a marshmallow heart."

"Send the young bastard in!" was Berlin's bellow to his secretary when she announced that the Vice President of Public Relations wanted to see him. Jason's entry into Berlin's office renewed the only twinge of envy he ever suffered at Trans-Coastal.

It was a huge room that was more like a cheerful den than an office. Seascapes in oils lined the paneled walls—Berlin loved the sea almost as much as he loved the sky and was fond of pontificating that "they have one thing in common: neither tolerates a mistake." The deep, built-in shelves on the wall directly behind the president's massive desk were filled with models of airliners, from the old M-2 to a Boeing supersonic transport painted in Trans-Coastal's green and gold colors. A big picture window overlooked adjacent Los Angeles International Airport. The thick, rust-colored carpet and soft blue drapes gave the room a touch of unobtrusive elegance, of unpretentious richness that impressed a visitor without overpowering him. Its awesome size was tempered by the president's habit of always working in his shirt sleeves.

"You picked a hell of a time to bother me," was Berlin's growled greeting. "Vic James just handed me IAM's new contract proposal."

James was the airline's Vice President, Labor Relations. Silvanius grinned as he sat down, *sans* invitation, in a chair directly facing Berlin's desk. "I take it our mechanics would like doubled wages, unlimited pass privileges, two months' vacation with pay and the keys to the executive washrooms."

"The keys are the only thing they didn't ask for. A thirty per cent wage increase, to start off with. I'm in a stinking mood, Jason, so whatever you're gonna ask me, the answer's no."

"I'm afraid in this case your answer may have to be yes. How does the thought of a woman flying for Trans-Coastal strike you?"

"Like a dose of clap on my wedding night," Berlin snapped. "Are you out of your goddamned mind?"

Silvanius shook his head. "We may have a problem, Tom. Horace Studebaker got an application from a woman pilot with around four thousand hours. If we go by the book, she's qualified for training."

"Bull," the president snorted. "Any time we can't find some small print in our book, we'd better rewrite it."

"Not this time, boss. We need 737 pilots but bad. Studebaker told me only a couple of weeks ago that we're scraping the proverbial barrel bottom for applicants. If this gal's really qualified and wants to take us before either a state or federal equal employment rights outfit, we're dead. Anyway, maybe it's not such a bad idea."

"You're nuts. A broad in the cockpit? The pilots wouldn't stand for it and neither would the public. Hell, I'd get off an airplane myself if I saw some damned skirt sitting in that right seat."

"I don't deny there'd by problems, Tom. But I'm afraid it's a decision every airline will have to face sooner or later. They're all getting applications from women. So far, nobody's managed to get through pre-training screening. But that won't last forever. Some gal's gonna pass everything they throw at her and a carrier will have to hire her. From what Horace tells me, our young lady may be just the one who opens the door."

Berlin lit a dirigible-sized cigar and puffed on it angrily rather than meditatively. "Let some other airline be the guinea pig, Jason. We got enough troubles without taking on another headache voluntarily."

Silvanius peered through the blue cigar smoke swirling around the president's head. He loved the old man but devoutly wished Hall Luther, Trans-Coastal's physician, could talk him into giving up those fat-bellied weeds that smelled like burning engine oil. He could not stifle a cough before replying, "I'm afraid we may already be the guinea pig, Tom. As I said, if this kid's qualified we might have to take her on."

Berlin took the cigar out of his mouth, not through any awareness of his public relations director's suffering but because the smoke was getting too thick even for him. He looked at Silvanius sharply, cognizant that Jason's advice was seldom off course. His respect for Jason was enormous, almost the equivalent of his affection for the younger man. Berlin was widower and childless, and Jason Silvanius was the closest he had ever come to a father-son relationship. It was Berlin who had sold the Board of Directors on elevating the post of public relations director into a vice presidency. He had given the Board plenty of valid, logical and antiseptically corporate reasons, even citing Jason's physical appearance as partial justification—an appearance that included such vice-presidential attributes as slightly graying temples, neatly pressed suits and conservative but fashionable ties.

"Dammit, he even *looks* like a vice president," he had rasped to the Board in his only illogical justification. What Berlin never admitted to himself on his future plans for Silvanius (probably because it was buried deep in his subconscious) was the natural desire of a father to pass on a business heritage to a son. In the back of Tom Berlin's wily mind was a notion that Jason Silvanius wouldn't make a bad successor when he decided to retire.

"You figure we're hooked?" Berlin mused.

"Very possibly. Of course she might do badly in the psychological testing or even the physical. But Horace says not to count on it. Besides, public relationswise it might not be a bad idea. To be the first airline that breaks the sex barrier in the cockpit, so to speak. Remember, Tom, we had some opposition within the company on hiring Negro pilots. But we've got five of them now and they've worked out well. It's like diving into cold water—once we're in, it's not as bad as we expected. Anyway, forty per cent of our passengers are women, if you'll excuse my bringing up the public relations aspects again. For that matter, hiring doesn't mean she'll be flying for us. She might never make it through training."

"I still think it's a lousy idea," Berlin said, putting the cigar back in his mouth and chomping on it hard as if he were attacking Jason's arguments with his teeth. "It's a lousy idea even if we include public relations. Suppose she does get through training. Then our troubles are just beginning. Men won't accept a woman pilot. Christ, Jason, they've never accepted women drivers. And women won't buy a female up front either. They go for that father image. Who the hell wants a mother image in that cockpit when things get hairy?"

"I repeat, forty per cent of airline passengers are women and we'll get a lot of mileage out of our enlightened policies."

"We'll also get a lot of static from the other sixty per cent—and maybe about half your distaff side you're so bloody sure of. No, sir, boy, we're begging trouble."

"Passenger acceptance won't be much of an argument at an FEPC hearing," Jason reminded him solemnly. "I'm just suggesting we hire her—and I'll handle *that* announcement personally. The odds are against her ever flying a trip. You know damned well a flight instructor could wash out Lindbergh if he wanted to."

Berlin scowled, but the scowl was accompanied by a sigh. "Tell you what, Jason. Have Studebaker run her through all the tests and Doc Luther can give her a real bastard of a physical—son of a bitch, I'll tell him to flunk her if she has only one tit. If she gets through all this, I'll have John Battles talk to her. The chief pilot's got the last say in hiring new pilots, anyway. Hell, he could turn down an applicant for something as nebulous as wrong attitude—which is probably what this stupid dame's got in the first place. Yeh, that's what we'll do, Jason. If Battles okays her I'll have to go along. I trust Johnny's judgment on any pilot—including one who menstruates. Then I'll just sit here and pray she washes out of training."

Silvanius was amused. "Johnny Battles won't be much of an obstacle compared to some of our line captains when and if she starts flying trips. I was just thinking of somebody like Crusty Callahan."

Berlin chuckled, in a nasty sort of way. "Yeh, that would be the day, when she drew Crusty in the left seat. I can just hear his opening line."

"Opening line?"

"Yep. It'll be 'Gear up, bitch!' "

The female half of that prediction was in her room at the Hacienda Motel, imprisoned by her thoughts and a silent telephone she wished would ring.

Dudney Devlin turned on the much-used television set and watched an old rerun of an Andy Griffith show, grateful for the escapist diversion offered by Sheriff Taylor and his bumbling deputy, Barney. A soap opera followed and she snapped off the set. She lay down on the bed, staring up at the ceiling without seeing anything, her mind a kaleidoscope of shifting reflections and memories and concerns.

She wondered if she had impressed Mr. Studebaker or merely irked him because she represented an annoyance, as frustrating and exasperating as a head cold. She *thought* she had handled herself well. Firm, but not too forward. She dreaded being taken for a belligerent suffragette and she had tried hard not to give the impression of a carping lobbyist for women's rights. She knew what she was facing in the way of male prejudice and intolerance. She even, if only to herself, agreed with it to some extent—enough so that if she had been in Studebaker's shoes she probably would have halfway resented the whole dilemma. It was typical of Dudney Devlin to look at virtually any given situation through what amounted to a man's eyes. Fault or virtue, and probably a little bit of both, it was the product of the relationship she had had with her father. He had given his daughter the kind of affection usually bestowed on a son, affection tempered by sternness and discipline, and he also had relied on her, even leaned on her, as a father does with a son he can trust and respect.

The death of his wife brought Ralph Devlin as close to his daughter as sweat on skin. With any other family it could have developed into that unnatural, uneasy relationship in which the daughter must try to substitute for the departed wife. Devlin was wise enough to know the perils and pitfalls of such stagnation, and he deliberately went in the other direction—making her more of a business partner than an immature homemaker trying to fill the void that death had carved into Ralph Devlin's heart. Yet he also was sage enough not to mold her completely into the image of a son. He let her retain her femininity in their predominantly masculine environment by the simple process of never letting her forget she was a woman. He insisted on her changing from the jeans she invariably wore during the day to a dress at every evening meal they had together; he observed such proprieties as holding her chair before she sat down and lighting her cigarette—except when he was preoccupied with business worries—and while he always seemed to be teetering on the precipice of bankruptcy, he still managed to dredge occasional clothing money for her out of his frayed finances.

Even in his loneliness for his wife and his reliance on Dudney for companionship, he insisted on her dating normally, although this phase of her young womanhood was not exactly a period filled with passionate nights and straining young bodies. She was too busy falling in love with airplanes to waste time on infatuations with mere men. Boys her age seemed hopelessly immature and silly; besides, none of them knew how to fly. Most of her social life involved pilots working for her father. She learned a hell of a lot about aviation this way but little about sex and men in general, for the pilots had too much respect for (and in a few cases, fear of) Ralph Devlin to attempt seduction of his daughter. They treated her more like a younger sister, told her filthy jokes, teased her unmercifully and taught her all they knew about flying.

She came home after her first year at Arizona State and told her father frankly that she was no longer a virgin. She had succumbed to the sheer masculinity of a football player, abetted by the aphrodisiac effects of four martinis. Ralph Devlin painted a tolerant smile on his face, quelled a natural paternal urge to murder the aforementioned football player and calmly discussed her introduction to sex.

"You pregnant, Dud?"

"No, Dad."

"This may seem like a heartless question, but did you enjoy it?"

"Very much. I was surprised how much. I was beginning to wonder if I had lesbian leanings."

"Good," he had chuckled as she looked surprised. "There's nothing wrong or immoral about enjoying sex, Dud. Someday you'll get married and find that it's a very important part of a happy life—not the only part or even the major part, but damned important. And I'm glad you told me the way you did—right out in the open where we can talk about it."

"I take it you'd like to talk about it further."

"Yep. Talk, not preach. Okay?"

"Okay."

"Couple of things I want you to think about." He had lit his pipe, a habit of his when he was trying to choose the right words and needed a little time to make sure his tongue would do justice to his mind. "First, I'm damned glad you're a perfectly normal young woman with normal desires. And I'm not going to hand you a bunch of do's and don'ts—you're a big girl. Just one bit of advice and one favor. Make it two favors."

Impulsively she reached out and took his big hand as he continued.

"Dud, sex gets people into trouble if their motives for sex differ too much. You go to bed with a guy because you love him, and he goes to bed with you just because he's horny, then you got built-in trouble. That's the way you can get hurt. His motive was different from yours. My advice, little gal, is simple. If you can, make sure you're going to have sex with a man for the same reason he wants to have sex with you. Read me?"

"Kind of. A bit oversimplified, isn't it? A guy can give you a phony reason for wanting sex."

"Granted. I'm not laying down any hard and fast rule. Life's like flying an airplane, Dud. You can operate any plane with a set of fine rules, but now and then you'll hit a situation the rule book doesn't quite cover. So you may have to bend the rule a little, or improvise, or maybe just ignore it, depending on common sense and judgment. Same thing's true in our relationships with other people. We can have the equivalent of rules and regulations—code of ethics, sense of values, even religious principles if you want. Whatever you decide is going to be your personal FARs, stick with them but be prepared to modify them if you have to. Christ, Dud, I'm getting philosophical."

"I like it," she had told him, squeezing his hand. "I like the way we can talk things out, Dad."

"Good. Now about those favors . . ."

"Ask and you shall receive."

"Watch the booze, Dud. A goddamned fink can look like Gregory Peck to a gal with a few drinks under her belt."

"Affirmative."

This time he squeezed her hand. "Dud, promise me if some bastard you don't love ever gets you pregnant, tell me about it. So you won't do anything foolish."

"Promise."

"That's all I need to hear. Now then, Dudney Amelia Devlin, we just changed number two engine on the Gooney. How about a little test hop? Just the two of us."

The two of them had charged out of the house like a couple of kids.

Flying was the summit, the peak, the epitome of their relationship. He had first let her handle the controls of a plane when she was eight, and he had started formal instruction six years later. He was a fair but ruthlessly tough teacher, capable of bringing tears to her eyes with anger that somehow never spilled over into impatience. He would correct her mistakes quietly—the first time. A repeat performance would draw a firm reprimand and if she made the same error a third time he would take over the controls, land the plane and make her write the correct procedure twenty times, longhand, in "Dudney's Dumb-Dumbs"—a notebook he had bought her in which to record her aeronautical transgressions.

She still had that notebook with her, crammed at the last minute into the bottom of her rather dilapidated suitcase along with a framed photograph of Ralph Devlin taken a year before his death. He had inscribed it: "To My Copilot Dudney from Her Father, the Captain."

Dudney Devlin was thinking of her father right now, aching with those memories of sweet sadness and sad sweetness that are the heritage a loved one leaves behind. Most of all she remembered, with an inner chill that almost approached nausea, the day he died. How he looked, gray and tired and sick, when he landed the Electra after a long flight from Seattle and Vancouver. He had just gotten over the flu and shouldn't have flown the trip, but Dudney had had a bad cold, two of his three pilots were hauling mining equipment in the DC-3 and he needed the revenue. His copilot was green, the youthful flight engineer even greener, and he had taken on about eighty per cent of the cockpit workload himself.

When Dudney saw him that night he seemed like an old man. At four the next morning, chest pains racked his burly frame. He died while she was phoning a doctor and there was no peace on his worn, still face—only the accumulated fatigue of too many hours wrestling danger in Alaskan storms and too many days of worrying on the ground.

In sorting out his effects, she came across his old American Airlines uniform. She could not bring herself to bury him in a business suit—somehow it seemed sacrilegious for a man who had loved the sky and the silver birds that thundered and screamed into its embrace. Flying for his own airline, he invariably had worn an ancient flight jacket too disreputable for a funeral, so Dudney had the old uniform cleaned and pressed. This was what she ordered the undertaker to put on the body. Even though the silver wings were tarnished, the braid on the sleeves faded and the cuffs frayed with age, she honestly believed it made him look younger and more at peace.

Fraternity of pilots, she was thinking now. That peculiar, intangible, elusive esprit de corps among airmen. That common denominator binding them together—sentimentality occasionally peeking through their masks of cynicism and fatalism. Maybe the uniform was a corny touch, but it was more the instinct of an airman than of a daughter that moved her to make the gesture. It was a pilot's farewell, not a woman's, and strangely enough it was this impulse that suddenly turned her rather vague dreams about the airlines into solid ambition. Not the uniform bit itself, but the reflective aftermath when she realized how beholden she was emotionally as well as professionally to civil aviation.

She had never even discussed the airline business with her father, committed as she was to his own troubled, shoestring operations. But when he died she knew she could not stay in Alaska even if his airline had been on solid financial ground. They had been too long dependent on each other and if his death brought terrible grief it also brought a kind of emancipation. Flying was her life, her love and her profession and the airlines were the ultimate and only goal she sought in fulfillment. She wanted no more part of Alaska—the void left by Ralph Devlin hurt too much—and besides, it was not even much of a challenge. She felt any flying job she took there would have been offered more in deference to her father than in acknowledgment of her own skills.

Every pilot she knew had at first scoffed at her announced intentions and then seriously tried to talk her out of applying to Trans-Coastal. Part of her resistance to their opposition, admittedly, was the recoil and resentment of sheer femininity. At any rate, even Sam Macklin, her favorite confidant among her father's pilots, caved in when she asked him pointedly, "Don't you think Dad would have been proud of me if I make the grade?"

"I guess he would have flown down to L.A. and pinned on your wings himself," Macklin had said gruffly. "But dammit, Dud, I also think he would have first taken you across his knee and walloped the hell out of you for even thinking about becoming an airline pilot."

"To all intents and purposes, I *am* an airline pilot," she had told Sam. "I'm just shifting from Air Alaska to Trans-Coastal. Cargo to passengers."

Her choice of Trans-Coastal was a matter of pure happenstance. The airline flew two daily flights into Anchorage and Dudney was looking aimlessly out of a window in her father's old office when a TCA 720 cut across her vision as it landed. Might as well start with them as anybody else, she had thought, and looked up Trans-Coastal's home office address that very afternoon.

Right now that afternoon seemed like a couple of hundred years away. She was scared, homesick and lonely and her self-confidence was evaporating like fog under a hot morning sun. On impulse, she reached into her still unpacked suitcase and dredged out her father's picture. Being a woman, she half expected it would open the faucets of some well-needed female tears. But when she looked at the image of Ralph Devlin, his thin, strong lips in a half-smile and his shaggy, unruly gray hair looking as if the wind was even then ruffling it with rough but affectionate fingers, she felt not sadness but closeness.

She was still gazing at the photograph when the telephone by her bed startled her with its rude, harsh jangle.

"Yes?"

"Miss Devlin," said the voice of Horace Studebaker, "if you'd be so good as to come right over, I've been told to start you on your psychological tests. And you're scheduled for a first-class physical at 3:00 P.M."

CHAPTER TWO

Never in her life had she quailed at the thought of a test—not in school nor in flying. Even before her first solo, she had exhibited more excitement than nervousness. Ralph Devlin, in fact, had been far more uptight than his eager daughter and it was Dudney who finally said, "Relax, Dad, there's nothing to worry about."

Now, however, she was ashamed and annoyed at the way her heart was pounding as she sat in a room adjoining New Personnel, awaiting the psychological testing. It didn't help much that Mr. Studebaker had seemed nervous too, fluttering around her with such admonitions as "Now, you'll find these tests very easy—nothing difficult about them" in that falsely soothing tone a doctor uses before committing a patient to potentially fatal surgery. She was too jittery herself to realize that Studebaker's paternalism was a matter of intense significance—he really wanted her to pass.

He had ushered her into the testing room and introduced her to Miss Frances Gillespie, the test monitor, with the air of a man confiding a state secret. "She's to take the, uh, pilot psychologicals"—sucking on the word "pilot" with special and absolutely unnecessary dramatic emphasis. Miss Gillespie already knew all about Dudney Devlin via the New Personnel gossip network, which was twenty-five per cent faster than a prison grapevine. She merely nodded with such unconcern that Mr. Studebaker was vastly disappointed.

Once the director of New Personnel had retreated to his own office, Miss Gillespie said simply with open friendliness, "Just have a seat," and pointed to one of the classroom-type wooden chairs with a writing armrest. Dudney felt as if she had been returned via time machine to grammar school, and sat down meekly. She was the only one undergoing testing, and she could not determine whether this should be reassuring or ominous. She decided it was more of the latter, but being Ralph Devlin's daughter, the expression she wore for the benefit of Miss Gillespie was one of unruffled composure.

"There are four tests," the monitor said. "Here's the first one. I'll give you five minutes to read the instructions, then I'll tell you when to start. Note the time limit for each test. It's ten minutes for the first and five minutes for the other three. Try to answer as many questions as possible. Any questions?"

Dudney, examining Test One—"Employee Aptitude Survey, Numerical Ability"—shook her head. It didn't look too bad. There were five sample problems with the correct answers supplied. The instructions advised that on the back of the sheet were seventy-five numerical problems, divided into three parts. She had two minutes for the first part and four minutes for each of the other two.

"I'm ready," she told Miss Gillespie, who went back to her desk, looked at her wristwatch as she waited for the second hand to sweep to 12, and nodded at the applicant. "Start."

Dudney's nervousness seemed to dissipate the very second she turned over the page. Math had never given her any particular trouble and she sailed through twenty-three of the twenty-five problems in Part One before Miss Gillespie's "Time—start Part Two" broke into her concentration. Part Two was considerably harder and well merited the additional two minutes, while Part Three—subtraction, addition, multiplication and division of fractions—was a mental obstacle course inasmuch as she hadn't worked with fractions for years. The nervousness returned as she struggled with $1\frac{1}{2} \times 4\frac{1}{4}$, $5\frac{1}{2} + 4\frac{1}{4}$ and a few others challenging her too dim memory of how to work fractions.

Because she had a methodical, meticulous mind, she resisted the temptation to sprint ahead to any problem that looked easier than the one on which she was struggling. She did the best she could, got through only nine of the last twenty-five and frowned miserably as Miss Gillespie called time and picked up her test paper. Dudney stifled the urge to ask how she was doing and lit a cigarette while the monitor handed her Test Two—"Visual Pursuit."

The back sheet of "Visual Pursuit" involved a bewildering maze of lines between two columns of letters. The trick was to start with a letter in the right column and follow the maze through to the correct letter in the left column. The sheet resembled the schematic wiring circuitry of an IBM computer and there were only five minutes given. Dudney worked carefully, traced eleven lines to what she prayed were the right destinations and felt ten years older when Miss Gillespie looked up from her watch and said—this time with unnecessary loudness—"Time."

"Space Visualization" was next—a series of lettered blocks, each the same size and shape. Her task was to look at each block and tell how many other blocks in the pile it touched. It was easier than "Visual Pursuit" and by the time Miss Gillespie's second hand had spun around to five minutes Dudney had solved (she hoped) six of the ten blocks.

"Last one," Miss Gillespie announced cheerfully. "Want to take a little break before you start?"

Dudney nodded gratefully, her mind weary from the strain of concentration and the tension of not knowing whether she was performing well, poorly or just adequately. She lit another cigarette and thought how good a chilled double martini would taste right now. She decided she might as well get the whole thing over with, put out the cigarette after a half dozen drags and told the monitor she was ready for the final test.

Test Four, "Symbolic Reasoning," appealed to her logical mind and in the allotted five minutes she raced through twenty-one of the thirty problems in which she had to decide whether each stated conclusion was definitely true, definitely false or impossible to determine definitely on the basis of the statement. Sample: A is larger than B which equals C, therefore A equals C. Or, A is not smaller and so is equal to or larger than B which is not equal and so is larger or smaller than C. Therefore A is larger or smaller than C.

Like nine hundred and ninety-nine out of every one thousand Trans-Coastal pilot applicants, she finished the testing with the firm conviction it had been grossly unfair, totally unconnected with either intelligence or flying ability, and obviously concocted by a borderline psychotic whose mother had once been raped by a pilot. She kept this opinion to herself, however, dutifully picked up her bag and left the testing room after Miss Gillespie politely instructed her to go to Mr. Studebaker's office.

He was so affable that for a moment she had a woman's wary suspicion of ulterior motives. Mr. Studebaker didn't look like the seducer type, she decided, purely on the basis of feminine intuition, and smiled back at him out of sheer gratitude that the testing was over.

"Had lunch yet?" he asked solicitously.

"No, I came right over after you called. I'm not really hungry." She was half afraid he was going to ask her to lunch and half afraid he wasn't, because she always hated to eat alone.

"There's an employees' cafeteria in the building right next to this one. Food's nothing fancy but it's passable. You should eat something, Miss Devlin. Don't want you fainting at your physical this afternoon, now, ha-ha." His little laugh would have sounded false and patronizing except that Dudney sensed he was trying, in his own pompous way, to put her at ease. Maybe she should eat something, she thought, even though she was far more tired than hungry.

"I'll just get a bite," she said. "When do you want me back?"

"Oh, let's say about thirty minutes. That give you enough time?"

"Plenty, Mr. Studebaker."

"Fine. When you get back I'll take you on the tour we give all new applicants. A look at your future surroundings, as it were. Provided you're hired, of course." The last was uttered hastily as the stern, professional side of Horace Studebaker took over momentarily, as if he had been reminded belatedly that all new applicants were to be treated alike—"with friendly firmness," as his own manual stated.

The cafeteria was a place of mausoleum gloom, located in a remodeled hangar and giving diners the impression that a plane was to be rolled in at any moment for an eight-thousand-hour overhaul. At one end of the room, beyond the steam tables, was the mockup of an airliner cabin, erected on a tall wooden frame and used—as Dudney found out later—for stewardess emergency evacuation training during non-eating periods. The structure was one more jarringly incongruous note of décor in the rather dingy cafeteria, all of which depressed her. It was bad enough to eat alone, listening to the chatter of mechanics, office workers and what must be a stewardess class—a dozen attractive girls dressed identically in green coveralls.

Dudney lackadaisically picked out a tired-looking tuna fish salad plate, a single roll and coffee. She found a long table occupied by a couple of rather elderly women and sat down to eat, uncomfortably conscious of their curious stares. She was afraid they would ask her if she were a new employee, a question that would inevitably lead to "What department?" and she didn't feel like stunning them with the answer, "I'm going into pilot training." She wondered if there were any flight crew trainees in the room but there seemed to be an absence of young men. She did notice two Trans-Coastal copilots eating together, the three gold stripes on their dark green uniforms so shiny that she assumed they must be fairly new. Somehow the glimpse of the airmen made her feel better, as if they had injected sudden familiarity into an atmosphere of uncertainty. She even had an urge to walk over and introduce herself, but the urge died even as it was born in her brain. They'd probably think she was some kind of nut, and even as she arrived at that probable appraisal, a feeling of dejection, a loss of self-confidence, enveloped her like a clammy fog.

She was back in Studebaker's office a scant twenty minutes after she had left, the tuna fish salad resting in her belly with all the comfort of an undigested rock. The director of New Personnel greeted her with a smile so broad and bright it came close to emitting light.

"Well now, I have some good news for you, Miss Devlin," he said with such enthusiasm she would not have been surprised if he had thrown his arms around her. "Good news, indeed. We ran your tests through the grading computer. Excellent, Miss Devlin, excellent results."

Her own face brightened so perceptibly that Studebaker was afraid he might have shown too much enthusiasm. "Of course, that's only the first stage, Miss Devlin. There's still your physical of course. And then an interview with Captain Battles, our chief pilot, either late this afternoon or first thing tomorrow."

She was quick to grasp what the latter would mean. "This Captain

Battles, Mr. Studebaker. Will he have the final say? Whether I'm accepted for pilot training?"

"That's what Jas—Mr. Silvanius, our public relations vice president, tells me. It seems he talked to our president, Mr. Berlin, about you and apparently they're . . . very sympathetic toward your . . . ah . . . ambitions."

"What's he like?" Dudney asked with feminine directness.

"Mr. Berlin? A very fine—"

"Not Mr. Berlin. Captain Battles."

Studebaker looked at her sadly. "Tough, I believe, is the word that best describes him. Very tough."

For no good reason she grinned and it was infectious.

"I rather expected as much," she said. "Or they wouldn't have left it all up to him. I take it I may be eaten alive."

"I'll say this much for John Battles," Studebaker responded soberly. "He's tough but he's fair. If he turns you down it'll be because he honestly doesn't think you'll make the grade. Don't expect any softness from him because you're a woman."

"I expect the opposite," Dudney smiled. "I figure he'll be harder on me *because* I'm a woman."

"That may be," Studebaker admitted unhappily. "You're a problem, Miss Devlin. A hot potato that's been tossed around all day until you finally wind up in the hands of a man who's used to hot potatoes. Let me put it this way: assuming you qualify in every technical sense, Captain Battles has the authority to reject you on other grounds. Such as attitude. Such as his believing that the presence of a woman in a pilot training class would be disruptive and unfair to the other trainees. Such as his being convinced a woman lacks the physical strength to be an airline pilot. Such as his being concerned over the effect a woman in the cockpit would have on our passengers. Such as his worrying about what effects your . . . uh . . . unusual status would have on non-flight deck personnel. Including stewardesses."

"You told me he was fair," she said quietly. "That's all I ask."

"Good, and I'm sure he will be. Now, Miss Devlin, you have about an hour before you see Dr. Luther. Suppose we go on that little tour."

"That little tour" consumed most of the hour and Dudney Devlin was convinced they had covered at least five miles in that time. She was shown classrooms for stewardess training, Mr. Studebaker pointing with patent pride and obvious motives to the bright, attractive cosmetics instruction room and the mockups for learning meal and liquor service. He lingered so long in the stewardess department that Dudney knew he would have been overjoyed if she had done a 180-degree turn and announced her intention of becoming a stewardess. She was properly and politely impressed but also a little amused when she suggested she'd like to see the pilot training center and Mr. Studebaker's face fell just a trifle.

There were no new pilot classes in progress, so Dudney had a chance to peek in on the classrooms, noting with interest the big, two-dimensional panels that were the schematic reproductions of jet systems—engines, electrical, controls, fuel, pressurization and landing gear. The brief glimpse not only fascinated her but gave her the same sense of delectable anticipation that a child enjoys in a toy department before Christmas. Yet simultaneously she felt a stir of resentment that the unknown, menacing quantity called Battles actually had the power to bar her from this world. The feeling was so strong that she abruptly, almost tartly told Studebaker she had seen enough. Wordlessly he escorted her out of the building toward the main maintenance hangars.

The familiar sight of airplanes in their disarrayed state of inspection and overhaul, like women in the early stages of dressing for dinner, restored her good mood. She noticed the well-posted signs reading DO NOT BRING FOOD OR DRINKS INTO THIS HANGAR: it reminded her of the time her father had been pestered by a mysterious rattle in one of their DC-3s. He never located the source until on a hunch he opened up a cabin ceiling panel and found an empty soft drink bottle left by some careless mechanic during a lunch break.

She related the incident to Studebaker, who laughed rather mirthlessly. He was one of those airline officials who would have died before confessing that he really hated airplanes and anything connected with them, including even humorous anecdotes. To him, the sight of the 737 and the 720B now being torn down in the hangar merely brought home their frailty and the incredible complexity of so many parts that could go wrong. To Dudney, the identical sight nurtured awe and pride; an airliner parked in the confines of even the biggest hangar took on new dimensions of size and power and imposing strength. Studebaker would gladly have left after the briefest of walk-throughs but Dudney insisted on walking around each plane several times, like an inquisitive puppy exploring a new back yard.

He finally got her to leave by reminding her that the appointment for the physical was only fifteen minutes away. He escorted her to the door of the medical department, opening it but not entering himself. "Call me when you're finished. Dr. Luther will have my number and by that time I'll know if Captain Battles will see you this afternoon."

"Thank you, Mr. Studebaker. I appreciated the tour."

He waved his farewell and she stepped inside, immediately confronting a nurse who asked, "May I help you?" with the same inflection she would have used saying, "What are you going to bother me with at this late hour?"

"I'm Dudney Devlin. I have an appointment with Dr. Luther."

"Devlin?" The nurse's eyebrows went up to half-staff and she peered at Dudney as an entomologist would examine an impaled bug. "Oh yes, Devlin." She spoke the name in a kind of snort. "Have a seat. The doctor will be right with you."

Dudney sat down in the rather large waiting room, picking up an ancient issue of *Life* and idly wondering why no doctor's office seemed to have a magazine less than two months old. She was just getting engrossed in it when a high-pitched voice interrupted. "Miss Devlin, I'm Dr. Luther."

The voice went with the person. The doctor was small, dapper and rather intense. He looked at Dudney Devlin in the same way his nurse had, but with a great deal more respect and even a touch of wryness.

"So you're the young lady who wants to be a pilot," he chuckled as she rose.

The chuckle bothered her.

"I'm already a pilot," she said in the same level, no-nonsense voice which had impressed Mr. Studebaker. "I'd like to become an airline pilot."

"Touché," the doctor said with a grin. "Well, I've been told to give you the works so let's get on with it."

Medically speaking, the works was what she got. For more than two hours he poked, probed, questioned and examined. Electrocardiograms, X rays, eye charts and a little soundproof booth where her hearing was tested—various sound frequencies at which she was to raise her hand the second they became audible.

Her head, face, neck and scalp were checked. Ditto nose, sinuses, mouth, throat, heart, eardrums, pupils, lungs, chest, breasts, abdomen, viscera, teeth, anus, rectum, mobility of limbs, vascular system, spine, skin, vagina and lymph glands. Blood pressure, urinalysis, red blood cells, white blood cells, hemoglobin, serology, sedimentation rate and cholesterol count. Color vision, depth perception and medical history—"Have you ever had allergy, amoebic dysentery, appendicitis, arthritis, asthma, backache, back injury, bone or joint injury, bronchitis, cancer, chronic cough, convulsions or fits, diabetes, epilepsy, gallstones, heart disease, hernia, hives, jaundice, kidney disease, lung disease, malaria, menstrual trouble, nervous breakdown, paralysis, pleurisy, pneumonia, rheumatic fever, scarlet fever, serious injury, skin disease, surgical operations, tuberculosis, ulcer of stomach or intestine, varicose veins or venereal disease?"

She liked him for not getting obviously cute or funny—refraining, for example, from remarking, "I never had to ask a pilot this before," when he questioned her on her menstrual periods.

"I just want to know if they're regular," he said.

"Very. Every twenty-eight days."

"Any particular problems? Heavy bleeding? Severe cramps?"

"Normal flow. Mild cramps."

"Ever fly with cramps?"

"Frequently."

"Bother you much?"

"No, sir."

"Has your period ever necessitated your taking time off from your job or school?"

"Never."

"Is your sex life normal?"

"Depends on what you mean by normal. I like men in a physical sense."

"Would you say you have intercourse frequently, occasionally or rarely?"

"Rarely, I suppose. Would five times since I lost my virginity—which was seven years ago—be considered rarely, occasionally or frequently?"

She said it without any note of resentment at his prying and he liked her for her own directness and honesty. "I'd classify it as rarely—and rare," he smiled. "I want it clearly understood, Miss Devlin, I'm not trying to disqualify you on the grounds of a rather limited sex life. I'm drawing up a total clinical picture and your sexual attitudes are a part of that picture."

She smiled too. "I imagine my attitudes might be described as extremely choosy, Doctor, if the rarity aspect bothers you."

"Not at all. And I appreciate your frankness. I've had stewardess applicants squirm at questions on menstrual difficulties and I had one girl slap my face when I asked her if her periods were regular."

"At no time have I felt like slapping your face, Doctor," she said with that sweet smile with which she had disarmed Mr. Studebaker. And, as had Studebaker, Luther also warmed to her.

"I apologize for putting you through a medical torture rack, Miss Devlin. I suspect you're well aware I was told to flunk you if I found the least thing wrong . . . the barest hint of some weakness or deficiency. And we've rushed through your lab tests and X rays so we could give you an immediate verdict."

"I don't blame them," she said. "I know I've created something of a problem. I would like to know right now if you did."

"If I did?"

"Find anything wrong."

He looked at the entries on the medical forms he had been filling out for the past two hours.

Blood pressure sitting: sys. 140 dias. 80 . . . standing: (3 mins) sys. 130 dias. 72 . . . recumbent: sys. 136 dias. 72 . . . pulse sitting: 64, after exercise: 72, 2 mins after exercise: 64, recumbent: 64, after standing 3 mins: 64 . . . red blood cells five million . . . hemoglobin 14.5 grams . . . white cells 5–10,000 . . . sedimentation rate 10 . . . serology and chest

X ray negative . . . specific gravity urine 1,018, zero sugar, albumin and microscopic . . . vision 20/20 right, 20/20 left . . .

He put the sheaf of papers in a folder. "Not a damned thing, Miss Devlin. Not a thing. You're as healthy a specimen as it has been my privilege to examine in many a month. In spite of the fact that we threw you a hell of a curve."

She looked the question without asking verbally.

"You showed me your first-class FAA physical ticket, still very much valid. By all rights, I shouldn't have had to give you any more than the same medical examination we give any new applicant, including pilots with the same ticket you have. What I just ran you through, young lady, was the FAA's first-class physical all over again with a few little addenda of my own. Congratulations. Or commiserations—you may wind up wishing I *had* found something wrong."

"You may be right, Doctor. But that's *my* problem."

"Anything more I can do for you? God knows, there's nothing else I can do *to* you."

"Mr. Studebaker said I was to call him when you finished with me. If you'd give me his extension . . ."

"I'll dial it myself." He was about to dial when his nurse entered.

"Miss Devlin," she said, "Mr. Studebaker called a little while ago with a message. He said Captain Battles will see you tomorrow morning at ten unless you hear differently—and you can go back to your motel whenever you're through here. And, Doctor, he wants you to phone him after Miss Devlin leaves."

"That answers my question," Dudney said. "Good-by, Doctor, and thanks for the good news."

He waited for her to leave before he reached Horace Studebaker. "Doc Luther, Horace. You can tell the brass hats I struck out. If there's a medical reason for flunking that Devlin kid, it hasn't been discovered yet."

It probably would have been small comfort to Dudney if she had known that Captain John Battles dreaded the interview as much as she.

His trouble was simple. He respected women, in a quaint, courtly, chivalrous way roughly comparable to that of a John Wayne movie cowboy. But he also had a quaint, courtly, not so chivalrous conviction that women didn't belong in certain professions, which resulted in what was known throughout Trans-Coastal as "Captain Battles' Shit List." On said list, in order of Captain Battles' prejudices, were women pilots, women doctors, women lawyers and women airline executives.

Jason Silvanius gave him a thorough briefing on Miss Devlin's background and Studebaker sent over his own files—including her test results, which were in the upper ten per cent of pilot applicants. Dr. Luther furnished him with her medical report along with an unappreciated opinion that "She's in a hell of a lot better shape than you are, you old goat." President Tom Berlin supplied his cautiously worded desire that Miss Devlin "be given the same impartial treatment you give all applicants, only for God's sake think of a way to get her the hell off our backs." All of which displeased Captain Battles no end, inasmuch as the voluminous verbal and written material on Dudney Devlin handed him gave him no legal loophole. He was fair enough to realize this, biased enough to swear he'd dismiss her on grounds of habitual tardiness if she was one minute late for the interview, and desperate enough to wish she'd break her leg on the way over.

Unfortunately for him, neither of the last two events transpired. She arrived at 9:55 A.M. on two healthy legs both of which, Battles reluctantly acknowledged to himself, were damned good-looking. The knight in him caused him to rise in graceful politeness when she was shown in and the anti-feminist in him painted a glowering frown on his face even as he got up to welcome her.

She sat directly across from him, a slight smile on her slightly parted lips, legs crossed discreetly but not too primly. She said nothing, which further disconcerted Battles, who—like Studebaker and Luther—instinctively and instantly liked her.

"Miss Devlin, you've given us something of a problem," he began —unwittingly echoing the sentiments of every Trans-Coastal executive whom she had met.

"Yes, sir, I realize that."

He examined her shrewdly, as if by staring at her he could penetrate and smash her armor plate of self-confidence and ambition.

"Exactly why the hell do you want to be the country's first female airline pilot?"

She did not answer him immediately, but merely stared back at this man in whose hands her future, her dreams and her hopes rested so precariously. There was something about him that reminded her of Ralph Devlin, although facially they were as different as cold and hot. Her father had been a handsome man with regular features. Battles was big, like Devlin, but he was almost totally bald and his strong face was pock-marked with the roughness of lunar terrain. His ears protruded at almost right angles, giving his head the appearance of a double-handled coffee mug. His big nose was thin, sharply hooked and totally out of proportion to a jutting, square jaw of bulldozer massiveness and strength. Someone had once said that John Battles resembled a lantern-jawed eagle. He was, in brief, an ugly man but ugly in a masculine way that made one forget his unattractiveness. And it was his eyes that recalled Ralph Devlin to Dudney—a light, icy blue; frank and direct, capable of cold fury and yet imparting an aura of trust and hidden warmth.

Those eyes were on her now, unblinking, emotionless, challenging. She wet her lips before replying, with no conscious thought of doing so.

"Captain Battles, I have no desire to be the first woman airline pilot in the United States. Or the second or third or tenth. I have no desire whatsoever to be an airborne Susan B. Anthony. I only want to fly for an airline. Trans-Coastal, at this moment. If I'm turned down I'll go elsewhere."

He was surprised. She herself had given him his loophole. "You mean if I say no, you'd try another airline? No running to the FEPC about women's rights?"

"I told you, I'm not interested in setting a precedent. I'd like to fly for you. If you don't want me and have a perfectly good reason for telling me I'm not good enough to fly for you, there won't be any running to anybody, except another carrier."

The blue eyes narrowed. "What may be a good reason to me might be an unacceptable reason to you."

"I know what *your* reason is, Captain Battles. I'm a woman."

"You read me loud and clear, Miss Devlin."

"Your reason is incomplete. I'd like to know why you think a woman wouldn't make a good airline pilot. If you can come up with a satisfactory answer, I'll stop wasting your time and mine."

He had anticipated this line of debate and he was ready for her. But even as he spoke, he was uncomfortably conscious of being glib rather than forceful.

"To begin with, I doubt the ability of a woman to cope with all aspects of airline flying. Her physical strength, or lack of it, would be a handicap. Her reactions in an emergency would be questionable. Her—"

"Captain Battles, I have four thousand hours, most of it multi-engine time. I won't say I've been at death's door on many occasions, but I have encountered a sufficient number of abnormal situations to deny that I'm not competent to handle any emergency. And in any airplane on which I'm qualified, provided I'm given the proper training. Which is why I'm sitting here today—to request such training."

"I must point—"

"And furthermore, your citing physical strength is a phony and you know it. I'll bet half your captains couldn't handle a total loss of control boost without help from a copilot. I'll even bet you'd be doing some sweating yourself."

He had to laugh, an act which put a warming sparkle into the cold blue eyes. "I'll withdraw—tentatively—comparative physical strength. Hell, I've got a few pilots who couldn't punch their way through wet Kleenex. Nor do I question your technical proficiency. You undoubtedly could fly as well as any rookie we hire, maybe better than most. By the time we got through training you in our way of doing things, I have no doubt you could pass any check ride. But that's not the point."

"I'm not trying to be argumentative, Captain Battles, but that seems to be precisely the point."

"Miss Devlin, I could teach a chimpanzee how to fly. But that doesn't make him a good airline pilot."

"I'd be interested in your definition of a good airline pilot."

The sparkle was gone from his eyes and his jaw was a taut vise.

"Simple. A good airline pilot is one who'll make a good airline *captain* someday."

"What makes you think—"

This time he interrupted her, and his words came out with staccato impact. "Miss Devlin, we don't hire copilots. We hire prospective captains. That eliminates you—or any other woman."

Her retort was calm, but it was calmness that hid anger mixed with near panic. "I think, Captain Battles, *that* judgment requires some justification."

"Very well. Suppose we took you on. Let's assume you sail through ground school and flight training. You're a qualified first officer. For all I know, you may even be a damned fine first officer. So good, in fact, that sooner or later you'd be eligible for that fourth stripe. And the sun will set in the east before I'll upgrade a woman to captain."

"You've stated an opinion," she snapped. "I'd appreciate your justifying that opinion."

The chief pilot had to grin mentally at the sight of her tightened lips, her jaw set belligerently, her own eyes flashing sparks, and her tiny, so very feminine nostrils flaring in resentful anger. She was a spunky little gamecock, that was for sure. But his admiration fell short of making him relax his attack.

"No woman," he said with a sudden trace of gentleness that still retained firmness, "is capable of the ability to command. Command authority, if you will—which is as much a part of an airline captain as his uniform—on Trans-Coastal or United or American or Western or any carrier. No, let me finish . . ."—she had started to say something—"I would not mind riding with you if I were in the left seat. I would be very much afraid to ride with you if *you* were in the left seat. I'd be worried about how you'd react to an emergency. Miss Devlin, my prime duty on this airline is to supply safe pilots, just as the prime responsibility of Trans-Coastal is to assure passengers of safe flight. They must put blind faith, unquestioning trust, in whatever crew we provide them. I could never give them complete assurance with a woman in that cockpit, simply because women are creatures of emotion and emotionalism has no place in a cockpit, not when the chips are down."

"You're giving me an answer that is emotionalism in its purest form," Dudney Devlin said. "You're substituting male prejudice for scientific evidence. Your so-called 'creatures of emotion' line is nothing but a male cliché, unsupported by any facts and, incidentally, contrary to specific evidence."

"I'm unaware of any scientific facts demonstrating that a woman thinks faster, clearer and more effectively in an emergency than a man," Battles said.

"I think you'll find that most psychologists will testify that under certain circumstances a woman will be braver and react more swiftly than a man. Such as protecting her children."

"The mother instinct is not what I'm looking for when something goes wrong at thirty-five thousand feet. Or when you come down to decision height out of a fog and you find a false ILS signal has lined you up two hundred yards to the right of your runway, smack over a bunch of houses, and you can't stop your sink rate. That, Miss Devlin, is when I want a goddamned man in that left seat, not a bloody female."

"I submit, Captain Battles, on more than one occasion the goddamned man in the left seat—as you phrase it—has pushed the panic button. I apologize for citing motherhood as an argument. I'll gladly concede that a father will be just as brave and react just as efficiently as his wife under the same circumstances. But by the same token there are a few women who'd be just as good as a man in an aircraft emergency."

"A few, you say. So damned few, I'd hate to take the chance of exposing a multimillion-dollar airplane loaded with innocent passengers to the possibility that I picked the wrong woman to test your theory."

"My theory might just possibly be as realistic as yours."

"Huh?"

"My theory is that a woman is capable of the right command decisions. Your theory is that she isn't. Neither of us can offer anything *but* theory. I can't prove mine and you can't prove yours. All I'm asking is that you let me at least prove I'm right, because you can't prove *you're* right unless you give me a chance first."

"I'm trying to be fair, Miss Devlin. After all, I could bring up a hell of a lot of other arguments—such as the fact that very few pilots will accept you, that most captains will make every minute you spend in their cockpits absolute torture, that you'll be walking on eggs all through training because every instructor will be panting for a chance to wash you out. Not to mention what passengers will think when they see a skirt up front. If we have customers boycotting a flight you're on, we'd have legal grounds for firing you—just as we could fire a copilot with a hippy hairdo that offended the public. My God, girl, do you really know what you're getting into? If you have any romantic ideas about this business, quit now before somebody breaks you in two—body and spirit."

"I don't think I'll break," she said slowly and distinctly. "All I'm asking is that you be fair. I want a chance. So help me, I'll take whatever you or anybody else throws at me—scorn, dirt, insults, ridicule or the bottom of the barrel on what trips you tell me to fly."

He looked at her as if he were seeing, for the first time, a person to know instead of a sickness to be cured. "Tell me about your dad," he said unexpectedly.

"He died three months ago."

"I know that. Studebaker told me. What kind of a pilot was he?"

"The best. He . . . he seemed to be a part of every plane he flew. He taught me more than just flying. He taught me not to fear the sky, but to respect it. His creed was fly by the book, and he made it my creed. I used to love to watch him work the throttles. Those big hands of his . . . all the knowledge and skill and instinct accumulated in all those years he flew seemed to culminate in his fingers, conning some tired old bucket of bolts into being young again." Dudney stopped, embarrassed, remembering acutely what Battles had said about women being too emotional. But she had gone too far down that path to turn back in total retreat. Now her voice was a little bitter, defiant, tinted with sarcasm. "I'm sorry, Captain Battles. Seems I forgot you have this thing about emotionalism."

The chief pilot shook his head. Ungrudging respect was etched into every line on his homely face. Studebaker had warned him. "She can get under your skin," Horace had said. And she had done just that. She had touched a chord buried deep in his airman's heart and the anger he felt for this unexpected weakness was not strong enough to override a surge of affection for her.

John Battles cleared his throat, a rasping sound that broke the silence hanging between them like an unspoken prayer. He said, very softly: "Miss Devlin, any time I label as emotionalism a daughter's pride in her father, or a pilot's feeling about the machines he flies, I'll tear up my ATR."

They studied each other, two combatants made wary by the sudden discovery that they had lost their zest for fighting.

"I take it you and your father were pretty close?"

"Yes, sir. Very close."

"Miss him?"

"Yes." A low voice, a trifle husky, but so intense she might as well have screamed her answer.

"Ever talk to him about this, this ambition of yours?"

"No, sir."

"Why not?"

"As long as he was alive, he needed me in his own work. Knowing that, it was a mental block against ever discussing it with him."

"When did he fly for American?"

"For about eight years before World War II. During the war he was in the Ferry Command and never went back to American."

"How do you feel about marriage?"

"As an institution or a personal achievement?"

Battles grinned, and when the chief pilot grinned the lines on his face crinkled, giving the effect of glass shattering without breaking. "I mean, do you want to get married someday?"

"Someday, yes. Not in the immediate or distant future."

"That's a woman's answer, Miss Devlin. And if you'll pardon my saying so, it's an answer that's one hundred per cent bullshit. I'd like to have a buck for every one of our stewardesses who's sworn by all that's holy she'd be married to Trans-Coastal *ad infinitum*. That's another thing I've got against a woman airline pilot. We'll spend fifty thousand dollars training you, after which you'll fall for some son of a bitch and you'll walk in here one fine day and tell me you want out."

Her retort was almost a spitting of the words. "If you hire me, Captain Battles, you'll get back every cent of your fifty thousand dollars, with interest—in loyalty, efficiency and dedication."

"What guarantee do I have that you won't fall in love? Or, assuming you're a red-blooded American girl, what guarantee do I have that some pilot won't knock you up?" He was being deliberately brutal in his gutter language, and he knew why just as she did.

"No guarantee. Any more than I could promise you I won't get killed driving to the airport, catch pneumonia or break my leg playing tennis. Nor could any other pilot. You're asking me to promise permanence. I can't, and neither could anyone else—man or woman."

"I'm asking for a reasonable assurance that you'd stay on the job a sufficient length of time to justify the training we'd give you."

"I don't know what you'd regard as sufficient length of time. Five years? Ten?"

"I want pilots willing to make a career out of flying," Battles snapped. "I'm afraid you want to play airline pilot until you're ready for your real career."

"I've already made a career out of flying," Dudney Devlin said with an intensity that renewed his respect. "I wasn't 'playing pilot,' as you put it, when I flew for my father."

Her mention of Ralph Devlin was an unintentioned stab at the chief pilot's conscience. He grimaced inwardly. It was strange, but it was almost as if he was vulnerable to a brother airman he had never met and yet somehow knew. Battles picked up her file more as a pretense at appearing busy while judgment wrestled with pilot loyalty, while his prejudices fought his liking for a girl he didn't want to like. He made his decision abruptly, camouflaging its core of sentimentality with the trappings of bluster.

"Devlin, you might as well know how things would stand if I let you go into training. I'd tell every instructor to wash you out if you're thirty seconds late to any class. You wouldn't get check rides. You'd get a deliberate attempt to make you come apart at the seams. If the miracle occurs and you come through, God help you when you start flying the line. The first time I see or even hear second hand that you shed tears in a cockpit, even if I ever see your eyes water in public, I'll cut those goddamned wings off your uniform myself. If you ever call in sick for anything as female as monthly cramps I'll ground you without pay for a month. If you're one second late for a trip sign-in, you're fired. In plain, simple language, Devlin, I'd make life so miserable for you that you'd want to quit—long before I ever had to face up to the day you'd be eligible for upgrading. You read me, Devlin?"

"Yes, sir."

"You'd still want to try? Knowing you're not just another trainee but a headache I'm gonna get rid of the first chance I get?"

"*Yes, sir!*" The words were hissed more than spoken.

The stern, rock-chiseled face, the angry eyes, softened. "You got yourself a deal, Devlin."

Being a man, John Battles would never know the effort it took Dudney to keep her eyes from glistening. She said simply, "Thank you, Captain Battles," stood up and put out her hand. Battles grasped it.

"How you fixed for dough?"

"I'm doing fine."

"Over the weekend, find yourself an apartment. There's a Boeing 737 class that starts Monday. You'll be with nine guys—all military-trained. Know anything about the bird?"

"I have never flown it. I've heard it's a fine airplane."

"It is, for the job it does. Okay, get going. You've done enough to ruin my day."

"Yes, sir."

She turned and started to walk from his office. As she reached the door Battles growled again. "Devlin!"

Startled, she turned around. He was still standing in back of his cluttered desk. His face was emotionless, except for an almost imperceptible working of his jaw muscles.

"Yes, sir?"

"Good luck, kid."

She nodded, her throat constricting, and left. Outside the Flight Operations Building, she looked up at the sound of screaming turbines. A Trans-Coastal 737 was coming in on final, flaps down. As she squinted against the sun, watching the jet settle toward its ribbon of concrete, it is entirely possible that even John Battles would have forgiven the tears that finally came to her eyes.

CHAPTER THREE

As he had promised Tom Berlin, Jason himself wrote the news release on Dudney Devlin's admission to flight training, composing it with both care and tongue in cheek, knowing what reaction it would cause among airline circles. He finished hammering it out with his old newspaperman's style of two forefingers and, per company protocol, brought it into Tom Berlin's office late Friday afternoon for approval. The president insisted that all major announcements affecting Trans-Coastal be cleared with him personally.

Berlin picked up the release with a grimace, as if Jason had handed him an overripe fish to be smelled suspiciously and disdainfully before attempting consumption.

"I don't like it. I don't like it at all, goddammit," he growled.

"You haven't read it yet," Silvanius protested.

"I'm not referring to what you wrote. That goddamned Battles must have been out of his mind to okay that dame's training. She's going to be nothing but trouble. Jason, maybe we oughta keep this out of the papers for a while. Then if she flunks out nobody's the wiser."

"She might not flunk out," Jason reminded him.

"She'll flunk out if I have to bribe somebody in her class to knock her up. Jason, what we should do is . . . oh hell, stop shaking your head. We're hooked, huh?"

"Read the release, Tom. It might make you feel a little better. There are some quotes in there from you that'll make you the most liberal-minded airline president in the history of commercial aviation."

"Or the stupidest," Berlin mumbled. "Okay, I'll read this bull." His tired old eyes swept over Jason's surprisingly neat typing.

FOR RELEASE A.M.'S SUNDAY

Los Angeles, April——. Trans-Coastal Airlines announced today it has accepted a veteran woman pilot for training as a Boeing 737 first officer.

If the applicant, Miss Dudney A. Devlin, 25, of Anchorage, Alaska, successfully completes TCA's rigorous flight course, she will become the nation's first female airline pilot.

President Thomas E. Berlin said the decision to admit Miss Devlin to flight training was based on "her excellent background, her admirable record as an already experienced pilot and her splendid attitude toward an admittedly difficult assignment."

"This airline has always adhered without exception to a policy of employing persons purely on the basis of qualification for specific jobs, without regard to sex, race, color or religion," Mr. Berlin stated. "Miss Devlin has been admitted to our flight school because she is qualified to undergo this training. We are not hiring her as a publicity stunt. We are hiring her because we believe she has the skill and sense of responsibility to become a trusted Trans-Coastal pilot."

Berlin laid down the paper at this point in the release and looked at Silvanius sharply. "I don't buy that last part, Jason."

"Which part?"

"That we're not hiring her as a publicity stunt. Hell, the minute we say that, every sonofabitch will assume that's exactly why we did hire her."

"Sort of a 'methinks Trans-Coastal doth protest too much'?" Silvanius asked.

"Right. You agree?"

"Possibly. But the publicity angle is gonna occur to practically everyone whether we mention it or not. I figured, by bringing it up ourselves, we'd be forestalling any criticism."

Berlin looked thoughtful. "There'd be an even better way of forestalling criticism, Jason. After you make this announcement I suppose you'll be getting requests for interviews with the girl?"

"Swamped with requests would be more likely."

"Fine. Turn 'em all down."

Jason Silvanius grinned. "Closely followed by my reassignment to duties other than public relations. Hell, Tom, when this whole thing first came up, good publicity was about the only benefit either one of us could dredge out of the mess."

"Think about it, while I finish reading this literary masterpiece." Berlin picked up the release again and resumed his perusal.

Miss Devlin is the daughter of the late Ralph Devlin, president and founder of Air Alaska, a cargo line. She flew for her father's company for several years, qualifying on such heavy aircraft equipment as DC-4s, DC-6s and Electras. Her logged flight time totals more than 4,000 hours, including several hundred hours of experience on twin-engine executive jets which she flew during a brief career with an air taxi company in Alaska.

There are approximately 1,700 women in the United States who hold commercial pilot licenses and another 500 who are licensed flight instructors. About 70 women hold Air Transport Ratings (ATRs) which qualify them to command aircraft flown for hire, but to date none has been accepted by a scheduled airline. The Soviet Union and several Communist-bloc nations have women airline pilots. The first free world carrier to hire a woman pilot was Scandinavian Airways System (SAS). Like Miss Devlin, the SAS pilot—Miss Turi Wideroe—came from a flying family. Her father was a former SAS pilot and later operated a small but prosperous seaplane line.

Miss Devlin is scheduled to start ground school next Monday with nine other pilots. If she attains passing grades in this course, she will undergo two weeks of flight training in Trans-Coastal's twin-engine Boeing 737s which serve more than a score of cities on TCA's routes.

(Editors: Miss Devlin will be available to the press, radio and television at 4 P.M. Monday in the Trans-Coastal employee auditorium, Building 3, 3985 Century Boulevard, Englewood.)

"For Christ's sake, Jason, you've already got her lined up for a press conference," Berlin complained as he handed back the release. "Does the dame know about it?"

"She will. She's due in my office in about fifteen minutes. If you go along with it. Release okay?"

"Oh hell," Berlin grumbled. "I'm not gonna tell you how to run your department. Go ahead—with one stipulation." The last three words halted Silvanius in mid-air as he rose off the chair in front of the president's frigate-sized desk.

"Stipulate away, Mr. President," Jason smiled, sitting down again.

"If she says no interviews, consider it the equivalent of an order from me."

The smile evaporated on Jason's face. "Dammit, Tom, that's not fair. The esteemed news media will clobber me if I put this girl under wraps. We're setting precedent and that's news!"

Berlin reached into a handsome humidor on his desk and pulled out a fat cigar. He lit it and languorously puffed a half dozen times before replying. "I'd like to meet this kid, Jason. Sort of get a line on her before we let anything out."

Silvanius looked dubious.

The president laughed. "I give you my word I won't try to influence her. I'll leave it strictly up to her. If she's willing to run that damned interview gantlet, you can issue your release as is. I won't even change a comma."

Jason's face brightened. "Fair enough. If you promise to keep quiet, I don't think I'll have any trouble with her. Come to think about it, I don't know why I should worry. She's probably so grateful about getting her foot in the door she'd pose topless on the Hollywood Freeway during rush hour if I asked her to. I'll call you when she comes in. Want me to bring her in here?"

"No, I'll come down to your office. Seeing mine might give her the idea this airline's wealthy."

"By the time you walk in," Jason enthused, "I'll have her more publicity-minded than a starving starlet."

"I'll bet," Berlin said in a tone that somehow transmitted to his vice president of public relations the president's conviction that Jason Silvanius was walking on soft-boiled eggs.

"No, sir," said Dudney Devlin, firmly and fervently.

Behind Jason, Tom Berlin's lined old face wore an expression that deftly mixed "I told you so" with "I like this girl."

"Why not?" demanded Silvanius, patiently but also firmly and fervently.

Dudney examined the vice president, a slight, wry smile on her wide lips. "Are any of the other pilots in my class being subjected to news interviews, Mr. Silvanius?"

"Of course not. For very obvious reasons. Conversely, for the same obvious reasons we're asking you to meet with reporters."

"Isn't it fairer," she said sweetly, "if I'm treated no differently from anyone else in training?"

"In training, yes. But before you actually start training, you must admit you *are* different. You're on your way to becoming the country's first woman airline pilot, Miss Devlin, and that makes you a most newsworthy subject. Look, I know you don't want to but it won't be as bad as you think."

"I'd rather not, Mr. Silvanius," she said with a little sigh. "I understand your position but I don't think you understand mine."

"I understand it very well," Jason said, somewhat stuffily. "It's my position you—"

She interrupted. "I'll make a deal with you, Mr. Silvanius. No interviews now. But if I get through training and actually start flying the line, I'll submit to this asinine ordeal for you. Before I take my first trip."

Jason hesitated, and his indecision was not helped by Berlin's low chuckle.

"Just why are you so opposed to this so-called ordeal right now?" he argued. "It won't be any rougher than it will be a few weeks from now."

"You said a woman airline pilot is news. I agree. But I'm not an airline pilot—yet. I'm just a hopeful. An untried question mark, same as the other nine students in my class. I'd rather prove myself before anyone makes a fuss about the whole thing. Isn't that being logical?"

"It's being goddamned feminine," Jason growled, "and nothing is as illogical as a female. Dammit, Miss Devlin, I can't really order you to—"

"Then don't. I'll feel better about it and so will you, in the long run. I'd be a pretty sad subject for an interview as of now. If I make the grade, I'd do a better job for you. A press conference would make me feel like a crusader for women's rights and that's exactly what I don't want."

Silvanius, although he was resigned to defeat, had one more shot to fire. "It's company policy, you know, for employees to cooperate with the press. Voluntarily, of course, but . . ." He shrugged his shoulders expressively, and waited for Dudney to say something. Typically, she didn't. She merely smiled at him and he frowned in frustration, turning to Berlin for support he half suspected was not forthcoming. The president, perched on one corner of Jason's desk, merely grinned and Silvanius turned back to the girl, totally defeated.

"I should let the both of you handle the calls I'll get when we put out the announcement—minus the news conference," he observed sadly. "Okay, Miss Devlin, you win. But I'll hold you to that promise —after you graduate. If you graduate." He regretted the latter sentence as soon as the words left his mouth, but Dudney was still wearing her tight little smile, no trace of rancor on her face. Tom Berlin cleared his throat.

"I might as well confess something to you, Miss Devlin," he said with a raspy, grudging kind of cordiality. "When Mr. Silvanius brought up the question of your meeting with the press, I tended to oppose it. Although I suspect my reasons weren't the same as yours."

"I'm curious to know your reasons, Mr. Berlin," she said with armed politeness.

"Frankly, I figured there was a damned good chance you'd make an ass out of yourself—and my airline. That you'd wind up sounding like a loud-mouth reformer."

"Frankly, that was what I was afraid of myself," she admitted, and both men laughed.

Jason had the virtue of being able to retreat without resentment; he nodded ruefully. "That's what could have happened, very easily. A news conference can make the Spanish Inquisition seem like high tea. Maybe you both had the right instinct about it, although I'll catch hell from our journalistic friends. Well, I'd like one favor from you, Miss Devlin. You too, Tom."

"Pictures," Berlin guessed.

"Correct. That okay with you, Miss Devlin?"

"It's fine with me if it's all right with Mr. Berlin."

"Then you two sit right here while I go drum up our photographer."

He left, the president wondering momentarily why Jason didn't use the simpler device of summoning the airline's photographer by phone. Wisely, he reasoned Silvanius had supposed he might like a few words alone with Trans-Coastal's Problem. He sat down in the chair behind Jason's desk and surveyed the girl from under his bushy eyebrows. Attractive kid, he thought. He liked her eyes. Clear and direct. He had a habit of judging people by their eyes.

"Everyone treating you right?" he ventured gruffly.

"No complaints," Dudney replied. Conscious that perhaps she was being too abrupt, she added, "By the way, Mr. Berlin, I am most grateful for . . . for the chance you're giving me."

Berlin's reply was an indistinguishable growl, a mongrel kind of sound between an angry snort and a reluctant acknowledgment. Then, uncomfortable at the silence that hung between them like a dark curtain, he blurted, "I find myself torn between wishing you luck and hoping you'll wash out, Miss Devlin."

"Well," Dudney murmured, "despite your indecision, I'm still grateful."

"Gratitude is considered by some to be a sign of weakness," Berlin observed, a note of challenging animosity in his rasping voice.

"So is hiring someone under duress," she came back, her own tone as sweetly gentle as his had been belligerent. The very contrast seemed to square them off against each other, a pair of wary duelists circling verbally as they awaited an opening.

"We didn't hire you under duress," Berlin retorted. "We weighed your qualifications and decided to at least let you try."

"Under the duress of fear that I might file suit charging discrimination because of sex," Dudney said, her voice still low and even.

He glared at her, but his anger disintegrated as his glare collided with the little smile around her mouth. He realized then she was baiting him, taunting him, and somehow it was a pleasant surprise to learn that she had no fear of him. Berlin despised fawners. Now he was smiling back, and by the time Silvanius returned with the photographer they were conversing volubly about Ralph Devlin and Air Alaska's operations.

The photographer was a bustling, officious little man with a noticeable lack of awe in the presence of company brass. He seemed more impressed, in fact, with Dudney or at least her legs, at which he kept casting surreptitious glances. Like most photographers dealing principally with news pictures, Arthur Smithfield always managed to resemble a man simultaneously bored and expert at what he was doing.

"Smitty, how about getting Mr. Berlin and Miss Devlin shaking hands under this picture of a 737?" Jason suggested, with a certain amount of advance resignation in his voice. He knew that Smithfield regarded advice like an airline captain listening to a flight engineer telling him how to land.

"She gonna fly 737s?" the photographer asked.

"Hopefully, yes," Silvanius told him.

"Is that model on your desk a 737?" Smithfield wanted to know.

"Goddammit, Smitty," Berlin complained, "haven't you shot enough pictures of our aircraft to recognize a 737?"

"The damned things all look alike to me," Smithfield confessed blandly.

"It's a 737," Silvanius assured him.

"Good. Miss Devlin, you sit on the edge of the desk, with your hand on that plane. Mr. Berlin, you just look at her—which ain't hard."

The principals complied. There is something about a photographer's orders which approximates the indisputable authority of a four-star general.

"Hoist your skirt a little higher, Miss Devlin."

Dudney flushed, started to say something, and looked at Berlin pleadingly.

"Her skirt's high enough," Berlin growled. "What the hell do you think you're photographing—the center spread for *Playboy?*"

"You want this printed anywheres?" Smithfield demanded disrespectfully—although he took the precaution of looking at Silvanius as he said it.

"We're not out for cheesecake today," Jason said soothingly. He had to work with Smithfield almost daily. "Just take her the way she is, Smitty."

"It'll never get used," the photographer predicted as his flash went off. "Let's take another one. Mr. Berlin, this time you put your hand on the plane, and Miss Devlin, you look at him. Smile, dammit. This is supposed to be the happiest day of your life." Dudney exposed her white teeth in what was supposed to be a demonstration of sheer joy, achieving the look of someone trying to smile in the face of onrushing seasickness.

"Wider!" bawled Smithfield. "You too, Mr. Berlin. Smile. That's better. Hold it. Fine, let's try another one just to make sure."

Silvanius stepped in, diplomatically. "I think we've got enough, Smitty. Thanks a lot. Appreciate your rushing 'em through. Eight by eleven glossies, about twenty-five copies, and send them up to me as soon as they're ready."

Smithfield grunted his assent, folded up his camera and marched out with a final look at Dudney's legs, muttering as he left, "Dame's got good legs, why hide 'em?"

Jason grinned wryly. "You're free to go, Miss Devlin. Your cooperation was appreciated, but sure you won't reconsider that news conference?"

Dudney shook her head. "After experiencing that . . . that man's obsession with legs, no, thanks. Mr. Silvanius, Mr. Berlin, I enjoyed meeting you both. If there's nothing else you want me for, I'm going apartment hunting."

The two men watched her trim figure go out of Jason's office.

"Nice girl," Silvanius said.

"Very," Tom Berlin agreed. "See her face when that goddamned Smithfield wanted more leg showing? Been a long time since I've seen a girl blush."

"All photographers are composed of at least one tenth sex fiend," Jason said in amused defense of his photographer.

"In Smithfield's case, nine tenths," Berlin snapped. "He'd have been happier if she had posed in the nude."

"So would I," Jason admitted. "Hell, she *does* have good legs."

"Her legs, my fine young friend, are going to be a Trans-Coastal problem on the upper-echelon executive level. Which includes you, so start thinking about them."

"They'll be a problem if I do start thinking about 'em," Silvanius protested. "I'm happily married, Tom. Let me just concentrate on Janet's legs, which, by the way—"

"I said they constitute a problem, Jason. A corporate problem. Don't you know why?"

Silvanius was honestly puzzled. "No, sir. What's the problem?"

The president was still staring at the door through which Dudney Devlin had departed.

"I'm thinking," he mused, "what the hell kind of uniform we'll have to put on her if she pulls off the miracle and flies for us."

Jason Silvanius whistled in sudden awareness.

"In other words," Berlin continued, "do we cover up those legs with slacks or let her wear a skirt in the cockpit?" He sighed heavily. "Jesus, Jason, I told you she'd be nothing but trouble. I wish I hadn't liked her so much."

The airline career of Dudney Amelia Devlin got under way at 8:00 A.M. the following Monday in Trans-Coastal's employee auditorium. It started officially as it had begun unofficially—listening to Horace Studebaker.

The Sunday papers had featured her story prominently—the *Herald-Examiner* putting it on page three with one of Smithfield's pictures. The *Times* did even better by Jason Silvanius, assigning it to page one along with a file picture of SAS pilot Wideroe, plus an editorial complimenting Trans-Coastal on its enlightened attitude.

"This is a red-letter day not only for women but for commercial aviation," the editorial writer enthused. "Trans-Coastal has recognized, albeit belatedly, there is no reason why females would not make safe, skilled and highly responsible airline pilots. Miss Devlin's triumph over Victorian prejudice is far more important than a mere victory for her sex; it is a step forward for all aviation, which by its own dynamic, ever expanding nature must not overlook any source of technically skilled personnel."

The *Herald-Examiner* didn't go as far as an editorial, but under the main story it ran a UPI dispatch from Stockholm quoting First Officer Wideroe as being "delighted that a U.S. airline has followed in the footsteps of my own progressive company at long last"—a statement which might have been dictated by the SAS counterpart of

Jason Silvanius—and assuring Dudney Devlin of "my very best wishes for her future success." The *Herald-Examiner's* final item of coverage was a series of brief interviews with various persons on the subject of women airline pilots.

Frank Kelly, film cutter: "If I ever see this babe in the cockpit of a plane I'm supposed to fly on, I'll get off."

Ruth Shub, housewife: "I think it's just great. She struck a blow for all of us."

Penelope Parker, TV actress: "She deserves a lot of credit, but I just don't know if it's really a good idea. Me, I'd feel better with a man flying my airplane."

John Cartwell, airline pilot: "The whole thing is stupid. Now I suppose we'll have fifteen-year-old pilots because some damned fool kid complained about age discrimination."

Peter Szymanski, student: "It's okay, but when are the airlines going to hire black women pilots?"

Thunder Storme, exotic dancer: "I'd feel perfectly safe flying with her, honest. Of course, you can carry equal rights too far. I hope men never get into my line of work."

This excellent cross section of public opinion was duly read and painfully digested by Tom Berlin, who resisted the urge to call Jason Silvanius and/or John Battles with a few well-chosen words of recrimination. Jason, who operated on the age-old axiom of public relations that any mention short of libel should be tolerated, was grateful for all the play—considering the fact that both Los Angeles papers, as well as the AP, UPI and all three networks had raised hell with him for refusing to allow interviews with Dudney.

Dudney herself had grimaced when she read the accounts. To see her name in prominent print was a new and embarrassing experience, giving her the uncomfortable feeling that she had suddenly found herself living in a house with transparent walls. She hoped her classmates hadn't seen the papers, although she quickly discarded this as silly. They would know soon enough, if they didn't already, that a girl was going to train with them. Still, it would be a lot better if they didn't have the idea she had sought publicity and the possibility really bothered her. Mingled with her self-admission that the class was likely to be hostile was her very natural and almost desperate desire to be accepted and also liked.

These thoughts were sprinting through her jittery, turbulent mind as she watched Horace Studebaker march up to the small podium on the auditorium stage. The room was relatively small and Dudney figured it probably held not more than a couple of hundred persons, three hundred at the most. There were about fifty present this morning and she wondered which of the dozen or so men in the room were her classmates. There was one group of seven rather handsome, healthy-looking young males sitting together. They were in their mid-twenties or early thirties at the most, and their neat, closely trimmed hair seemed to stamp them as recently military. This could be part of her class, she decided, and she was examining them curiously when Mr. Studebaker's voice interrupted.

"Good morning," he began in a voice so cheery that Dudney half expected the audience to rise and sing, "Good morning, Mr. Studebaker," in the manner of dutiful kindergarten students.

He gazed around the room and was momentarily flustered when his eyes intercepted Dudney's. He had spent considerable time worrying about whether he should mention her presence to the other new employees, cognizant that she would resent it and yet figuring that, thanks to all the publicity in yesterday's papers, most of them might welcome his pointing her out.

"Ladies and gentlemen, my name, as some of you already know, is Horace Studebaker. I'm the director of New Personnel and it is my pleasant duty to welcome you to the family of Trans-Coastal Airlines. This morning we have with us a new stewardess class—those thirteen lovely girls to my right"—all eyes swiveled to the thirteen girls, who fortunately were unaware that Jason Silvanius had wagered five dollars with another vice president that one girl in this class was doomed to flunk because George Moore, head of cabin attendant training, was so superstitious he would never permit a thirteen-girl graduating class.

Studebaker was continuing. "For this orientation meeting, of course, we make no attempt to differentiate between employees. In addition to the stewardess class I just mentioned, we also have several new office workers, a new mechanics and a new pilot class—

these men will be first officers on our Boeing 737s." He glanced at Dudney again, beaming as he did so, and she cringed inwardly in anticipation of what was coming. "I said we had a new pilot class and I said something about these men becoming first officers, well, uh, as many of you may know by reading yesterday's papers, this particular class will not be one hundred per cent male. It will include our first woman pilot trainee, Miss Dudney Devlin, that very lovely young lady sitting over there . . ."

Dudney's face was scarlet, the product of embarrassment and anger mixed in equal proportions. She had two violent urges—to dig a hole into which she could crawl, and to shoot Horace Studebaker. She felt about fifty pairs of eyes turned toward her like a battery of searchlights impaling an enemy night bomber, and all she could do was glare at Studebaker. The look she gave him was so patently disgusted that he blushed himself, retreating hurriedly to his usual welcoming remarks delivered in a less than normally assured fashion.

He discussed the history of Trans-Coastal, its route structure, the types of aircraft it flew (with slides) and the future aircraft it had on order. Next came the functions and operations of the Civil Aeronautics Board, the Federal Aviation Administration, the Air Transport Association, the International Air Transport Association, the Department of Transportation and the National Transportation Safety Board. This brought them to the lunch break, which Dudney both dreaded and welcomed. Most of what Studebaker had been saying was old hat to her and she was frankly bored. Yet his orientation lecture had been a kind of verbal sanctuary, allowing her to hide anonymously behind his droning voice, the attention of everyone else drawn safely away from her. Now she was exposed to their hungry curiosity again, maybe their unspoken ridicule, and she started to walk hurriedly out of the auditorium in what amounted to near panic. She was halfway up the aisle, heading for a rear exit, when she felt a hand on her elbow and heard a male voice that brought her to a halt. "Miss Devlin, wait a sec."

She turned. The interceptor was a young man, only an inch or so taller than she, but husky, with a shock of black hair and deep brown eyes that were almost doelike in their softness. He was grinning broadly, and the unexpected friendliness in his smile made her smile back, a reflex as spontaneous as breathing.

"I'm Al Miller. I'm in your class." Only the "I'm" came out "Ah'm" —he was as Southern as hominy grits, with an accent so thick it was close to a parody.

"Hi," said Dudney uncertainly.

"We thought you might like to eat with some of us," Miller said. "Give us a chance to get acquainted."

"You want to eat with me?" The question was a statement of gratitude rather than interrogation.

"Sure thing. We read all about you. And we . . . we figured you might be a little lonesome."

She could have kissed him.

"I'd love to have lunch with you," she said, conscious that her answer might have sounded too much like a feminine response to a social invitation. She wished she had said "like," not "love."

"Good. Come along outside. You won't meet everybody right off. Two guys are getting special physicals. Mike's already latched onto a couple of gals from that stew class, and Doug's with him. They're two of our three bachelors. Rest of us are old married men." By now he was already propelling her up the aisle, his hand on her elbow again, and she could not help resenting the gesture as hinting of patronization, of sex distinction, of unwelcome male-female protocol. She scolded herself for this throb of what she knew was phony independence, maybe aloofness, but even as Dudney warmed anew to his drawling chatter she had to push back a feeling of wariness and suspicion. She was not quite sure whether they were accepting her as a fellow pilot, a potential sex target, or some kind of a feminist freak. She was actually nervous when they reached the door and stepped out into the warm spring air.

There were four men waiting for them, all dressed conservatively in business suits and all looking at Dudney with frank curiosity.

"This here's"—it came out "heah's"—"Dudney Devlin, fellas. Want you to meet Bob Tarkington, Frank Webster, Hank Mitchell and Ernie Crum."

One by one, as Miller went through the introductions and they offered handshakes, she inspected them and categorized them, knowing that the niches to which she assigned them temporarily could very well be inaccurate ones. Mitchell was the surprise. He was a Negro with a skin so black it had almost a bluish cast to it. His features were regular—he resembled Harry Belafonte to some degree —and he had none of the rather thickish lips and nose Dudney usually associated with Negroes as dark as he. He was big, too, taller by several inches than the others, with wide shoulders and a prize fighter's slim waist.

Mitchell was grinning at her as if he could read her thoughts.

"Surprised to find you're not the only minority member of our group, Miss Devlin?"

"Somewhat," she admitted. "They didn't tell me there'd be a Neg— black in the class."

He smiled at her discomfiture. "Negro's fine, Miss Devlin. Always did think that using 'black' instead of 'Negro' was more a matter of semantics than racial pride."

"Hank doesn't care as long as you don't say 'nigger,' " Miller said. That ugly word coming from the Southerner's mouth shocked Dudney, but Mitchell laughed easily and Dudney instinctively realized there was a bond between the two men which surprised her further. Miller, with that thick, drawl-saturated accent, had to be Deep South while the big colored man was the kind of black who attracts the bigotry of the ignorant—his voice was soft, cultured, almost melodious, with a kind of singsong lilt to it that reminded Dudney of a Jamaican Negro.

Webster was a big man, too, and Dudney put him in the stuffed shirt category—somewhat wrongly, she was to find out later. He had sparse, sandy hair, a thin nose with pinched nostrils, and a rather formalized way of speaking that reeked of conceit. Tarkington was handsome, mature, quiet, polite and reserved but it was a deceptive reserve that evaporated the minute he smiled—a boyish, mischievous smile that seemed to erase years from his stern face. Ernie Crum, Dudney decided, was a pixie—a small, wiry youngster with red hair, freckles and a grin that crinkled his face into dimples so big they came close to being ridges.

There was a moment of uncomfortable silence before Miller suggested that they eat. "Employees' cafeteria okay?" he asked.

"It's pretty dull food," Tarkington complained. "We got time to find a good restaurant? Miss Devlin, you know any place around here?"

She fervently wished she could have come through this first test of her knowledge, good-fellowship and culinary acumen. But she had been eating in a small, cheap restaurant near the Hacienda which was too far away, and she had to confess she was no expert on dining places in the proximity of Trans-Coastal's headquarters. She was grateful when Mitchell offered the opinion that the employees' cafeteria was the most convenient choice until they had scouted the area.

Dudney walked next to Miller on the way over, learning among other things that his friends called him Dixie, he was from Mobile, Alabama, had slightly more than three thousand hours of logged flight time—most of it in Navy transport aircraft—and was happily married to a former Alabama cheer leader named Norma Jean, who was due to join him in another week "provided I find a decent apartment."

"Your wife was a cheer leader?" Dudney commented. "Did you play football?"

"Yep. Defensive halfback. Kinda light, but Coach Bryant liked speed and hittin' more than he did heft. Pleasure to play for that man. Boy, he was tough but he knows football. You like football?"

"Very much," and she smiled to herself, remembering the player who had been her "first."

"Good game. Y'know, I played against Hank Mitchell there."

"No fooling?"

"Sure did. In the Orange Bowl, now when the hell was it? Play on New Year's Day, I keep getting the year mixed up. Anyway, Hank was a fullback at Syracuse. Remember first time I ever hit him in the open. He came through on a trap and it was head-on, Katy bar the door. Boy, like running into a truck. Hell of a player, Hank. We both went down but I was the last one up and I was hearing birds and bells. Ole Hank picked me up and laughed at me. Said something like 'Welcome to Eastern football, rebel.' We whomped 'em but it was a tough game. Hank came up to me afterwards and said nobody ever hit him harder than me. Made me feel pretty damned good. That boy was all man. Hell, he *is* all man. Make this airline a fine pilot, I'll bet."

"Frankly," Dudney said, "I'm a little surprised to see you getting along as well as you do with a Negro. A Southerner and all that."

Miller slowed down to light a cigarette, then resumed talking with it dangling from one corner of his mouth. It gave him the appearance of an amiable delinquent. "Tell you something, Miss Devlin. You hear a lot about the evils of football. How most of the guys playing at the big schools are dumb Polacks who couldn't get into college any other way. How the game's overemphasized and coaches make more dough than full professors. Maybe some of the mud's valid, but football's done more for good race relations than most of your reformers like to admit or even know. Baseball too, but not on the college level. You take me, for instance. Hell, when I was in high school I called guys like Hank niggers and I thought they were scum. Big, dumb animals. But when I started playing college ball, 'Bama played a lot of teams with colored kids on their squads. I learned in a hurry. They had just as much guts and sometimes a hell of a lot more skill than any white boy. They played hard and they played clean. In football, Miss Devlin, you get down to the nitty gritty when it comes to judging another man—in the best way to judge him. When he's playing against you and you both want something awful bad. Namely, to win. So you find out right quick that football uniforms come in the same color, no matter what the face is under that helmet. Well, I learned all this in football. I learned it again flying for the Navy—we all wore the same uniform and only a damned fool would say 'nigger' to a colored guy flying as your wingman or maybe working as your crew chief or bringing you in safe and sound on a carrier with the deck bucking like an ole bronc. Maybe I would have learned this in the Navy if I had never played football, but I don't think I would have been as pliable to that kind of teaching if I hadn't hit guys like Hank Mitchell in the open first. End sermon, Miss Devlin."

"Dixie, I wish you'd call me Dudney. Or Dud, like my friends do."

He looked at her as they walked along, then at his four friends trudging ahead. "Be easy for me to call you Dud," he said soberly. "But in a way you're like Hank, up there. Colored guys had to prove themselves before rednecks like me got off our prejudice platform.

So do you, as a pilot. As a good guy. Won't do any good for me to call you Dudney, when the others will keep calling you Miss Devlin. Until you're accepted."

She was shaken, hurt, but she hid it under the cloak of a tart retort. "I was sort of hoping I was accepted when you asked me to eat with all of you."

Miller threw away his cigarette before replying, started to light another and then changed his mind. "Felt kinda sorry for you, mostly. Just like I felt a little sorry last week when I bumped into Hank— first time since that bowl game. I went out of my way to be nice to him in front of the other guys. But I didn't expect them to accept him just on my say. Sorta paved the way a bit, I guess. Soon's they got to know him, no trouble. Maybe it'll be that way with you. I dunno, Miss Devlin. Most of the guys don't know how to take you. Some of them figure you're nothing but a crusader with a little flight time, which doesn't make you an airline pilot. Maybe . . . maybe they aren't convinced you're serious about training. That you're just trying to prove a point."

Dudney was angry. "I want to be an airline pilot as much as anyone else in the class, but I'll be damned if I know how to prove it to a bunch of conceited males."

Dixie shrugged, unoffended. "Give 'em a little time, Miss Devlin. Just like they'll give you a little time before they make up their minds about you." He chuckled as he remembered something. "Matter of fact, it wasn't me who suggested taking you along to lunch."

"It wasn't? Then . . ."

"Nope, it was Hank. Well, here's the caf."

The lunch was quiet and, worse, uneasy. Dixie Miller tried to be funny, Mitchell tried to be polite, Crum tried to be friendly and Webster tried to be patronizing. Nobody succeeded but Webster, who was the kind of person who could make a compliment sound like a thinly disguised insult and an innocuous remark resemble a deliberate barb.

In desperation Dudney asked them about their military backgrounds. All four had around three thousand hours. Crum and Miller had been Navy lieutenants, Mitchell an Air Force captain and Webster—it figured, Dudney thought—a major. An aircraft commander, at that. He had flown the left seat in Globemasters, C-130s and C-141s, a record which he recited modestly enough but with an air that gave her the notion he was listing his combat decorations.

"Be kind of hard to be a copilot after being an aircraft commander, and a major," she ventured.

Webster shrugged. "A bit. I expect it'll be difficult taking orders from some character who might not be able to fly as well as I can."

Dudney must have looked her disgust, for Dixie put in wryly, "One thing you might as well get used to about military pilots, Miss Devlin. We're a cocky bunch because we had to be—sort of walking a tightrope between cockiness and overconfidence."

"I'd prefer confidence to cockiness," she observed with a touch of defiance.

"You're confident, not cocky, I take it," Webster said.

"Reasonably confident, yes. But not so much that I don't think I've got a lot to learn about flying for a scheduled airline."

"Of that, I have no doubt," Webster murmured.

Dudney flushed, and she bent over her food as if she wanted to hide under the chopped beefsteak. It was Mitchell who eased matters slightly by asking her if she had ever flown Constellations.

"Never did," she said almost eagerly, "but I always wanted to. One of my dad's competitors had five of them—the Super-Gs, I think. Dad said they were sweet-flying but he never thought much of their power plants." She hoped she was not sounding falsely technical, as if she were showing off with her use of aviation jargon so natural to any airman.

The Negro nodded. "Your dad was right. Good engines for power but temperamental. I flew Connies out of Andrews for about six months. I think in just that time I had seven shutdowns."

"Connies had those Wright 3350s, didn't they?" Crum asked.

"Yep. Around thirty-two hundred horsepower, turbo-compounds."

"Best reciprocal engine they ever put into an airplane was that Pratt and Whitney R-2800," Webster said. "Our C-112s had 'em. And the airlines used them on the 6-Bs—I know a couple of United pilots who told me it was the finest recip ever made."

Dudney swallowed an overlarge hunk of chopped beefsteak,

coughed a little and mentally gritted her teeth before speaking. "The DC-6B had R-2800s, but they were the CB-17 model. The 6 used the CB-15 and that was four hundred horses less than the 17 and with overhauls about a third more frequent."

They stared at her as if they had just heard a nun utter a four-letter word.

"You memorize that out of some book last night, just to impress us?" Webster asked with open rudeness.

Now she was regretting that smart-ass impulse and her answer to Webster approached the status of humility. "I wasn't trying to impress anybody," she said, so softly that they could hardly hear her. "You made a little mistake and I was just trying to correct you." Her voice rose, and she was smiling bitterly. "No, that's not true. I was trying to show off—or maybe trying to get across to you that I know a little bit about airplanes. I'm sorry."

Dixie was looking at her reproachfully, Mitchell a bit sadly and Crum with a touch of awe. Surprisingly, it was the pontifical Webster who was graciously forgiving—if her leaping at a minor technicality really called for forgiveness. Actually, there was friendliness if not respect in his voice. "Well, can't say that I blame you. Guess you're on a spot with us, Miss Devlin. Natural to show off a little."

"If any of *us* had brought up the exact model number of the DC-6B engine," Mitchell commented sagely, "we wouldn't have been accused of showing off."

"Yeah," agreed Dixie. "No hard feelings, Miss Devlin?"

"No hard feelings," she said, but the fight had gone out of her. While the four pilots discussed various aeronautical matters during the rest of the lunch break, she remained silent—hoping that silence would not be mistaken for pouting or sulking. She knew she had just been given a disturbingly accurate measurement of the ice on which she was skating—and it was razor-thin, its fragility ready to crack at the slightest mistake either in her relationships with the rest of the class or, in all probability, with her instructors.

It was with relief that she accompanied them back to the auditorium for the afternoon session, at which Studebaker continued with a recitation of Trans-Coastal's corporate structure, the employees' credit union, the pass privileges and mechanics of obtaining reduced-rate transportation on TCA and other carriers. Two girls from his office handed out various booklets which contained, Dudney discovered as she glanced through them, all the information Studebaker had imparted orally and so laboriously.

"I would like to conclude," Studebaker was saying, "by wishing each and every one of you the best of luck in your new career. As a representative of management I want to assure you that merit means everything in this company—merit along with loyalty and responsibility. We promote on ability, not on politics or who you know." He fought off a twinge of cynicism as he spoke those words, being only too well aware that a recently appointed vice president was an incompetent slob who had buttered up a large TCA stockholder with what was rumored to have been an effective job of pimping. "Tomorrow, you can report to your respective departments for your first day of work and/or training. I think you new mechanics already have been informed of where and when to report, and also our new office workers. The stewardess class will meet with our chief stewardess instructor, Miss Gillholland, at 8:30 A.M. in Room 301 of the main Administration Building. And I've been asked to tell you new pilots that your 737 first officer school starts at 0730 in Room 200 of the Flight Training Center. Now then"—and he could not help looking at Dudney for a split second—"I wish you all not only the best of luck but congratulations on your new career with the world's finest airline. Thank you."

There was a smattering of applause which stemmed as much from relief as appreciation, and the auditorium emptied quickly. Dudney was walking behind the four pilots with whom she had lunched, plus the five other members of the class. She hung back deliberately, but not so far that she could not hear their chatter.

"Let's go find a good steak house," Dixie was saying. "Have a little celebration before all the classroom shit hits the fan."

"I got a date with that little blonde from the stew class," one of the pilots she had not met said. "Count me out—sex interests me more than food." She could not see his face, but he was a tall youngster with a crew cut and a waddling kind of walk that made her suspect his fashionably narrow trousers hid a pair of bowlegs.

"A steak sounds fine with me," Ernie Crum said. "How about you, Hank?"

The big Negro shook his head. "I'd better keep looking for a place to live. My wife's due in here next Wednesday and I can't afford many more nights in that motel. Tell you what, Dixie. Leave word at the motel where you'll be and if I get through in time I'll join you."

"Okay. Mike, you gonna come along or are you stew-chasin' with Doug?"

Dudney didn't hear the answer. She dropped farther behind, out of range of their voices, conscious that her fear of a snub had overridden her desire to be asked along. By the time she reached the street they were already out of sight.

She had found a furnished efficiency apartment the day before, a somewhat dilapidated two-story building on Maple Street just off Sepulveda and only a five-minute taxi ride from Trans-Coastal. It was a bit dingy but had window air conditioners, a reasonably modern refrigerator and a bright if tiny kitchen. The creaky convertible sofa bed might have been the prototype of all sofa beds but there was a fairly new dinette table with two chairs and a large, well-stuffed easy chair with a good floor lamp next to it.

She decided she might as well move in that night, then changed her mind because it was far past the Hacienda's checkout time. Maybe she should go over to the apartment and clean up a bit, she thought, but the prospect of solo housework merely accentuated her loneliness. She found herself walking by the Flight Training Center and on impulse walked in, examining the cluttered bulletin board that hung on the wall across from an unmanned reception desk. Idly, she scanned the multitude of announcements and advertisements that included the inevitable three-by-five cards offering such bargains as "1961 Plymouth convertible, good rubber, excellent mech. condition, needs new top, $250 or best offer." She would need a car eventually, Dudney told herself, having already discovered that Los Angeles public transportation was woefully inadequate and cabs were woefully overpriced.

Bored, she turned away and was about to walk out when she noticed a large framed blackboard suspended over the closed-down switchboard in the reception area. It reminded her of the squadron flight boards she used to see in World War I movies, the ones containing the pilot roster with a few names always erased by the grim-faced adjutant at the end of a day's mission in those flying coffins, while Captain Geoffrey Thorp (played by Errol Flynn) gulped down a shot of whiskey and threw the empty glass into the big fireplace as a last salute to a dead comrade.

She was laughing to herself, recalling those corny but wonderful old films, when the first line on the blackboard caught her eye.

"0730—NEW HIRES CLASS B-737—ROOM 200."

Uncertainty and fear flooded her mind, but it was only momentary —a flush of quickly doused fever.

She was Ralph Devlin's daughter, and she marched out of the Training Center with her head high and her jaw set stubbornly as if the memory of the man who had been friend and teacher as well as father had conquered the loneliness of the empty twilight.

CHAPTER FOUR

The class reported to Room 200 not only on time but ranging from fifteen to thirty minutes early—a demonstration more of anxiety than punctuality.

Every one of her nine classmates, Dudney noted, was spruced up with conservative ties, clean shirts and freshly pressed suits—in marked contrast to an older-looking Boeing 720 recurrent training class which reported to an adjacent room outfitted in loud sport shirts and not a tie or suit coat in sight.

She had worried and fussed over her own clothes for the first day of class. She finally decided on a simple black skirt, with a white blouse and a black cardigan sweater—knowing that her trim, slim figure looked good in a blouse. She had left her packed bag at the Hacienda, planning to pick it up after class so she could move into the apartment.

A few of her new comrades seemed a little hung over—Dixie Miller being one and Doug Worthington, the pilot who had already started his Trans-Coastal social life with a stewardess trainee, being another. Their cleanly shaven faces merely accentuated the incongruity of their bloodshot eyes, like heavy make-up applied to mask wrinkles of age on a woman. Dixie's greeting to Dudney, in truth, was sheepish, as if her clear, bright eyes were a symbol of superiority over this debauched male.

"Hi, Miss Devlin. Uh, get a good sleep?"

She had slept poorly, as a matter of fact, but she was not going to admit it. "Very well, Dixie." The use of his nickname was a curious mixture of deference and defiance. And it did not go over his head.

"You, uh, sort of disappeared after orientation yesterday," he remarked in a tone of false offhandedness. "We were going to ask you if you had any dinner plans."

She felt like saying bullshit but decided it was neither ladylike nor diplomatic. "I would have been too busy anyway. I was moving things into the apartment."

"I wish I had done something constructive like that," Dixie confided. "Too much to drink—I feel like a wet dishrag. Some of us went—"

His accounting of the previous evening's activities was interrupted by the arrival of a well-built man in his mid-thirties, wearing a loud checked sports jacket and a natty bow tie which somehow meshed beautifully with his bristly crew cut. He also wore an air of brisk authority which managed to douse the students' chatter before he said a word.

"Gentlemen—and the young lady—if you'll take your seats, we've got a lot of ground to cover and you can have your bull sessions on your own time."

They took their seats, hurriedly and rather quietly, Dudney noted. The seats were uncomfortable, unpadded wooden chairs in back of several rows of long tables, six chairs to a table. Three men grabbed seats in the first row, four occupied the second row, the remainder settled down in the third row and Dudney, hesitating uncertainly for a moment, sat alone in the fourth row. The man in the bow tie watched her as she isolated herself, and she could have sworn a look of sympathy crossed his square face.

"Good morning," he began. "For the record, I'm Dave Robinson, director of the Training Center. From right now to the day you graduate I'm your boss, disciplinarian and the chaplain if you need a shoulder to cry on. The first week will be relatively easy—we'll go through what we call company indoctrination, a forty-hour course required by the FAA. After that, things will get a little rougher."

As he was speaking, another man entered Room 200—like Robinson, of medium height but husky build, with graying hair and a brown business suit whose simplicity was jarred by a purple shirt and a screaming surrealist tie. The latter reminded Dudney of something that might have been selected by the dubious taste of a five-year-old boy buying a gift for Father's Day.

Robinson nodded at the newcomer but didn't introduce him, continuing instead with his opening remarks. "The indoctrination course will take up the rest of this week and will include a morning session on Saturday." There were groans at this announcement but Robinson merely smiled. "The following week will be devoted to B-737 systems, in other words, your ground school phase of training, and if you survive"—he paused, for obvious dramatic emphasis, and looked pleased at the solemn young faces in front of him—"if you survive, then will come two weeks of flight training. Now, anybody here who hasn't shown us your FAA ticket and your radiotelephone permit?"

Everyone, it seemed, had. "Fine," Robinson said, grinning "Haul 'em out again—for a double check."

There were murmurs at this unexpected order. The smile departed Robinson's face as he explained. "We're not questioning anybody's honesty, but a few years ago Eastern and the whole bloody industry, not to mention the FAA, were damned embarrassed when they discovered a very highly regarded captain was flying around with phony credentials. I don't know if any of you recall the incident, but due to some sloppy checking this character worked his way up to captain on nothing but an altered private pilot's license and what was obviously a hell of a lot of innate flying skill. Since then, we're making damned sure you're legally qualified for training. This gentleman here, by the way"—he was looking at the man in the loudly hued tie—"is George Le Baron, chief of our ground school. George, if you'll get the first two rows I'll check the rest."

While Robinson and Le Baron were examining the FAA certificates, Dudney had a chance to gaze around the classroom, being particularly fascinated by the large systems panels she had noticed on her earlier tour with Studebaker. About four feet tall and six feet wide, they amounted to two-dimensional, workable reproductions of such major 737 components as the electrical, hydraulics, landing gear, air conditioning, fire protection, fuel and flaps/spoilers systems. A big blackboard faced the class, with two hand-printed signs tacked above it: "No Food or Beverages in Classroom" and "WELCOME TO CONFUSIONVILLE." She also examined the classmates she had not met yet, amused at the way all nine men were fishing their pilot credentials out of their wallets like motorists nervously locating drivers' licenses under the impatient stare of a policeman. She had her commercial ticket and radio permit out of her own wallet long before Robinson reached her.

"Miss Devlin," was his laconic greeting when he reached her seat. He inspected them carefully, although no more diligently than he had the others, handing them back with just a suggestion of a smile that managed to unnerve her more than if he had frowned at her. She could not tell whether the smile was one of friendly understanding or along the ominous lines of "I can't wait to throw the book at you."

All tickets examined, Robinson returned to the front of the room and resumed. "I know all of you, except for Miss Devlin, are ex-military. Let me assure you we have utmost respect for your military training—if it hadn't been good, you wouldn't be here today. So we don't mean to disparage your service flying when we tell you we're going to teach you all over again. What makes a good military pilot doesn't necessarily make a good airline pilot. Your responsibilities, in some respect even your flying techniques, will be different with Trans-Coastal. I hope none of you will approach any phase of training with the idea you're Einstein being asked to go through kindergarten again. A lot of this stuff will be old hat, maybe even boring, but bear with us. In the airline business we can't assume a damned thing so we operate on the theory that everyone is starting out from the level of complete ignorance, at least about the aircraft on which you'll be qualifying. Now, do you all know each other?"

There was general nodding. Dudney kept silent. She was unhappy when Robinson continued, "Well, just to make sure George and I can start telling you apart, I'd appreciate each one standing up and giving us your name—including any nickname you might prefer our using—and give us a little background on your military or other flying experience. Okay, we'll start here in the first row and go around the room clockwise."

The tall pilot with the duck walk and what apparently was a most active libido arose. "Doug Worthington, and I'm Navy. PB-5 Marlin flying boats, Lockheed Neptunes and Orions. Home town's Phoenix, Arizona."

Crum, the pixie, was next. "Ernie Crum, Navy. From Hartford,

Connecticut. Strictly a fighter pilot, I'm afraid—F-6s, F-4B Phantoms, and a few hours in the Crusader."

"Don't apologize for the fighter background, Mr. Crum," Robinson said. "Some of our instructors prefer ex-fighter pilots, although others would rather get men with transport experience. We'll be happy to give you the latter. Next."

The third man in the front row was stocky, with black wavy hair and a solemn face. "Mike Kalinka, Air Force—hell, I've moved around so much I forgot what's supposed to be my home town. Make it Chicago—that's where I was born. Let's see—I've flown C-131s, C-123s and C-135 tankers."

Webster stood up. "Frank Webster, Air Force, Miami, Florida Globemasters, C-130s and C-141s." His voice was clipped, as if he were barking orders to a non-com.

Miller announced, in his molasses-thick drawl, "I'm Dixie Miller, Mobile, Alabama, Navy."

"Confederate Navy, I assume," Robinson interposed as the class laughed.

"I'm strictly a Lockheed man—mostly Orions, about one hundred and fifty hours in Neptunes," Dixie finished.

Hank Mitchell was next and Dudney thought she saw a shadow of approval flit over Robinson's face as the black rested a huge hand on Miller's shoulder while he spoke. "Henry Mitchell, otherwise known as Hank, and I'm Air Force. Boeing C-135, mostly, although I've flown Connies and a couple of other recip transports." He started to sit down, then rose again briefly. "Oh, I forgot—I'm from Binghamton, New York."

The handsome Tarkington got to his feet hurriedly and spoke even more hurriedly, like an embarrassed schoolboy trying to race through a recitation. "Bob Tarkington, Navy, Marlins and Neptunes." He sat down so quickly the words "and Neptunes" were still floating in the air as his buttocks touched the chair. Dudney decided she liked him; a good-looking man who was shy was refreshing as well as unusual.

"Where you from, Mr. Tarkington?" Robinson asked.

"Uh, Boise, sir. In Idaho."

"Your cabin PAs may be on the brief side, I'm afraid," Robinson remarked good-naturedly as he nodded at the next man, sitting directly in front of Dudney. He seemed to be the eldest of the nine, tall but thin, with blond hair and a rather sad face. His large brown eyes turned down at the corners, giving him a somewhat spaniel appearance.

"Harrison McCrae, and I prefer to be called Mac. Air Force. C-119s originally and then B-52s. Originally from Minneapolis." His voice was a surprise. Deep, modulated, even cultured with no trace of affectation—like that of a self-assured veteran radio announcer.

"Bill O'Brien," said the last man, a sandy-haired youngster of pudgy, well-fed build. "Navy, Grumman S-2A Trackers, Marlins. I'm from Marinette, Wisconsin, and don't hold this against me—I've been checked out in helicopters."

"I won't hold it against you," Robinson smiled, "but I trust you'll forget everything you learned on those choppers." He started to nod at Dudney, but even before his head moved a fraction of an inch, every neck in the room had swiveled toward her. Her chair scraped noisily as she pushed it back and stood up. "Dudney Devlin, Anchorage. DC-3s, DC-6, Electras and Jetstars, mostly." She could not stifle a smile as she added, "No military experience, I'm afraid." There were a few chuckles, whether from humor or politeness she could not tell. At this moment the faces staring at her were blurred. Robinson resumed even before she sat down.

"Very good, gentlemen and Miss Devlin. We're glad to see so much heavy transport time in this class." Ernie Crum grimaced but Robinson did not seem to notice. "Matter of fact, you men who've flown equipment like the C-135 may find Fat Albert a letdown." He paused. "I take it from your puzzled expressions you've never heard of Fat Albert?"

The class shook its collective head, Dudney excepted. She was well aware that the stubby, potbellied Boeing 737 had been dubbed Fat Albert almost from the day it first flew, but after her experience of the previous day she was not going to be caught showing off again. Anyway, she was uncertain of the nickname's origin and she was glad when Robinson went on to explain.

"Some engineer at Boeing gave the 737 the name Fat Albert, after Bill Cosby's famous friend. It just seemed to fit the bird. Most air-lincs flying the 737 don't care for the nickname—Trans-Coastal, in fact, has ordered pilots not to use it in public. Supposed to be disrespectful, but frankly I can't buy that. The 737 will be Fat Albert until the day it makes its last flight. Which brings me to the airplane itself. It's easy to fly, honest, extremely strong and rugged—all in all, a very, very fine short- to medium-range jet. Like any jet, it won't forgive mistakes and it won't tolerate sloppiness. But give it an even break and it'll do the job for you. Question, Mr. McCrae?"

"Yes, sir. How come Trans-Coastal doesn't operate the 737 with three-man crews, like most of the airlines that bought it?"

"Good question, Mr. McCrae, and a controversial one. I don't want to get involved in the pros and cons of the three-man crew donnybrook at this time—you'll hear plenty of it when you join ALPA, the Air Line Pilots Association, as I expect most or all of you will. But for the benefit of those who aren't aware of the three-man issue, I'll explain the background briefly. The 737, like the DC-9 and BAC-111, were certificated for operation by two-man crews. The BAC-111 and DC-9 went into operation ahead of the 737. Before the latter entered service, ALPA laid down a policy that all future turbine aircraft must have a third man in the cockpit, as an additional safety measure. Primarily as a collision lookout and also to handle any trouble in the cabin while the captain and first officer are busy with cockpit duties. United's pilots were the first to apply the new ALPA policy and United eventually started flying the 737 with three men. So did Western and other carriers. A few airlines, like Trans-Coastal, stayed with two men. Our guys weren't happy about it and they damned near struck. They got a pretty fat wage boost and a flock of new fringe benefits by agreeing to a compromise —TCA would fly the 737 with two men for a period of three years, and we've got two more years to go on that contract. ALPA's warned it'll demand a GIB in the next negotiations but you don't have to worry about that for the time being."

"What's a GIB?" Dixie wanted to know.

"Stands for Guy In Back—in other words, the third man who occupies the jump seat. I think GIB originated with Western, although like Fat Albert it's not considered kosher to use the phrase. Seems somebody at Western happened to come across the word 'gib' in a dictionary. It means castrated tomcat, so from then on Western insisted that its pilots refer to GIBs as second officers. Naturally, it didn't do a damned bit of good; they're still known as GIBs, unofficially, anyway."

The class laughed and Robinson looked appreciative.

"Let's get something straight," he continued seriously. "I don't want to influence you one way or another on this third-man business. For what it's worth, I'll give you my personal opinion. I think it's a damned good idea to have three men in the cockpit of any high-performance airplane, even if ninety-nine per cent of the time the third man's about as useful as tits on a boar hog." He glanced at Dudney as if expecting her to object to his phraseology, but she didn't even blink and merely looked intensely interested. "The only trouble with ALPA's policy is that it's unfair to the 737. I've got a hell of a lot of respect for the DC-9 or any plane built by Douglas. I don't know much about the BAC-111, although guys I know with Braniff and American tell me it's a fine little bird. But of the three airplanes, Fat Albert, for my dough, is the easiest to fly with only two men. If ALPA wants to be consistent in a matter of safety, then it should be fighting to put a third man in DC-9s and BAC-111s instead of limiting all the bloodshed to the 737. When you start flying the line, you're gonna find that ninety-nine times out of a hundred you don't need any third guy in that cockpit any more than you need three testicles." This time he didn't bother to glance at the lone woman in the room and she wondered if his mild profanity was deliberate.

"But along comes that one hundredth occasion," Robinson continued, "like when some stupid ass flying a Cessna with about twenty-five hours' logged experience blunders toward your windshield, and you're up to your armpits with a final approach checklist, and the third man is the only one who can spot the bastard in time for evasion. That's when you gotta weigh the two million bucks a year Trans-Coastal would have to spend on generally useless GIBs against the maybe once a year he'd save a three-and-a-half-million-dollar airplane from a mid-air."

There were several hands raised for more questioning, but Robinson shook his head. "We'll have some time for questions later today, but let's get a few of the required formalities over with first. George, help me hand out this stuff."

"This stuff" included an eight-by-eleven mimeographed notebook with a gray cover bearing the title, "737 First Officer Course"; a smaller booklet with a green cover labeled "Pilot Agreement, Trans-Coastal Airlines, May 1, 1969"; a large yellow card with black lettering, "PILOT TRAINING, TEMPORARY PARKING, EMPLOYEES LOT"; two Trans-Coastal baggage tags per student; a loose-leaf notebook for lecture notes; a wallet-sized temporary trainee identification card, and —the class looked with wonderment at this item—a postcard with a beautiful color shot of a TCA 720 in flight over a mountain range.

"The postcard's for writing home," Robinson informed them with a straight face. "We're just like the Army—we encourage you to write home to mother."

"I can't afford the postage," Dixie murmured. "When do we get paid?"

"The fifth and twentieth of each month," Robinson said. "So your first check will be issued on May fifth. May I have your attention, please?" The class was chattering again as it pored through the material just handed out. "I told you, we'll save some time for questions this afternoon. We've got a lot to do so let's settle down. This course outline in the gray notebook we've just handed out will answer a lot of your questions, anyway. If you'll open it to the first page, you'll get an idea of what the schedule will be for the rest of the week."

The class turned to the first page.

DATE	SUBJECT	ROOM	INSTRUCTOR
April 29 (Tues)			
0730	Ground School Indoctrination	200	Robinson
0930	Coffee		
1000	Stores	Bldg C	
1100	Domiciles	200	Robinson
1130	Lunch		
1230	Ops Manual	200	Croyden
1400	I.D. Photos (G/O–2nd flr)		
1500	Ops Manual	200	Croyden

April 30 (Wed)
0730	Flight Dispatch	200	Willis
0930	Coffee		
1000	Tailors	200	

That last item caught Dudney's eye just as Robinson suggested they turn to the second page. It was very *un*womanlike, but she never really had given any thought to what she was supposed to wear as a legitimate TCA first officer. Sam Macklin had kidded her about it once. "I saw some Polish women airline pilots at the Warsaw airport last summer," he had recalled, "and they looked about as sexy as a pro defensive tackle. They had on short skirts and boots that came up to their knees." Probably, she reasoned, Trans-Coastal would put her in slacks; she hoped they wouldn't go for anything as far out as the miniskirts worn by stewardesses. Her mental meanderings on this vital topic were interrupted by Robinson's voice.

"These are the general rules for ground school training, our policies for the classroom and outside the classroom, to some extent. Read them carefully. As of 0730 tomorrow, we'll take it for granted you know the rules and we expect you to follow same. Not knowing them won't be any excuse if you get into trouble. Let me emphasize a couple of items. Later today you'll be given your Jeppesen Manual, and when you start Systems you'll be handed the 737 Operations Manual. Don't make lecture notes in the manuals—that's why we gave you this little classroom notebook. Technically, the manuals are on loan to you as long as you fly for Trans-Coastal. Actually, we don't give a damn what you write in them after you start flying the line, but if you wash out of training you're expected to return every manual, and if you don't, you'll be charged for them. I might add, they're mighty expensive publications. One more item—drinking. Refresh my memory—what's the military policy on alcohol?"

"Don't drink within fifty feet of an airplane," Dixie said, "and no more than twenty-four drinks an hour before takeoff." Robinson joined in the laughter.

"Hell," the training chief said, "you're all grown men and pilots as well. You know what too much drinking can do to your flying proficiency and I'm not gonna deliver any temperance lecture. But some of you came in here this morning with eyeballs that should have been donated to a blood bank. What you do is your own business once you leave this classroom, but if booze affects the learning process, it's damned well going to be our business. Just let me give you this little advice: don't think for one minute that you can get through ground school on the basis of what you learned flying for the Navy or Air Force. Make up your minds you're gonna have to hit the books from now on—so watch the booze, and the broads, if you're so inclined. That reminds me, how many of you are married?"

The reply came from Dixie Miller, who seemed to have appointed himself class spokesman. "Doug, Mike and Ernie are bachelors, rest of us are married. Except Miss Devlin." The last was a rather gratuitous afterthought, Dudney said to herself.

"Three swingers, six prisoners and I'll let Miss Devlin put herself into her own category," Robinson said. "Of you married men, whose wives are already here?"

Again, Dixie supplied the data. "Only McCrae's and Tarkington's. I guess most of the guys expect their wives later this week. Mine's due in Thursday."

Robinson's eyes narrowed. "Well, I suppose you'd be asking for time off if your wives arrived at the airport during class hours. I'd like to avoid this if possible. It would be a good idea if you could contact your families tonight and arrange for them to arrive in L.A. after class is over. We'll try to finish up no later than 1630 for the rest of this week, but I can't promise anything. One more thing before we resume—have you all found places to live?"

There were general murmurs of assent and Robinson nodded with satisfaction. "Fine, that'll be one less distraction. Now . . ."

"It wasn't easy," Dixie called out. "I went to a hundred places—eighty of them wouldn't take my dog and the other twenty wouldn't take my wife."

The class roared and so did Robinson, who already had resigned himself to the fact that every pilot class had to have at least one clown. He made a mental note to mention Miller's name to John Battles when it came time to report on ground school personnel and progress. The chief pilot had an unshakable theory that pilots with senses of humor invariably were good captain material. And it wasn't a bad theory, either, for it was based on a statistically unverified but logical assumption that such men were happy at their work, relaxed, unruffled by tension and rock-solid under the outer crust of horseplay.

"All right," he resumed, "let's go through the rest of this course outline. Turn to page 3. This is a list of Trans-Coastal's executive officers in Flight Operations. I suggest you memorize it tonight— particularly the first five names on the list. One, several or all names will be on the test you're given Saturday morning." The titles, if not the names, were imposing. Vice President, Flight Operations, Jerome Norgaard. System Chief Pilot, John Battles. Regional Chief Pilot, LAX, Rudolph Coston. Regional Chief Pilot, DEN, Eric Henzey. . . .

Robinson's voice droned on, delivery dulled by familiarity. . . . "Page 4 includes the general duties of a first officer and these, too, will be a test item Saturday. These are generalized and will be more detailed in your Jeppesen. We'll go over these briefly. Note your check-in time of one hour before estimated departure. That's *in person*—no check-ins by proxy on this or any other airline. After signing in with Crew Schedule, you're to check the first officer bulletin board. Be sure and always check and empty your mailbox. In the event of a delayed departure, you're to—yes, Mr. Worthington?"

"Sir, where are the mailboxes? I mean, the ones we get before we start flying? Or don't we get any?"

"You do. You'll find them in Operations. Right in the crew lounge, there's a rack of temporary mailboxes designated for flight trainees. Later, you'll get a permanent box located adjacent to Dispatch. Gentlemen, I'd appreciate your refraining from further questions until this afternoon. Now, if you'll just glance over the next few items which are self-explanatory. As I was saying, if your departure is delayed, you're to wait in the crew lounge for further instructions from the captain. Your duties as to flight plan data are spelled out, also the rules for reporting to aircraft—that's at least forty-five minutes before ETD, and you're to be in the cockpit no later than fifteen minutes prior to departure. Anyone know why?"

Typically, the class found itself stricken with temporary speechlessness and ignorance at an unexpected question. Again, Dudney knew the answer—as did everyone else if they had been thinking— but she was determined not to volunteer the time of day unless asked directly. Robinson grimaced impatiently. "It's a very simple question and you should have known the answer just by being a pilot. You need that fifteen minutes for accomplishing the pre-taxi check- list. Now, let's go on to required first officer equipment. This may be another test question. Flight computer—and you'll be able to buy this handy little item at Stores after our coffee break. A standard two-cell flashlight. A—I hope it's important, Mr. Miller."

"I think so, sir. My question is, uh, financial. Germane to your mention of flight computers."

"You'll find out how much a computer costs when we get to Stores."

"Sir, what I mean is that some of us already have our computers, the ones we used in service. Mine's almost brand-new. I was wondering—"

"Trans-Coastal doesn't give a damn where you bought your flight computer so long as you have it with you every time you board an airplane. Its purchase in Stores is not mandatory. I suggest you check yours with the type Stores is selling. If they're the same, you don't have to buy one. Now, going on with the required equipment. Pen- light, aircraft and cockpit door key, fuse puller, and the following tools: standard, Phillips and pen-size screwdrivers; water pump and diagonal pliers, and a crescent wrench. You're also expected to have with you your fuel loading charts, aircraft Operations Manual and spare copies of checklists and power charts . . ."

Every succeeding page discussed by the training chief brought the repeated admonition, "This may be a test item Saturday." Es- pecially alarming was Robinson's assignment of that warning to page seven, a list of the fifty-four cities served by Trans-Coastal and the airport code letters for the fifty-four airports, starting with ACA for Acapulco and ending with YAK for Yakutat. When at 0930 sharp he mercifully announced a thirty-minute coffee break, Dudney over- heard Dixie Miller complain mournfully to Webster: "My God, if he includes everything he mentioned as part of that Saturday test, we'll be there for six hours."

"Well," Webster replied stodgily, "he also told us we'd better hit the books and that's exactly what I'm going to do, starting tonight."

"Yeah," Dixie breathed in fervent agreement. "Those airport codes—Jesus."

Dudney had planned to at least sit down with some of her classmates for coffee, but as she was leaving Room 200 Robinson stopped her.

"Miss Devlin, may I see you a moment?"

Dixie and Hank Mitchell tossed glances of curiosity at her as they left. She felt a sudden surge of fear that somehow the brass hats had changed their minds by finding some legal loophole to block her.

"I just wanted to apologize for some of the language I used," the training chief said. "No—that's not quite right. I'm not apologizing, just explaining. I am sorry if I sounded a bit foulmouthed, but I can't clean up my vocabulary for the benefit of the one female in the class. Hope you understand."

She not only understood but was relieved. "Mr. Robinson, I was brought up by a pilot and I've spent most of my young life among pilots—a career which of necessity included exposure to quite a few four-letter words. I've used some of them myself, on occasions. So don't be sorry, and do me a favor—please don't bring up the subject again."

He looked relieved in turn, conscious that John Battles had advised him, "Talk as dirty as you want to—maybe we can embarrass her into quitting." He prayed Battles would never hear that he had apologized to her, but he couldn't help feeling guilty. She was such an attractive, personable kid and he liked her attentiveness and obvious alertness. Wisely, he suspected that with her civil aviation background she was ahead of her military-acclimated classmates in some respects and yet, at least on this first day, she had made no effort to flaunt this aspect.

"Okay, go have your coffee," he urged.

The brief delay cost her any chance to sit with the others. When she arrived at the cafeteria the nine pilots were occupying an entire table and there was no room for her. She skirted the area without their seeing her, found an empty table in the rear of the caf out of their sight, and she sipped her coffee alone, feeling a little sorry for herself and simultaneously scolding herself anew for self-pity. She had expected some ostracizing and in some ways it hadn't been as bad as it might have been. Dixie Miller had exhibited some friendliness and so had Hank Mitchell and the others she had met—along with Dixie's advice not to expect immediate acceptance, advice she knew was fair.

Still, she was basically a warm and affectionate person who liked people, who liked being with people and talking with people. If it was easy to accept the logic of this form of Coventry, it was not easy to bear it uncomplainingly. She had much in common with her classmates, and she was starved for the kind of friendships she had treasured with fellow airmen in Alaska: the easy, pleasant sharing of mutual interests and experiences; the taken-for-granted comradeship that went doubly deep because it was taken for granted only outwardly; the sentimentality so poorly hidden under brusqueness and profanity; the loyalties occasionally emerging from surface coldness to be thawed by real necessity.

It bothered her that the excitement of training was tempered by this unexpectedly strong need for companionship. It was a strange alchemy, an alloy of bitterness and ambition, of resolve weakened by unhappiness. She was angry at her emotions, which she considered moral and professional flabbiness, never stopping to realize that it took courage to admit those emotions without letting them override everything else. And when she returned to class after the coffee break, the interlude of self-flagellation had strengthened her, shame dispelling pity and determination once again displacing loneliness.

The class resumption lasted only long enough for Robinson to announce a visit to Stores—"the Neiman-Marcus of Trans-Coastal," he explained, "where you can pick up your flight bags, otherwise known as brainbags, also the pocket computers I mentioned and a separate attaché case. The latter's not absolutely necessary but the brainbag is—you'll need it for all your manuals."

"Do they accept Diners or Carte Blanche?" Dixie wanted to know.

"You can pay for anything you buy by personal check, or sign an authorization to deduct specified amounts from future pay checks," Robinson said. "The brainbag sells for twenty-nine ninety-five and the special attaché case for eighteen bucks. Eighteen's not a bad buy, either, if you have the dough. They retail for damned near forty dollars. There are two flight computers—a large, fancy one for eight bucks and a smaller one for six. I'll give you a tip—the little one's perfectly acceptable and the big one won't fit into anything but a brainbag. Okay, let's go."

Stores may have been "the Neiman-Marcus of Trans-Coastal" in Robinson's words but to Dudney and the rest of the class it more closely resembled what it really was—a huge warehouse located on the second floor of an older building, and from the looks of it containing everything but spare wings and engines. Dudney saw pile after pile of company stationery, manuals, seatback cards, schedules and voluminous other items in such variety that an accountant taking inventory probably would have gone into a state of shock.

She bought a brainbag, making out a check on her Anchorage bank, but along with everyone else resisted the attractive attaché case. She already had a pocket computer, one her father had given her only a few months before his death. Webster and McCrae also made out checks for their brainbags, the others signing the payroll deduction forms. They were all a little self-conscious as they marched back to Room 200; a shiny new bag was about as conspicuous as a clean football uniform on a muddy gridiron, stamping them instantly as rookies. It was almost inevitable that the class en route should pass a couple of Trans-Coastal captains who grinned a faint wisp of disdainful superiority.

The first agenda item on their return was Domiciles, which turned out to be the low point of their day. Robinson handed out a small sheet of paper at the top of which was the legend: "BASE PREFERENCE SHEET." Under this was:

> First Choice_____
>
> Second Choice_____
>
> Third Choice_____
>
> Fourth Choice_____

"We'd better have a brief discussion about this," Robinson announced. "Trans-Coastal has four pilot domiciles, or bases if you're more used to that word. Los Angeles, San Francisco, Seattle and

Denver. List your preferences one through four in that order. But I'll be honest with you—the chances are about ninety per cent all of you will be based in Los Angeles." Loud groans greeted this news. "There's a reason for this; most of our 737 trips originate in L.A. and it makes sense to domicile Fat Albert's crews right here. This doesn't mean you'll be stuck in L.A. forever. After your first two years you can bid for a transfer, and no city, even if you get your fourth choice, is unbearable for twenty-four months."

"When's the soonest we can find out where we'll be based?" O'Brien asked.

"The day you get there," Dixie muttered before Robinson had a chance to answer. The training chief chuckled and then got serious again.

"We'll do our damnedest to place you where you'd like to go," he assured the class, "but until you acquire some seniority, system needs will have priority over personal preferences. And now's as good a time as any to drum something into your skulls. Seniority. *Seniority.* From this first day of training to the last flight you'll take with TCA, that one word will govern your lives, your profession. Seniority will dictate the type of aircraft you fly, the times you fly, the places you fly, your vacations, your days off, your upgrading either to captain or to bigger equipment. It may seem cold-blooded, but if you hear that a pilot's been killed in a crash, your first instinct will be to ask what his seniority number was."

He knew he had suddenly impressed them. The mumbling and subdued chatter that followed his pessimism on base assignments had ceased. "I think you're getting the message. Remember seniority before you make any major decision affecting your flying career. If you want to change domiciles, for example, find out first how far down the seniority ladder you'll be at the new base—you might wind up flying milk runs with nine takeoffs and landings a day. Or suppose I told you there's an opening in a 720B first officer class that starts May 10. Four-engine equipment, higher pay. Who'd be interested?"

They hesitated momentarily, then seven of the ten raised their hands. Dudney was one of the three who didn't, largely because she suspected the offer was loaded.

Robinson shook his head in half-mocking disapproval. "The seven who'd drop out of this 737 class right now to start a 720B class later are damned fools—because they'd be giving up about ten days' seniority. I'll give you this illustration of how important seniority can be over the long haul, and why you seven would be making the mistake of your young lives. When I was flying the line some years ago, a good friend of mine started out in Convair 240 school. On the second day he heard there'd be an opening in DC-6 school two weeks later. So he drops out of the 240 class and waits for the DC-6 class to start. He lost the seniority he had acquired in the original class. It took him four years before he upgraded to a DC-6 captain—and that little decision to go for the bigger equipment and higher seniority number cost him about twenty-five thousand bucks in salary. In other words, your seniority with Trans-Coastal started as of the moment you entered this classroom."

Webster raised his hand. "If all nine of—I mean ten—of us started today, how do we determine who's senior in this class?"

"By birthdays. The oldest person in this room gets the lowest seniority number. If any two or more of you were born the same day, we'd have to boil it down to hour of birth and even the time zone if that was the only way to decide it. We've already got your birth dates from your applications, but after you fill out these base preference sheets I'll give you five minutes to swap birthday data so you can tell where you stand in this class."

"Navy pilots should get seniority credit just for joining the Navy," Miller argued as he entered his four choices. "The Air Force, now—that's like retiring."

Dudney was at a brief loss as to what to list. She had never given the base problem any thought, and she finally decided on Los Angeles primarily because she already was there. She put down Denver second, having heard it was a clean, pleasant city; San Francisco third on its reputation for being cosmopolitan, and Seattle last, with no particular prejudice against it. It didn't make much difference, she figured, inasmuch as Robinson already had warned them they'd probably be based in L.A.

Robinson collected the sheets and glanced through them.

"Worthington, Kalinka and Devlin are the only ones who listed

L.A. first," he announced. "Crum picked San Francisco and the rest chose Denver. All you married guys want to live in Denver. Very interesting. The bachelors picked L.A., I assume on the theory it's a great place for swingers—no offense, Miss Devlin, I was referring to the males in the class. Mr. Crum, may I ask the reason for your minority dissent?"

"I got a girl in San Francisco," Crum said with a nervous giggle.

"Miss Devlin?"

"I guess I just hate to pack," Dudney explained.

"Logical," Robinson agreed. "You family men, I'm afraid, are going to be disappointed, not only now but later. There's quite a waiting list for Denver. Those of you who picked San Francisco or Seattle as second choices have a better shot—the openings are more frequent for those bases. Don't ask me when, because I'd be giving you a SWAG, otherwise known as a Sophisticated Wild-Assed Guess. Okay, you can start swapping birthdays."

As Dudney had suspected, McCrae was the oldest by a full year. Ernie Crum was the youngest, followed by Tarkington, O'Brien and Dudney, who was glad to be that far down in seniority and not for reasons of pure feminine vanity. She had a hunch her topping the seniority list would have been deeply if foolishly resented, and she already had enough strikes against her.

The lunch break a few minutes later, however, was in welcome contrast to the earlier coffee break. Dixie fell alongside her as they left the classroom, offhandedly said "Join us for lunch," in a tone that blessedly sounded more like an invitation than an order, and she found herself eating with Mitchell, McCrae and Kalinka as well as Dixie. True, they tended to leave her out of the conversation but she reasoned realistically that she was a latecomer to an away-from-class companionship that had started almost a week before training. She munched lackadaisically and yet contentedly on a ham and cheese sandwich, listening to her three companions discuss their impressions of Trans-Coastal.

"I kinda like the way they run things around here," Dixie was saying. "Treat you like adults and not immature kids."

"You guys apply to any other airline before you tried Trans-Coastal?" McCrae asked.

Dixie, his mouth full of hamburger, shook his head and so did Mitchell. "Frankly I picked TCA because I heard they already had about a half dozen black pilots," the Negro said.

"I was accepted by Pacific Northwest," Kalinka told them. "Went through all the tests—including that goddamned one they call, uh, what the hell do they call it? Stanford or something?"

"Stanine," Mitchell supplied. "It's supposed to be a bastard."

"It sure was," Kalinka recalled gloomily. "Somebody told me it costs Pacific a hundred and forty bucks per test and how the hell it can tell whether a guy's gonna be a good airline pilot is beyond me. I think there were eight hundred and fifty questions—including one like do you hate your mother worse than your father."

"But you said you were accepted," said Dixie, "so how come you went with Trans-Coastal?"

"Just didn't like the setup," Kalinka explained. "That test bugged me, for one thing. And the character who interviewed me—I got the idea Pacific Northwest was doing me a favor. So after I got TCA's telegram offering me a job, I trotted down here and applied."

"I dunno," Dixie drawled placidly, "in a sense an airline *is* doing you a favor. That guy Battles, the chief pilot—he told me he's turned down guys just for having the wrong attitude. The ones who asked him all about the fringe benefits and what the company could do for them. Hell, I wanted to but I was too damned scared to ask him anything. That sonofabitch was tough."

Hank Mitchell smiled. "If Captain Battles had suggested I pay Trans-Coastal for training, all I would have said is 'Fine, what do I owe you?'"

"Me too," McCrae agreed. "That Battles could scare the cigar right out of Curtis LeMay's mouth. I wonder if he gives the check rides."

Mitchell shook his head. "I've heard they have special check pilots, but that Battles will check-ride a marginal case."

"If my flying's like my finances," Dixie sighed, "I'm marginal."

The chore of eating silenced them for a few minutes, before Hank looked over at Dudney. "Why'd you pick this airline, Miss Devlin?"

Quietly, she explained her choice was almost pure accident—that she had seen TCA jets come into Anchorage and knew it was an expanding, aggressive carrier with a good reputation.

"My dad always thought a lot of TCA," she added.

"We read about your dad in that newspaper article Sunday," Dixie said. "He ran a cargo line or something like that?"

She could not help it, but the very mention of her father was like turning on a faucet. She tried and succeeded in keeping her tone matter-of-fact as she told them about Ralph Devlin. How he taught her to fly. How he had loved airplanes and airmen. How he had cut his pilot's teeth on Alaskan storms and regarded any ceiling of more than three hundred feet as CAVU weather. And she was suddenly conscious that a look of new respect had flitted across every earnest young face.

"Quite a guy," Hank Mitchell murmured. "You've got a lot to live up to."

Her comment on this was not quite matter-of-fact; it was thinly coated with fervor. "If I make it on my own, I'll be living up to him."

Somehow, this brief glimpse into the past of their freakish classmate seemed to sober them. The rest of the lunch was consumed in relative solemnity, an atmosphere extended during the first ninety minutes of the afternoon session. Robinson introduced a new instructor, a man with a fireplug body, a shining, totally bald head and friendly, laughing eyes.

"I'd like you to meet Rufus Croyden, one of our ground school instructors," Robinson announced. "You'll be in his charge for the rest of the day. Rufe, take over."

The training chief left the room, and Croyden surveyed the class —mentally concluding that it looked exactly the same as the other forty-two classes he had taught previously. Except, of course, for that girl in the back row. Croyden, like every instructor in the training department, had moaned loudly at the news of a woman trainee— he more than anyone, for he was an earthy, ribald character who loved to tell dirty stories at the start of every class. Robinson had relayed to all members of his department John Battles' warning not to pull any punches in the foul language department, but Croyden found it was one thing to be given carte blanche for profanity and another to look at this Dudney Devlin's composed, completely absorbed expression.

He decided to abandon the latest joke he had heard, one involving the allegedly questionable morals of stewardesses on crew layovers (in its original version, born in whatever mysterious factory produces off-color stories, it was about doctors and their nurses).

"Any glider pilots in here?" he started out.

No one responded, although all looked surprised.

"Too bad," Croyden went on. "Gliding is the greatest sport of all. I happen to be president of the Orange County Glider Enthusiasts Club and I'm definitely partial to anyone who knows how to fly a glider. He automatically gets a passing grade and two months' free membership. Well, sorry about that. We'll get on with our work. If one of you gentlemen will help me with the contents of that box, we'll distribute the Jeppesen manuals."

Ernie Crum, sitting in the front row, volunteered and with Croyden handed out the manuals—small and very thick loose-leaf books bound in heavy leather. If someone had reduced the Manhattan telephone directory to a volume slightly larger than a copy of *Reader's Digest,* that would have approximated the Jeppesen manual.

"This is your bible," Croyden said, holding up one of them. "This is the book you will live by. This is the book you will fly by. You will learn its contents, adhere to its contents and keep those contents up to date at all times. The most important item you will find in your mailbox is manual revisions, outside of pay checks and bid sheets, of course." The class dutifully chuckled at the last, although all ten were busy admiring the brown leather covers with the gold inscription:

JEPPESEN
AIRWAY MANUAL

Dudney wondered, and probably so did most or all of the others, how many years would elapse before the gold lettering faded to illegibility . . . how many times the leaf rings would be snapped open to insert revisions and remove the pages they replaced. This futuristic nostalgia was interrupted by Croyden's voice, launching into a brief outline of what the manual contained and how much they were expected to learn by the Saturday test. Basically, the Jeppesen manual was a rules book, most of it containing the Federal Aviation Regulations applying to scheduled airline operations but with considerable space devoted to Trans-Coastal rules approved by the FAA for inclusion in the official manual. Dudney had used an old one given to her by her father, in comparison one that was both slimmer and simpler. The Jeppesen the class had just been handed was labeled Volume 1 and not until the trainees had won their wings would they be given the airway maps and airport approach charts included in Volume 2.

Croyden devoted only a few minutes to each section, marked in the outer margin by a white tab listing the section subject matter. TCA administrative organization and company policies. General procedures. Flight procedures. Non-scheduled procedures. Communications. Operations specifications. FARs. Air Traffic Control. Emergencies and irregularities (this tab was in brilliant red, so naturally most of the class kept flipping to this section and sneaking interested if worried looks at the contents). Foreign operations. En route procedures.

"As you can tell from our just skimming over this material," Croyden finally wound up, "there isn't time for lengthy class discussion. You're expected to study this stuff at night and I might warn you some of it will be in the test next Saturday." Nervously, a few of them flipped through the hundreds of small-type pages, a wordless gesture of protest against this unfair attack on their out-of-class hours. There were audible sighs of relief as Croyden added, "But I'll also tip you off that the test questions will be drawn only from Sections 1 through 3—administration, company policies and general procedures. The gentleman in the first row, with the striped shirt and maroon tie."

Doug Worthington looked up, startled.

"Me, sir?"

"Those sideburns of yours. Would you all turn to Section 2, page 5."

A rustling of paper.

"Note company rule 2.3.5. Personal appearance. Let me quote. 'A Flight Officer will present a neat, well-groomed appearance. Extreme hair styles and excessively long sideburns. Sideburns will be trimmed in length to mid-ear. Mustaches may be worn if kept neatly trimmed.' Okay, this is as good a time as any to give you the facts of life about this manual. The rules contained herein are in black and white. They're inviolate. There are no exceptions, no deviations. However, we have a few unwritten rules which go a bit beyond the black and white print. Some of them involve personal idiosyncrasies of individual Trans-Coastal officials. For example, if there's one thing our chief pilot hates it's long sideburns. Captain Battles carries a ruler around with him. If he thinks your sideburns are too long, he's liable to whip out that ruler and measure the distance between the bottom of the sideburn and the middle of your ear—if the space is too narrow, your next port of call had damned well better be a barber. I'm surprised our friend here didn't collide with one of Captain Battles' pet prejudices when he was interviewed."

"He didn't mention my sideburns," Worthington objected, his face red.

"You're lucky you were accepted for training. Battles must have had something else on his mind—or you happened to hit him on the one day a month he's reasonably human. No matter. I suggest you get those trimmed to regulation length, as per 2.3.5. To continue the subject of idiosyncrasies, we come now to the president of Trans-Coastal, Mr. Tom Berlin. Mr. Berlin, it seems, detests mustaches, whether they're visible on a picture of Adolf Hitler or on one of his pilots. Now the manual states mustaches are allowed provided they're neatly trimmed. Unfortunately, Mr. Berlin being the president, the manual doesn't go quite far enough. Mr. Berlin, out of the kindness of his heart and to demonstrate his humanity, fairness and reasonable attitude, has unofficially decreed that only captains may wear mustaches. Captains, but not first officers or flight engineers. This means if any of you is tempted to grow one, refrain until the day you're upgraded to captain. At Trans-Coastal, mustaches may be added only with the fourth stripe on your uniform. There are no exceptions. If you think I'm kidding, Tom Berlin fired a new copilot who insisted that a mustache was a constitutional right—and he made it stick. It took the whole Trans-Coastal ALPA Master Executive Council to talk the kid into shaving it off before Berlin would take him back."

"Christ, that's silly," somebody in a rear row blurted.

"Silly it may be, but it's an unofficial rule and Mr. Berlin means it. The only wrong decision he's ever really made while he's been president was the wad of dough he lost betting on the Baltimore Colts to beat the Jets in the Super Bowl back in '69. Rumor has it that the only reason he went overboard was because he hated Joe Namath's mustache. Which brings me to another unwritten law which I personally think makes more sense than the mustache business. This one represents the very strong views of Mr. Silvanius, our vice president of public relations. Jason Silvanius will report to Captain Battles the name of any flight officer he catches with his uniform coat unbuttoned in public. Silvanius is a hell of a nice guy, as you'll find out if you ever get to know him personally, but he has this thing about our public image and God help you if he ever catches you with an unbuttoned coat. Battles will back him up and so will Mr. Berlin. He nailed one of our senior captains once and, so help me, Battles grounded him for a week. Actually, Item B under Personal Appearance gives the company a legal right to enforce what may seem arbitrary to a few of you rugged individualists. I suggest you glance at B."

They did. Item B proclaimed:

It is the responsibility of the Flight Officer to keep his entire uniform neat, cleaned and pressed at all times. No ornaments, emblems or pins shall be added other than the official TCA flight officer wings and the appropriate number of stripes on the sleeves, with the following exception: a TCA service pin and/or an ALPA pin may be worn centered one (1) inch above the flight officer wings. Unkempt personal appearance, unshined shoes, dirty or greasy visor, frayed collar, cuffs, buttonholes, pocket edges, flight bag of shabby appearance or in poor repair, etc., will be cause for removal of the Flight Officer from flight schedule.

"The 'etc.' covers anything that isn't spelled out," Croyden continued. "To be honest with you, I've never seen anyone taken off flight schedule for a shabby brainbag—hell, some of the brainbags

I've seen around this airline belong in a museum—but don't let yourself get sloppy in appearance. An airline pilot *does* have a public image
and not even ALPA will protect you if somebody lowers the boom
on you for needing a haircut or a shave, or showing up at an airport
with a uniform you must have slept in. Which reminds me, Captain
Mark Ashlock—he's membership chairman for ALPA's TCA Council—has asked me to make this announcement: you're invited to attend
a briefing on ALPA membership tonight. It's"—he consulted a slip
of paper—"at the International Hotel, Paladin Suite, 7:00 P.M. The
International's that big hotel right near the airport. Any questions?"

There were whispered consultations among the class before Dixie
Miller asked the question Dudney wanted to ask. "Do we have to
join ALPA?"

"Negative," Croyden told them. "But I'll give you a little free
advice and then you can make up your own minds. First, Trans-
Coastal has damned near a thousand pilots and only five of them are
non-ALPA. Second, even if you're not exactly pro-union, don't let
that be the only factor in your decision. Sure, the Air Line Pilots
Association is a labor union, but it's also a professional organization
with a hell of a lot of benefits for its members—a fine group life insurance program, to mention just one. Its work in air safety, for my
dough, has been underrated for years. So listen to what Ashlock
has to say tonight and keep an open mind."

"Do you instructors belong?" Hank Mitchell wanted to know.

"All but the boss—Dave Robinson. And he holds an honorable
withdrawal card from ALPA. So does John Battles. The pilots in
management feel the company deserves priority on their loyalties,
particularly in case of a pilot strike, which is where I suppose you
have to draw a loyalty line. The five men who won't join ALPA
believe this way—namely, they say they wouldn't walk out in a labor
dispute so there's no point in belonging to a union."

"Are those five guys sort of ostracized?" That one came from
McCrae.

"Negative. Oh, a few ALPA members won't exactly fraternize
with them, so to speak, but generally they get along with almost
everybody. Okay, it's almost 1400 so we'll break for those I.D.
photos. Go up to the second floor of the General Offices—that's

the big building with all the shrubs in front. The receptionist will tell you what room to go to. Be back here by 1500. Miss Devlin, I'd like to see you a minute."

The trainees already had started out the room as Croyden finished, and a few heads pivoted back to stare at Dudney in renewed curiosity. She heard Webster whisper to McCrae, "Maybe they're going to give her the boot." It gave her the jitters but the expression on her face, as she approached Croyden, was her inevitable mask of unruffled calm.

"Yes, sir?"

Croyden was ill at ease. "Miss Devlin, Mark Ashlock told me to tell you, uh, that it, uh, won't be necessary for you to attend the ALPA briefing tonight."

"Did Captain Ashlock say I was not to attend, or just that it wasn't necessary?"

"I, uh, think he thought it, ah, inadvisable." Croyden looked unhappy.

Dudney's mouth tightened, a muscular roadblock to an angry retort.

"Thank you, Mr. Croyden. If you like, you may tell Captain Ashlock I'm thinking it over."

She walked out. Rufus Croyden said aloud, to no one in particular:

"Over to *you*, Captain Ashlock."

CHAPTER FIVE

Her instinct told her not to attend the ALPA meeting, but it clashed fiercely with hurt pride and anger. At first, she resolved to stay home that night, studying the course outline and Jeppesen manual. She fixed herself a sandwich, opened a bottle of Coors beer and sat curled up in the easy chair like a relaxed kitten, the Jeppesen unfolded on her lap to Section 2.3.1, labeled "Flight Officer Conduct," which Croyden had warned would be the source for a certain Saturday test question and which started out with the stern declaration that "a Flight Officer wearing a Trans-Coastal Airlines uniform is a representative of management and his deportment must create trust and confidence in him and the Company."

That was Rule A under Section 2.3.1. She read the others.

B. The use of alcoholic beverages by a flight crew requires a maximum amount of discretion. A Flight Officer is prohibited from drinking alcoholic beverages of any kind during the 12 hours preceding a flight on which he is scheduled as a crew member. In addition, a Flight Officer is prohibited from drinking any alcoholic beverage during any calendar day that he is scheduled as a crew member. Violation of this policy will be cause for immediate removal from flight duty and will subject the Flight Officer involved to dismissal from the Company.

C. A Flight Officer in uniform is restricted from public places devoted primarily to the sale of alcoholic beverages.

D. A Flight Officer shall conduct himself in the cockpit with due regard to the standing of his profession. His attention must be devoted only to those details relevant to the operation of the aircraft and the management of the flight.

E. A Flight Officer who is deadheading, regardless of the mode of transportation, is considered on duty and shall conduct himself accordingly.

Well, she thought, the rules were simple and made sense. The twelve-hour ban against drinking surprised her; it was a company regulation, not FAA, and she always had assumed it was a federal ban for twenty-four hours, not twelve. Rule D amused her, inasmuch as she suspected (correctly) it was put into effect after the big public flap about alleged hanky-panky in the cockpit—stewardesses had been photographed sitting on pilots' laps, apparently during scheduled flights. The outcry from self-righteous Congressmen and an avidly panting press was horrendous—ignoring, naturally, certain facts which came out later but which were not widely played on front pages. Such as the revelation that one of the most prominently used stewardess-on-pilot's-lap pictures turned out to be a photograph of the captain's wife, snapped in the cockpit not in flight but in a hangar during off-duty time, and as a gag.

No matter, Dudney reasoned, it still was a sensible rule and so was the warning not to drink in bars while in uniform. She remembered the night she and Sam Macklin had been having a couple of quiet drinks with an airline captain on an Anchorage layover. They were engaged in some pleasant hangar flying when the captain's complexion caught fire. He had spotted, at a nearby table, a young copilot still in uniform, coat unbuttoned and tie askew, drinking what obviously was a martini. The captain rose, went over to the copilot, and although he kept his voice low Dudney and Sam could hear what he said to the offending crew member.

"Get your ass back to the hotel, you stupid bastard! And when you're in your room, you latch onto some paper and write one thousand times, 'I will never again drink in public while in uniform.' Repeat, one thousand times, you dumb shit, and you better have it ready for me to look at when you report to Dispatch in the morning. Now wipe that dying-cow expression off your stupid face and consider yourself lucky I don't pull you off schedule and report you to the chief pilot. Beat it!"

The copilot, literally trembling with fear and shame, departed in disheveled haste. The captain, still seething, returned to their table carrying the copilot's unfinished martini which he handed to Dudney.

"No use wasting the damned drink," he said gruffly. "Hell, I just thought of something. Now I've got to pay for it—I scared him off before he got his check."

It was those occasional contacts with the responsible side of the airline breed that had nurtured her dreams. But at this moment today's snub popped back into her mind in jarring contrast to the half-worshipful attitude she had created toward captains. Resentment suddenly displaced nostalgia. She tried to study further, contemplating Section 2.3.2, which forbade the use of any antihistamine drug twenty-four hours before a scheduled flight, the use of any sulfa drug twelve hours before a trip, the use of narcotics in any form at any time unless under the direct care or supervision of a doctor, and SCUBA diving regardless of depth during the twenty-four hours preceding flight duty.

She looked at her wristwatch. Six-fifteen P.M. She turned to the pages in the Jeppesen containing Part 121 of the Federal Air Regulations. Part 121, Croyden had emphasized, contained the major certification and operating rules for all common carriers, their aircraft and their crews, and those FARs affecting the latter had to be memorized. She gulped down the last of the beer, considered pouring a second, changed her mind and continued reading desultorily, one corner of her brain persisting to dwell, with nagging intensity, on the ALPA meeting,

Again, she consulted her watch. Six-thirty. She closed the Jeppesen with a firm smack and, not bothering to change the outfit she had worn to class, ran down the apartment stairs to the street where she waited for a passing taxi.

The International was only about five minutes from her apartment, but she had trouble getting a cab and it was ten after seven when she located the Paladin Room.

Her class was there in force—including the rather austere Webster, whose presence surprised her. She had guessed that he would be one of those rare pilots who considered joining a labor union beneath his dignity. They all had drinks in their hands, most of the trainees clustered around a wiry man of medium height, his thin but strong face topped by a thatch of tousled, sand-colored hair. He looked to be in his late thirties or early forties. The thought flashed through her head that facially he resembled Paul Newman but this purely feminine reaction was derailed quickly by Dixie and Hank Mitchell, who spotted her as she entered the room and walked over to her.

"Hi, Miss Devlin," Dixie said cheerfully and with no sign of astonishment that she had showed up. Apparently her classmates were unaware of the informal suggestion that she stay away.

"You're a little late," Hank greeted her. "Can I get you a drink?"

"Scotch and water, please," she asked gratefully, conscious that the sight of his friendly black face gave her a feeling of comfortable familiarity in a potentially hostile atmosphere. She was, Dudney admitted to herself, nervous and even scared, and her jitters increased to the flutter stage when she heard Dixie say, "Come on, meet Captain Ashlock."

The face of the captain was a blur to her at first, focusing to reality only at the sound of his voice—pleasant, though touched with an edge of querulous disbelief that she had ignored the rebuff. "Miss Devlin, glad you could make it."

I'll just bet you are, you hypocritical sonofabitch, was what she wanted to say but she settled instead for an equally hypocritical answer. "Nice of you to invite me."

There was just enough sarcasm in her tone to lift his eyebrows to half-staff. Then he grinned, and it was a grin of admitted guilt, apology and proffered friendship. Mark Ashlock already had talked to Croyden, receiving the latter's assurance that he had implied to Miss Devlin her presence at the briefing would not be particularly welcome. But Croyden had added:

"Don't be surprised if she shows up anyway, Mark. The word is that the kid's got spunk."

That she did, Ashlock was telling himself now. He knew her coming was more of a gesture of defiance than interest in ALPA, but he still respected her for it. She could not know, of course, that a few of Ashlock's fellow pilots had talked him into the snub and that he had gone along with it only because he honestly believed Dudney would not want to join the union. One of them had been Captain Callahan, whose opinion of women pilots paralleled those of John Battles except that, by comparison, Battles' were relatively favorable. It occurred to Ashlock that the Paladin Room might be a scene of combat; Crusty Callahan was head of the ALPA local and was due any minute to join the meeting. Ashlock looked at Dudney with an unexpected surge of pity, as Mitchell handed her a drink. Crusty had a tongue like barbed wire and heaven help anyone he decided to cut up verbally. It also bothered Ashlock that only Miller and Mitchell were paying any attention to Dudney; her other classmates seemed to be ignoring her and when Captain Callahan arrived . . .

Inevitably, Captain Callahan chose this timely moment to arrive on the scene, heading right for Ashlock and the group around him and then literally skidding to a halt, like a panicky driver applying brakes, as soon as he saw Dudney. The expression on his froggy face was a shifting panorama of surprise followed by concern followed by disbelief followed by disapproval, which shifted temporarily back to concern because he was not quite sure if she was the girl he feared she was.

Before anyone had a chance to speak, Callahan did—in a voice that matched his face, a cross between a deep croak and a bellow.

"I hope to hell you're married to one of these guys," he roared to Dudney. "Or his girl friend. Or his mother—anything but that goddamned bitch who thinks she can be an airline pilot."

Even Ashlock was taken back by his rudeness, let alone Dudney and her fellow trainees. Yet she was the first to recover, her face flushed but taut with righteous indignation. For a split second she glared down at him—and down it had to be, for Captain Artemus Callahan was almost three inches shorter than Dudney, a wizened, ugly, fire hydrant of a man who looked more like one of the seven dwarfs than a Greek god airline captain. That advantage in altitude seemed to add icy calm to her answer.

"Sorry to disappoint you," she said, "but I'm the goddamned bitch."

"Who the hell invited you?" Callahan snapped.

Ashlock started to say something, but Dudney beat him to the punch. "I understand it was a blanket invitation from ALPA to the new 737 class, and I happen to be a member of that class. So I came. And if it's all the same to you, I intend to stay and listen to what ALPA has to say. In somewhat politer terms, I trust, than those I just heard from what I assume is one of its members."

"Well, it's *not* all the same to me, young lady, and furthermore—"

Ashlock interrupted. "Just a minute, Crusty. Calm down and let's get on with the meeting. She has a perfect right to be here."

"She's got as much right to be here as I've got to piss in the lady's crapper. There won't be any meeting as long as she stays."

Someone off to the side sucked in his breath. Dixie Miller opened his mouth, then shut it. Hank Mitchell also started to utter an apparent protest, but stopped and looked at Dudney miserably, a mute acknowledgment of fear and embarrassment.

"That's not being fair to the others," Dudney said, still flushed but still calm with the silent strength of a massive iceberg.

"Screw the others." Callahan glared at Dudney and then glanced at Ashlock, half defiantly and halfway asking for support.

The latter frowned unhappily, not quite certain whether his anger should fall on the girl for showing up or on Callahan for his barnacled attitude.

"Come on, Crusty," he finally said. "She's here and she's right—it's not fair to these guys if you call off the meeting."

"No!" The little captain was adamant. "There's no room in this airline for a goddamned female pilot and there's no place in ALPA for any"—he was fumbling for the most effective epithet—"for any bitch with radical ideas."

"She's not an airline pilot yet," Ashlock argued. "If she gets through training and wants to join ALPA, that's a matter for the whole Executive Council to decide. You can't decide it here, Crusty, all by your lonesome."

"The hell I can't, Mark. This is an official ALPA function to which she was *not,* repeat *not* invited."

Dudney was conscious of the murmurs around her, her shaken classmates whispering among themselves. That very awareness diluted her fury with uncertainty, for she was afraid their reaction was one of resentment toward her. But when she again looked down on Callahan, contempt oozed out of both eyes and hate was painted in a thin line on her tightened lips. "I'd like to say something after I'm formally introduced to this . . . person." The accent on "person" left no doubt she meant it as a synonym for any four-letter word the others would like to substitute.

Ashlock laughed, but it was more of a nervous giggle. "Miss Devlin, may I present Captain Artemus Callahan, otherwise known as Crusty Callahan, of ALPA's Trans-Coastal Executive Council."

"Shit!" Callahan barked.

Dudney surveyed him for a long moment, with the expression of one who has just been handed a decaying fish. When she spoke, it was in a tone saturated with scorn.

"Captain Callahan," she said slowly and distinctly, "you are a foul-mouthed, rude, contemptible bigot with the limited vocabulary of a skid-row bum and the sickening prejudices of a Gestapo agent. If you are representative of the ALPA membership, I would sooner join the Communist Party. Keep your damned mouth shut until I finish" —Callahan, his eyes wide in shocked surprise, had started to speak —"but inasmuch as I seem to be spoiling the evening for the rest of the class, I'll depart quietly. And a very pleasant good evening to you, *sir*."

She turned to leave, the "sir" hanging in the air like an unfinished curse.

"If she goes, I go." That was Hank Mitchell, his black face tense.

"Ditto." That was Dixie Miller, looking at the Negro with something akin to gratitude.

"That goes for me too." Dudney's eyes widened. That had been Webster, tall and arrogant as if he were the only one in the room with the right to wear the four stripes of a captain.

"Well I'll be a sonofabitch!" That was Captain Callahan, weakly resorting to profanity to cover up the fact that he was flustered.

Ashlock, failing completely to keep delighted glee out of his voice, observed, "That leaves only six men to proselyte, Crusty. Better pull in your fangs and let's get on with business."

If Callahan was going to surrender, Dudney took the painful decision out of his hands before he had a chance to be humiliated.

"No," she said with the quiet firmness so typical of her under stress. "If I stay, there'll be too much thinking of what just happened. Too much distraction, instead of listening to what's said about ALPA. Too much"—she looked squarely at Callahan, a look of faint amusement crossing her features—"too much suspense waiting for Captain Callahan's bias to erupt again. It's best I do leave. Captain Ashlock, thank you for your courtesy. I think I'll go home and reread the section in the manual on the responsibilities of an airline captain. It's too bad they don't include fairness."

She was out of the room before her three allies—Miller, Mitchell and Webster—could say a word. For one strained moment they seemed ready to walk out after her and, if any of the trio had started, the others would have fallen in step. The black trainee was the closest to making the move, but he hesitated a fraction too long and the mood of belligerence evaporated into uncomfortable silence.

"Well I'll be a sonofabitch!" Callahan blustered again.

No one else, including Ashlock, was quite sure whether his repeated expletive was in relief, triumph or admiration, blurted involuntarily like an unwanted belch.

The first thing Dudney noticed at class the next morning was the marked change—for the worse—in her classmates' apparel. From the sartorial perfection of laundered shirts, ties and business suits, they had deteriorated to a motley collection of sports shirts ranging from a nauseating green number dotted with cigarette burns and worn by Dixie Miller to Webster's, which evidently was the result of cross-breeding between a Hawaiian motif and a psychedelic nightmare. On the regal, fastidious Webster, it was as startling as seeing Chet Huntley appear before camera in a sweat shirt.

Dixie and Hank arrived just before the 7:30 A.M. starting time so she had no chance to thank them for their spoken loyalty of the previous night. She would have thanked Webster except she was not sure how words of gratitude would be received. She had an idea that Webster's reaction would be supercilious—a kind of "Tut-tut, my girl, don't thank me for exhibiting natural chivalry." She could not know that Webster expected her to say something in the way of appreciation, that he was disappointed she didn't, and that he also had his reply all formulated—"Miss Devlin, don't mistake a man's natural chivalry for approval of your professional plans."

George Le Baron, head of ground school, took over the morning class but only long enough to introduce Herb Willis, Trans-Coastal's chief dispatcher, an elderly man with a thatch of hair so white it looked dyed. Willis lectured for more than an hour on the functions of the Dispatch Department, in a dry, pedantic manner which managed to preclude boredom by the sheer interest of his subject. Being military, most of the class had little idea of what an airline dispatcher did; even Dudney's knowledge was vague, inasmuch as Air Alaska had never been able to afford such personnel. The class was surprised to learn that a dispatcher can overrule a captain or even an airline president in determining when and whether a flight can depart, and that the predeparture conference between dispatcher and captain is the catalytic agent of an efficient, safe flight.

Willis also reviewed Trans-Coastal's major operating rules, the trainees taking voluminous notes in the suspicion (a correct one) that the forthcoming test would include a few questions on the dispatch side of airline life. When they broke for coffee, Dudney intercepted Dixie and Hank.

"I just want you to know I appreciated your standing by me last night," she said with the first iota of shyness they had ever seen her display. Hank muttered, "Forget it." Dixie—demonstrating the standard embarrassment of a male caught doing the decent thing—merely patted her on the shoulder and added, "Come on, get some coffee with us, Miss Devlin," the use of her last name again a tacit warning that she remained a creature apart.

The break was followed by the brief appearance of Robinson, who announced that the two company-approved uniform suppliers were waiting outside to make their sales pitch.

"Trans-Coastal doesn't take sides," he added. "You're free to choose either one. Mr. Miller?"

"Sir, if we all decide on a single manufacturer, is it kosher to ask for a class discount?"

"It's kosher to ask, but I doubt if you'll get one. Any more questions before I tell the first one to come on in?"

Dudney lacked the nerve to ask if any higher-echelon decision had been made on what uniform she would be wearing, contenting herself with the hope that mental osmosis or telepathy or maybe the half-pleading look she aimed in Robinson's direction would lead him to volunteer the information. He didn't, and she settled back in her chair to await—according to the training chief's introduction— Mr. Lawrence Ferranti of Sawtell Clothiers.

Mr. Ferranti bounced into the room with the fervor and aplomb of an actor getting the cue for his big scene, a broad smile on his swarthy face but one that looked as if it had been painted on, like that of a chorus girl.

"Good morning, good morning, good morning," he proclaimed in the manner of a college cheerleader delivering the first three lines of a locomotive yell. He was carrying a long garment bag and a rectangular box, both of which he laid on the instructor's table that faced the class. "On behalf of Sawtell Clothiers, a firm which has been proud to outfit Trans-Coastal's great pilots for the past ten consecutive years, I am here to solicit your business. Not only your first uniform, but for as long as you fly. Now I won't keep you in suspense another second—I know this is what you want to see."

Mr. Ferranti unzipped the garment bag with a proud flourish that would have done justice to the first unveiling of an original Rodin. He took out the green TCA pilot's uniform and held it up for inspection. "This garment is individually tailored, gentlemen"—apparently no one had informed him of Dudney's presence beforehand and evidently he had not even seen her in the rear row—"and we can supply linings at a very nominal charge. At absolutely no charge, we'll sew your name into the pants and sleeve."

"How much?" Dixie asked.

"I'm glad you asked, because this is the pleasantest part of my presentation. We at Sawtell Clothiers are only too well aware that for a year you new pilots will be in a bit of a financial bind—"

"You're sure as hell right," Worthington muttered.

"—and we are glad to make allowances for this." Mr. Ferranti was used to such interruptions. "Our price is a special promotional one, for new trainees. We want to make it as easy on you as humanly possible. You'll be happy to know, gentlemen, that Trans-Coastal pays us for your first uniform—but, of course, the company will deduct this amount from your salary at the modest sum of ten dollars a month."

The class did not seem particularly grateful but Mr. Ferranti showed no sign of discouragement. If anything, his demeanor increased in enthusiasm. "Now for the biggest surprise of all, gentlemen. This uniform coat, with trousers, both individually tailored as I said, is only eighty-seven dollars. I recommend, for only an additional twenty-two fifty, a second pair of extra trousers, in case the stewardess spills coffee on you some morning, ha-ha."

Nobody laughed. Undeterred, Mr. Ferranti went into high gear. Out of the garment bag he took a green topcoat—"thirty-four fifty," he said proudly as the class began taking notes of the prices. He opened the box and removed the contents. "This uniform cap is ten dollars, permanent-press shirt for three dollars—a real bargain, that's virtually at cost—this handsome tie matching your uniform is one dollar, and finally we furnish a belt for a dollar and a half. Oh, I almost forgot—in the event you don't feel you can afford the combination topcoat-raincoat, we have a dacron raincoat available for just twelve dollars. And one more thing, gentlemen, the uniform itself is available in two weights, one rather light and the other amounting to a year-round outfit. We recommend the latter as more practical. Same price, by the way. Yes, my friend, you have a question?"

Dixie wanted to know about the chances for a class discount if everyone ordered from Sawtell. Mr. Ferranti seemed hurt by the very suggestion. "In effect, gentlemen, you're already getting a discount price. As I said, our price scale is based on our desire to serve you in the future as well as the present. I myself have been with Sawtell Clothiers for thirty-two years, and believe me when I say you won't find a better bargain than what I've just quoted you. I don't wish to knock my competitor, who's waiting in the hallway, but we at Sawtell are absolutely convinced we're giving you the best buy in the airline business. Tell you what, I'll just pass this uniform jacket around so you can judge the material—a combination of worsted and wool that will stand up to the, ha-ha, rigors of your profession."

While the trainees examined the uniform, with the false assurance of a man kicking the tires of a used car because he doesn't know a carburetor from a spark plug, Mr. Ferranti sweetened the pot.

"If you do favor me with your business, gentlemen, we'll have transportation here at five o'clock to take you to our showrooms on Sepulveda. While you're being measured for your uniforms, there'll be refreshments"—his voice dropped an octave as if he was conspiring with them—"plenty of scotch and bourbon."

"How long before we get delivery?" Kalinka asked.

"Twelve working days after you're measured. And we guarantee a perfect fit. Believe me, as perfect as the suit you see me wearing."

The class looked impressed; fortunately Mr. Ferranti did not pass around *his* well-tailored jacket for inspection, inasmuch as it bore a Hickey-Freeman label. He gathered up his display, zipped the garment bag closed and bounced out of the room—nodding cordially at his competitor, who came in as Mr. Ferranti left.

The second clothing representative introduced himself as Mr. Weber of Baldwin Uniforms, Inc. He delivered his sales pitch with all the warmth of an undertaker.

"We take three weeks to complete the basic uniform of coat jacket and trousers," he informed them with no other preliminaries. "Another two weeks for the raincoat. Our prices are as follows: one coat and trousers, ninety-nine fifty; extra trousers, twenty-six dollars; uniform cap, twelve dollars; white shirts, five-fifty; combination topcoat-raincoat, thirty-five dollars; plain raincoat, fifteen twenty-five; belt, two-fifty, and tie, three dollars. If you're interested, the address of Baldwin Uniforms is 1490 Monaco Drive. Thank you for your attention."

The class examined him in disbelief. This was a sales pitch?

"Don't you have any samples?" Webster asked.

"No. They're the same quality we make for all the airlines."

"Your prices are all higher than Sawtell," Dixie observed. "About two or three bucks for each item."

"We feel our product is better than anyone else's, and we charge a slightly higher price."

"If we all ordered from you, could we get a discount?" Kalinka put in.

"Sorry, but we don't discount to classes. We feel if we do we'd have to discount to line pilots as well. Gentlemen, that completes my presentation. Good morning."

He marched out, the trainees waiting until the door was shut before they started discussing the economics of the uniform business.

"There's something goddamned fishy," Dixie announced. "That last guy acted like he didn't even want us to order."

"Yeah," Kalinka agreed sourly, "higher prices, longer delivery dates and a take-it-or-leave-it attitude."

"No booze, either," Dixie remembered.

Webster's reaction was pontifical and decidedly suspicious. "I smell a deal between the two firms. One makes a pretty good pitch and the other just about forfeits the whole thing. They must be splitting up business between them. Sawtell gets Trans-Coastal and lets Baldwin have some other airline."

Dudney, who still was wondering what kind of uniform to order, remained silent but she agreed privately with Webster. (She was to learn, much later, that his analysis was only too accurate—the two companies had divvied up airline orders, Sawtell concentrating on the pilots and Baldwin selling the stewardesses, while going through the motions of competition.)

"Well, there doesn't seem to be much choice," McCrae said. "I guess it's Sawtell. That the way you guys feel?"

It was. Robinson was so advised and the class settled back to hear Rufus Croyden lecture further on Part 121 of the FARs before they broke for lunch. Dudney, whose curiosity overrode her pride, used the walk to the caf for asking Dixie about the ALPA meeting. "Did you all decide to join?"

"Yep. Seems like a good deal, Miss Devlin. The first year, the one we spend on probation, we don't pay any dues but we get all the benefits from the day we join, as associate members, soon's we go on the line."

"Are the benefits good?"

"Sure are. Real cheap life insurance. Great pension plan under the contract ALPA's got with Trans-Coastal. Loss of license insurance, too—some outfit in Atlanta underwrites it for ALPA. Like I said, we all decided to join. By the way, Miss Devlin . . ."

He hesitated, and she guessed what was on his mind. "I wanted to thank you and Hank again for what . . . what you did last night."

"Yeah. It sorta came up later at the meeting."

"Oh?"

"Hank, he asked if a Negro could join ALPA. That Callahan character said ALPA didn't care if a pilot was a full-blooded Sioux so long as he met the qualifications and was a loyal member. Then Hank said how about letting a woman pilot join. Captain Callahan started to cuss again—he sure has one fine repertoire of four-letter words."

"I'm only too well acquainted with his repertoire. Go ahead, you're keeping me in suspense."

"Well, Captain Ashlock said ALPA had females in the union—they're in the stewardess division of ALPA—so there wasn't any discrimination because of sex. Hank said he was evading the question—would they let a woman pilot in? Callahan said it would be over his dead body but Ashlock kinda eased things a bit—he told Hank that if you won your wings ALPA would consider you as a probationary member, same as anyone else, in the first year. Then Hank—" Dixie chuckled in admiring recollection.

"Go on."

"Then Hank said he didn't want to belong to any organization which discriminated against anybody, and would ALPA let him resign if they turned you down?"

Dudney was touched and she could not hide it. "Hank said that?"

"He sure as hell did. Callahan fumed and fussed for a while, and Ashlock hemmed and hawed around until he finally told Hank that Captain Callahan's personal beliefs didn't necessarily coincide with ALPA's official policy. Ashlock said he couldn't honestly answer Hank because the issue of a woman pilot had never come up before, but that he felt sure the union would do the right thing and that if the rest of us felt the same way Hank did, we shouldn't let that interfere with our joining before, uh, before your problem was settled. So we all signed up, including Hank."

Dudney pondered this account briefly before another question occurred. "Dixie, the others—did the rest of the class, well, agree with Hank?"

He did not reply at first, reluctant to hurt her and reluctant to lie.

"He felt the strongest about it, if I can put it that way," he said carefully. "Nobody else had much to say. I guess we all were a little afraid of Callahan—hell, Miss Devlin, some of us may have to fly with him one of these days. He's a 737 captain. He's not a bad guy, by the way. Told us a lot of funny stories."

"Some of them involving women pilots, no doubt." She could not hold back the sarcasm any more than she could stop breathing.

"No, but he did tell us that one airline—I think he said it was Northwest—has a minimum height rule of five-ten for all pilots, for the express purpose of discouraging women from flying."

"Five-ten would eliminate Captain Callahan," Dudney noted smugly.

Miller ignored this. "Captain Ashlock, he was, well, uh, more sympathetic. Said he met a gal who teaches simulator training for El Al. He claimed she was better than most of the men she was checking out."

"And Captain Callahan, I presume, thereupon displayed prejudice against female pilots who happen to be Jewish? I wouldn't put anti-semitism beyond him."

Dixie was a little nettled. "Look, I told you, he wasn't a bad guy. You might be surprised to hear he told us he knew a lot of damned good women pilots. He said he just didn't think they belonged in the airline business. He even said you seemed like a nice gal—that he doesn't have anything personal against you."

"You sure he used 'gal'? Or was it broad? Or maybe bitch. Or that other word."

They were almost to the employees' cafeteria. "I honestly think he was sorry about . . . about the language he used," Dixie said slowly. "He's a tough little rooster, that Callahan. Even Hank figures he was rough on you because he was surprised you showed up."

"Dixie, did any of you know I was invited *not* to show up, in so many words?"

"Nope. Not till everything hit the fan at the meeting. Some of us were talking about it later. Nobody was particularly surprised when you walked in, but nobody would have been surprised if you hadn't."

"Well, at least you're all neutral—that's something. And what did they think about my walking out?"

Dixie gave a little laugh. "Same thing. They wouldn't have been surprised if you had stayed—and they weren't surprised when you didn't."

"In other words, I'm holding my own."

Miller stopped her as they were about to enter the caf. "Miss Devlin, I said it before and I'll say it again. Be patient. They still don't know what to make of you—and that includes me. You're a long way from being accepted. Maybe you will, eventually, and maybe you won't, but for now just don't expect too much and don't push it."

"That include Hank?"

"It does. Hank, well, he's for the underdog because he's been one himself. But he doesn't differentiate between female underdogs and male underdogs. He's for giving everyone a chance, and that's why he stuck up for you last night—and stuck his neck out in the process. It was a matter of principle to him. It doesn't mean he approves of you specifically or of women airline pilots generally. It means he's just against discrimination, no matter what the format happens to be. For all I know, he wouldn't be sorry to see you wash out."

Her eyes narrowed. "You wouldn't be sorry, either, would you, Dixie?"

He looked straight at her, a glance as penetrating as an arrow, not a vestige of friendship or sympathy on his face. "Miss Devlin, the entire class hopes you'll fall flat on your duff. Let's eat."

It was just as well she had no way of knowing that the identical sentiment was being expressed at that very moment, in a dining room considerably more posh than the employees' cafeteria.

Tom Berlin had gathered four vice presidents including Jason Silvanius, plus Captain Battles, around a luncheon table to discuss a vexing corporate problem—namely, Dudney Devlin's uniform.

"Robinson told me he didn't say anything to her when the uniform suppliers were there, and she didn't ask him," Berlin informed the others. "Dave says her class is due for a fitting session at Sawtell's later today, so we've got to make up our minds."

"Maybe if we don't reach a decision she'll get the idea we hope she'll never wear a TCA uniform when she shows up for a fitting." That came from Paul Brandon, Vice President, Marketing.

"Does anyone know for sure she'll be there?" Silvanius asked. Berlin shook his head. "The trainees all voted for Sawtell, the girl included, according to Dave. We've got to assume she expects to be measured."

Jason was dubious. "Not necessarily. She might be waiting for someone to tell her what she's supposed to wear in the cockpit. It would be damned embarrassing for her if Sawtell didn't know what to do about her—and refused to fit her. In fact, she'd be more likely to ask first. She's no dumbbell."

John Battles cleared his throat, unafraid of all the brass but nevertheless somewhat ill at ease among them. "She's no shrinking violet, either, Jason. She barged into an ALPA meeting for new pilots last night and, from what I hear, she reamed out Crusty Callahan like an avenging proctoscope."

"Crusty?" demanded Berlin incredulously. "Where did you hear that?"

"From the recipient of the reaming job—namely, Captain Callahan. He told me she showed up after being advised not to, and when Crusty got a little rough with her she gave it right back," Battles chuckled. "In fact, Crusty seemed a bit shaken. Anyway, he informed me that if she ever gets into a right seat the pilots will walk out. So I informed Captain Callahan in turn there was nothing in our contract with ALPA which cites our hiring a woman pilot as a legitimate reason for a strike."

"Good for you," Berlin said.

"There will be in the next ALPA contract," Vic James, Vice President, Labor Relations, dourly predicted.

"It'll never come to that," Berlin said with more outward confidence than he felt inwardly. "Anyway, we've got to be very careful to give every indication we're treating this girl with utmost fairness. We must forget the odds against her ever flying for us, which means we have to go through the motions of letting her get a uniform along with the rest of her class. So we're back to our problem, gentlemen —what the hell should she wear?"

"A maxicoat, at all times," James growled.

"Strictly from the standpoint of public relations," Jason advised,

"I'd suggest a specially tailored jacket with a miniskirt, and boots about up to her knees."

"She'll look like a Russian Army nurse," Berlin objected. "What the hell's wrong with just matching slacks, to go with our regular pilot's jacket?"

"On a woman," Battles pointed out, "that jacket will be like outfitting a cheer leader with shoulder pads and a football jersey. They're double-breasted."

"So's Miss Devlin," Jason murmured.

"Let's get serious," Berlin growled. "How about putting her in one of our stewardess jackets, with some kind of slacks?"

"She'll look too much like a stewardess," Jason said. "Besides, the stewardesses might object. That'll be great—the pilots walk out because she's in their cockpit and the stews strike because she's wearing their uniform."

Jerome Norgaard, a big Norwegian who was Vice President, Flight Operations, beamed. "Got an idea. Why not have Sawtell fix her up with a regular pilot's jacket but make it single-breasted? Then just add some tailored slacks. A single-breasted coat would cut down the shoulders and the slacks could be the same color as the pilots' pants, only tailored for a woman."

"Not bad," Battles conceded. "At least she wouldn't look like a dame going to a Halloween party masquerading as a pilot."

The cash register imbedded in Tom Berlin's mind began its monetary revolutions. "How much would a special single-breasted jacket and matching slacks cost us?"

"Nothing," Vic James pointed out. "She'd have to pay for the uniform like any new pilot."

Jason was inclined to support Norgaard, partially because he had more respect for him than any other VP and partially because he honestly thought Jerry's idea had merit. But he had to relieve himself of one nagging doubt. "A specially made uniform is likely to cost her more than the rest of the trainees are paying. That's not quite fair."

"So what?" James demanded. "It serves her right for getting us into this silly bind. Christ, the president of Trans-Coastal, four vice presidents and the chief pilot all wasting a whole lunch session on a uniform for a female copilot. We should be discussing that IAM contract."

"We can discuss IAM right now," Berlin decreed. "Personally, I go for Jerry's idea. You all agreed?"

Jason shook his head. "On the idea, yes. But I still don't think the kid should have to pay more for her uniform than the others in her class."

Berlin sighed in resignation. When Silvanius decided to take a stand, he was harder to move than a Boeing 747 mired in mud five feet deep. "Okay, Jason. We'll deduct the regular uniform cost from her salary and pay the difference ourselves. That satisfy you?"

"Yep."

"Fine, it's decided. John, why don't you call Sawtell's yourself and tell them what we've got in mind? And better advise Robinson he can tell the girl to go along with the rest of the class for that fitting. Now, about that goddamned IAM . . ."

The Thursday session included more lecturing on the manual and its voluminous contents . . . more rules and regulations and procedures and advice and warnings.

"*. . . if you want to know how important good flight planning is, if you pilots could save one minute of fuel on each trip segment over a one-year period, Trans-Coastal would have an additional three million bucks in revenue. . . .*"

"*. . . learn the cockpit-to-cabin-to-cockpit bell signal system. One ring from the cockpit to the cabin to advise the stewardess that you're starting takeoff. Two rings from the cabin to the cockpit mean the stewardesses want the cockpit door unlocked. Three rings means routine business in either direction, cockpit to cabin or cabin to cockpit. Four rings call for a prayer or singing 'Nearer, My God, to Thee' —cockpit to cabin or cabin to cockpit, signifying any unusual or hazardous situation. It is mandatory to answer the interphone immediately if you hear four bells, even if you're in the middle of an ILS approach and you've just passed the inner marker. Question, Mr. Worthington?*"

"*Sir, if one bell means you're advising the cabin attendants of takeoff clearance, how do you signal you're about to land?*"

"A bell sounds automatically when you flick on the seat belt and/or no smoking signs. Now if you'll turn to Section 5.1.9, the use of the public address system, note that Trans-Coastal encourages the use of this system on a regular basis in such areas as a welcome aboard announcement before each leg flown, any explanation for delays or unusual maneuvers, any alarming weather phenomena in flight such as rough air, St. Elmo's fire, rain, lightning—as reassurance for passengers, plus announcements of expected turbulence with an estimate of how long the turbulence may last, a brief description of points of interest but avoiding lengthy accounts and running commentaries; in addition announcements of unusual news events—for example you may pick up a World Series score via radio that the passengers would be interested in—and finally it's our policy to include terminal weather conditions, ground temperature and any precipitation at destination —without making it sound the least bit hairy, of course. . . ."

". . . don't ever use the word 'fire' in the presence of a passenger. There'd be too much chance of panic. . . ."

". . . Never, but never, forget that you and your captain—and someday you as a captain—have as your prime responsibility the safety of your passengers and that multimillion-dollar piece of equipment on which they're riding. Trans-Coastal and the other U.S. airlines have committed themselves to ordering eight billion dollars' worth of new airplanes between now and 1974. Repeat, eight billion dollars. If any of you don't feel like gawking at that figure, just remember that to get one billion dollars you'd have to receive one thousand bucks every day for thirty-five hundred years. . . ."

". . . if you ever have to operate at a non-tower airport, remember that the FARs require all turns to be made to the left unless a right-hand traffic pattern has been established for that particular airport. . . ."

". . . At thru stations, you're to give a 'fuel on arrival' figure on ramp frequency 130.1 as soon as practical after landing. Remember that frequency—if you ask a captain what the ramp frequency is, he'll chop your head off in the approximate region of the gonads. 130.1—write it down. Now, this fuel figure should be the estimated total on arrival without allowance for taxiing. . . ."

". . . and as soon as possible after landing, 'on' and 'block' arrival times are to be reported to the company by radio. . . ."

Rules. Regulations. Procedures. Advice. Warnings.

". . . make sure you know the definitions of turbulence. The difference between light, moderate, severe and extreme. In light turbulence, occupants may be required to use seat belts, but objects in the airplane remain at rest. Air speed may fluctuate five to fifteen knots. In moderate turbulence, air speed may fluctuate from fifteen to twenty-five knots . . ."

". . . it is advisable to know your TERPs, which stands for Terminal Instrument Procedures as they apply to the category of aircraft in which you're qualified and flying. For the Boeing 737, the category is C as defined in Section 5.1.17 of your Jeppesen—Category C affecting approach speeds of one hundred and twenty-one knots or more but less than one hundred and forty-one knots, and a gross landing weight of sixty thousand and one pounds or more, but less than one hundred and fifty thousand and one pounds. The gross allowable landing weight for a B-737 is one hundred and four thousand pounds . . ."

More rules. Regulations. Procedures. Warnings. All hammered into their tiring young minds until the ordeal of the Saturday test assumed benevolent proportions—a welcome relief from listening and learning, as one would look forward to even a painful extraction as surcease from a toothache.

Training films were a pleasant interlude. They watched movies on how to combat the turbulence upset problem. On the techniques of artificial respiration. On decompression—a film produced by United but made available to other airlines, in which the class watched the effects of lack of oxygen on crew members placed in a special decompression chamber. The volunteer pilots and stewardesses performed simple tasks, like adding a few numbers, putting varied-shaped blocks in the correctly shaped receptacles, and playing patty-cake, while the chamber lost pressurization. As the oxygen content diminished, the participants' actions were those of happy drunks, with all coordination lost. One stewardess in the film keeled over and an oxygen mask was quickly applied. The class was impressed, not only with the movie but with Robinson's telling them that "one of the major items on your check ride will be the speed and efficiency with which you don an oxygen mask at the first indication of decompression."

The trainees were even more impressed with the subsequent film. "This one was put out by the Los Angeles Fire Department," Robinson announced. "It's on the techniques of fire fighting—very interesting job, and I can tell you there will be at least one question on the test derived from this film. Mr. O'Brien, you're closest to the projector. If you'll turn it on and run the film, I've got a couple of phone calls to make. Lights."

The training chief left just as the lights were turned out. O'Brien flicked the projector switch. The class settled back to learn all about fire fighting, as filmed by the Los Angeles Fire Department, then looked puzzled at the title on the screen.

BIRTH OF A BABY

Produced for the Los Angeles Police Department

by

PACKER PRODUCTIONS, INC.

*(Use restricted for training purposes; not
for public distribution or showing.)*

The class sat upright in a hurry, all eyes on the screen.

> Opening shot, a car speeding down a highway at night. Interior of car, two women, the driver and a companion—the latter obviously pregnant. The latter murmurs dramatically, "Louise, I . . . I think it's time. The pains . . . the pains are terrible." Long shot of car pulling over to curb. Louise jumps out, starts to flag down other cars. Finally a Los Angeles police car squeals to a stop. "Officer, my friend's having a baby!" Young policeman looks in front seat and dashes back to scout car where he radios for an ambulance.

"What the hell has this got to do with fire fighting?" demanded Worthington.

"Shut up and watch," Dixie hissed.

Policeman returns to car. "I've just sent for medical aid," he tells the distraught driver. "Officer, there isn't time—she's started!" Sound track of exciting music, rising to crescendo as close-up shot of officer reveals concerned but steely look on his handsome face. "I'll take over," he assures the driver. Close-up, exterior, policeman helps pregnant woman out of front seat and into back of car.

"They've got the wrong film," McCrae worried in a loud whisper.

"It's better than fire fighting," Dixie countered. "Dammit, just look."

They did. At full-color films of an actual birth, with enough blood to satisfy Cecil B. De Mille and including a close-up of the young policeman cutting the umbilical cord.

THUMP!

"Jesus Christ," Ernie Crum wailed. "Worthington's fainted!"

"Turn on the lights," Webster ordered.

O'Brien snapped the switch. Doug Worthington had fallen off his chair and was lying on the floor, curled up in a ball, his face drained of color.

"Somebody get smelling salts!" Crum yelled. Worthington groaned feebly. Kalinka started to rush out the door and bumped into Robinson.

"Where do you think you're—" The training chief broke off the question when he saw the terrified look on Kalinka's face.

"Wrong film. My God, all that blood. Doug's fainted. We need ammonia—"

"Calm down, Mr. Kalinka. Now what's—holy cow, he did faint."

The movie was still running. The unctuous voice of the film commentator boomed through the classroom as Robinson bent over the half-conscious Worthington.

". . . and the quick response of this policeman, thanks to his thorough training, not only may have saved the life of a panic-stricken mother but that of her baby as well. Proper training is designed to turn any emergency into a routine chore in the daily life of a Los Angeles police officer." Up music.

"Amen," breathed Dixie.

"He's coming around," Robinson said. "No need for smelling salts. Mr. Worthington, how do you feel?"

"My God," the white-faced trainee muttered. "All that blood . . . oh hell, I'm going to get sick."

Somebody with both foresight and quick reaction shoved a waste-basket under Worthington's face and he retched. Inevitably, it was contagious. Mike Kalinka also turned pale and dashed out for the men's room, handkerchief over his mouth.

Robinson shook his head. "Take a ten-minute break and lemme see that film can."

He looked at the label on the can. "FIRE-FIGHTING TECHNIQUES— PROPERTY OF TRANS-COASTAL AIRLINES TRAINING DEPARTMENT."

The training chief sighed. "Well, I guess she did it again."

"Did what again?" Webster asked. "Who did what?"

"Jean Gillholland, head of stewardess training. About twice a year she'll switch films. Puts that damned birth film she uses for stews into the can holding the fire-fighting movie. And every time she pulls it I lose one or two of you brave bastards for the rest of the day. I'll kill her."

"Worthington and Kalinka—the class Casanovas," Dixie marveled. "I never figured it would affect them that way."

"Bachelors," Robinson chuckled. "Hits the bachelors in a class nine times out of ten. I'll bet they won't be able to even think about sex until tomorrow. You okay now, Mr. Worthington?"

"Yes, sir." The color had returned to his face, although about fifty per cent of it could have been traced to embarrassment rather than recovery. "Jesus, I think I'll break that date tonight."

Robinson rose, a rueful smile on his face. "You guys might as well get some coffee—and, Mr. Worthington, you go outside and get some fresh air. Somebody go check out Kalinka and take him outside too. I'll go get the fire-fighting film from Jean—damn her hide, I'll bet she's been laughing all day. Be back in ten minutes."

Dixie fell in alongside Dudney as they headed out of the room on their unscheduled break.

"What did you think of it—the film, Miss Devlin?" he asked, a note of awed respect creeping unwanted into his voice.

"I couldn't help thinking it reminded me of a certain fact of life."

"From that movie?"

She nodded, a tiny grin on her lips. "There's nothing a man can do that a woman can't do also, Dixie. But there's one thing a woman can do that a man can't—and you just saw it."

Friday.

Again, rules. Regulations. Procedures. Advice. Warnings.

Plus an announcement, delivered by Robinson. "Mr. Kalinka, Mr. Worthington, Miss Devlin, I have good news for you. You'll be based in Los Angeles as requested. Mr. Crum, Mr. McCrae, Mr. Webster, Mr. Mitchell, Mr. Miller, Mr. Tarkington and Mr. O'Brien—I've got bad news for you. You'll also be based in Los Angeles. Sorry, gentlemen, but the coordinator of domiciles says there are no openings for 737 crews either in Denver or San Francisco at the present time. San Francisco looks like the best bet if you can't stand L.A. Short waiting list—might be able to transfer there about a month after you start flying. At your own expense, incidentally. Mr. Mitchell?"

"Sir, what's the outlook for Denver?"

"Not very good, I'm afraid. Denver has a waiting list of at least twenty pilots, all of them with more seniority. I'd guess at least a year, and I wouldn't make book on that. Mr. Webster?"

"I understood that the company pays for moving to another base."

"Only when the move is at the company's request. If you ask for a transfer you pay your own way. If there are no more questions, the first subject of the day is bidding—something you won't have to worry about for the first month or two after you graduate, inasmuch as you'll be on reserve. But as you move up the seniority ladder, after the first year bidding gets to be pretty much of a cutthroat operation because you'd stab your best friend in the back to get a better sequence of trips. If you've got one day's seniority on him, you'll bump him if you want a certain sequence that he wants too. Now, have you all seen those pink sheets in your gray manual? The sample bid sheets? Good, did you all understand them?"

There was mass groaning at the question. Dixie spoke up. "Sir, if my career depends on knowing how to bid flights, where do I go to resign?"

"It's not as tough as it seems at first," Robinson assured the class. "Remember, the stewardesses have much the same bidding procedure—not quite as involved as the pilots but still pretty complex. If they can figure out the process, so can you and, believe me, it's easy once you get the hang of it."

Dudney, along with everyone else, had her doubts about the training chief's optimism. A stewardess friend had once told her that bidding was the hardest part of her job and that some girls continue to make mistakes after a year of flying. The samples in the pilots' manual, at this stage of training, might as well have been reproductions of a Chinese crossword puzzle—a bewildering maze of dates, figures, hours, bases, aircraft types and schedules.

Patiently, Robinson explained the bidding mechanism. How once a month Crew Schedule issued a list of blocks—each block consisting of a sequence of several flights, no block totaling more than eighty hours, which under the ALPA contract was the maximum flying time allowed per month. How each bid information sheet supplied the flight schedules involved in a single block, the total scheduled flying time for every trip listed, the total on-duty time, the number of hours for which the pilot would be paid and whether the individual trip called for day or night flying. The pink sheets slowly began to make sense.

". . . it pays to know your schedules, believe me. On page 3, for example, look at that fourth line—'Flight 22 LAX–YYC' with a scheduled flying time of three hours and fifty-three minutes. Seems like a good trip, but Flight 22 between L.A. and Calgary happens to be a three-stopper. The bid sheets just give the originating airport and the final destination—you've got to know what might be in between. . . ."

It was not only beginning to make sense, Dudney thought, but it was starting to become exciting. Seniority. Bidding. Trip sequences. Flight pairings. Turn-around schedules. Bumping. Blocks. All part of the litany of the airline pilot. Words that were not just words but a way of life that someday might be hers. Even as she listened to Robinson drone on, she had a new feeling of belonging, of becoming a part, and the slurs, the frustrations, the prejudice, the loneliness of the past week, all paled like night giving way to dawn.

". . . *hell, I remember getting careless with a bid one month because I didn't study the sequences after the first day. I got one landing the first day, eight the second and eleven the third. . . ."*

The rest must feel the same as me, she thought. From her seat in the last row, she could see young heads tilted up toward Robinson in a mass mimicry of total absorption.

". . . *you're paid either for actual flight time or scheduled flight time, whichever is greater. If you forget to bid, or turn in a late bid, or make out an incorrect or incomplete bid, you'll get the thick end of the shaft—namely, for any of those reasons, Crew Schedule can assign you to any remaining unbid blocks and those unbid blocks are dogs. Such as being on reserve for a whole month. . . ."*

It was a glimpse of the future, sensed more than seen, and Dudney knew that even after less than a week the magic alchemy that was crew training had begun to take hold. To form the molds and forge the habits and carve the image.

". . . *deadheading calls for one half flight time credit, and that's for pay as well as flight time. Note that for every one and a half hours of duty time between 2200 and 0559 you get one hour's pay and one hour's flight time. . . ."*

The class listened with rapt attention to Robinson's accounting of pay differentials and flight time credit rules. Dudney listened, but with less concentration. She was not averse to making a good salary, but her involvement and her motivation were as much emotional as financial.

". . . *and one more thing before I forget, don't try to swap days off for a while. You'll make a lot more friends and influence Crew Schedule if you stick to your assigned trips. . . ."*

She was wondering, in blissful anticipation, if Sam Macklin could possibly arrange to fly down to L.A. for graduation and pin on her wings. Or did Trans-Coastal even have anything resembling a formal graduation ceremony for new pilots? No matter, Sam would get to see her in that new uniform. Mr. Ferranti certainly had been nice about explaining how they were going to cut the jacket for her. . . .

Saturday.

The first test. "Passing grade is seventy, but if any of you get that low a grade you've got troubles," Robinson said sternly, just before handing out the test papers.

Actually, the company indoctrination examination was not as difficult as most of them feared. It was primarily a multiple-choice test which allowed them to rely on common sense as well as memory. Dudney knew she was going to get a high grade at her first cursory glance at the questions and she had to resist racing through the test.

TRANS-COASTAL AIRLINES, INC.

NAME_____

DATE_____

GRADE_____

Answer by circling the letter corresponding to the correct answer.

1. The TCA NOTAM contains summary of pertinent NOTAM Summaries and Airman's Information Manual data which is prepared:

    a. every 6 hours at LAX FLT CNTC.
    b. daily at LAX FLT CNTC.
    c. daily by NOTAM service.
    d. every 12 hours by FAA NOTAM service.

2. A First Officer will report to Crew Schedule in person at least:

    a. 30 minutes before estimated departure.
    b. 45 minutes before estimated departure.
    c. 1 hour before estimated departure.
    d. 2 hours before estimated departure.

3. Normally, the complete TCA uniform requires the jacket to be worn. During warm weather it:

a.   must be worn in public view.
b.   need not be worn at individual's option.
c.   need not be worn if entire crew is uniform.

4.   A Flight Officer is scheduled for a series of flights on the same day with a total schedule time of 7 hours and 20 minutes. Before departing on the last flight it is evident that he will exceed 8 hours for the series because the previous flight ran over schedule time due to traffic delays. Under these circumstances, the Flight Officer:

a.   can take the last flight if he is given at least 16 hours for rest after completing the series.
b.   cannot take the last flight.
c.   can take the last flight if he had at least 24 hours for rest prior to starting the series.
d.   cannot take the last flight if instrument conditions are expected.

5.   Basic minimum fuel requirements for a flight that has two alternatives specified are a total of taxi-runup fuel; takeoff, climb and cruise fuel to destination plus:

a.   fuel for 45 minutes at normal cruise consumption.
b.   fuel to proceed from destination to nearest alternate with reserve fuel for 45 minutes at normal cruise consumption.
c.   fuel to proceed from destination to furthest alternate with reserve fuel for 45 minutes at normal cruise consumption.
d.   fuel to proceed from destination to both alternates with reserve fuel for 45 minutes at normal cruise consumption.

6.   The authority for a flight to operate is in the form of a dispatch release issued and signed by the dispatcher and is valid:

a.   after being signed by the captain.
b.   immediately.

    c.   after being signed by the station manager and captain.

    d.   after being submitted to ATC.

7.   Ramp control frequency at TCA terminals:

    a.   121.5

    b.   126.7

    c.   131.6

    d.   130.1

8.   To summon the stewardess to the cockpit, you should ring the bell system:

    a.   once.

    b.   twice.

    c.   three times.

    d.   four times.

There were thirty of these multiple-choice questions, followed by ten true or false of such variety as . . .

Taxi fuel is included in the amount of fuel shown on the weight manifest.

The primary consideration in decision making in the cockpit is passenger comfort.

Rime ice is usually more dangerous than clear ice.

The allowable trip takeoff gross weight for any TCA flight is the certificated takeoff weight of the aircraft.

Finally, there were ten questions calling on pure memory, none of them giving Dudney any trouble except for the fiftieth and final one—"name the Vice President of Flight Operations." She could not remember that name at all, wrote down "John Battles" knowing it was wrong, and turned in her test paper just behind Webster, who finished ten minutes ahead of everyone else. Robinson, after collecting the last paper from Ernie Crum, smiled at their hopeful and tired visages.

"I was going to have George Le Baron come in and give you an hour's rundown on the Systems course," he said—smiling at the way the hopeful looks gave way to expressions of dismay. "However, I know it's been a tough week so I think I'll just let you go for the weekend. Just a second"—five trainees already were on their feet—"one word of caution."

He paused a good minute. "Get the hell out of here and have some fun—only lay off any heavy drinking Sunday night. If you think this week has been rough, it's kindergarten compared to Systems. I'll give you these test grades first thing Monday morning. Okay—dismissed!"

Dudney was in back of Dixie and Hank as the class left the room.

"When's your wife coming in, Dixie?" the Negro asked.

"Four forty-five this afternoon, on Delta. I'd ask you and Judy over, Hank, but Jesus, I haven't seen Norma Jean for—"

"Yeah, you wanna be alone. Don't blame you. Give us a call Sunday—maybe we can have dinner together."

"Sure thing."

Outside the Training Center, as most of them headed for the parking lot, Dudney saw Hank Mitchell look back at her. He hesitated, then continued toward the lot.

But today she didn't care. She didn't mind being alone. She felt confident and brave, buoyed by a sense of accomplishment.

The first week of training was behind her.

CHAPTER SIX

The first thing Dudney noticed Monday morning was that Doug Worthington's sideburns were gone. He tried hard to joke about it but achieved mostly an air of overly desperate nonchalance.

"I was getting a haircut anyway," he was explaining weakly to Mike Kalinka as Dudney entered the classroom, "and I noticed they *were* a little longer than I've ever worn them. So I—"

"You would have shaved off your pubic hair if Battles told you to," Kalinka snorted.

All eyes were clear this morning, too, Dudney also noted. This and the missing sideburns were pretty good indications of a class upon whom had dawned the realization that it had one hell of a lot to learn about the airline business in one hell of a hurry. It was just as well they were in a serious mood anyway, because Robinson himself was in a stern one.

"I'm going to read your grades on the Saturday test," he opened up. "Some of you should be ashamed of yourselves. That exam was the easiest one you'll get in ground school—there was no excuse for pulling down anything lower than a ninety. Repeat, ninety. Now you just listen to these grades."

He glared at the trainees before resuming, reading the grades from the test papers themselves as he shuffled through them. "Mitchell, ninety. McCrae, eighty-five. Kalinka, eighty. Worthington, seventy-five. Webster, ninety-five. Devlin, ninety-five. Crum, sixty-five." Every head in the room, Dudney's included, swiveled in Ernie Crum's direction and Dixie muttered, "Jesus, Ernie," in a tone that was part surprise, part castigation. "Tarkington, seventy. O'Brien, seventy-five. Miller, eighty. Over all, that's a pretty sloppy performance. Mr. Crum, you'll have to take the test over. After class, tomorrow. When I return these papers later today, take a look at the ones you missed and make damned sure you know the answers Tuesday. For a retest, you'll have to get at least an eighty-five. Dammit, you guys, I told you at the very start you'd have to hit the books at night. I don't care if you're Baron Von Richthofen when you're in an airplane—the FAA says you've got to pass ground school before we even let you near any cockpit. So shape up—or else."

His anger was real. Every trainee was sobered, including Dudney despite her high grade and Webster, who was trying to figure out which question he could have missed. He had confidently told McCrae after the exam, "A snap—I'll be surprised at anything below one hundred," and what would have been satisfaction at still getting the highest grade was watered down considerably by Dudney's achieving the same score.

Robinson stalked out, after turning the class over to George Le Baron with a whispered "I think these jokers will be on the attentive side today." The ground school director surveyed the class briefly, as if judging the degree of predicted attentiveness, then reached down under the instructor's desk and brought up two big boxes. Out of one he lifted a thick loose-leaf book with a bright orange cover and silver lettering, "B-737 OPERATIONS MANUAL," a smaller "Property of Trans-Coastal Airlines" in the lower right-hand corner. He held up the book for the class to see, drawing a few whistles as he announced, "This is our textbook for the next five days—take it home with you every night and study everything covered in class during the day. Mr. Worthington and Mr. Crum, if you'll help me hand these out . . ."

While the manuals were being distributed a wiry, dapper little man with salt-and-pepper hair and a loud sports jacket entered, nodding smilingly at Le Baron, who grinned back and waited for Worthington and Crum to finish before introducing the newcomer.

"Gentlemen and Miss Devlin, this is Vic Haines, who'll be your Systems instructor. He knows Fat Albert like a man knows a wife after twenty years. There isn't a better Systems man in the business, so if you goof up in this stage of your training, blame yourselves and not Vic. Now, before I turn you over to him, I'd like to leave you with this word of advice. I told you to study this manual every night. Perhaps 'review' is a better word than 'study.' Don't try to read ahead. Don't try to study in advance. Wait for Vic to cover the subject in class, then go over it at home There will be a written exam next Saturday morning. But don't think that'll be the end of Systems. After you finish simulator and flight training, before you take your final check ride, we'll have a one-day refresher course. Before you graduate into that right seat, you'll be standing up in front of an examiner for about an hour and answering questions on Systems. A lot of guys who've gone through this will tell you it's the toughest part of qualification—a hell of a lot tougher, in some ways, than flying the airplane. So I don't think I have to tell you to stay awake the rest of this week. Vic, they're all yours."

Le Baron departed and Haines, whose voice was incongruously deep and mellifluous for a small person, wasted no time in getting to the subject of Fat Albert.

"Our little pea-shooter," he began, "is one hell of a fine airplane. Very stable, very sensitive—almost like a fighter plane. Some of our 720 copilots who've transitioned to Fat Albert for upgrading have a tendency to overcontrol—the 737 is that easy to fly. It's like picking up a live fish by the tail, as you'll find out when you go into flight training. There's ten per cent less sweepback than the bigger Boeings and absolutely no tendency to Dutch roll. It has one peculiarity common to Boeing airplanes, sort of a family characteristic. Boeing builds square airplanes"—the class chuckled—"and by this I mean the fuselage length and the wingspan are almost identical. Albert's a money-making little beast, too. Excellent passenger capacity for a small plane—we operate the 737 with one hundred and seven passengers, compared to one hundred and fourteen in a 720, which is about twice its size. Albert's a better airplane today, by the way, than the day we took delivery on the first one. We've got a new thrust reverser system that wasn't on the airplane originally. This really improves its short-field capability. Just to give you an idea of how profitable Albert can be, the 737 can make money on almost every trip with a stage length of more than one hundred and fifty miles. By comparison, the 707 won't fly into black ink until the stage lengths reach at least seven hundred miles.

"Now a word about this Systems course. First, you military pilots may find yourselves looking down your noses at the 737. In many ways, military airplanes are far more sophisticated in such areas as systems and nav aids. Well, the military can afford more cost and weight than an airline and sophistication adds weight and cost. As far as this course is concerned, we're not only dealing with a relatively simple machine, but we've eliminated a lot of nuts and bolts from the curriculum itself. Basically, we don't expect you to become a 737 mechanic. All you need to know is how everything is screwed in or screwed on, so that when you move a lever or see a light or hear a noise, you'll know what the hell is happening—normal or abnormal. And that, gentlemen and, uh, Miss, uh . . . what's your name, young lady?"

"Devlin."

"Miss Devlin. Well, as I was saying, Systems is designed for training you to understand your airplane, not to fix it if anything goes wrong. To know how to write up a malfunction in the logbook so the mechanic will understand what's wrong. It'll take a couple of days before you feel comfortable, before you grasp what we're looking for. In simplest terms, by the end of the week you'll be able to separate what you should know from what it would be nice to know. I've got one rule: there's no such thing as a stupid question. Maybe you'll be asking something which I've covered while you were taking a nap. That doesn't make any difference. A question is not stupid when you don't know the answer, so don't be afraid to ask. I see we've got one already. The gentleman with the Hawaiian sports shirt. At least, I think it's Hawaiian."

"Sir, I'd like to ask—"

"Suppose you give me your name when you have a question—for a couple of days, anyway, so I can get to know you."

"Webster, sir. I wanted to ask why the 737 was certificated with inadequate thrust reversers. You said the plane has a new—"

"We didn't know they weren't as good as they could be until we had some operating experience."

"But how come the FAA certificated the plane anyway?"

"Because the certification process doesn't include thrust reversers as a primary stopping device. The primary items are spoilers, flaps and brakes. Thrust reversers are regarded as auxiliary. By using them, we save five minutes' taxi time and five minutes adds up to a lot of dough. Okay, let's go on. The first subject we'll cover today is the jet engine itself. For those of you who've had turbine experience in the military, we'll be covering familiar ground but the FAA requires it, so bear with me. After the power plant we'll go into the electrical system, fuel system, instrumentation, fire protection, flight controls, flaps and spoilers, hydraulics, landing gear, pressurization and air conditioning and finally a three-hour summary and review Friday afternoon to wrap up everything before the Saturday final.

"One more thing. Remember, I said the purpose of this course is to teach you to understand what's happening when you pull a lever, see a light or hear a noise. The lights, in a sense, are the most important. They're literally a mirror in which you can see the functioning components of your aircraft. The cockpit of any transport plane qualifies as a pinball machine—and the 737 is no exception. We started out with ninety-one lights in Fat Albert's cockpit and we're now up to ninety-six. Idiot lights, you might call them. They're easy to understand and interpret if you remember this simple guideline: warning or emergency lights are red; caution lights are amber or yellow; advisory lights are blue, green or white. That's probably old hat to a military pilot but in some cases you'll find Fat Albert has more lights than you're used to, so just follow those guidelines. I'm glad to see you writing this down . . . any pertinent points I emphasize during class that you can put down on paper will help you commit them to memory. Now, let's talk about the power plant. . . ."

By the time they broke for lunch Haines had not only covered the theory of the turbine engine and its operating characteristics but had begun discussion of the 737's electrical system. Some of it was dully familiar to them, with their military backgrounds (and Dudney's civilian), but the familiarity was only in a general sense; the specific innards of the 737 were totally new. So, they discovered anew, were the airlines' ways of operating those innards even when some were virtually identical to what they had been used to in the service. All ten were getting it drummed into their skulls that safety followed by comfort and economical operation were the cornerstones on which every flight was built, and that the airplane itself fitted into that pattern in the same manner the wings were an integral part of the 737's total design.

Dudney heard Dixie say something at lunch with which she had to agree and which summed up an attitude that had been seeded in their minds almost from the very first day of training and already was sprouting into convictions and philosophies. "Dammit, I've got nearly four thousand hours and I know I'm a better pilot than some of the captains I'll be ass-kissing for the next few years—but I also know I've got to learn the airline way of doing things." Dudney, who knew from her father's precarious existence that just the right altitude selected for cruise could supply the blade-edge difference between profit and loss, breathed a silent amen.

That same afternoon Haines finished up the electrical system and dismissed them with the warning to review this subject and power plants before the next session. On Tuesday he covered fire protection and hydraulics, and managed to add fifteen minutes on the pressurization system by the time he dismissed the class. Pressurization was concluded Wednesday morning, followed by flight controls and instrumentation. The work was hard and the laughs were few, one of the blessed lighter moments occurring Wednesday when Haines released them for lunch. Dixie, Mike Kalinka and Doug Worthington announced their intention of forgoing the employees' cafeteria for a topless restaurant.

"The Wild Goose is the one I heard about," Mike said. "It's on Sepulveda, I think. Mr. Haines, would you know where it is?"

"I haven't the slightest idea," Haines said virtuously.

"It's 8814 Sepulveda, if I remember the address in the phone book," Doug offered.

"8816," Haines blurted impulsively, and then joined the laughter himself. The instructor promptly announced, "Inasmuch as my secret has been exposed anyway, I might as well join you guys at the Wild Goose."

The entire class, Dudney excepted, trooped off in three cars. She was disappointed, not at the latest snub but because she was curious about such establishments. Resigned to eating alone once more, she sat down in the caf and was surprised to see Ernie Crum also eating by himself—reading at the same time from the 737 Operations

Manual propped up in front of him. When she finished her meal she stopped by his table.

"Hi. Didn't you feel like going to the Wild Duck or whatever you call it?"

Ernie shook his head glumly. "I felt like it, Miss Devlin, but I figured I'd be better off if I studied this stuff. To tell you the truth, it's pretty thick going."

"A lot of material to remember," she agreed, "but it shouldn't be hard for anyone with your logged time."

"Flight time is one thing. Book learning is another. I'm a pretty damned good airplane jockey, Miss Devlin, but the classroom stuff always bugged me. I just about scraped through Navy ground school. Hell, I got only an eighty-five on that indoctrination retest Tuesday."

He looked so unhappy and worried that she almost sat down to keep him company, then decided if he wanted to study he didn't need any distractive conversation. She settled for an inadequate "Well, have fun," and went back to the classroom where she proceeded to get in some book time herself. Not that she was having Crum's difficulties; for Dudney, memorization came easily if she knew the subject at hand, and with her aeronautical engineering background, Systems was merely interesting and fairly unexacting.

Haines polished off instrumentation that Wednesday afternoon with enough time left over for a few minutes on the fuel system. The next morning he opened the class as usual by asking if the trainees had any questions on the material covered the previous day.

"Mr. Haines?"

"Mr. Crum."

"Sir, would you go over the fuel transfer arrangement again? I don't quite understand the valve sequence."

Haines frowned, a little puzzled. "Mr. Crum, we haven't come to fuel transfer yet."

Ernie turned red and there was some tittering behind him.

"Oh," he said weakly. "I guess that's why I don't understand it."

The laughing was louder this time, but Ernie Crum didn't join in and neither did Dudney. She was watching the little trainee with curiosity bordering on concern. It *had* been stupid of him, asking about something that hadn't been covered up to now. It was obvious that Crum had been reading ahead, a sign of apparent panic. If he was having trouble grasping past material, he must have plunged ahead in a desperate effort to get an advance inkling of what the instructor would be dealing with the next day. Or, Dudney reasoned, Ernie might even have so poor an understanding of the subject that he never recognized fuel transfer as something Haines did not touch on Wednesday in his brief introductory discussion of the fuel system.

She was surprised at her concern, recognizing it as symptomatic of growing affection for her classmates, and then also being surprised at this sudden awareness. They were emerging as individuals, warm, likable, fun and generally sharp—in other words, she realized, fellow pilots. Their aloofness, their refusal to accept her, their rejection of her socially and their suspicious, even jealous attitude professionally —all these negatives, she conceded, were natural if unfair and discouraging. In brief, she found herself liking them in spite of everything, and if she felt sorry for Ernie Crum, it was more an emotion of comradeship than an urge of motherhood.

Even Dudney, who relished almost every minute of class as an exciting adventure, a preview of a promising future, was tired when the last session ended Friday. The subjectiveness of the test loomed menacingly, its reliance on memory as much as understanding and its loaded technique of spot-checking knowledge taking on the frightening form of a trap. There had been so much to learn so fast. . . .

". . . the Auxiliary Power Unit or APU has only fifty pounds of thrust and its primary function is to take in bleed air from the engines and cool it. . . ."

". . . there are three transformer rectifiers which cut voltage or change current. . . ."

". . . the 737, like virtually all modern transports, does not contain fuel cells as such but utilizes the wings themselves for fuel storage. This is the so-called wet wing, and it is a design which not only adds to the strength of the wing but reduces oscillation and virtually eliminates fuel leakage. . . ."

". . . the initials MEL stand for Minimum Equipment List and if you see any amber light on your panel corresponding to a component on that list, you must return to the gate for a maintenance check. . . ."

". . . you're guaranteed a positive start on the APU up to twenty-five thousand feet, although the 737's capability goes up to thirty-five thousand. . . ."

". . . another little tip, to extinguish a fire in the wheel well, all you have to do is drop the gear. . . ."

". . . the battery switch is the most important switch in the airplane. It's the first thing you turn on and the last thing you turn off. . . ."

". . . between one hundred and twenty and one hundred and fifty-seven degrees, you'll get an oil temperature warning. If she reads above one fifty-seven, it's a mandatory shutdown. . . ."

". . . never underestimate an electrical fire. If you can smell electrical smoke, you've got troubles because things are going wrong that you can't see. . . ."

". . . and if you don't think this air conditioning system is effective, believe me, you can park this bird at Phoenix in mid-August, a hundred and twenty-five degrees Fahrenheit outside, turn on the unit full blast and eventually you'd be able to throw snowballs in the cockpit if it weren't for an automatic cutoff device which is this circuit here. . . ."

". . . this airplane can be flown safely with only the battery working. If you should lose all generators, which is the worst possible situation, you'd still retain power for your basic instruments for up to thirty minutes. Question, Mr. Mitchell?"

"Sir, assuming you did suffer total generator failure, does the emergency checklist call for immediate throwing of the battery switch before determining the source of the generator trouble?"

"You wouldn't have time to look for the source, Mr. Mitchell. In the event of total generator loss, the battery switch is activated automatically—that's only on the 737, by the way. On the 727–200 series, the battery switch is entirely manual. Now if you'll look at this schematic panel, you'll understand the importance of this bypass circuitry. . . ."

". . . I cannot emphasize this too strongly—all systems are fail-safe, and if anything craps out you'll get a warning light. . . ."

The instructor's departing words Friday afternoon were coated with foreboding. "The test tomorrow will last about two hours. . . . Report at 0730 as usual. You're free for a coffee break after the test, but you're to pick up your I.D. cards at 1100, same place where the I.D. pictures were taken. Starting at 1300, you'll report to Mr. Robinson's office to receive your test grades and your schedule for simulator training next week—if you've gotten by the test. You're to see Mr. Robinson individually and in alphabetical order, starting at 1300. Mr. Tarkington?"

"Sir, what's the passing grade?"

"Seventy. Mr. O'Brien?"

"If we flunk, Mr. Haines, will there be a chance for a retest like we had in the indoctrination exam?"

"Negative." There were a few gasps of anxiety but Haines added, "However, Mr. Robinson or Mr. Le Baron has the prerogative of ordering a retest if either feels the individual warrants another shot. In that case, the retest will be given at 0730 next Monday in Mr. Le Baron's office. It's only fair to warn you, though, that unlike the indoctrination exam—which merely involved taking the same test over again—a second Systems examination will be even harder than the original test. And I might also warn you that neither Mr. Robinson nor Mr. Le Baron is in the habit of granting second chances—the circumstances would have to be *very* extenuating."

There were more murmurs of fresh concern tinged with protest and Haines continued. "I want you to know we're not being cold-blooded about this. We simply feel that if you can't hack it in ground school your chances of making the grade as pilot are reduced. Now inasmuch as we'll be spending a minimum of ten thousand dollars per man just in the initial phases of your flight training, we don't have the time or money to waste on marginal cases. So hit those books tonight—and good luck."

Dudney noticed that Ernie Crum was pale as the class filed out. She was not the only one. Dixie Miller was watching the little trainee too, an expression of worry flitting across his face when he saw Crum stuff the manuals into his new brainbag and leave without a word to anyone.

"Ernie's got troubles," she heard Dixie say to Mitchell and Webster. "Wonder if we shouldn't help him study tonight?"

"I've got enough studying to do on my own without worrying about Crum," Webster snapped.

Even Hank was reticent. "Frank's right, Dixie. If anyone tried to nurse Ernie through at this stage, he'd be hurting himself. I'd like to help him but I can't study for two people—I'm not that sure of what they've been throwing at us all week."

"We might call him around midnight and see how he's doing," Dixie argued. "Then maybe an hour or so of cramming . . ."

"He doesn't have a phone," Hank said.

"Then we could go down to the Purple Eagle later and see if he's there. That's where he'd probably head after studying—he's been at that bar with us a dozen times."

"Maybe," Hank said doubtfully. "But by the time I get through with my own cramming I'm gonna be too tired to hold Ernie's hand."

"Well, Jesus, I hate to see our little chum wash out. . . ." Dudney heard Miller's Samaritanism fade into futility as he followed Mitchell and Webster from the room. She packed her own manuals and left.

She had been studying for a couple of hours, after a light supper, when the first stirrings of intuition invaded her consciousness. It was intuition, perhaps, summoned from her own confidence in what she had learned and absorbed during the week. Her reviewing was almost perfunctory, an assurance born of not only knowing a subject but understanding it thoroughly. In that mood, she found herself thinking of Ernie Crum.

Exactly forty-two minutes later she had found her way to the Purple Eagle Cocktail Lounge and was peering around through the dimness and stale smoke. The Purple Eagle was one of those bars making a pretense at intimacy by utilizing bad lighting, which not only hid the place's dinginess but also covered up such unaesthetic and unsanitary aspects as poorly washed glasses. Even as she looked for her fellow trainee she wondered what appeal this dubious Mecca had for the class and decided it had to be the scantily clad waitresses, surprisingly pretty in a hard sort of way. She was following one of them, a blonde with pendulous breasts, with her eyes when Ernie came into her field of vision, sitting morosely in a dark corner. A half-finished scotch and water was in front of him, and he seemed to be doing more brooding than drinking.

"Hello, Ernie," she greeted him.

He looked up in surprise, bordering on shock. The expression on his face reminded her of that uniformed copilot caught by the captain in the Anchorage bar.

"You're a damned fool. Mind if I sit down?"

He motioned a surly invitation. "Don't start preaching, Miss Devlin."

"Okay. But I'd like to ask why. You should be home studying. And don't tell me you're finished or don't have to."

He did not answer her directly. "What the hell are you doing here?"

"Some of your classmates were a little concerned about you. I thought I'd just make sure you were in good shape for that test."

Suspiciously, belligerently, defensively. "Any of those guys send you? They don't have any right—"

"Nobody sent me. I overheard Dixie Miller say you hung out at the Purple Eagle on occasion. So I came over. I repeat, Ernie, why?"

"I'll ask you the same question. Why'd *you* come?"

"I don't want to see you flunk. And I'll give you ten to one you're not ready for that Systems test."

"Make it twenty to one, Miss Devlin. I don't have a chance. I started to study. Honest to Christ, I tried. For more than a hour. That's when I shut up the goddamned manual and came over here. I knew it was hopeless."

"Bull, my friend. Nothing's hopeless. If you could get to be a Navy fighter pilot you can pass that test tomorrow. With a little help. Finish your drink and let's go back to my apartment. We've got some cramming to do."

Even in the semidarkness she saw a look of hope cross over his features. He lifted his glass but did not touch the contents. "Why are you helping me, Miss Devlin? You've got your own studying to do. How come . . ."

She glared at him. "You can bet your sweet butt it's not because of any mother instinct. You're a pilot, Ernie. You had to be damned good to fly for the Navy. I suspect you're also good enough to fly for Trans-Coastal, provided you get rid of that silly damned mental block you have on books. So come on, chum, let's get rid of it."

A final, flabby gesture of protest, of reluctant martyrdom. "But how about *your* studying . . ."

"It's all done. I could pass that test in my sleep. And so will you when I get through with you. Pay the check and let's get out of here."

They studied her manual for more than five hours. She was sympathetic but insistent. More than once he wavered on the precipice of surrender, only to be pulled back by her ability to combine firmness with patience. She cajoled, scolded, soothed and lectured. Above all, she taught—not just the memorization of facts but making sure he understood the theory and/or reasons behind those facts. She quickly established that he had three major areas of weakness—electrical, hydraulics and fuel—and she concentrated on these after making sure he had the other systems under control. She never let him off the hook by accepting a correct answer as proof of learning; she kept coming back to the same question a few minutes later, and then asking why he answered it the way he did.

At 2:00 A.M. she wearily but with great satisfaction told him, "Ernie, you're as primed as I am. Let's have a beer or a nightcap and you can go home and get some sleep."

"I'll forget all this by morning," he worried.

"Probably. But it'll come back to you the minute they shove the test in front of you."

They sipped two cold beers while Ernie told her about himself. His ambition had been to go to the Naval Academy but his Annapolis dreams foundered when he flunked the entrance exams. Flight school at Pensacola was a second choice and a fortunate one, for he proved to be a natural flier.

"I suppose failing those entrance exams built up that mental block you were talking about," he theorized cheerfully. "Funny, but everything seemed to fall into place when you explained everything the way you did. I wish Haines had."

"He didn't have time, Ernie. But you're right—it was a mental block and not inability to learn. Tell me about your girl in San Francisco."

"She's a nurse. Two inches shorter than me, regular kewpie doll, Nancy is. You'll like her, Miss Devlin. I'm gonna have her down here when we graduate."

They talked about Nancy briefly before Dudney sent him home. She was exhausted but happy with that special breed of happiness that comes only from a sense of accomplishment. It never entered her head that she had done something decent and unselfish. It merely pleased her when he said, simply, "Thanks, Miss Devlin," as he left. She knew he was neither glib nor particularly articulate, and the way he said that one word of gratitude was stamped with sincerity. Her last word to him was an offhand "By the way, Ernie, this session is just between the two of us." He looked puzzled but nodded agreement.

The test the next morning *was* tough, yet not unreasonably so. Ernie Crum was the last one to finish but this stemmed more from carefulness than panic or lack of knowledge. Dudney badly wanted to ask him how he thought he had done but she had no chance to talk to him alone, and she was afraid that seeking him out when others were in hearing distance might disclose her own role. Helping Crum, she was positive, would be interpreted in the same spirit as her correcting Webster on the rated power of the DC-6B's engines. Thus, she avoided her classmates until it was time to gather outside of Robinson's office on the first floor of the Training Center.

At 1300 sharp Robinson opened his door, called out, "Mr. Crum," and closed it as soon as Ernie entered.

"Christ, I hope he passed," Dixie muttered.

"He didn't seem too worried at lunch," Hank noted.

"Nope," Dixie observed, "but he didn't say much, either. Said he crammed until the wee hours, that's about all. Dammit, I wish somebody would have helped him."

Dudney said nothing. The others seemed to be pacing mentally, conversing in low tones that reminded her of people outside a hospital room occupied by a dying relative. Robinson's door opened and Ernie Crum emerged from—no, shot out of—the office, his grin stretching nearly the width of his face.

"I passed!" he yelped.

The class crowded around him, Dudney on the fringes until Ernie saw her and yelled, "You're to go in, Miss Devlin."

She left the other trainees still congratulating Crum. Robinson welcomed her with a small smile, held out his hand and shook hers with a single pump. "Congratulations, Miss Devlin," he said, and handed her a pair of white, wallet-sized cards. She glanced at them eagerly. The first:

TRANS-COASTAL AIRLINES

This certifies that DUDNEY DEVLIN

has completed the Basic Indoctrination Course

The second:

TRANS-COASTAL AIRLINES

This certifies that DUDNEY DEVLIN

has completed the 737 Initial Transitional Course

Both were signed by "David Robinson, Director—Flight Training," and "George Le Baron, Manager—Ground School Training."

"Your first diplomas, so to speak," Robinson informed her pleasantly. "Now, Miss Devlin, you're down to start simulator training next Tuesday at 1300. There will be a general class meeting at 0730 Monday, Room 200 as usual. Simulator school is on the first-floor level, at the end of this hall. Any questions?"

"No, sir. Except"—she hesitated—"did everyone pass?"

"Everyone, I'm glad to say. But don't tell them that when you go out. Kinda like to break the good news myself." He waved her out with a "Send in Mr. Kalinka." She departed, completely forgetting to ask him for her test grade until she was out of his office and in the hallway with the others. She was about to turn back when she became aware that the entire class was inspecting her, every man with a grin on his face. Dixie broke the silence.

"Ernie just told us what you did for him last night. Uh, we're having a little celebration at my apartment tonight. And—*Dudney*—we'd be damned glad if you'd join us."

It was one hell of a party.

For the nine men, it was relief from the tensions of two tough weeks. For Dudney, it was the same plus even more blessed relief from loneliness and rejection. And she had to admit that the class did a one-eighty maneuver in going from aloofness to acceptance. They treated her with a combination of equality and respect, largely—she suspected—because every one of them knew that he should have done what she did for Ernie Crum.

They told off-color jokes which accelerated rapidly in raunchiness as the evening progressed and the deftness of mixing drinks deteriorated. For a time the stories were accompanied by discreet apologies —noticeably directed at Dudney, not at wives or dates—along the lines of "Excuse me, Dudney, but I gotta use a four-letter word in this one . . ." Eventually and inevitably, the apologetic prefaces were abandoned, along with the use of "Dudney," which quickly was shortened to "Dud" and then expanded temporarily, in direct correlation to alcoholic consumption, to "good ole Dud."

She was both amused and surprised at the way some of their temperaments altered under inebriation—and at the individuals so affected. Webster, for example, did a Hyde-to-Jekyll transformation of sorts, shedding his mantle of supercilious pomposity and becoming maudlin and even humble. He did insist on calling her Dudney throughout the party, but for him even the use of her full first name was a retreat from his attitude of superiority. She liked his relationship with his wife, a tall, slender brunette named Betty, who regarded his gradual descent into mild intoxication with amused tolerance.

"It does Frank good to climb off his high horse now and then," Betty Webster confided to Dudney in refreshing awareness of her husband's starched-shirt personality. "He's not really as stuffy as he seems to most people—a pretty sentimental, very considerate guy, as a matter of fact. You just have to get to know him and, believe me, I did. When we first started dating I couldn't stand the bastard. Then one night he took me to visit the widow of a pilot in his squadron who had just been killed. The way he handled her, his tenderness and thoughtfulness—I figured there was a human being under all those layers of arrogance and I wound up falling in love with him."

Dudney found herself wondering curiously about the pairings in the married couples she met. All her life she had seen some stunning contrasts and incongruities among married persons, challenging any logic in their mating process. The handsome Tarkington, for example, in-

troduced her to a wife whose mousy plainness was next door to home-
liness. Dudney figured his shyness was probably the catalytic factor
—she obviously worshiped him and that was an effective antidote for
shyness.

Norma Jean Miller, on the other hand, was just as Dudney had
imagined she'd look—a tiny, honey-haired, pug-nosed girl who was
extremely cute rather than beautiful, and as effervescent as Dixie.
Dudney liked her instantly, something she was not prepared for
inasmuch as she had always assumed Southern women were simpering
epitomes of cloying coyness. The only thing Southern about Norma
Jean was her thick accent; she was sharp, quick-tongued and handled Dixie with a kind of discipline that stretched like a rubber
band. She let him tell dirty jokes—up to a point. She let him flirt with
the dates Kalinka and Worthington brought—up to a point. Then,
Dudney noticed, she apparently decided the band was stretching a
little too much and she brought him back with a mere look or word.

Dudney warmed to Judy Mitchell, too. Hank's wife was almost as
tall as the husky Negro—lighter-complexioned, patrician in both appearance and vocabulary, and with a figure that made Dudney feel
flat-chested. She and Hank sat in one corner for most of the night,
holding hands, laughing politely at the ribald joke-telling, and quietly
enjoying themselves with the somewhat tolerant air of adults watching
teen-agers cavort at a loosely chaperoned party. The looks she occasionally sneaked at her husband gave Dudney a glow. They bal-
anced pride with love, respect with devotion.

"I met him at Syracuse his senior year," she told Dudney when the
two had a moment by themselves in Dixie's small kitchen. "I guess
what attracted me the most was his gentleness—so many big men are
that way, a sort of childlike gentleness that makes their strength
stand out even more."

"Everyone in the class seems to like him," Dudney ventured.

Judy Mitchell smiled. "Yes, and we can thank Dixie for at least
some of it. Hank figures that, when a Southerner like Dixie accepted
him so openly, it practically immunized the class from prejudice. I
hear, Dudney"—she smiled again as she said it—"you had more
trouble than Hank when it came to prejudice."

"I think I learned how a black person must feel," Dudney said.

"But you expected it, didn't you?"

"To some extent, yes. But even when you expect something, it doesn't always ease the pain when it actually happens. We all expect death, yet very few of us welcome it or even adjust to the prospect."

"Very true," Judy agreed. "Anyway, that was a fine thing you did for that Crum boy. It's too bad it took something like that to make them all act sensibly. You know, Hank was ready to welcome you to the fold right from the start. But . . ." She paused, uncertain of her next words.

"But if he had, the others might have put him out in the cold," Dudney finished for her, and Judy Mitchell nodded, her dark brown eyes reflecting the wisdom born of knowing bigotry.

If the class had taken Dudney to its collective bosom, the reaction of the wives definitely was mixed. She got along well with Judy, Norma Jean and Betty, but some of the other women present seemed to regard her as a combined menace and fluke. McCrae's wife, a woman of Amazon proportions, was neutral—a status dictated by her inability to hold liquor. She started out primly, shifted early to raucous laughter, and eventually began telling worse stories than the men. Tarkington's spouse was cool, and O'Brien's outright hostile.

Kalinka brought a quiet, well-behaved girl Dudney could swear she had seen waiting tables at the Purple Eagle, Ernie came sans female and Worthington's date was the blonde from the stewardess class she had heard him mention. Dudney's introduction to the latter, a pretty girl with cropped red hair, was a shocker. They came later than any-one else and neither was feeling any pain.

"Want you to meet our most celebrated classmate," Doug said in presentation. "Dudney Devlin, this is Shirley Melton."

"Boy, I envy you," Shirley announced immediately. "All that lap time you'll be getting—and perfectly legal, too."

Dudney, who was on the verge of a polite thanks for the envy, gaped.

"Suppose you'll feel pretty high and mighty up there in the cock-pit," Shirley continued in a slurred tone. "But lemme tell you some-thing, don't expect to lord it over us poor slobs back in the cabin. If I ever get you on a flight, I'll treat you same as any other copilot—'cept I won't go out with you, will I, Dougie baby?"

Drunk or not, Worthington was embarrassed and angered. "Don't be an ass, Shirley. Dud's not gonna lord it over anybody—she's not that kind of person."

Dudney was more amused than miffed, deciding wisely that a retort would lead to an unpleasant argument. "Come on, Shirley, I'll get you a drink," she laughed, putting her arm around the girl and leading her toward the kitchen. But for the rest of the night, she noticed, the stewardess trainee kept staring at her with looks ranging from curiosity to belligerence. Most of the class was getting too bombed to notice the one-sided friction, but Norma Jean Miller did.

She came into the kitchen when Dudney was alone, mixing herself a last drink. "That little would-be stew getting you down, Dud?"

"Not really. She's feeling her drinks—and I can't blame her for being antagonistic. I must seem like a freak to her."

"More of a threat than a freak. I heard her tell Mike Kalinka none of the girls in her class ever want to fly with you."

"Oh? I'd like to know why."

"Something about women making poor bosses. They figure you'd be kind of uppity toward them."

Dudney shrugged good-naturedly. "I might, I suppose, if I don't watch myself. I'll be low man on the totem pole in every cockpit. Be rather natural to take that status out on the next lower echelon."

"You're not the type," Norma Jean said. "To tell you the truth, when Dixie told me all about you, I didn't feel any fondness toward you. But he put me straight—said you were a fine girl who just wanted to be an airline pilot, and if you got through training you deserved a medal."

"Why did you resent me, Norma Jean?" Dudney asked with typical directness.

"Jealousy."

"Jealousy? That's foolish. I don't have designs on any man in the class, including the bachelors, let alone the married ones. I have all the predatory instincts of an altered cat."

Norma Jean stirred a bourbon and water, the movement seeming to reflect a stirring of thoughts and words in her mind. "Not jealous of you personally. I guess I'm jealous of Dixie's job. The attractive girls he'll fly with. The temptations he'll be exposed to. Maybe 'worry' is a better word than 'jealousy.' "

"Either one is a form of insecurity, Norma Jean. From what I've seen of Dixie, you shouldn't feel insecure. Anyway, I'm the last one you should worry about."

Dixie's wife surveyed her with a wry look. "I suppose it's not fair to put you in the category of home-wrecking, wife-stealing stewardesses —but you're pretty enough to be a stewardess, so you're included in that cross of insecurity I'm hauling around."

"I'm climbing off the cross. And where did you get the idea stews are wife-stealers?"

"I've heard."

"Some are, I imagine. So are a few secretaries I know. Also teachers, store clerks, nurses and any other branch of our sex you could mention—including some wives. You can't indict all stewardesses because a few of them are bitches. Like I said, our sex contains a certain number of bitches and it has nothing to do with their profession."

"It has in the case of stewardesses. They have more opportunity to get their hooks into married men—pilots in particular."

McCrae and his wife came in for refills at that moment, and Dudney diplomatically ended the discussion with a cryptic "I think you're overestimating the possibility, Norma Jean." McCrae looked puzzled and his wife oozed curiosity but Dudney simply said, "Hi," and went back to the party.

Yet the brief conversation, plus the remark from Worthington's date, upset her. She had enough to worry about as far as her male colleagues and superiors were concerned. Now she had been handed a glimpse of resentment on the part of her own sex, something she had never included in her forecast of obstacles. Funny it hadn't occurred to her before. She should have anticipated opposition from this source, certainly from stewardesses and other airline distaffers if not from pilot wives. Shirley Melton's hostility was not dictated by liquor; drunkenness had merely triggered it and under the words spoken by a thickened tongue was uneasiness—a kind of unspoken fear as prickling as that of Norma Jean Miller's. Some of it, Dudney recognized, was covetous envy in the massive proportions that could only be stewed up by one woman toward another. But there also had to be an element of concern over her higher status—women, Dudney conceded, often *did* make poor bosses. The fact that the concern was first expressed by a lowly stewardess trainee didn't lessen its potential adoption by any other outranked girl if and when she began flying the line.

This, plus the coolness of a couple of the wives and Norma Jean's temporary jealousy, were storm warnings. A fresh batch of emotional worries clouding her technical competence, invading her new-found happiness like the vague aches preceding a bout of flu. It was not enough to spoil her evening, but when Ernie Crum took her home she was rather quiet, responding to his cheerful chatter with monosyllables.

Ernie—spurred by the whiskey he had consumed, a male sense of duty, the fact that his girl was a couple of hundred miles away, gratitude and Dudney's admitted attractiveness—kissed her good night. She was jolted when she had to resist an urge to open her mouth for a French kiss; she suddenly realized she wanted a man, although even as normal desire flared, a corner of her brain opened a cold-water faucet. Instinctively, she knew that sleeping with a classmate could involve professional suicide, altering her new-found standing as a comrade and colleague into that of a target and, worse, just another woman. She shut the door on Ernie with as much politeness as abruptness would allow, and he never guessed the turmoil that had boiled within her for a dangerous moment.

Well, Dudney told herself, at least her libido hadn't died. But she had done the right thing. Ernie was a good kid but he still was a male and males seldom could resist bragging any time one scored; the boasting seemed to be a post-sex inevitability, much as doubtful regrets are part of a woman's sexual pattern after an affair. She was not a little startled that Ernie of all people had aroused her, but with her faculty for introspection she concluded correctly that it just happened to be Ernie who lit the fuse at a vulnerable moment. She merely had been ripe for sex with any decent man for whom she felt friendship and perhaps affection, her natural embers of passion stoked into flames by a man's nearness, her long celibacy, too much alcohol and —she laughed to herself at this theory—maybe a subconscious reaction to the women who had resented her that night.

She had trouble falling asleep. A man would have said she was horny, a woman would have explained it as being mixed up, but Dudney herself abandoned any self-analysis of insomnia—deliberately, coolly and most wisely, she sublimated career for sex and finally dozed off while thinking about the flight training that would start next week.

The Monday session turned out to be more of an informal bull session than a class, Robinson surprising them first with the announcement that their uniforms were ready.

"Mr. Ferranti says you can pick them up any time," he informed the trainees.

"He said it would take twelve working days," Dixie commented. "It's only been"—he counted on his fingers the days that had elapsed since the fittings—"nine."

"Small class," Robinson explained laconically. He refrained from disclosing that Mr. Ferranti regarded the nine-day performance as a feat roughly comparable to Boeing's turning out a 747 in three hours. "This session today is mostly to wrap up any loose ends, answer any questions, stuff like that. We should be through in a couple of hours, maybe less—that'll give all of you time to pick up your uniforms. However, before you start simulator training tomorrow, a word of advice. We've got a Link trainer downstairs. The simulator department has reserved it for the exclusive use of this class the rest of the day. I suggest that before you head for Sawtell's you make an appointment for about thirty minutes of Link time. It's probably been some time since any of you have flown a plane and the Link will be a good refresher. Kind of a warm-up for the 737 simulator. Okay, any questions? Mr. Kalinka?"

"Sir, if we wash out of flight training, do we get to keep the uniform? Or will the company refund what they've already taken out of our pay?"

"I don't know why the hell anyone would want to wear a uniform they weren't qualified to wear. Anyway, the answer to your question is negative—if you flunk, you're to return the uniform and there will be no refunds on what you've already paid. A few years ago we had a trainee who was fired and he tried to get his dough back—about twenty bucks, if I remember right. The company refused. He not only wouldn't give back the uniform, but the crazy bastard wore it to the airport with a whiskey bottle sticking out of a pocket. He paraded up and down in front of our ticket counter scaring the hell out of passengers until somebody had him arrested. Then the sonofabitch gets himself a lawyer and threatens to sue for the twenty dollars, so we gave in and sent him a check. I don't recommend any of you trying this drastic course of action, however. Mr. Worthington?"

Doug cleared his throat, looked around as if pleading for moral support, cleared his throat again and glanced at Dudney.

"Well, Mr. Worthington? You did have your hand up, didn't you?"

"Uh, sir, I was wondering, uh, well, what's the policy, uh, about dipping your pen in company ink?"

There was loud laughter in which Robinson joined.

"You're a little late with the question, Doug," Dixie chortled.

"Is your question hypothetical, Mr. Worthington?" Robinson asked wryly.

"Retroactive," Kalinka murmured, which drew more laughs.

"Before answering Mr. Worthington," the training chief said with mock coldness, "I think he should explain to Miss Devlin the meaning of the phrase, 'dipping your pen in company ink.' "

"Dudney already knows—don't you, Dud?" Doug said imploringly.

"I haven't the faintest idea," Dudney lied.

"I'm a bit vague on the matter myself, Dudney," Webster announced in a surprising revelation of a lighter side.

"Elucidate, Mr. Worthington," Robinson ordered.

"I withdraw the question," Doug said, his face red.

"Negative on the withdrawal," Robinson grinned. "You will explain to Miss Devlin, in front of the class, the meaning of the phrase you used. And that's an order."

"I meant, well, what I was getting at . . . oh hell, what's the policy about scr . . . having an affair with somebody else who works for Trans-Coastal? Like stewardesses."

"Succinctly put, Mr. Worthington. At least, for me it was. Miss Devlin, do you desire a fuller explanation?"

"No, sir. It was a very lucid explanation." Dudney was not sure whether the training chief was trying to embarrass Worthington or her.

"Fine. Then I'll answer the question. Which, by the way, isn't a bad one. I'd be a hypocrite if I told you there's no hanky-panky among flight crews and I'd be a damned fool if I told you the company condones it. There's no policy except one of common sense and common decency. No airline can legislate against human nature, but as far as Trans-Coastal's concerned, all we ask is that you be discreet when you're wearing that uniform in public. We frown on public displays of affection—innocent or otherwise. Don't hold hands with a stew, for example, where passengers might see you. Don't try to paw one in an elevator going up to your rooms on a layover—even if she wants to be pawed. I think you know what I mean. As airline pilots you have an image we're pretty proud of and of which you should be equally proud. The same thing goes for our gals. If a pilot wants to shack up with a stew, that's his private business and hers too. But we don't want you wearing public signs boasting about it. The word is discreet. And that's the policy—be discreet. Next question. Mr. O'Brien?"

"Sir, some of us have heard some scuttlebutt that Trans-Coastal is going to sell all its 737s to Air West along with its short-haul routes. Do you know anything about those rumors?"

"I do. There's nothing to them. Let me talk briefly about the subject of rumors. There's a saying which you'd do well to remember—'Rumor is halfway around the world before Truth can get its boots on.' This is not only an excellent aphorism but it's one that's especially applicable to the airline business. Because of our communications network, not to mention the fact that our planes and our crews fly to a hell of a lot of places, our own rumors are spread very fast and they also get screwed up very fast. I know one captain who deliberately invented a rumor and mentioned it to another pilot. In two days it came back to him in a form he hardly recognized. My advice is, don't believe what you hear. This is a pretty good company for keeping its employees well informed. A rumor is nothing but garbled gossip. Mr. Tarkington?"

"Mr. Robinson, I couldn't find anything in the Jeppesen or anywhere else about rules concerning cabin PA announcements.

Whether they're required of pilots, how often, and are copilots supposed to do them or just captains. What's the company policy on
this?"

Robinson appeared a little surprised. This was Tarkington's first
question in two weeks. The training chief's lips curled up into a little
smile; it figured that Tarkington's only question would concern the
one area which scared the hell out of him. The shy rookie probably
would welcome in-flight fires, jammed landing gears and extreme
turbulence in preference to making a cabin PA.

"Well, let's say there's an unofficial policy if not a formal one.
Trans-Coastal would like captains—or copilots, at the discretion of
the captain—to make announcements from the flight deck at oppor-
tune times. At least one right after takeoff, for example, letting the
passengers know the flight plan, whether arrival will be on schedule
and the weather at destination. Occasional PAs during the flight are
welcomed, provided they aren't done in excess and don't bother the
customers. You're going to find, gentlemen and Miss Devlin, that the
attitude toward the PA varies according to what captain you're flying
with. Some of them like to talk to the public, most perform it as an
unpleasant but necessary chore, and a few would rather lose an engine
than pick up that mike. I'd suggest you play it by ear. Any more questions?"

There weren't, right at this moment, and Robinson continued.
"You'll get a lot of valuable tips from captains on this PA business.
As I said, we don't have any hard and fast rules—common sense,
again, is the best rule to follow. For example, I think most of our
captains will tell their passengers when something's wrong—and
they'll explain what and why. The guys know they'll get more cooperation from people who understand a situation than if a captain
just gets them scared. Let's say you lose an engine. Fat Albert likes
to fly straight and passengers will know something's up when they
hear thrust applied on only one side. That's the time to calmly explain
the situation—without throwing them into a panic. Sometimes you
can sugar-coat the truth a little. Like when you throw a turbine
blade, which can be hairy, instead of saying, 'Folks, we've had engine
failure and we're returning to the airport,' make it 'Folks, we've lost
some oil pressure in our starboard engine, and as a precautionary

measure, I've shut it down and we'll return to the airport to find the trouble.' See what I mean?"

The class nodded in newly acquired wisdom of flight deck etiquette.

"Even the judicious use of certain words can help allay panic," Robinson went on. "For instance, most people get petrified at the word 'fire.' Avoid it if at all possible. And God knows what your stews will come up with. We had one flight delayed in Salt Lake City while mechanics put glycol on the wings to get the snow and ice off. They were using a spray unit and one of the stewardesses decided she should explain the delay to the passengers. 'They're doing a blow job on the airplane,' she tells them—and then wonders why half the men on board started laughing."

The class was laughing too and Robinson could not quite decide whether he was pleased or disappointed that Miss Devlin, while she wasn't exactly holding her sides, definitely was chuckling. More than two weeks had gone by since the brass had issued the edict: embarrass the hell out of the dame on the off chance she'll walk out in a huff. She might have been embarrassed on occasions, he thought, but she showed no indication of walking out and her classroom performance had been superb. That previous Saturday afternoon he had called John Battles to pass on the news.

"Thought I'd better let you know how your pigeon is doing," he told Battles.

"Pigeon? What pigeon?"

"Miss Dudney Devlin, John."

"She flunked Systems, I hope."

"Your pigeon, esteemed Chief Pilot, is a goddamned eagle. With the exception of an ex-Air Force major, she pulled down the highest grade in the final."

Battles groaned. "Oh hell, that means simulators next. Maybe we can sink her then."

"Don't count on it," Robinson said sweetly and hung up, somehow perversely satisfied at Battles' unhappiness. Now he was glancing at her, her pretty face alive with something more than a residue of humor from his stewardess anecdote. She was chattering with the others, and Robinson was not only aware of her changed relationship within the class but he also knew why. George Le Baron had pumped somebody else in the class on Ernie Crum's mysterious scholastic recovery. "It was that Devlin kid who pulled him through," Le Baron told him. "She stayed up with him all night long and she must have crammed Systems up his butt and into his navel. Crum got the fourth best grade in the class and I had him pegged as a copper-riveted cinch to flunk."

In spite of himself, in spite of the front office's wishes, a wave of warm feeling washed over Robinson and the thirty minutes in which he had intended to review flight dispatch procedures he devoted instead to funny airline stories. After answering a few more questions and dispensing a few more items of advice, such as keeping their manuals up to date, he decided to dismiss them.

"I want to say one more word," he concluded as they were closing their new brainbags. "You've been a damned good class, one of the best we've turned out of ground school. On behalf of your instructors and myself—good luck to you."

There was applause, a scraping of chairs on the floor, and the ten trainees filed out. As Dudney passed Robinson, the training chief called out softly, "Miss Devlin."

"Yes, sir?"

He could not know that he was echoing the words of another man who had been told to get rid of her by any legal means possible.

"Good luck, kid," said Dave Robinson.

With Dixie, Ernie, Hank and Webster, she raced down to the Simulator Department where they arranged for thirty minutes of Link time apiece that afternoon. Then they piled into Webster's station wagon for a quick trip to Sawtell's where Mr. Ferranti himself greeted them with no less hand-rubbing eagerness than he would have displayed to Jackie Onassis. All the men's uniforms except Ernie's fitted well; his resembled the indifferent offering of an Army supply sergeant.

"Not bad at all," Mr. Ferranti clucked. "Just an inch or so shorter on the sleeves and maybe an inch off on the trousers."

"You'd better take in the back of those pants, too," the fastidious Webster suggested. "Ernie, that rear end looks like an empty sack of potatoes."

"Yeah," Dixie agreed. "For Christ's sake, Mr. Ferranti, who did you think you were measuring—King Kong?"

"With just a few alterations, it'll fit him perfectly," Ferranti said hastily. "If you'll just hold still, Mr. Crum, I'll—Ah . . . !"

The "ah" was exhaled, a sound of sheer admiration, and the four trainees followed the direction of his eyes. Dudney had just emerged from a dressing room—the green slacks hugging her trim hips and the smart, single-breasted jacket, even with its masculine lines, not quite hiding the swell of her firm breasts.

"Wow!" said Dixie.

"God, Dud," breathed Ernie.

"Very nice," allowed Webster. Then, as if ashamed at the inadequacy of this verdict, he added: "*Very* nice, Dudney."

Hank Mitchell just examined her silently for a moment before chuckling, "Dud, you may not become the best airline pilot in the United States but you're sure as hell going to be the most beautiful."

"You guys look pretty good yourselves," she said sincerely.

"Not me," Ernie complained. "There's something lacking in mine."

"Style," said Dixie.

"We all lack something," Hank murmured. "The wings."

"Amen," Dudney said, her eyes shining.

"Two more weeks," Dixie added, and for no particular reason reached out and grabbed Hank's black hand.

CHAPTER SEVEN

Dudney had all of Tuesday morning to herself before reporting for simulator training, and she consumed most of it by buying a car—an investment which depleted her checking account but gave her a delicious sense of independence from both the Los Angeles public transportation system and its overpriced cabs.

She did not really know much about automobiles and, a little embarrassed, asked Dixie to accompany her inasmuch as he had the morning free too. She was self-conscious at having to admit a lack of knowledge in this area, as if it were a confession of a typically feminine weakness, but Dixie shrugged it off generously—possibly because he actually didn't know much about cars either. In fact, he managed to ask Hank—outside Dudney's hearing—"What should I tell her to look for?"

"Get an idea first what she wants a car for. Just driving to the airport and around town, or maybe for weekend trips. Frankly, I'd advise her to spend a little more if she has to and get something dependable. And listen, Dixie, stay away from used car dealers—she'll be safer if she goes to a new car dealer and gets some wheels somebody's traded in. And if she does that, tell her to pick a Ford dealer if she wants a Ford product, a GM dealer if she wants a GM car, or a Chrysler Motors dealer if she wants a Plymouth or Dodge."

"Why's that?"

"Chances are that a guy who's traded in a Ford, say, for another Ford was satisfied with the first car. Same thing with a Chevvy. An owner who turns in a Ford for a Chevrolet might have been unhappy with the Ford, or vice versa if she tries to buy a Chevvy from a Ford dealer. Get it?"

"Got it."

Dudney, it turned out, was thinking mostly of a used Mustang, which narrowed the search. Dixie, with a learned air, suggested they visit a few Ford dealers and grandly explained why—neglecting, naturally, to credit the source of his automotive acumen. It turned out she found what she was looking for at the very first dealer—a turquoise 1968 Mustang with air conditioning, automatic transmission and power steering. The mileage was a little high, more than the 40,000 the odometer showed, but the car was clean, the tires good and the price reasonable at $1495.

"It's in good shape," Dixie ruled professionally after opening the hood and then examining the brake and accelerator pedals (he had read somewhere that if these pedals were worn, they could be a sign of more accumulated mileage than appeared on an odometer).

"I like it," Dudney decided.

"Shouldn't we go to a few more places?" Dixie asked, not wanting to admit he was as inexperienced as she but a little worried that he might be giving her a wrong steer.

"Why waste time, Dixie? The price is good—I checked the *Times* classified this morning and '68 Mustangs ran about $1400 to $1600. And you said it's in good shape . . ."

"Yeah. Okay, Dud, go ahead. I guess you won't do much better."

She paid for the car with a check written on the Los Angeles bank to which she had just transferred her Anchorage account. The salesman, elated at her quick choice, engaged in some pleasant conversation while the necessary paperwork was being done and her bank balance was checked.

"An excellent buy, Miss Devlin. I'll bet you take a lot of trips in her."

"Mostly to and from the airport, I'm afraid."

"Oh? You work for one of the airlines?"

"Trans-Coastal."

"A stewardess, I'll bet." His look walked a tightrope between an interested smile and a lecherous leer.

"Yes."

Five minutes later he handed her the keys and she walked with Dixie over to his own car. "Thanks for the ride and the help, Dixie. Sure appreciated it."

"Dud, why did you tell him you were a stewardess? Hell, you're a pilot. You ashamed of it?"

"Of course I'm not ashamed. But if I told him I was in pilot training he either wouldn't have believed me or it would have taken an hour's explaining. Thanks again, Dixie."

He climbed into his car, waved and headed for home. Dudney walked back to her new acquisition. She had a propensity for naming cars—a nondescript gray Plymouth she owned in Anchorage had been christened Mosby. She already had decided on Misty for this car. Misty the Mustang. Apropos and euphonious. Her proud inspection of the little car was interrupted by the salesman.

"Uh, Miss Devlin, perhaps you'd like to celebrate by having dinner with me tonight."

She was flattered by the invitation, the first purely boy vs. girl one she had received since coming to Los Angeles, and she tried hard to make her refusal polite. "No, thanks, but I go pretty steady. With a captain."

"Oh. Well, uh, I suppose they lead quite an interesting life, these airline pilots."

"Very. Thanks, Mr. Johnson. If Misty gives me any trouble, I'll come back to see you."

"Misty? Oh, your car. Very cute. Any time, Miss Devlin. Any time. Within the first ninety days or the first four thousand miles. If you and that pilot friend, ha-ha, ever break up, maybe you'll give me a rain check?"

"Could be, but don't count on it. Good-by." She drove away, thinking not of the indirect compliment he had paid her but of her reluctance to identify herself as a pilot trainee. It had been the easy way out, of course, preferable to wisecracks, gibes or questions, but she still was not pleased with herself. She wondered if her avoiding the subject was merely prudent or a sliver of sagging confidence. Then she decided that the latter possibility was foolish; she recalled how well she had handled the tricky little Link the day before, even though it was only her second time in a procedural trainer. The Link offered a good test of instrument flight and she had expected some rustiness in her instrument proficiency, but the instructor—after watching her work for a half hour—had grinned at her with a "Nice going."

She parked in the employees' lot, using the yellow and black card that had been handed out on the first day of ground school and noting with satisfaction that the gate guard glanced at the "PILOT TRAINING" on the card without a remark or any challenge. She had time for a quick sandwich in the caf, joining Webster and O'Brien, who had just finished their initial simulator sessions.

"How was it?" Dudney asked eagerly.

"No sweat," Webster said. "It's got the feel of a real airplane, that's for sure. Control forces seemed a little stiff but I didn't have any trouble."

"Instructor's a hell of a nice guy," O'Brien put in. "Used to be a captain with Trans-Coastal but he got beached with a heart condition. Very patient."

"Were you in there together?" Dudney wanted to know.

"Yep," Webster replied. "I flew for a couple of hours; Bill had it for another two hours and then we switched again for two more hours each. I was kind of bushed when I got out of there."

"You ever flown a simulator, Dud?" O'Brien asked.

"Negative, and I can't wait. If they're putting two of us through at a time, wonder who my partner'll be."

It turned out there was no partner. When she reported to Simulator Training at 1300 sharp, no one else from the class was there and she had an uneasy premonition that she was going "solo" so no other trainee could witness the process of tossing her into an aeronautical meat grinder. This was not apparent from the demeanor of the instructor, however. He was a pleasant, heavy-set man with curly gray hair and eyes that looked sad even when he smiled. He rose from behind his desk when she entered his small office.

"Miss Devlin, I take it?"

"Yes, sir. I believe I'm down for simulator time at 1300."

"You are. I'm Art Prentice. Welcome to the world of make-believe. Ever flown a simulator?"

"No, sir. Heard a lot about them."

"Favorable, I hope."

"Yes, sir."

"Good. Sit down here, Miss Devlin, and we'll chat for a few moments before we go across the hall and introduce to you the 737 trainer."

She sat where he indicated, in a chair facing his desk, conscious that he was inspecting her as if the visual scrutiny could provide him with advance judgment of her flying skills.

"You've flown our Link, I understand."

"Yes, sir. I spent thirty minutes in it yesterday." She decided it was unnecessary to volunteer that she apparently had done well.

Prentice cupped his fingers, leaning back in his chair as he did so. "Most of our new pilots have a built-in prejudice against synthetic trainers, to use the technical nomenclature for simulators. Some of it stems from their experience with Links, which is understandable. The Link is a valuable primary training tool but it's relatively simple and even primitive. The average pilot finds it hard to believe he can be taught to fly a new piece of equipment in a cockpit located on the ground, even a sophisticated cockpit. But believe me, he can. In less time and with a great deal less expense than if we used a real airplane. We used to average seventeen hours for initial flight training—qualification in a specific type airplane. We've cut this down to ten, thanks to the simulator. Matter of fact, Miss Devlin, we can transition a captain from his old equipment to a new plane in about an hour. It used to take six when we didn't have simulators."

"We'll be getting some actual flight time, won't we?" she said anxiously.

"Oh yes. But after you spend twenty hours in the simulator this week, your flight training will consist largely of two or three flights and if you're good—or maybe lucky—a single check ride for your type rating. Starting this afternoon and going through next Saturday afternoon, you'll have four hours' daily simulator time. And let me make one thing clear—if I can teach you to fly a simulator, you should have no trouble in a real 737. Your attitude, however, is most important."

Dudney smiled. "I think if my performance matches my attitude, you won't have any difficulty teaching me."

"Then we'll get along fine, Miss Devlin. Just keep an open mind. I'm not going to insult your intelligence and claim this simulator is exactly like an actual 737. But in many areas, key areas, it is. Listen to me, do what I tell you, and I'll not only teach you to fly it but you'll enjoy it in the process and you'll be a better 737 pilot for having gone through simulator training. I don't care if a guy's got ten thousand hours logged, he can't get into the cockpit of an unfamiliar airplane cold and fly it right the first time. Okay, let's go across the hall and start work."

Her first glimpse of the simulator carried the impression that she had walked into a Hollywood set to take part in the filming of a cockpit scene. From the outside, it looked like a huge shipping crate with the nose of an airplane sticking out the front end, except that the crate was mounted on movable jacks. But, inside, it *was* the cockpit of an airliner to Dudney, who was warmed by nostalgia the minute she saw the gray cockpit seats, the red fire-warning lights and CO_2 discharge knobs, the communications panel between the two seats, the big landing gear lever protruding from the instrument panel with the gear-raised and gear-down lights just above it. Her eyes swept over the scores of round dials on the panel, the basic instruments arranged in the shape of a T, and she quickly located the altimeter, airspeed indicator, rate of climb indicator and all the others as familiar to her as the instruments in an automobile would appear to a motorist. She had a feeling of intimacy that thrilled her and she had to suppress a chortle of sheer glee. Only her eyes betrayed her excitement and they did not escape Prentice, who let her bask in the intoxication of the homecoming for a moment before he said quietly, "Suppose you get into that right seat, Miss Devlin, and we'll take a little flight."

Although she knew something about simulators, she still was not prepared for the realism of the cockpit and its illusion of flying. She was aware that the so-called synthetic trainer was a direct descendant of the original Link, invented by a young piano manufacturer named Edwin Link, whose first "trainer" was an imitation airplane mounted on organ-style bellows that provided limited motion. The device actually was used in a children's amusement park before Link got the idea it could be used for instrument flight training and sold ten to the U. S. Army Air Corps in the 1930s. She understood how the modern simulator worked, that its instruments and controls were hooked electronically to a computer into which had been fed all the performance characteristics and reactions of a real plane, and that whatever a pilot did on his make-believe controls was fed back into the simulator by the computer.

She was surprised, nevertheless. Trans-Coastal's 737 simulator was a sophisticated monster, weighing as much as a fully loaded DC-3. The start of the "engines" produced a screaming sound almost identical to that of live turbines and there was even a feeling of forward motion despite the opaque cockpit windows that blocked any visual reference—"It substitutes for that feeling in the ass," Prentice explained. The control forces were a little stiffer than Dudney anticipated, Prentice nodding knowingly when she commented that the Electra she had flown seemed lighter on the controls.

"I don't think anyone will ever build a plane easier to fly than the Electra," he told her, "but this little bird is no truck, either. Once you get used to the 737, you'll find it an amazingly docile airplane."

She did. For the rest of that day he nursed her through speed and flap management, letting her get the feel of the airplane and gaining confidence with every maneuver. He was a gentle, tolerant, understanding man who found it impossible to follow John Battles' barked dictate: "Throw the book at the dame, Art—make her sweat." Prentice was tough and demanding, but he also was patient with Dudney because he could not bring himself to handle her differently than he treated any other trainee. Patience was the key to overcoming the fear, suspicion and even contempt most pilots aimed at simulators before they accepted them as the most valuable training aid ever developed. Even Dudney, so eager to learn and anxious to succeed, was not immune to this prejudice, particularly when she made a mistake and tended to blame it on the simulator instead of herself.

"I wouldn't have done that on a real airplane," she insisted after Prentice pointed out she had used too much flap on one approach. "I would have felt something was wrong."

"Maybe," Prentice said calmly, "but you've got to remember, Miss Devlin, that the cockpit workload in a two-man, high-performance aircraft lessens the possibility of 'feeling something's wrong,' as you put it. There isn't enough time to sense difficulty, particularly under the stress of a final approach. You'll be concentrating too much on your checklist, on your instruments, to be conscious of anything else. That's why we've had several mid-air collisions in which cockpit work-

to flush the head in a submarine, you can fix a simple old toilet. Hell, that sub john had to have a list of instructions posted for flushing—if you didn't follow the list, you could get into a lot of trouble. Like finding yourself glued to the toilet seat because of back pressure. There must have been seven valves to open or close before you could pull the lever and get the right results. Man, after that one trip in a submarine's can I'm a hydrostatic expert. Dud, all I need is a wrench and maybe a screwdriver."

"I don't have any tools," Dudney said, with a surge of unspoken gratitude for this equipment oversight.

"I've got a wrench and screwdriver in my car," Hank offered. "But, Dixie, maybe you'd better let Dud call—"

"You heard her say she's already called, didn't you? Get the tools."

Hank complied. Dixie retired to the bathroom accompanied by supervisors Mitchell and Webster, neither of whom knew anything about the innards of a toilet, whether submarine or landlocked. Dixie confidently took the commode apart, tinkered with the components, and put it back together, standing by the flushing lever with a look of magnificent triumph on his face. Everyone crowded around the bathroom door to witness the results.

"Orville Wright must have worn your expression that day at Kitty Hawk," Hank marveled.

"To paraphrase a certain astronaut," Dixie proclaimed, "a small step for Dudney, a great step for mankind."

He flushed the toilet.

Nothing happened. Absolutely nothing.

"You got rid of the hissing," Dudney said kindly.

"Maybe it would work if we were under water," Kalinka suggested unkindly.

"I must have forgotten to hook something up," Dixie said, unperturbed. "Everyone out—I'll fix this bloody thing."

"This may end the drinking," McCrae worried. "Nobody'll be able to go to the john."

"I told you guys, I'll fix it. I just didn't—"

"Dixie," said Norma Jean, "leave well enough alone and come back to the living room."

"Nothing doing, Norma Jean. Hell, I can't leave Dud's toilet so it won't flush at all."

"I'll settle for your reviving the python," Webster said.

"So will I," Dudney murmured.

"Out!"

The party went on for another forty minutes while plumber Miller tugged, pulled, wrenched and cursed. From the bathroom there came the familiar hissing sound and from the living room came loud cheers and from the bathroom emerged Dixie, face grimy and wrench in hand. "The snake's back," he announced.

"Thanks, Dixie," Dudney said. "I'm grateful for returning to status quo."

"You're not exactly back to status quo," Dixie admitted sheepishly. "It hisses, but now it won't flush at all."

Inasmuch as the inexorable laws of nature, gravity and bladders dictate that what goes down must eventually come out, Dixie's flushing failure broke up the party. The well-meaning amateur plumber was properly apologetic, and after everyone had left, Dudney called the apartment manager to demand a plumber—Sunday or no Sunday —but carefully avoided any mention of the reason for the complete breakdown.

She loafed around the apartment all Sunday, welcoming the plumber's surly arrival as pleasant relief from boredom. She could never quite stop thinking about the forthcoming week. Prentice had told her to report to Captain Smith of the flight school at 0800 Monday. She wished she had a small television set to keep her mind off what loomed as an ordeal and she thought mournfully that what the party had cost her could have been a down payment for a TV. Restless, excited and a bit jittery, she had trouble falling asleep and wound up reading the 737 manual until exhaustion weighted her eyelids. Her last conscious thought before sleep overtook her was a kaleidoscope of figures on approach speeds and flap settings, a blurred pinwheel spinning through her tired mind. . . .

Captain Daniel Smith's office was more of a cubbyhole than an office, even smaller than Prentice's, with only enough room for his desk and chair, plus two uncomfortable wooden chairs facing him.

At 0800 sharp he motioned Dudney into one of them, with a curt "Good morning, Miss Devlin," uttered in a tone that could have been translated into "Good morning, headache."

He inspected her critically and she inspected him worriedly, searching his stern face for a clue as to how he was going to handle her—with the patience of an Art Prentice, the harsh discipline of a John Battles or the blind bigotry of a Crusty Callahan. She found no clue at all. Smith was younger than she expected, a slim man of medium height with sharp features and wavy brown hair. On a coat rack behind him was his pilot's green uniform jacket, the four gold stripes of a captain as glaringly visible to her as a neon sign on a misty night. His dark green tie, immaculately knotted, carried a gold tiepin which she recognized as a miniature 737. He was freshly shaved, his brown eyes alert and penetrating, and the aroma of a subtly masculine aftershave lotion seemed to fill the tiny office. It was silly and stupid, but the combination of that odor and the sight of the four stripes on his uniform infused her with dread—twin symbols that spoke of male dominance and awesome command authority.

His first remark was friendly enough. "I'd like to congratulate you on your accomplishments thus far, Miss Devlin. You've come a long way."

She could not think of anything startlingly original to say, so she resorted to a simple "Thank you, Captain Smith."

"Well, in about ten minutes I'm going to take you up for your first training flight. Let you get the feel of the airplane mostly. We'll go out to Palmdale—there's a military field there and they let us use it for training. Not much traffic to worry about and long runways. I'd like you to try a couple of takeoffs and maybe a landing or two. Art Prentice tells me you handled that simulator like you were born in one."

"Mr. Prentice was an excellent teacher."

"We don't have much trouble with the students he turns over to us. I hope you won't spoil the record."

"I'll try." The way she said it, the two words were a bugle call sounding "Charge!"

His lips formed a cynical little smile. "We're throwing you a little curve, in case you haven't heard."

"A curve?"

"Your flight training will be solo—just you and me. The rest of the class will go up in twos, which gives each man a little break on every flight and also a chance to observe somebody else's performance."

She was puzzled. "There are ten in the class, Captain Smith. If I fly by myself, that leaves nine and you can't divide nine by two."

"That leaves eight, Miss Devlin. We're sending Kalinka home today."

"Mike? But why? . . ."

"Police picked him up last night. He started a fight in some bar. He was charged with drunk and disorderly. Captain Battles bailed him out and also fired him as soon as he got him sobered up enough to understand plain English. I guess I assumed you had already heard."

She shook her head, stunned. "I'm still waiting for a phone to be installed. Somebody would have had to drive over to tell me."

"No phone yet?"

"No, sir."

"Why the hell didn't you say something? You can't be without a telephone." He dialed a number on his own phone. "Mrs. Ridgway, this is Dan Smith. Would you call that contact of yours at Pacific Telephone and get some priority on an installation? Name's Devlin. Dudney Devlin. Yeah, that's the one." He grinned at Dudney. "Her address is—what's the address, Miss Devlin?"

"6016 Maple, in El Segundo." She could hardly get the words out, still shocked at Mike Kalinka's swift, merciless destruction. It was like hearing of a totally unexpected death.

"6016 Maple, El Segundo, Mrs. Ridgway. That's right. Thanks."

He hung up and looked sharply at Dudney, ready to leap viciously at the first sign of emotional reaction to her classmate's dismissal. But by now she had rescued her composure and was staring back at him almost phlegmatically. Smith grunted, a sound that combined disappointment and surprise. "Let's go down to Hangar 3, Miss Devlin, and pick up our airplane."

They rode one of the airline's trams—a pint-sized bus—from the Training Center to Hangar 3, Smith confining his conversation to two topics. He briefly complimented her for wearing slacks—"That's to be your uniform for the week"—and he noted they were lucky to get an airplane for training at this time of the morning.

"I've got you down for 0600 Wednesday," he added, "and unless you hear differently that'll be your reporting time for the rest of flight school. We grab whatever 737's available between regular trips."

She was curious about his own background and could not refrain from asking, "Were you a line pilot, Captain Smith?"

"Sure was. For nine years before they offered me this training job."

"You miss line flying?"

The question seemed to soften his sternness. "Yeah, I suppose I miss it, sometimes. But this job's a challenge. I get a kick out of qualifying a new pilot. They come to me soaked behind their ears and they don't know their ass from the well-known hole in the ground. That's no reflection on Art's precious simulators, mind you, but it's when they get into the real thing that they find out how good they are —or how much they've got to learn. By their second flight, you can see them improving and on the third or fourth you get a feeling of pride at how sharp they've become. I suppose I'll go back to the line one of these days but training has its rewards."

His words were prophetic. Dudney's initial performance was uncertain, obviously nervous and sloppy in the early stages. She got a momentary kick out of boarding the plane, the long rows of empty seats in the cabin instantly accentuating the difference between a live 737 and the cockpit simulator, but at the same time literally bringing the jitters right out of her pores; she was sweating as she sat down in the right seat.

Smith did the takeoff, Dudney retracting the gear and flaps on command and hating her nervousness as she did so because she knew it was the simplest chore a copilot could execute. There was even a brief second of panic when Smith called out, "Gear up," and she was able to move the lever only with a hard tug. Miserably, she remembered Battles' arguing with her that a woman lacked sufficient physical strength to fly an airliner regularly. But Smith restored her confidence by matter-of-factly commenting, "Don't worry about that gear handle —this is ship 321 and that goddamned lever's been written up three times for sticking. I almost broke my arm trying to raise it the other day."

It was after he established a heading for Palmdale that he let her take the controls, putting her through some easy banks and seeing how she responded when he altered their course headings. At Palmdale he did one touch-and-go, Dudney following him through on the controls, and then told her to try one. On the first attempt she came in too high and bounced with a sickening thud, but Smith seemed unperturbed.

"If you were perfect the first time, it would be strictly accidental," he remarked patiently. "Let's do it again."

That "Let's do it again" was uttered too frequently for Dudney's pride and confidence. In the first two hours Smith had at least one criticism for every maneuver she accomplished. He was surprisingly mild about it—she expected him to breathe fire at every mistake—but the mildness itself disturbed her. She figured he might already have determined to wash her out and was just going through the motions. The notion bothered her enough to put some steel in her spine. Her nervousness disappeared and she began to fly the 737 with her old natural ease, with that slick, effortless coordination between pilot and machine. Her control input was firm but smooth, the power changes and flap settings perfectly timed. Her third touch-and-go landing at Palmdale was a runway paint job, so beautiful that Smith turned his head away so she could not see him grin in pure admiration.

"Not bad," he conceded grudgingly.

He thought, I'd like to see John Battles' face if he went through a landing like that with her.

She thought, Not bad my ass, you male sonofabitch—it was perfect and you know it.

By the end of the third hour he was putting her through some emergency maneuvers, something he seldom let a trainee do on the first flight. She started off well but as they progressed into the fourth hour her proficiency deteriorated. He once more began to correct and criticize, but always constructively because he recognized why—she was getting tired and her coordination was slipping. They had been up just eleven minutes short of four hours when he suddenly said, "Let's go home, Dudney. I'll take it—you earned a rest."

She slumped a little in her seat and lit a cigarette, realizing with alarm that her hand was shaking and glancing over at the captain to see if he had noticed it. He had, and he smiled sympathetically.

"Tired, Dudney?"

"Don't you know it," she answered but she grinned back at him. He had used her first name twice and if he had ordered another four hours at that point she would not have uttered one word of protest.

They flew back to Los Angeles International with no further conversation except for the items and responses on the checklist. As tired as she was, she was disappointed that he did the final landing himself—and she noted ruefully it was just as good as that cream-smooth one she had performed at Palmdale.

"Not bad," she could not resist mimicking as they turned into the taxiway.

"Didn't want you to get a swelled head," he said.

"A swelled head is not my problem, Captain Smith. A sore butt is more like it."

"Four hours is too long a session," he admitted. "But you're a special case, as you know only too damned well. If it'll make you feel any better, I'll try to cut down Wednesday's session a bit. One thing I liked about your performance today is that you don't seem to have any ingrained bad habits or particular fears. Funny how most pilots have pet nightmares. I've known some who have a mental block on short runways. Others are petrified in turbulence. They may hate to fly at night or land in a cross wind. I've got one myself—fog. Ever read David Beaty's *The Human Factor?*"

Dudney shook her head.

"You should. It's a study of why pilots make mistakes. Beaty's an ex-BOAC captain. He has a pretty well substantiated theory that these special fears can be traced to an experience early in a man's flying career. And he figures some accidents can be traced to a kind of regression, where in spite of all the training and testing we give a man he may encounter his pet nightmare in an exaggerated form. His reaction is to fight the situation with his old behavior pattern instead of the one he's been taught."

"I would think," Dudney said, "that a weakness along those lines would be brought out in simulator training."

"Sometimes, but not always. Simulators occasionally are too perfect. For example, a foreign carrier had an accident a few years ago when the copilot flew a Vanguard right into the ground. He was executing a missed approach and he swore his Vertical Speed Indicator showed he was climbing out. He was wrong, obviously, because VSIs all have a lamentable tendency to lag. But some smart investigator found out that the simulator on which he'd been trained showed instant and accurate readings with no lag. The copilot had been lulled into a mistake because he was used to a simulator VSI instead of the real thing. We modified our VSIs on all simulators after that accident. There's one thing we can't change, though, either in a synthetic trainer or the actual airplane, and that's a pilot's reactions when he's faced with a real nut-twister. All we can do is hope that the training prepared him for it—which is why we're being tough on you and everyone else."

They went back to his office for a debriefing after leaving Fat Albert 321 in the hands of a lead mechanic at whom Smith barked, "That gear lever still sticks, Bill—I had to write it up again."

Sipping welcome hot coffee, they went over the training flight, discussing Dudney's weaknesses and strengths, and she was grateful that he spent more time on the former. She had never been a prima donna about criticism and she soaked up the instructor's corrective suggestions like a thirsty sponge. As for Smith, out of deference to John Battles' orders to "Break her spirit if you can," he never got around to telling her that her performance was among the best first-timers he had ever seen in a pilot. As for Dudney, she was so engrossed in what she had learned in those two hundred and twenty-nine minutes of a flying classroom that not until she walked out of the Training Center did she remember, with a pang of pity, Mike Kalinka.

Dixie and Norma Jean Miller had invited her to supper that night, along with the Mitchells, and Kalinka's downfall was the chief topic of conversation.

"Doug Worthington's the only one who talked to him," Dixie said. "He saw Mike off at the airport. Said he was pretty shook up but that he was gonna apply to another airline. You heard anything more, Hank?"

"Negative. I saw Doug at the mailboxes this afternoon. He said he had thought of having the whole class get up a petition asking Battles to give Mike another chance. But hell, by that time Mike was gone. They sure didn't waste any time lowering the boom."

Dudney shivered. She knew the "boom" was hanging over her head, a figurative sword of Damocles. When Dixie and Hank asked her how she did on her first flight, she murmured an "Oh, so-so, I guess," that stemmed more from worry than modesty.

"I thought it was pretty unfair, firing a man because of one slip," Norma Jean said indignantly, and Judy Mitchell nodded in feminine solidarity.

"No," Hank disagreed. "He was a damned fool, going out on a bat the night before flight training started. You've got to remember, Norma Jean, if he was stupid enough to pull that stunt in training, he could have done the same thing while he was flying the line. He didn't deserve a second chance because a second chance probably wouldn't have done any good."

Dixie nodded slowly. "Hank's right. Anyone that dumb lacked the maturity to be an airline pilot. That the way you feel, Dud?"

Dudney hesitated, the woman in her siding with Norma Jean and Judy and the pilot in her knowing that the two men were right. "I can't pass judgment," she said finally. "I'd like to know if Battles made any effort to find out why Mike did it. He might have had some bad news or a quarrel with a girl friend—I suppose I'd go along with the firing provided there wasn't any good reason for his getting drunk."

"Are you all telling me no airline pilot gets bombed occasionally?" Norma Jean argued. "If Mike had been a captain, that Battles person wouldn't have fired him so fast. He'd have gotten off with a bawling out and nothing more."

"Sure pilots get drunk," Dixie told his wife. "But there's a difference between doing it in private and getting looped in public—and starting a fight to cap it all off. Battles would have clobbered even a senior captain if the slob got arrested the way Mike did."

"Well," Hank said doubtfully, "he wouldn't be likely to fire a senior captain. Probably ground him for a couple of weeks or longer. And I suppose ALPA would go to bat for a member who got canned for one foolish stunt, particularly if his record was clean."

"Mike's record was clean," Judy reminded him.

"Mike didn't have any record at all, clean or otherwise," Dixie pointed out. "That's the real issue, Judy. He was nothing but a trainee, on probation. The whole damned class has been doing a lot of drinking, me and Hank included, but most of it's been in private. And nobody but Mike wound up on a police blotter. I feel sorry for him, believe me, I really do. But he got what was coming to him."

Dudney shivered again. "Let's change the subject. It hurts to even think about it."

"He got what was coming to him and—" Dixie stopped, seeing the imploring look on Dudney's face and intuitively realizing she was thinking, There but for the grace of God go I. The same ax that had fallen on Mike Kalinka was waiting for her and for less serious transgressions—she had told Dixie once, after they became friends as well as classmates, that Battles had warned her she would be fired if she were only thirty seconds late for a class.

She spent most of Tuesday studying the 737 manual, devoting most of the time to emergency procedures. It was a wise decision because on Wednesday Smith's preflight briefing consisted mainly of an oral quiz on those procedures and the two-and-a-half-hour training flight was largely a relentless emergencies drill. He was far less patient than he had been in their first flight and far more sharply critical. On Thursday, not more than ten minutes after her phone was installed, he called her to say there was a 737 free for a couple of hours and to get out to the airport. For an hour she practiced takeoffs and landings at Palmdale and more emergency drills in the second hour.

Smith took over one takeoff, much to her mystification. She found out why in a hurry. They had just broken ground when he suddenly took his hands off the yoke and leaned back in his seat.

"I'm having a heart attack," he said. "She's all yours."

She grabbed her own yoke quickly and completed the takeoff, raising the gear and handling the throttles herself while worriedly asking, "Captain Smith, I'd better land . . ."

"Nope. Keep going. This is what we call the incapacitated captain drill. I may pull it on you again sometime when I'm making a landing and I keel over just as we're flaring out for touchdown. Or at some other crucial spot. You never know when you'll have to take over, and you might as well get used to it. Too many copilots subconsciously rely on a captain and they come apart if something happens to the guy in the left seat."

He pulled the drill again Friday, during another three-hour session. He was flying the airplane under the pretense of demonstrating a stall recovery and he yelled, "Heart attack," just as the stick shaker began violent gyrations and the stall warning horn emitted its nasty blare. Throughout the three hours he snapped and snarled at every mistake until she was ready to crown him with a fire extinguisher. "Pretty good, but" was the closest he came to praise and his "Let's try it again" was an incessant drumbeat on her nerves. After this grueling session and the 737 had been parked at the ramp, Smith stopped her as she started to board the tram for the Training Center.

"No debriefing today, Dudney," he told her. "Be here at 0600 tomorrow—general oral quiz and a rating ride."

How she slept at all Friday night she would never know. She ate hurriedly, turned down Ernie Crum's dinner invitation, and buried herself in the manual. She was too tired to sleep and even when she finally dozed off she tossed restlessly in a crazy quilt of dreams about oral exams and check rides.

She was waiting for Smith outside his office five minutes before 0600, idly examining, as one would read the label on a catsup bottle for want of anything else to peruse, a note on the flight instruction bulletin board.

> B-737 Instructors:
>
> When returning to LAX, do NOT call Ramp Control to determine where they want the aircraft. Bring the aircraft to the hangar EVERY TIME UNLESS they call you with other instructions.
>
> Robinson

When Smith came in, he was accompanied by Captain Battles. The chief pilot growled a "Mornin'" with all the pleasantry of an executioner and Dudney felt a jolt of fear. There were no preliminaries. Battles nodded at the instructor, who opened fire like a prosecuting attorney.

"You're the captain and you get a fire warning. What would you do?"

"Push the master fire warning light, power lever to idle, cut off the start lever, pull and rotate the engine fire warning switch."

"That's all?"

"No, sir. If the fire warning light remained on for longer than thirty seconds, I'd rotate the fire warning switch to the remaining CO_2 bottle."

Battles rasped, "Then I'd suppose you'd cruise toward destination congratulating yourself."

"No, sir. I'd land at the nearest suitable airport."

Smith fired again. "In the event of an engine fire, what are the sec ondary duties of the first officer?"

"Close the isolation valve, turn off the APU bleed valve."

"You have an engine fire at an altitude of fifteen thousand. Would you start your APU?"

She hesitated just a second, knowing it was a trick question. "No, sir, not below twenty-five thousand."

"What about opening your isolation or APU bleed valves?"

"Not until the fire had been extinguished."

Battles took over. "What's the required engine oil pressure during flight?"

"Forty to fifty-five pounds per square inch."

"What PSI would you tolerate to complete a flight without a shut-down?"

"Between thirty-five and forty, preferably at reduced power."

Smith resumed. "If you needed extra power for takeoff, what procedures would you follow?"

"I'd utilize APU bleed instead of engine bleed for air conditioning and pressurization during takeoff."

"Step by step, please."

"Leave APU and APU bleed on. Turn off both engine bleed valves. Turn on one air conditioning pack and . . . and . . ."

"And what?"

"Add point-zero-three to takeoff EPR setting."

"Okay, you've established your climb. Now what?"

"Simultaneously turn on number one bleed and turn off the APU bleed. Then . . . then turn number two bleed on, turn on the remaining air conditioning pack and turn off the APU after it's cooled."

"What's the emergency transponder code?" Battles barked.

"Seven-seven." She knew they were shifting from subject to subject deliberately, trying to rattle her.

"What's the maximum cross-wind component for a B-737?" Smith snapped.

"Twenty-eight knots."

"Tail wind?"

"Ten knots."

"Under what circumstances would you be likely to use rudder on a 737?"

"If you lost an engine and to make a final adjustment in lining up the aircraft correctly just before touchdown."

"You've lost both hydraulic systems, A and B. Give me the manual reversion procedures."

"Control wheel, neutral. Speedbrake lev—"

"You're the first officer, not the captain."

"First officer would turn off System A and B hydraulic pumps."

"Immediately?"

"No, sir. The captain would down and detent on the speedbrake lever after neutralizing the control yoke. He'd then stand by on the System A and B flight control switches. He then . . . then . . ." Oh, God, what's the next step? She could feel their eyes on her without looking at their faces. "Then . . . he'd . . . he'd . . . turn off the A and B spoiler switches."

"What flap setting would you use for a landing in the event of losing both hydraulic systems?"

"Fifteen degrees."

"Okay, your gear is down, flaps fifteen degrees, no hydraulic system A or B. You overshoot and have to go around. How do you get your gear up?"

You bastards, another curve, she thought. "Under those conditions, once the gear is extended you can't retract it." She probably was imagining it, but was there a faint smile on Smith's tight lips?

Battles resumed. "You've got unsymmetrical or jammed trailing edge flaps. What's the procedure?"

"Move flap lever to the detent nearest the actual flap position." She hesitated again, only momentarily but long enough for Battles to snarl, "Well?" Her finely honed memory came to her rescue. "I'd land at the V reference corresponding to the smallest flap angle."

"Then what would your V-ref threshold speed be if you were grossing eighty thousand pounds?"

This time, she did not answer.

"Eighty thousand pounds gross, Miss Devlin. I want the V-ref threshold speed."

"I'd look it up in the emergency checklist," she said desperately.

"You've lost the checklist. Come on, what's that threshold speed?"

"I can't remember . . . wait a minute, what flaps do I have?" Memory had surged from brain to tongue again.

"Five degrees."

"At eighty thousand pounds, let's see. One hundred and forty knots." The last figure was uttered triumphantly. Now Smith was grinning openly and from the chief pilot's barrel chest came the low rumble of a laugh he could not quite suppress. But his expression still was grim as he continued. "Okay, with jammed or unsymmetrical flaps, what's the limit on your bank angle?"

"Fifteen degrees."

"Over to you, Dan." Battles tilted back in his chair, his cold eyes fixed on the girl.

"If your Mach trim light failed, what's your airspeed limit?"

"Uh . . . oh-point-seven-four."

"Your wing anti-ice valve is inoperative. What are the two procedures you'd follow if the valve failed in the closed position?"

"Turn off—" she started to say, then realized it was another trap. "If it failed in the closed position, I'd avoid any icing areas."

"It fails in the open position. What do you do?"

"Turn off the bleed air switch and close the isolation valve switch."

They hammered at her for another thirty minutes. She faltered several times, fatigue enveloping memory and knowledge, and missed two questions completely. Battles finally brought the verbal lashing to an abrupt halt after she stumbled miserably over a relatively easy one.

"Let's go out to the airplane," he said, rising.

Smith looked at Dudney. "She could probably use some coffee first," he suggested in open sympathy. The girl looked beat.

"No," Battles ruled. "We've got ship 328 and Dispatch told us they gotta have it back for a noon trip. She can get coffee after the rating ride."

"I don't need any coffee," Dudney fibbed, knowing she would have given a week's salary for just a fifteen-minute break. "I'm ready now."

Smith shrugged. "Okay, Dudney. Let's get it over with."

They stopped at Dispatch to file for a local flight clearance, and Dudney watched him fill in the blanks on a piece of paper that meant her professional future.

TRANS-COASTAL AIRLINES, INC.

Plane 328   Fuel 23,300   Date May 24, 1970

Captain D. Smith   First Officer D. Devlin

Estimated duration of flight three hours

Flight plan LAX-PMD-LAX

Purpose of flight F/O 737 rating check

She was more angry than upset by Battles' presence, cognizant that his motive was to rattle her. The big chief pilot heaved his bulk into the jump seat behind Smith, while Dudney settled in the right seat and picked up the pre-start checklist.

"I'll read it," Smith said, and she handed him the printed list.

"Logbook."

"Checked and on board."

"Oxygen and interphone."

"Checked."

"Yaw damper."

"On."

Twenty-one items on the pre-start list. Four more just before she pushed the start buttons and watched the engine gauges spin to proper settings as the turbines spooled up.

"Generators."

"On buses."

"Pitot heat."

"On."

"Door lights."

"Out."

"Air conditioning packs."

"On."

"APU bleed."

"Off."

Seven items after a mechanic waved them off and she headed for the assigned runway. Five more before the clipped, filtered voice of the tower told them, "TCA training flight, cleared for takeoff."

As the heel of her left hand fondled the two throttles, shoving them forward, she forgot the presence of the chief pilot. She was concentrating too hard to notice that he had taken a mimeographed sheet of paper out of a small briefcase and was starting to grade her on each category.

Maneuver	Satisfactory	Unsatisfactory
1. *Before start scan and checklist*	X	
2. *APU operation—engine starts—pre-t.o. scan & checklists*	X	
3. *Takeoff normal climb*	X	
4. *Area departure procedures*	X	

"All right, Dudney," Smith said quietly. "We won't try any maneuver you haven't already gone through. In effect, you're the captain. You call the shots. If you're not satisfied with your execution in any category, tell me and we'll try it over. I want you to satisfy yourself as well as me. That clear?"

"Yes, sir."

"Okay. Your takeoff and climb were very good. You had an excellent fifteen-degree deck angle right up to fifteen hundred feet. Now I'll remind you what I've told you on previous flights. Below ten thousand I don't want to see that airspeed go above two hundred and fifty knots—make it two-forty just to be on the safe side. Above ten thousand, we'll want two-eighty. Any questions?"

"No, sir."

"Fine. Let's try some steep turns."

They did steep banks. Also a demonstration of Mach and G buffeting. An emergency descent. Engine-out handling. High-rate descent and recovery. Slow flight. Stalls and stall recovery. Simulated engine fire with shutdown and restart. Simulated APU fire drill. Runway stabilizer drill. An ILS approach followed by an aborted landing. An ILS approach with one engine out. Engine failure on takeoff, prior to V_1. Engine failure on takeoff after V_1. Normal approaches. Approaches with no flaps. Jammed stabilizer approach. Autopilot approach. Manual reversion approach. Simulated flameout and in-flight start. Wheel well fire drill. System A hydraulic failure with alternate gear and flap operation. System B hydraulic failure drill. Approach with manual trim. Electrical fire drill. Smoke evacuation drill. Navigation failure drill . . .

She would hear the instructor's voice, calm, patient but cruelly incessant, for weeks to come. . . .

". . . a little slow with that oxygen mask. Remember if you have to go into an emergency descent after pressurization failure you've got to get that mask on in seconds or you'll wipe out not only yourself but everybody else. . . .

". . . always tell me what you're going to do. Keep your crew informed any time you're doing anything out of the ordinary. . . ."

"That was fairly good on your speedbrake but a little bit too hard. Remember that old lady back in the cabin who's scared to death. . . ."

". . . beautiful, Dudney. You rolled out right on the money—two hundred and eighty knots on the nose. . . ."

". . . descent was okay, but you didn't tighten your mask. Dammit, an unconcious pilot isn't gonna do anybody any good. . . ."

"Fair, just fair. Make sure you've got forty-five degrees bank on your indicator. Do it again. . . ."

"Better, but I didn't notice any application of power through thirty degrees. Gotta keep that nose up. Keep it up. . . ."

"Relax a little. You were in too much of a hurry. You know you can do better. Try it again. . . ."

". . . not bad, but you asked for forty-degree flaps too soon. Try *twenty-five on the base leg and forty as you turn into final. Do it again. . . ."*

". . . make it a touch-and-go this time. I want to see your flap management and I want a square pattern. . . ."

"That was a beaut. You painted it on. . . ."

". . . still too slow on that mask. You've got fifteen seconds and the lives of one hundred and seven persons depending on how fast you don that mask. It's all that's between you and trouble. . . ."

". . . come on a little smoother on that speedbrake. . . ."

". . . once more. . . ."

"Try it again . . . good but not perfect. . . ."

". . . do it again. . . ."

"Beautiful! That's the way to fly an airplane. . . ."

"Nice work . . . beautiful job. . . ."

She felt more like crawling out of the airplane than walking off. With Battles not saying a word, they returned to Smith's office. The chief pilot sat next to the instructor in back of the latter's desk, Dudney facing them and feeling like a failing pupil called before both the principal and her teacher.

"Any comments or questions?" Smith asked pleasantly enough.

"No, sir. I wished I had done better on the mask drill and the circling approach."

"There was room for improvement on her patterns," Battles grumbled, and she almost started at the unexpected sound of his voice.

"Well," Smith said amiably, "her high work wasn't too bad. Even the FAA requires only seventy for passing."

"I'm going back to my office, Dan," Battles said. He tossed the grading sheet in front of the instructor, muttered, "Mornin', Miss Devlin," and stalked out.

Smith waited several minutes after the chief pilot left before resuming the debriefing, making sure Battles could not hear him. He lit a cigarette and surveyed Dudney with an enigmatic stare.

"We threw you another curve, you know," he finally said.

"It was a tough check ride, Captain Smith. But I didn't think it was unfair."

"The hell it wasn't. I didn't want Battles along—he did it deliberately just to make you fall apart. And that wasn't an ordinary rating ride."

Her forehead furrowed in puzzlement.

"Nope, young lady. What we just put you through was the ATR check ride given to copilots upgrading to captain."

She felt limp, almost nauseated.

"And what made it rougher was that Battles insisted on grading you himself. Normally that would have been my job. For my dough, you didn't do badly. I liked your decision to go around after you screwed up that circling approach. That showed class. Any pilot, even the good ones, can louse up a maneuver. It takes guts to admit you're doing something wrong and it takes intelligence to recognize it. Did I do anything to confuse you?"

She could not keep the hoarseness out of her voice when she replied. "Well, you cautioned me for being too tight on a circling approach the second time we flew. Today you said I wasn't tight enough."

"I just wanted you to slow down a little. You're allowed one and a half miles and I was just trying to keep you in that pattern. Anything else?"

"I'm sorry about that one missed approach when I touched down. I thought the gear was coming up through the floor. But I knew what I did wrong."

"Good. You can see now why I stressed that fifteen-degree rotation. You've got to get that nose up on a go-around or you'll sink. To get an airplane to perform the way you want, fly it the way it was designed to be flown. You must realize how slow those engines spool up once you've reduced thrust. That's why I jumped down your throat for letting your power spool down at low altitudes. When you're a quarter of a mile from touchdown, don't screw around if you have an engine out. It's a damned critical maneuver. On one of those approaches, if I hadn't called out your airspeed you would have sunk. I couldn't bust you on that maneuver because you corrected nicely and in time."

"I guess it's time to ask how many maneuvers Captain Battles busted me on," she said in a low voice.

Smith picked up the grading sheet, scanned it briefly and handed it to her wordlessly. At the bottom of the page, after the words "Instructor's comments," she read the verdict.

"Excellent flight under difficult circumstances. Handles a/c well. Knows procedures. Good attitude. Recommended for probationary f/o.

J. Battles

CHAPTER EIGHT

In the excitement of winning her airline wings, Dudney had forgotten completely about the promise she had made to Jason Silvanius.

Unhappily for her, Jason remembered it only too well and called her at her apartment only an hour after she had returned from the rating ride.

"Congratulations," he said cheerfully and with sufficient sincerity to douse the quick throb of annoyance that sprinted through her. "Like to take you up on that offer you made a few weeks ago."

"Press conference," she remembered unhappily.

"Right, Miss Devlin. Seems you performed the miracle and I'm afraid that's definitely in the category of a news story."

"When?" She was abrupt, not in a rude sense but with impatience to get an unpleasant task finished.

"How about Monday morning, ten o'clock, in my office?"

"I might have to fly. I haven't heard from crew sked yet."

"I've already talked to crew sked. You won't be flying Monday."

"I'd still like to get out of it, if I could, Mr. Silvanius. I'm pretty tired. It's been rough . . ."

"I know it's been rough, Miss Devlin. But you're going to have to go through with it eventually and you might as well get it over with."

"Well . . ." She hesitated so long that Jason leaped into the breach and shut off further debate.

"I'll be there to help you over any uneasy spots," he said with friendly reassurance. "Unless you have any legitimate objections, Miss Devlin, I'll go ahead and set it up for 10:00 A.M. Monday. Can I count on you?"

"I guess so," she said doubtfully. "I'd still rather not but I know I promised you."

"Good. See you Monday morning. By the way, be a good idea if you'd come over no later than nine-thirty. It'll give me a chance to brief you and kind of ease the ordeal."

"I'll be there, Mr. Silvanius."

"Oh, I forgot," he added. "Wear your uniform." He hung up before she could give him any argument.

She relieved herself of a few unfeminine words of profanity which made her feel better to some extent. She knew the Public Relations Department had its own job to do and that what she had just accomplished was definitely news, however distasteful meeting with reporters seemed to her. That line of logic brought sharply home what she *had* achieved, and not even Jason's call could spoil a feeling of pride. But with the pride came a sudden pang of longing for her father. She resisted an impulse to call Sam Macklin in Anchorage, entirely on penurious grounds, and sat down to write him a short letter instead.

Dear Sam:

I just wanted you and Helen to know I start flying for Trans-Coastal next week, as a 737 first officer. Yes, I made it! They were pretty hard on me but now that it's all over, I can admit that they had to be.

It would be great if you two could come down here, Sam. Hope you're flying again and that things are fine with you. I had to write to you because I can't write to Dad. I'd like to think he'd be proud of me—just as I'm grateful to him. I would never have come through if it were not for the things he taught me, both in and out of flying, and I guess I miss him right now more than ever before. I miss you, too, you old unreconstructed bush pilot, so please write soon and let me know how things are up there.

Love,

Dud

Naturally, there was a class party—at the Websters'—that night and, also naturally, it topped all the others—if the conclusions of ground school and simulator training had provided reasonable excuses for celebrating, the occasion of nine brand-new first officers was even more so. All had passed, and there was voluminous swapping of experiences on their rating flights and orals.

Ernie Crum's little nurse came down from San Francisco, an event which severed First Officer Ernest Leonard Crum and Miss Nancy Elaine Foster, R.N., from the rest of the party participants and, perhaps, the rest of the world. They sat in a corner by themselves, holding hands and occasionally sneaking a chaste kiss. Every time Dudney saw them she congratulated herself on not succumbing to her libido two weeks ago; she could not have looked Nancy in the face.

Doug Worthington brought some movie starlet—he never explained where he had met such a celebrity—who did not endear herself to Dudney when she gushed, "If they ever make a movie of your life, I'd love to play you."

"I think Doris Day's already bid for the screen rights," Dudney told her with a straight face.

"Oh, not Doris Day," the starlet protested. "Isn't she kind of old for the part?"

"After the last few weeks," Dudney assured her, "I'd be too old for the part."

The celebration took her mind off the Monday press conference, at least temporarily. So, but not as enjoyably, did Worthington's vapid-faced date, who proved to be a chain drinker. She downed one martini after another with the alacrity of a 707 taking on fuel for a transatlantic flight, and with each drink her fascination with Dudney seemed to swell. The party was in its last stages when the actress cornered Dudney coming out of the bathroom. The starlet was outwardly sober by her walk and unslurred voice, but her slightly glazed eyes betrayed her.

"Before we go back to the others, I'd like to tell you something," she whispered.

"Go ahead," Dudney said with as much pleasantness as she could muster.

"I go both ways, and any time you . . ."

"Both ways? What the devil—"

"Don't play coy with me, Dudney. I dig boys and I dig girls. And any female nutty enough to be an airline pilot must be a dyke. I'll give you my phone number so we can get together—"

"You're wasting your time," Dudney snapped, flushing in anger and shock. She stalked away from the girl, almost trembling with embarrassment, and it did not help when the starlet came back to the living room, gave her the sly, intimate smile of a fellow conspirator, and promptly flung herself into Doug's unprotesting arms as if she were taunting another lover.

Dudney thought about the incident driving home alone, her very solitude reminding her anew that it was going to be difficult being an airline pilot and a normal woman simultaneously. She realized with sharp clarity what she had only sensed the night she was tempted to take Ernie Crum into bed—her vocational success carried an ugly penalty, a kind of enforced aloofness from normal relationships with either men or women who worked with her. Both sexes tended to regard her as something of a freak. Yet a close relationship with a man could weaken her professional status, while her own sex would likely reject her as an oddball with suspicious masculinity. I'm an airline pilot now, she thought with a degree of bitterness, so I can expect propositions from men who want to brag they proved I'm nothing but a susceptible female and from lesbians who figure I must be one of them.

Her mood was not exactly happy when she reported to Silvanius Monday morning, a fact which Jason recognized instantly and which he handled astutely.

"I appreciate this, Miss Devlin," he told her. "I know how reluctant you were. And thanks for bringing your uniform—that is the uniform, I take it?"

It was. She had carried it in with her on a clothes hanger, covered by a plastic garment bag.

"I only hope this won't last too long, Mr. Silvanius. Is it just newspapermen or will there be"—he was nodding sympathetically before she could finish the question and on anyone else her disappointed look would have been called a pout—"television?"

"I've already told them you'd like to make it as short as possible. Maybe about a half hour. By the way, President Berlin will be here—he'll pin on your wings in sort of a little advance ceremony."

"Advance ceremony?"

"I guess you haven't been told yet. Mr. Berlin decided the occasion of the first woman airline pilot deserved some special recognition. He's having a little cocktail party tonight for your class. The real presentation of your wings will take place then—and you're to wear that uniform."

"I was wondering if there'd be a sort of graduation," she said, pleased. "Doesn't anyone in the class have to fly?"

Silvanius laughed. "I think Mr. Berlin fixed it up with crew sked—amid loud protests, I'm afraid. Two of your classmates were supposed to take trips today but we changed things around a bit."

She was about to ask him if he had heard when she was supposed to fly the line for the first time, but Tom Berlin entered at this point and if there was any discontent at his possible problem having become a distinct reality, he kept it well hidden under a cloak of cordial congratulations.

"I never thought you'd make it—in fact, I was hoping you wouldn't," he said candidly.

Her eyes twinkled. "Sorry to disappoint you, Mr. Berlin."

"I'll bet your father would have been damned proud of you," Berlin rasped, and enough warmth peeked through the gruffness so that she was touched.

"I only wish he could be here tonight," she replied, "and incidentally, Mr. Berlin, I know all of us in the class appreciate that little party tonight."

"It was Jason's idea," he growled. "Personally, I—"

Whatever attack he was going to make on the PR vice president's judgment was interrupted by Jason's secretary poking her head into his office and announcing, "The press is here—in force."

"Go down to the ladies' room and put on your uniform," Jason ordered. "You can do that while they're setting up the lights and stuff."

She complied, cringing inwardly as she walked by the mob of reporters and cameramen gathering in Silvanius' outer office. By the time she returned, Jason's own office was brightly lit by the TV spots and, self-consciously, she took her place by Berlin's side as if his very presence was a kind of fatherly protection.

"Ladies and gentlemen," Jason called out—Dudney noticed for the first time there were two women in the crowd—"if I may have your attention, please. I'd like to introduce Miss Dudney Devlin, who as of last Saturday afternoon successfully completed four weeks of very rigorous training as a first officer for Trans-Coastal Airlines. I might add that as far as our Flight Training Department is concerned she is eminently qualified to serve as a copilot on scheduled flights. Her grades in ground school and her performance in the airplane itself were not only good but excellent. I'm speaking for President Tom Berlin and all officers of Trans-Coastal when I say that we are proud to have her as a bona fide member of our flight crews, and we know she's going to be a credit not only to this company and commercial aviation but to herself and her sex. Okay, Miss Devlin is yours."

There was a smattering of applause which, while well meant, unnerved Dudney to the point of having to suppress a desire to run from the room. Her face was flushed, her throat dry and the people in front of her were a mass blur.

"Miss Devlin," said a man from UP, "was the training harder than you expected?"

"No. It was hard but I thought—"

"Louder, please," someone in the back of the room yelled, and beads of sweat glistened on Dudney's forehead as she started over. "It was tough but I thought everyone was fair. I've got no complaints."

"When do you start flying regular trips?" the AP asked.

She hesitated and looked first at Berlin, then Silvanius. "I haven't heard from crew sked . . . schedule . . . yet," she finally answered.

"Sometime this week," Jason put in. "Her schedule hasn't been decided yet. I'll let you all know." Dudney frowned.

A reporter from the Los Angeles *Times* asked, "Do you anticipate any problems in your relationships with other crew members? Pilots and stewardesses, for example?"

"Neg . . . no, I don't. At least, I hope I won't. I hope I'm judged as a pilot, not as a woman. I know I'll have problems if I make a lot of stupid mistakes."

One of the two women reporters, rather patronizingly, Dudney thought, chirped, "If you fell in love with a handsome captain, would you quit flying?"

Dudney gritted her teeth. "Falling in love is not on my agenda."

"But suppose you did?"

"Well, stewardesses often keep flying after they're married. I expect I would too."

The woman persisted. "Do you think you could combine a career of flying and a career of marriage?"

"Up to a point. Until one career conflicted with the other. Then I'd have to make a choice—in favor of a happy marriage, I suppose. I couldn't fly if I were pregnant, of course."

"Do you want children someday?" the second woman reporter asked.

"Yes, I do. But not in the foreseeable future."

The flashbulbs were popping intermittently, the TV lights were uncomfortably hot, and the whir of the cameras was grating on her nerves.

"Miss Devlin," said an NBC reporter, "do you think you've broken the barrier against women airline pilots? Uh, established a precedent that will lead to more women flying for the airlines?"

"I couldn't care less," Dudney said with such surprising firmness that Tom Berlin grinned.

"I don't understand," NBC pressed. "You mean, it's immaterial to you whether more women do what you're doing, or about to do?"

"I mean I didn't intend to establish any precedent. Flying is my profession and I wanted to fly for an airline. Trans-Coastal gave me a chance, for which I'm grateful. Very grateful. What other women do is up to them, and other airlines."

"Women's rights aren't of any concern to you?" a CBS man said.

"I'm interested in them as any citizen should be. But I don't picture myself as a crusader for them. I don't like to think I've set some shining example for others to follow. I don't regard myself as a test case."

"Well, that's a switch," UPI commented.

Jason, seeing the disdainful looks that appeared on the faces of the two women reporters, intervened. "I think it's only fair to tell you that Miss Devlin made her views perfectly clear to us when she first applied and was interviewed. I think she told one of our officials that she'd rather be the tenth woman airline pilot, not the first."

Dudney nodded gratefully.

"Nevertheless, Miss Devlin," CBS commented, "the fact is that you have set a precedent, and a very important one. Wouldn't you agree that what happens to you with this airline will affect the rest of the industry?"

"I suppose so. Look, I'm not against women airline pilots. I didn't mean to give that impression. It's just that I want to do my job with Trans-Coastal as ably as I can. It's . . . it's my motive you seem to have trouble understanding. I wasn't motivated by any strong feelings about sex discrimination, by equal rights for women. I wasn't trying to prove a point."

"Wouldn't you like to see other women flying for the airlines?" the *Herald-Examiner* asked.

"If they're good pilots, qualified pilots, who'll make capable airline crew members, yes. But not just because they're members of my own sex. If I were an airline official, I'd hire pilots on the basis of ability, regardless of sex. If some were female, so much the better. I'm certainly not ashamed of being a woman."

The AP tossed her a question that brought an enigmatic smile to Jason's face. "Suppose you *were* an airline official and you had to choose between two equally qualified applicants, one male and the other female. You could hire only one. Which one?"

She answered without hesitation. "The man." One of the two women reporters gurgled in mixed surprise and resentment. Berlin's smile duplicated Jason's.

"Why?"

"Because, assuming they were identical in flying proficiency, the man's adjustment to an airline career would be easier for obvious reasons. He'd . . . he'd be accepted by his fellow pilots while a woman would have to overcome a . . . a certain amount of prejudice. In sufficient proportion, perhaps, to affect her flying ability. If I did have the authority to make the hiring choice you posed, I'd have to take factors other than proficiency into consideration. Such as relationships with other crew members."

"It sounds to me, Miss Devlin," one of the women said, "that you expect to have difficulty in your own relationships—despite what you told us about not expecting any."

"I didn't say I didn't anticipate difficulties. I said I hoped what troubles I do run into involve cockpit performance, not my sex."

"What will your attitude be if captains make passes at you?" the second woman asked.

Dudney felt a strong impulse to glare and managed to look merely resigned. "I think the crew of a Boeing 737 is too busy to have the subject come up," she answered.

"Oh, come now," the woman said. "You're attractive enough to have the subject come up."

This time she didn't resist and did glare. "Any passes occurring in the cockpit will be resisted. Passes occurring while I'm off duty are my own business."

Most of the men in the room laughed and someone murmured, "That's a damned good answer."

"You got a steady boy friend, Miss Devlin?" She couldn't see who asked that one, which was hurled from a back row.

"No, I don't. Or any boy friend right now."

"Too bad," the voice said. "I was going to ask how he was gonna like that uniform."

"How do you like it?" UPI interjected.

"I think it's attractive and I hope I'll always wear it with pride."

"Who designed it, Miss Devlin—you?" That from a Mutual newsman.

"I don't know," Dudney replied as she looked to Jason for guidance.

"It was the selection of an executive committee," Silvanius informed the press conference. "Frankly, we couldn't decide whether she should wear a skirt or slacks but we finally chose slacks as both practical and less distracting." The last word had scarcely left his mouth when out of the corner of one eye he saw a frown creasing the stern features of Tom Berlin, and he hastily diverted the press to another topic. "For the benefit of those who may not have seen the first news release we put out when Miss Devlin was accepted for training, we've run off a few more copies and they'll be available as you leave. Gentlemen and ladies, Miss Devlin has just completed a pretty strenuous four weeks and I know she's tired. I'd like to wrap this up with just one or two more questions."

"I've got one," the *Herald-Examiner* said. "Miss Devlin, did you encounter any—well, let's call it prejudice—did you meet up with any of this during training?"

Both Jason and Berlin held their breaths, the latter recalling the number of times he had deliberately ordered subordinates to make life miserable for the girl.

"No more than I anticipated, under the circumstances," Dudney said after a brief pause. "After all, Trans-Coastal was on something of a spot too."

"You did encounter prejudice?"

"Prejudice is too strong a word. I encountered a . . . a determination to make me prove I could fly a 737 as well as or better than any man. If I had been in Trans-Coastal's shoes, I would have acted no differently."

The *Times* man asked shrewdly, "Would you say your training was stiffer than that given the men in your class?"

"I wouldn't know. From my conversations with my classmates, I'd say their training was just as tough as it had to be." She had phrased this with deliberate care, but the *Times* reporter was not fooled.

"You're implying, then, that your own training may have been tougher—because it had to be?"

She was too honest to continue any deception. "Yes, I think it had to be tougher."

"Because of prejudice." It was a statement, not a question.

"Because they had to make sure. Prejudice against a woman airline pilot was not, is not and may never be the exclusive property of airline management. The men I'll be flying with will look askance on a woman pilot—and I can't very well blame them. So will the public. A lot of you in this room may feel like getting off my airplane if you see me sitting in the right seat before takeoff. That's what I meant when I said Trans-Coastal had to make sure of me—for the sake of those whom I'll fly with and those whom I'll be flying."

"In what stage of your training do you think there was anti-female prejudice?" UPI asked.

"My final check ride, or 737 rating ride, as we call it. They put me through a wringer. And I'm damned glad they did—for my sake as well as theirs."

The room was suddenly quiet, stilled by the intensity, the open honesty of her responses. One of the TV technicians turned off his lights and it was as if a breath of cool air had been pumped into the office.

"Thank you very much—and good luck, Miss Devlin," the AP called out.

A photographer yelled to Jason, "We'd like to get some shots of her with Mr. Berlin—pinning on her wings or something."

"Sure," Jason said, pleased at the way the girl had handled herself. "Ladies and gentlemen, thank you for coming. My secretary will give you the biographical background material as you leave."

The picture-taking took only a few minutes and when the last photographer left, Berlin turned to his new first officer. "Dudney, I think you performed admirably. I'm very grateful for the things you said."

"Also the things you didn't say," Jason chuckled disrespectfully.

Dudney smiled but was silent, reaching into the pocket of her slacks for a handkerchief to wipe her brow and then realizing she had none. Berlin gave her his. She returned the handkerchief to the president and had turned to leave when he stopped her. "Better take off the wings, Dudney. That pinning was just for the cameras—I'll put them on permanently at the party tonight."

She took them off reluctantly, like a child who has been loaned a toy with which to play, and handed them back to Berlin.

"I'll see you tonight, sir," she said. "Mr. Silvanius—thank you. Will you be there? And I almost forgot—where is it?"

"Board of Directors room, right on this floor. Six o'clock. We've notified the rest of the class by now." He walked her to the door, shook hands and said matter-of-factly, "When you've flown a couple of trips and are settled down, Janet and I would like to have you over for dinner some night."

"I'd like that, Mr. Silvanius."

"After one month on the line," he smiled, "you can start calling me Jason."

"I'd call you the great, kindhearted, understanding Mr. Silvanius if you'd do me a favor."

"After what you did for us today, name it."

"You told the reporters you'd let them know when I took out my first trip. Don't."

"Oh, come on now, Dudney. I—"

"Please. No more fuss."

"Well . . ."

"That first day on the line is the start of a whole career for me. It's just a one-day story to them. It'll be hard enough for me without distractions."

He almost squirmed under her direct gaze. "Mean that much to you, Dudney?"

"It does."

"Okay. No press coverage. Until the day you make captain."

She smiled. "*That's* a deal, Mr. Silvanius."

"Favor."

"Name it."

"Maybe you'd better start calling me Jason as of now."

Dixie, naturally, called the vice president of public relations by his first name as soon as they were introduced at the graduation party. Jason took no offense, inured as he was to overly excited new first officers. Dixie's irreverence was not extended to Tom Berlin—the entire class was virtually speechless in the awesome presence of the president, not to mention the overpowering enormity of the paneled board room.

Only Webster retained his calm poise and, on him, the three stripes of an F/O looked as out of place as a sergeant's chevrons on a West Point graduate. Tall, straight, almost haughty, he seemed more the model of an airline captain than a mere first officer and Dudney wished she could look that self-possessed. She was quiet, staying close to Hank and Dixie and nursing a single highball as if it were the last drop of scotch left in Southern California. She noticed with silent amusement that the bartender, apparently on orders from above, was mixing rather weak drinks; there was not much chance that the nine fresh additions to Trans-Coastal's flight crews could get bombed. It was, as Berlin told them on at least four occasions, the last time in their airline careers they could drink in uniform without getting fired.

Dudney was surprised to see John Battles show up, his dour, massive, homely face glum and giving the impression he had been summoned under duress. Dudney wondered why he was in uniform but this question was answered when company photographer Arthur Smithfield bustled in and suggested officiously to Silvanius, "All right, Jason, let's get the show on the road—have Battles pin on the dame's wings so I can go home and take my wife to a movie." The chief pilot was standing by Jason, and Dudney was disturbed to see him give Smithfield a glare that would have burned through asbestos.

"Might as well get started," Jason said easily and diplomatically. His voice rose. "Gentlemen and Miss Devlin, we'd like to welcome you officially into the ranks. Mr. Berlin has a few words he'd like to say."

The class stood in a semicircle facing the three brass hats and the photographer. Berlin cleared his throat.

"I doubt if any of you know I used to be a line pilot myself. Trans-Coastal always has been known as a pilots' airline. That doesn't mean our crews run this company. It does mean that major executive decisions are based primarily on operational safety and efficiency—and that in turn means that, whenever we have to make a major decision, every top official must take pilot attitude, pilot judgment, pilot opinion, into consideration. I'm not going to hand you any guff about loving you one and all—when contract negotiation time comes around, I consider you all a bunch of overpaid prima donnas"—the class laughed a little weakly—"but that's S.O.P. for any labor-management relationship. Down deep, I regard our flight crews with respect, not to mention gratitude, for their professional skill, devotion to duty and mutual interest in what has to be the top priority on this or any other airline—safety. When it comes to safety, you'll find me on your side. If you ever do anything to jeopardize safety, you'll find me ruthless and unforgiving. It's as simple as that. On behalf of the Board of Directors of Trans-Coastal Airlines and all of us in management, I congratulate you for having completed your most difficult training, and I also congratulate you as you embark on what I hope will be a long and honorable career—the finest career in the world. As I call your names, please step forward and Captain Battles, whom you all know and I trust will get to know better"—the class laughed again, not quite so weakly—"Captain Battles will pin on your wings."

One by one they answered the roll call. Their shoulders were back, their young faces stony, and in more than one instance their eyes glistening. Dudney, whose name was called last, thought some of them were going to salute Battles as he attached the gold first officer wings and pumped their hands. Her turn finally came.

"Dudney Devlin," Berlin said softly.

Her heart was thudding and she had an irresistible urge to cry. Only the stern face of the chief pilot dammed up the tears; she could still hear his voice, warning her in his office a long four weeks ago:

"*. . . if I ever see your eyes water in public, I'll cut those god-damned wings off your uniform myself. . . .*"

She found herself staring at his dark green tie as his big hands fumbled with the wings. His sudden clumsiness was a godsend, for now she felt more like laughing because he obviously was nervous. She heard the dim, tiny click of the clasp as the wings were attached and she stepped back, looking directly into Battles' cold eyes. Only for a split second, they were not cold; they were kind and under-standing and maybe, although she could be wrong, there was even a touch of paternal pride. She had a strange, chilling feeling that Ralph Devlin had put on her wings. Then the eyes narrowed again, the warmth replaced by that icy curtain of unyielding discipline.

"Congratulations, Miss Devlin," the chief pilot said stiffly.

"Thank you, Captain Battles." Her voice was calm, but she came close to giggling because now she, too, had an impulse to salute. The impulse was drowned by what she heard—applause from her class-mates. Silvanius was saying, "Well, one more round in honor of the occasion," when Dixie interrupted.

"Just a minute, Jason, we've got a little ceremony of our own."

Webster was handing him a gift-wrapped box that somehow they had kept hidden. Dixie held it and, with his eight male colleagues clustered around him, he addressed the girl who had won their friendship.

"Dud, all of us wanted to make this occasion a bit more special for you. We, especially, know what you've gone through the last four weeks and what those wings mean to you. We have a pretty good idea that, more than anything else, you would have liked your father here tonight. He's here in spirit, Dud, and I guess this is from him as well as us—it represents pride, affection and our heartfelt congratulations."

He handed her the box. She managed to tear off the paper with trembling hands and took out the contents. The leather attaché case she had admired in Stores, with the letters "D. Devlin" embossed in gold on one side.

Now she was crying unashamedly, thinking and almost saying it aloud, as the emotional dam of four weeks burst and the tears cascaded, and she hugged Dixie: *Screw you, John Battles . . . go ahead and fire me, you bastard. . . .*

He didn't. He mixed her a drink himself and it was a hell of a lot stronger than what the bartender had been dishing out. Tom Berlin put his arms around her and his old eyes were suspiciously misty.

It was about a half hour later, when the party was breaking up, that Battles came over to her and drew her to one side. "I suggest you call crew sked when you get home, Dudney. I happen to know you'll be flying a trip tomorrow morning."

"That's great," she said, so enthusiastic that his use of her first name went unnoticed. "Maybe I should find a phone now and—"

"When you get home will be time enough." He was studying her as he had that day he had cleared her for training, paternalism and admiration struggling with prejudice and self-justification. "You know, we have our new F/Os fly with one captain for the first twenty-five hours—supervised line flying while you're on reserve."

"Yes, I know." She could not figure out what he was getting at.

"I've assigned you to a captain I consider an excellent teacher and pilot."

"That's fine, Captain Battles. I appreciate—"

He interrupted her, his tone strangely one of apology and even regret.

"Crusty Callahan," he said.

She reported to Crew Schedule for her trip sign-in at 5:45 A.M., fifteen minutes ahead of the required time for a flight that left at 7:00 A.M.—above-and-beyond duty that was more a demonstration of insomnia than punctuality. She had slept poorly the night before, a combination of excitement and worrying about her first captain, and this repeated insomnia before crisis bothered her.

She had wondered what motive Battles could have had in assigning her—deliberately—to the one person with whom she had clashed, openly and violently. The chief pilot had emphasized that Callahan was a good teacher, but he must have heard about the incident at the ALPA meeting. Dudney was more prone to suspect that Battles figured Callahan was likely to break her spirit. Even, she thought, to the point of goading her into a disciplinary violation that could result in her dismissal. Talking back to a captain, she knew, was grounds for firing any copilot, let alone one who—as Battles himself had phrased it a month ago—would be walking on eggs every day.

The day's schedule looked easy. Los Angeles to Las Vegas, then Vegas down to Phoenix and Tucson and back to Los Angeles before dark—a trip with three different flight numbers but the same airplane and crew. Yet the thrill of her first trip, the prospects of all-daylight flights into modern, well-equipped airports, were watered by the small but menacing figure of Captain Callahan.

The big Operations room was fairly crowded when she entered and walked up to the Crew Schedule counter for her sign-in. The crew scheduler on duty grinned at her as she put her brainbag down next to a long row of similar but more weather-beaten bags and self-consciously introduced herself.

"Hi, I'm Devlin."

"Hi. Max Graham." He was a small, elderly man with twinkling eyes and frosted, wavy hair. "You signing in?"

"Flight 340. Where do I . . . ?"

"Right here, next to the trip number, second line." He handed her a mimeographed sign-in sheet and she started to squeeze "D. Devlin" into an allotted space of not more than a half inch. "Just initial it," he told her dryly. "Your name's already on the sheet, in the first row." She felt two feet shorter until she sneaked a glance at her name where he had indicated. There it was. Right underneath "Captain: A. Callahan."

"*F/O: D. Devlin.*"

It stood out like Braille. It shined and glowed and sparkled like a diamond under a bright light. Even more than her wings, it signified victory and achievement. Cheered by the simple symbolism, she was emboldened enough to ask, "Has Captain Callahan come in yet?"

Graham looked disappointed, as if the question was unworthy of her. "If you don't see his initials on the sign-in, he hasn't showed yet."

"Oh." Deflated, she started to turn away, rather aimlessly, when the crew scheduler took pity on her.

"There's a coffee urn in the crew lounge—next room to the right. Just grab a cup and introduce yourself around. The stews working 340 are in there."

"Thanks," Dudney said gratefully. She could use some coffee and a cigarette—usually the only time she smoked was after coffee and eating. She marched toward the lounge, looking straight ahead, miserably conscious of the curious eyes following her and the whispers of recognition from pilots and stewardesses. She almost wished she had reported in a dress; the new uniform felt ostentatious and even bizarre.

A tall stewardess in her late twenties was at the urn ahead of her and smiled as she moved aside to let Dudney hold a paper cup under the spigot.

"You must be Wonder Woman herself," she said breezily, but in a manner that was more teasing than sarcastic. "I heard you were gonna be on our trip today."

"Is that what the crews are calling me—Wonder Woman?"

"Don't take it to heart. It's what they'll call you in a month or two from now that counts."

"I'd rather be called Dudney, or better yet, Dud, if it's okay with you."

The stewardess put out her hand. "I'm Del Fitzgerald. The Del is for Delfinia so for God's sake forget I ever told you. Take sugar and cream?"

"Just sugar, Del."

"It's over on that small table. You met the other stew?"

"I haven't met anyone yet—except Captain Callahan."

"Crusty here already? He's usually fifteen minutes late for sign-in. I'll bet he even shaved for the occasion."

"I met him a few weeks ago," Dudney said, avoiding the details for strategic reasons. "He hasn't signed in yet." She was amused at the stewardess using his nickname while she, the first officer, was confined by protocol to more a respectful form of address. She had heard that most captains invariably told new copilots to use their first names right from the start, but her class also had been warned in ground school that it still was safer to say "Captain" and even toss in an occasional "sir" just in case the captain might be a stickler for cockpit etiquette. Dudney was taking no chances, particularly with Callahan.

"Here's your other stew, Dud," Del was saying as a petite, pretty girl with close-cropped brown hair approached the urn. "Susie, meet Dudney Devlin. Dud, this is Susie Russell."

Like Del, Susie was friendly without being disrespectful. "Hi. So you're the famous Miss Devlin. Congratulations—you've struck a blow for womanhood. Our captain is signing in, by the way. He looks unhappy—I guess his wife didn't give him any last night."

Del laughed. "She probably hasn't given him any for six months and Crusty just found out about it."

Dudney smiled but not very hard, deducing that Captain Callahan's mood this morning had no connection with his sex life.

"She's already met our captain, Susie," Del informed the other stewardess. "He's a lovable old bear, isn't he, Dud?"

"A very interesting man," Dudney said evasively. She had an impulse to confide in them, but even as she stifled it she was surprised to discover she had missed the companionship of her own sex more than she had realized. Right now she actually felt close to the first stewardesses she had met, not counting Worthington's trainee, and she was not quite sure whether this was a portent of smooth rapport or something to worry about.

Del was looking at her curiously, suspecting with the shrewd intuition of a woman that the new first officer had not only met Captain Callahan but had already clashed with the little man. She decided to change the subject and was aided by the arrival of Captain Mark Ashlock, whom Dudney had not seen since the ALPA meeting.

"Morning, Del, Susie," he said pleasantly as he filled his cup under the spigot. He straightened up and inspected Dudney, and for the life of her she could not tell whether he was looking at her as a girl or a new fellow pilot.

"Congratulations," he said simply, offering his hand. "Welcome to the line."

She appreciated his firm handshake, and she liked his eyes, which she had failed to notice at their first meeting. They were gray, with a hint of sadness as if they somehow recovered a past tragedy with the permanence of a photograph.

"She drew Crusty Callahan for her first trip, Mark," Del said.

Ashlock whistled, an inadvertent reflex. "Oh? Well, you'd better get over to the Dispatch desk then, Miss Devlin. Crusty's probably looking for you."

He couldn't have been looking very hard, Dudney thought, but aloud all she said, in one nervous breath, was "I'm-on-my-way-nice-to-have-met-you-Captain-Ashlock-see-you-aboard-Susie-and-Del," and she was off, heading briskly toward Operations, when she suddenly did a one-eighty and dashed back to the stewardesses.

"How does he like his coffee, Del?" she asked.

"Crusty? Black, I think. But . . ."

Dudney already was pouring a cup. "I think I'd better score some brownie points," she explained, and then raced toward Operations again.

Callahan was standing in front of the Dispatch desk talking to a dispatcher when she came up alongside him and offered the coffee as a way of greeting. The captain took it, looked to see if it was black, and snorted.

"What the hell are you supposed to be, the stewardess or my first officer?"

She flushed but held back a retort. She knew she was brown-nosing, if a peace gesture could be called that. "I just thought you might like a cup," she finally mumbled.

"Thanks." The way he said it, it was a word of scorn, not gratitude. He turned back to the dispatcher and resumed their conversation as if she were not even present. Dudney felt sick, angry at him for his rudeness and angrier at herself for the impulse that had prompted her to bring him the coffee. It was weak, it was apple-polishing and it was feminine, she admitted, and the fact that it also was well-meaning didn't help. She waited for a pause in the dialogue between Callahan and the dispatcher before trying to repair the damage.

"Captain, is there anything you'd like me to do before boarding? I'll be glad to make out the flight plan if you'll tell—"

He turned to her with the force of a cracking whip and his voice was so loud, other crew members stared at them.

"No, you may not make out the flight plan. Nor the takeoff data. And I'll do the walk-around myself. You may, Miss Devlin, ride in the cockpit but only because the FARs say I gotta have a copilot. I only wish to hell I could put you where you belong—back in the cabin with the rest of the broads. Go get yourself some coffee and leave me alone!"

Her fists were clenched, her face crimson. But she kept her own voice low.

"Yes, *sir!*" It was an expletive, not an acknowledgment of a command. She walked away, but not toward the crew lounge. She could not face anyone after this public humiliation and it did not ease her rage and pain that several pilots—one of them Captain Ashlock—were watching her with expressions of sympathy. Instead, she looked up at the big Dispatch board and located her flight number. Next to it, under a column marked "Ship No," she saw the numerals "328." The same plane on which she had taken her rating ride. Miraculously, it served to infuse her with fresh courage, and she marched right back to Callahan. This time, her voice rose to a level that nearly matched the decibels he had achieved in humiliating her.

"Captain Callahan, I'm going out to the aircraft and perform the walk-around, in accordance with the company manual which pre-scribes this as the first officer's responsibility. If you don't like it, you can go tell Captain Battles you're pulling me off the trip and you can goddamned well tell him why!"

She was out of Operations and striding toward the ramp area before Crusty Callahan could get his mouth closed. In her wake she also left pilots and stewardesses who were almost as stunned as Captain Callahan, and one girl actually applauded twice—a loud if brief clap-ping that died under a look from Crusty that was more hurt than angry.

The two stewardesses on Dudney's trip had come into Operations just as their first officer delivered her curtain line.

"It should be an interesting flight," Del murmured to Susie, and Captain Ashlock, standing behind them, nodded gravely.

Susie clucked sympathetically as she watched Callahan, his face burgundy-hued, stomp by them in ignominious retreat to the crew lounge.

"I haven't seen him so shaken since that United stew told him he couldn't score if he walked into a woman's prison with a handful of pardons," she recalled.

"I think," Ashlock said, "I'd better talk to him."

He found Callahan pouring another cup of coffee and as soon as he saw Ashlock he started sputtering indignantly. "You hear what she said? You hear what that damned broad said to me? Goddammit, Mark, I'm gonna ream—"

"Crusty, shut up," Ashlock said quietly but with intensity.

"Huh?"

"There isn't a pilot on the line who hasn't heard what you tried to do to her when she came to that ALPA educational meeting. You not only didn't have any right to speak for ALPA, but if you'll pardon my saying so, you were a horse's ass. The kid's supposed to be a damned good pilot, so why don't you give her a chance?"

"I'll give her a good boot in the butt," Callahan raged. "No wet-behind-the-ears, snot-nosed dame who thinks she's a copilot is gonna talk to me like that."

"She would have been justified if she had gone right to Battles and reported you."

"Reported me? What the hell for? Since when can't a captain chew out a smart-aleck first officer?"

"She wasn't being smart-aleck and you know it. That walk-around's the copilot's job and you were off base telling her she couldn't do it."

"The hell I couldn't. You show me where in the manual it says a captain can't perform the walk-around at his own discretion."

"You show me a captain who's ever done it, Crusty. If I ever took the walk-around myself, it would be only because I didn't have any confidence in my copilot."

"Hah!" chortled Callahan. "You just said the magic words. No, sir, Mark, I don't have any confidence in *that* particular copilot. Jesus, a goddamned broad playing airline pilot!"

"Look, chum, Dan Smith told me she can fly circles around ninety per cent of the copilots we've got on the 737. Give her a break, Crusty."

"Smitty told you that?" For the first time, the little captain's indignation seemed diluted by uncertainty.

"Damn right. And Battles graded her himself on her rating ride. So who the hell are you to pass judgment before you ever fly with her?"

Callahan shook his head, puzzled. "Battles didn't tell me that when he wished the dame on me."

Ashlock looked surprised. "Johnny assigned her to you?"

"He sure did. I screamed like a raped panther but he said I was the most senior 737 captain and he wanted her to fly with me. When I screamed again he made it an order. And I ain't gonna argue with our chief pilot."

"That's funny," Ashlock mused, "he must have heard about that run-in you had with her. He should have known you'd give her a bad time. Did he tell you to rough her up?"

Callahan stared at his coffee, crestfallen. "No, I can't say that he did. Hell, Mark, I don't mean to be unfair. She's got guts, I'll concede that much. But Jesus, we need woman pilots like we need structural failure."

"Judge her as a pilot, not a female, Crusty. That's all she'd ask."

Callahan gulped down the last of the coffee, sighed unhappily and then—almost unwillingly and reluctantly—he started to chuckle in that froggy voice of his. "Goddamn, she sure as hell put me down, didn't she? You weren't kidding me, were you, Mark—did Smitty really say she could fly rings around most of our first officers?"

"May I lose an engine on my next takeoff if that's not the absolute truth."

"Well," Callahan said grudgingly, "a new first officer who can fly will be a welcome change." He poked a pudgy fist playfully into Ashlock's mid-section. "Never let it be said that Artemus Callahan isn't fair. I'll give her a break. Don't expect me to be sweetness and light, though—she'd damned well better be perfect or I'll chew her up and spit the pieces in Battles' face."

He left Ashlock in the crew lounge, the slim captain seeming pleased but still a little doubtful at Callahan's transformation. He liked Crusty; the little guy ordinarily was an ideal captain for a new copilot. Bawdy, irreverent and enormously skilled at his job—that was Crusty. He had the outward disposition of an IRS investigator with ulcers and the charming personality of an emotionally disturbed bear, but he was a solid pilot, a somewhat impatient yet effective teacher, and the most loyal of friends once he made up his mind to admit anyone to friendship. He also was the most inveterate and unpredictable practical joker on the line, the type who played jokes on impulse rather than with elaborate planning. Ashlock had heard of the time Callahan took a sudden dislike to his wife's regular Wednesday afternoon bridge party. He was watering his front lawn on the occasion and somehow the chatter from the bridge table occupants in his living room got on his nerves.

He shut off the water at the nozzle and shoved the garden hose through a side window that opened on a downstairs bathroom adjacent to the living room. Casually, he strolled into the house and by the bridge players, remarking loudly, "I gotta take a leak," and avoiding his wife's angry stare as he made the announcement. Once inside the bathroom, he turned on the hose nozzle and aimed a gentle stream into the commode—with just enough force so that the sound of the water stream could be heard in the living room. He ran the hose, with an occasional flushing to prevent overflowing, for a good twenty-five minutes—until the bridge game broke up in disarray, giggles and perhaps a certain amount of awe at the apparent capacity of Captain Callahan's kidneys.

Like many men pretending sourness and gruffness, he was pudding-soft, deathly afraid that somebody might discover it, and naïvely unaware that the news had leaked out. Not even his fellow pilots were aware of all his good deeds. They knew he was the easiest target on the airline for a hard-luck story, but they never realized how many hard-luck stories he had actually bought. Crusty greeted every request for aid with profane bellows, adamant refusals and dyspeptic lectures—followed a few hours later by a check he would sneak into the imploring pilot's or stewardess' mailbox along with a note that usually read something like "Pay me back when you can and stop being a stupid slob."

Ashlock had heard rumors that Crusty had loaned more than one stewardess, ticket agent or secretary money for abortions which he arranged himself through a doctor he trusted. He also knew of a probationary copilot who hated Callahan's guts for riding him unmercifully, who had threatened to "kill the little bastard the minute I get my fourth stripe," and who was totally unaware that Crusty had gone to bat for him with Battles when the youngster overslept, missed a trip and faced grounding or even dismissal.

"He's one of the best damned copilots I ever had," Callahan solemnly informed Battles, having only two days earlier informed the same first officer, "You're the stupidest copilot I ever had."

Ashlock himself personally had encountered Callahan's gift for hiding (he thought) a heart the size of a 747 wheel under foul, even cruel invective. When Mark's wife had been ill with terminal cancer and medical bills were straining even his captain's salary, Crusty was asked to contribute ten dollars to a fund the pilots were raising. Callahan went into a tantrum, telling the solicitor, "There are too goddamned many charity drives around this airline—why the hell should I fork out dough because Ashlock was too dumb to take out enough hospitalization?" That same afternoon, Ashlock found Crusty's check for five hundred dollars in his mailbox, plus this note: "I doubt if the good Lord listens to dirty old men like me, so this is in lieu of a prayer. P.S.—it's a loan, of course."

Still, Ashlock was wary of Callahan's too sudden willingness to handle the Devlin girl with a modicum of fairness. He knew that Crusty could be a mean s.o.b. when he had a grudge against or didn't like somebody, and he was not sure whether Captain Callahan's belligerence was personal or merely anti-feminine in a general sense. His wariness was partially justified; by the time Callahan reached Ship 328, he hadn't really made up his mind whether to ride the girl, ignore her or treat her like he would any new first officer—which, admittedly, would not be with tenderness. I'll see how the bitch does, he decided—if Smitty and Battles say she can fly, I'll give her the benefit of the doubt . . . temporarily.

Dudney already was studying the cardboard checklist when Captain Callahan came into the cockpit, squeezing his fat little bulk into the left seat and adjusting both the seat and the rudder pedals to his short stature.

"Guy who flew this the last time must have been John Wayne," he grumbled. Then he handsomely, graciously and gallantly apologized to her by remarking, "We've got a good day for flying, Miss Devlin," which for Crusty Callahan actually *was* a handsome, gracious and gallant format of apology.

"Walk-around completed, Captain," she said calmly. Determination to make the best of an uncomforable situation had frozen her anger into icy self-control. "And I'm ready on the checklist."

He looked at her quizzically, his reaction that of a professor who has just heard a ten-year-old suddenly recite an Einstein formula. He could not grasp the logic of a mere woman exhibiting the brisk efficiency of a well-trained, disciplined first officer and, faced with his own illogic, not to mention confusion, he retreated behind his usual wall of gruffness.

He made no move to let Dudney fly any portion of the Los Angeles–Las Vegas leg. He did allow her to perform routine first officer chores, such as communications, raising the gear and handling flap settings as they climbed to cruise altitude. For her part, she responded to his commands quickly and smoothly and they conversed solely in the technical litany of the cockpit. It was in this armed truce atmosphere that they began to achieve grudging, unspoken respect for one another. Callahan was surprised at her performance—what little he did give her to do, she executed flawlessly and with such uncanny swiftness that she seemed to be anticipating his orders. He was enough of a veteran pilot to know the reason—she was mentally flying the airplane herself, not satisfied to sit there like a ventriloquist's dummy, unable to act until he moved his own muscles and mouth. Crusty had remarked to fellow captains on several occasions that a good copilot was an extension of a captain's hands, legs and brain and he admitted to himself—grudgingly—that this girl met that stiff standard.

As for Dudney, she admitted to herself—also grudgingly—that he was one hell of a good pilot. Watching him, something her father had told her came back to her in sharp clarity: "Dud, always handle an airplane like a lover should handle a young girl. Be gentle, but be persuasive and firm if you have to be." She observed that Callahan never wasted a motion, worked with deliberate speed and flew Fat Albert in exactly the manner her father had prescribed—like a skilled seducer coaxing a passionate but balky virgin into submission. He had a technique that was nonchalance personified, yet nonchalance with an undercurrent of alertness that was velvet draped over sharp spurs.

Susie Russell brought them coffee once, utilizing the visit to sneak a few drags on a cigarette that was illegal to smoke in the cabin. She nodded to Dudney, spoke a few pleasantries to Captain Callahan, and returned to the passengers where Del immediately queried, "Any bloodshed up there yet?"

"Well," Susie reported, "they don't seem to be speaking to each other but there aren't any wounds on either of them."

"The way she clobbered him in Operations, he must be bleeding internally. Poor Crusty."

"Poor Dudney," Susie corrected. "If she so much as breathes the wrong way, he'll crucify her. What did you think of her, Del?"

"I liked her. I was afraid she'd act kind of superior, but she didn't put on any airs. That cup of coffee she got for Crusty was a dumb move."

"She was just trying to be friendly. God, Del, her first trip—I've seen a lot of new first officers practically get down on their knees and genuflect to captains."

"I suppose so, but . . . oh damn, there's 6A again—he must have been weaned on coffee. Hey, Susie, was she flying the plane when you went up?"

The other stewardess shook her head. "Not when I was there. I'll bet Crusty wouldn't let her flush the john in the Blue Room, let alone fly this bucket."

They had a one-hour layover in Las Vegas before Ship 328 changed from Flight 340 to 352, Vegas–Phoenix–Tucson. Callahan, in what for him was a major concession as well as a form of additional apology, casually remarked after the Las Vegas landing, "I'll check weather while you're doing the walk-around."

"Yes, sir," she said obediently—and with a decided effort not to sound grateful. She would have enjoyed a longer stop in Las Vegas, never having seen the play city and deciding right then and there she would use a pass some weekend and spend a couple of nights touring its Babylonish resort hotels. She had heard that the Sahara gave a nice discount to airline personnel and Dixie had raved frequently about the Tropicana's superb service. For that matter, she looked forward to the Phoenix leg. She had not been back to Arizona since graduating from college, and she loved Phoenix for its casual sophistication—"San Francisco in a ten-gallon hat," a college classmate had once described this desert oasis.

On the approach to the Phoenix airport she resisted the temptation to look down at familiar landmarks—those she had seen so often when she was flying in the area. It was well she did resist, in favor of one of her prime duties: watching out for other traffic. Crusty was peering at the oil gauge on number two; it had been running slightly higher than normal, and his eyes were on the instrument panel. Dudney had just lowered the flaps to an approach setting when she spotted disaster in the form of a twin-engine Cessna, coming smack on a collision course from above and slightly to their left, descending as they were.

Her shout was startled and loud but devoid of panic. "Traffic ten o'clock descending!" Instinctively she grabbed the yoke even before Callahan could, rolling hard right and pulling the wheel back almost to her lap.

"Power!" she yelled simultaneously and the captain's right hand was shoving both throttles forward even as his left hand grabbed his yoke and followed through Dudney's evasive maneuver. The turbines screamed in protest at the sudden abuse, but now they were in a steady, steep climbing turn. Out of the corner of his eye, Callahan saw the blue Cessna flash by—not more than fifty feet away—and drop out of sight as they continued their rolling climb.

"Jesus," was Crusty's only comment for the first fifteen seconds. Dudney's hands were shaking slightly but she rolled back to level flight, still flying the airplane as Callahan reduced power.

"I'll take it," he almost whispered, and she relinquished the yoke gladly. "You okay?"

"Yes, sir." It was more of a sigh than a response.

"Good. I'd better see if we broke anything in the cabin." He rang the intercom bell three times. "Del—everyone okay back there?"

Dudney could hear the stewardess' reply, somewhat breathless but calm. "All passengers okay, Crusty—good thing you had the seat belt sign on. Susie's bruised her leg a little, I think—she fell against the galley. What happened?"

"Near miss with some damned fool Cessna driver. I'd better apologize to the customers. You all right?"

"I'm fine. I landed in somebody's lap—hell of a way to meet a guy."

"Good girl. Better check again and make sure we haven't busted any bones." He was about to flick the PA switch when Phoenix Approach Control paged them.

"Trans-Coastal 352, any reason for your abandoning that approach?"

Dudney started to reply but Callahan, fuming, barked, "You take it. Lemme talk to those bastards." He picked up his radio microphone. "Phoenix, this is 352. We just had a near miss with a light twin, a blue Cessna, I think. Didn't you see the sonofabitch?"

"Negative, 352. No conflicting traffic on our scope. Will you be filing a near-miss report?"

"You're goddamned right I'll be filing a report!" the captain roared. "And I'd like to shove it right up—" He realized hurriedly it was useless and possibly hazardous to insult ATC, and amended his remarks. "He damned near creamed us. Missed us by about fifty feet. I'll see you guys when we land. We cleared for another approach?"

"Trans-Coastal 352, you're cleared for approach. Contact the tower on 124.6."

"Roger, 352." Callahan released his transmitting button, advising Dudney, "Okay, I've got her. Give the tower a buzz after I make Jason Silvanius happy." He picked up the cabin PA mike and Dudney admired the soothing quality of his voice, so matter-of-fact that he might have been giving the Phoenix weather. "Ladies and gentlemen, this is Captain Callahan. I'd like to apologize for that abrupt maneuver but we had a private airplane in our way and we had to take evasive action. We'll be landing in Phoenix in about five minutes. Thank you." He put the mike back in its steel-pronged nest and looked at his copilot. She was a little pale, her eyes roving the sky in front of them as if expecting another near miss.

"Better raise the tower," he said and she complied—her voice firmer than she imagined it would be. She then used the company frequency to report the near miss and requested the station manager to meet the flight.

When they landed, the station manager was at the ramp to check each passenger individually. One man, limping down the aircraft stairs in exaggerated pain, was holding his back.

"It's whiplash," he moaned. "My lawyers will be in touch with you. Never saw such careless flying. . . ."

The captain had opened the cockpit window on his side and heard the passenger as well as saw him. Crusty's lips curled before he turned back to Dudney. "The lousy, phony crumb—he isn't hurt any more than I am. And some airborne ambulance chaser will talk him into suing us. The creep's lucky to be alive."

Dudney couldn't see the disembarking area from her right seat. "Somebody claiming they were hurt, Captain?"

"Yeah, one guy's holding his back screaming 'whiplash.' I'd better go back and see how Susie is."

It turned out the stewardess fortunately escaped with a small but painful bruise. She insisted on working the Phoenix–Tucson–Los Angeles legs after promising Callahan she would see Dr. Luther as soon as they got in. Crusty spent twenty minutes of their forty-five-minute layover telling the FAA verbally about the near miss, and promised to file a full report in Los Angeles. He met Dudney in Phoenix Operations and filled her in while he was making out a flight plan for the final leg.

"Radar never spotted that Cessna," he told her. "It figures—small target that never registered on their scope. Some asshole of a student pilot wandering VFR in terminal airspace, probably. I'll bet he never saw us."

He made no mention of Dudney's actions. She had half expected him to raise hell about her grabbing the controls, although she knew they would have collided if she hadn't, and she figured that his not mentioning it was his way of approving it. On the last leg, halfway to Los Angeles, he casually suggested, "Maybe I'd better let you get in some flying time," and he let her fly the 737 right up to the time they were turned over from Enroute Control to Approach Control.

She was signing her flight pay log when Crusty came up behind her and touched her elbow. He was holding several booklets and pamphlets which he handed her.

"Some stuff about ALPA," he explained in a tone that was so falsely harsh that she almost laughed at him. "And, uh, I left a membership application blank in your mailbox."

CHAPTER NINE

The close call at Phoenix was the only non-routine event that occurred in her first six months on the line, bringing home the truth of the timeworn axiom that airline flying consists of hours of boredom punctuated by seconds of sheer terror.

Yet it definitely was not a dull existence, not in an industry where no two trips are ever the same. Because she loved flying and those who made it a profession and a way of life, every takeoff was exciting and every landing a challenge and every flight a fresh opportunity to enjoy the moods of the sky—benign or angry, it made no difference. She relished its beauty and respected its fury. She was sublimely confident in her machine and the men who commanded it, but never forgetful of the frailties of each.

It was only too true that every new captain with whom she flew had to be won over. Invariably he would start out with doubts, suspicion and occasionally open hostility, but she was too good at her job to warrant any permanent negativism. Her experience with Callahan had given her a kind of immunity from captains who might otherwise have been antagonistic. In typical fashion, Crusty had done a complete course reversal and would extoll her proficiency, attitude and personality at the drop of a "Waddaya think of that Devlin gal?" The general feeling among Trans-Coastal's flight crews was that anyone who had punctured Crusty Callahan's hide couldn't be all bad.

She kept up her contacts with most of her classmates, Dixie, Hank, Frank and Ernie mostly, but not to the degree she had expected or wanted. Inevitably, their own circle of friends expanded even as their immediate need for one another—forged under the stresses of training—diminished. The closeness of the classroom weakened once they were out of that atmosphere of sharing a single environment and mutual problems. It would return someday to some of them, depending on the depth of their earlier comradeship, but in the initial weeks and months of line flying they were too busy meeting new people and solving new problems—such as pleasing a variety of highly individualistic captains.

The result was that professional acceptance failed again to cure personal loneliness. Her happiest hours were spent in the comparative cubbyhole that is an airliner cockpit, with its distinctive leathery odor—almost like the smell of a new car. The familiarity of the multi-dialed instrument panel was security and companionship; the spinning fuel-flow gauges were friendly winking eyes. She felt even more at home on a late night flight, the instruments dancing with graceful coordination in their tiny, glass-enclosed cages under the soft red illumination. The muffled hum of the turbines, the clipped, impersonal metallic voices of controllers that were gossamer threads linking their flight to the earth below. The brief moment the cockpit door might be open and she could sneak a glimpse of the long, dimly lit cabin behind them with its sleeping, trusting passengers—this was the world of the pilot. This was her world, one of symmetry molded in metal and sound and smell.

The cockpit was the culmination of all that had gone before the flight—advertising, ticketing, meteorology, maintenance, dispatch, boarding and commissary. A flight crew was the cast in a drama, the team that takes the field. It needed a script. It needed plays to run. It needed plans and strategy and coaching and directing. But a takeoff was a curtain going up, a referee's opening whistle, and from then on the crew was alone in its tubular shell—a stage, an arena, made up of schedules and weather and traffic and winds and clouds. Of unwinding altimeters and the white-hot heat of ignited kerosene roaring through compressors and madly racing shafts. Of invisible electronic fingers guiding and informing and cautioning. Of gently flexing wings with sinews of metal and filled with the lifeblood of fuel. Of hydraulic lines that were an extension of a pilot's biceps and instruments that were an extension of his brain. Of engineered reliability—human as well as mechanical, for in every cockpit there sat the products of scientific training and preparation. The perfect combination of man and machine mutually dependent on each other, one trusting design and the other trusting skill and judgment.

This was Dudney Devlin's world, where an airplane became a living creature—a loyal friend to be loved, an enemy to be respected, a child to be spoiled, an ally to depend on, a temperamental prima donna to be coaxed and sometimes cursed. The world of flight crews, where distance was measured in hours instead of miles and where time was dominant, from the cold print of airline schedules to flight plans; from flight pay logs to fuel consumption.

She made friends, but they were mostly older captains. On lay-overs or in their homes, she uncomplainingly would listen to their stories and anecdotes for hours—nostalgia and history substituting for contacts with people nearer her own age, almost a re-enactment of her life with Ralph Devlin. The younger captains and copilots, she was convinced, would have liked to brag they were the first to seduce her. It was quite possible she was wrong in some cases, but the caution she had imposed on herself during training lapped over into her new life. She wanted to socialize with stewardesses, confide in them, like them—but on their part they regarded her either in awe or with wary aloofness as if she was a kind of airborne half man, half woman. Unwittingly, or perhaps reluctantly, she sentenced herself to a form of self-exile that was unnatural but an almost inescapable penalty for a healthy, normal, attractive young woman who had chosen what was essentially a man's existence.

Crusty she not only liked but began to worship, not as a father replacement but as an older brother she never had. Once she had seen his bluster and bombast for the sham they were, she found herself able to tease and taunt him. He gave her more flying time than any other captain and he also taught her more. It was part of his one-eighty-degree turn, and his own feeling toward her grew from one of respect to unquestioning friendship. She knew part of his changed attitude was the product of a guilty conscience as much as anything else, but this was in the early stages of their association. She admitted to herself on more than one occasion, when loneliness choked her like a clammy fog, that she would have gone to bed with this ugly little man—not only from sheer need for affection and satisfied desire but from gratitude. Yet she also discovered that Crusty regarded marital fidelity in the same spirit as he regarded friendship —once he had decided to bestow either sacred trust, nothing could have weakened his loyalty.

Once, on a layover in Salt Lake City, she asked him about pilot morals and whether their reputation for extracurricular promiscuity was justified.

"Depends on the individual, Dud," Crusty said soberly. "Some cheat occasionally, some cheat frequently and some never cheat. But you can say that about all men—pilots take the rap because their opportunity for straying off the reservation is greater than most guys have."

"How about yourself?"

"Hell, I've been tempted. Layovers can be lonely and if some stew with an obvious case of hot pants gets across the idea she's willing, it takes a cargo bin of will power to get out of her way. Any time I run into that situation, all I gotta think of is my wife. Martha was a stew with Western—never did tell you that, did I? Well, Martha's a damned good-looking gal and damned good in bed. Man couldn't ask for anything more. And look at what she married—a sawed-off bastard with a foul mouth, a lousy temper and a face like the puss on an English bulldog. She picked me over guys I'd have given the last five years of my life to look like. That's what I think of when I'm tempted—how much Martha must have loved me to marry what she did. And I'm so goddamned grateful for what she's given me that I'd die before I'd hurt her."

"Snap judgments stink," Dudney said abruptly.

"Huh?"

"Snap judgments. The kind I made on you the first night I met you—at the ALPA meeting. I thought you were a fourteen-carat, undersized creep and you turned out to be a giant."

Crusty chuckled in mixed embarrassment and appreciation. "Don't pin any medals on me, goddammit. I'm not the only guy on this airline who walks the straight and narrow, although I'll admit we might be in the minority. Mark Ashlock's another. Or was."

"Was?"

"When his wife was alive. She was one of our stews. Hell of a beautiful gal. Died of cancer about two years ago. Mark's played the field since but never seriously. It's like he was looking for her twin and never finds her. In fact, he's kind of a lone wolf now—something like you, Dud. Hell, I'd like to see you date him."

"Don't start playing Cupid, Crusty. I'm not going to get involved with any pilot."

"Who the hell are you gonna get involved with—a stew? Far as I know, Dud, you aren't dating anybody, in or out of the airline. It ain't natural."

She smiled, albeit sadly. "No, it's not natural. But preferable to being known as an easy lay. Which is what I'd be tagged by the first pilot I said yes to."

"Goddammit, so don't go out with pilots. For Christ's sake, there are other honorable professions."

"I don't know anybody but pilots. Besides, they're all that interest me. Can you imagine me having anything in common with an insurance salesman? Or a lawyer?"

"Football player," Callahan said in sudden inspiration. "Say, I know a good kid who plays defensive halfback for the Rams. Bachelor, about your age, has—"

"No," Dudney said with more than necessary emphasis.

"Why the hell not? He's a—"

"I'm not interested in football players."

"That's being stupid. Would you mind—"

"I knew one once." The way she said it was sufficient to steer him away from the subject and toward another of more mutual interest— the handling of Fat Albert in turbulence.

Dudney figured at one time she had softened Crusty up, but an experience Dixie had with the redoubtable Captain Callahan taught her otherwise. Dixie drew him for a trip when the Southerner was on reserve. Dixie worried loud and clear and his fears were justified because for some reason Crusty was in a bad mood when he greeted First Officer Miller in Operations at eight o'clock on a beautiful moonlit night.

"It's real pretty outside, Captain," Dixie informed him politely. "Full moon."

"Shit!" Crusty bellowed. "That means I'll have the goddamned moon in my eyes all night!"

Dixie unfortunately picked this flight on which to woolgather—understandable and forgivable inasmuch as Norma Jean had told him only that morning that they were going to have a baby. Not suspecting that his copilot's mind was not on his work, Crusty let him fly a Las Vegas–Denver leg and was handling the radio as they approached Denver's Stapleton Field.

Dixie, flying, was only half listening.

"Denver Center, this is Trans-Coastal 344 inbound five miles southwest of Gunnison VOR. Request approach clearance."

"Roger, 344. Squawk ident over Gunnison. What is your altitude?"

"Flight level three-one-zero, Denver, for Trans-Coastal 344."

"Roger. You're southwest of the Gunnison VOR on Jetway one-four-six, right?"

The dialogue suddenly registered—but only partially—in Dixie's brain. He paled, grabbed his mike and yelled, "Denver Center, Trans-Coastal 344! I'm also at three-one-zero southwest of Gunnison on J one-four-six!"

Denver Center possibly would not have needed a radio communication to hear Callahan's scream of rage.

"YOU SHOULD BE, YOU CHOWDER-HEADED MORON! YOU'RE MY COPILOT!"

The shattered Dixie lived for one week in mortal fear that Crusty would report him to Battles, a belief nurtured by the fact that the captain had not spoken to him for the rest of their trip except for necessary commands. The copilot never found out that Crusty told the story to Dudney, laughing so hard that he had to wipe the tears from his eyes. "But don't you tell that Alabama asshole I thought it was funny," he added hastily. "I got him scared to death I'll turn him in and it'll do him good to worry about it for a while. I'll bet the poor sonofabitch listens to ATC from now on."

Crusty was not the only colorful captain she encountered. She drew Carl Redmond for one month and Redmond's personality was best described by what the other pilots called him behind his back because he was six-five and boulder-solid—"old Stone Face." Crusty at least had a sense of humor, however hard it was to extract, but nobody could recall ever seeing Captain Redmond smile. Unlike Callahan, he never swore; he merely looked disgusted and this was signaled by the slight curling of the left side of his upper lip and an equally slight lowering of his eyelids, as if he had started to doze off with a half snarl frozen on his mouth. He had two idiosyncrasies, neither necessarily evil, and in fact quite commendable for an airline captain. Redmond had a fetish for keeping to a schedule that was close to being fanatical. He also insisted on copilots, particularly new ones, knowing the answer to every question he might ask if it bore the faintest connection with the day's trip.

Crusty alerted her to this latter menace when she told him she was flying with Redmond.

"Where?" Callahan demanded.

"L.A., Salt Lake City, Pocatello and Idaho Falls."

"Get out your Jeppesen charts and a good atlas, if you have to. Study every damned landmark on the route. You never know what Stone Face is liable to ask you—such as the height of the main steeple on the Mormon Tabernacle, or how deep is the Great Salt Lake. He flies the same trip almost every month and he knows it like he knows the way to his own bathroom."

She didn't quite believe Crusty but she did her homework. Leaving Pocatello the next morning at the exact scheduled time of 10:00 A.M., they banked over a large gray building just off their right wing.

"What's the time?" Redmond demanded.

"A minute after ten, Captain."

"What's that gray building?"

She answered triumphantly and not without a touch of smugness, "That's the Idaho State Penitentiary, sir."

He made no further reference to the subject. But three days later, on the same schedule, they broke ground at Pocatello and one minute later, as they banked over the prison, the captain asked it again.

"What's the time?"

"Ten-oh-one, sir."

"What's that gray building down there?"

She was bewildered but stuck to protocol. "That's the Idaho State Penitentiary, sir."

They came into Pocatello the following week. Redmond asked the same two questions and got the same answers. Once more four days later. On their last trip of the month, they had a minor mechanical before leaving Pocatello and the takeoff was delayed twenty minutes.

"What time is it?" the captain asked as they turned over the prison.

"Ten-twenty," she answered dutifully.

"What's that gray building?"

"That's the Idaho State Penitentiary, Captain." A trace of impatience.

They flew on, the captain silent for about three minutes at most.

"Too bad," he finally sighed.

"What's too bad?" Dudney inquired, mystified.

His reply put him in that very special category to which she had assigned a chosen few. Captain Redmond, too, was a Character.

"Do you realize, Dudney," he said in the tone of a reformer citing some woeful statistical fact, "that every poor guy in that prison is gonna think his watch is wrong?"

Not all her Characters were lovable, funny or deserving of respect. A few merely were interesting, such as Captain McPherson, a pilot known to his Trans-Coastal brethren as "Alibi Angus," a fast man with an excuse. His worst failing was his devout conviction that he knew every checklist by heart. No one in authority had ever caught him relying on memory, for he was one of those captains who wore a halo in the cockpit when a check pilot was aboard. Out of supervisory sight, he reverted to form, which was not really dangerous but occasionally embarrassing.

Dudney flew with him only once, in uneasy anticipation, having heard about his nickname, and reported to Crusty that his reputation was undeserved. "He used the checklist as thoroughly as you do, only he's not so grouchy," she informed Captain Callahan.

"He's reformed somewhat," Crusty said. "He doesn't take the chances with a jet that he did when he was flying pistons. I remember once when he figured he had a Convair 240 checklist memorized and he starts to take off without setting his fuel mixture to full rich. When he tries to give it full throttle, both engines cough like they're running on tap water. Angus realizes his mistake, calls for full rich and they take off okay—but only the copilot's laundry knew how scared he was. Anyway, when they get to cruise altitude, one of the stews comes up and asks Angus what the hell happened on takeoff.

'Some of the passengers were scared because they thought we had engine failure,' she tells McPherson. Angus doesn't bat an eyelash. He picks up the PA mike and gives them this spiel: 'Folks, some of you may have thought we had a little mechanical difficulty when we took off. Actually, just when we were about to leave, a small dog ran across the runway and I momentarily reduced power to let the little fella get out of our way safely. I hope you enjoy your flight and thank you.' Well, Angus must have had half the plane filled with dog-lovers because about twenty passenger commendation letters wound up on John Battles' desk. I always figured Johnny suspected right away that there wasn't a dog within fifty miles of that runway but he couldn't prove it. It would have been forgotten except that one of the passengers was on the Board of Directors of the Humane Society, or the SPCA—I can't remember which—and he decides Angus should receive a medal. Jason Silvanius gets all excited about it and arranges some public ceremony. That damned McPherson was ready to accept the medal, too, except that he neglected to make sure the copilot didn't squeal on him. Silvanius interviewed the kid to find out exactly what happened for a publicity release, and the copilot was so damned vague and hesitant that Jason got suspicious. He confided his doubts to Battles and Johnny finally pried the truth outta McPherson. I don't know what the hell baloney they gave the guy from the Humane Society—I suppose Silvanius told him Captain McPherson was too modest and wanted to avoid publicity."

Jason confirmed that story when he and his wife Janet, a former Trans-Coastal stewardess, had Dudney for dinner at their house one night. Silvanius, too, was a storehouse of airline anecdotes—including one on Crusty which she hadn't heard, probably because Callahan was loath to admit possessing anything as human as a sense of humor.

"It happened when he was a fairly new captain," Jason was recalling to Janet and Dudney when the talk got around to funny airline incidents. "He almost got fired for it, too. It seems Crusty had the world's largest hangover one flight and he kept leaving the cockpit to get a glass of water in the galley. After the fifth or sixth trip, a passenger who'd been watching him grabs Crusty as he walked back to the cockpit. 'Got a hangover, Captain?' he asks kind of sarcastically.

Crusty gives him that patented Callahan glare and says, 'No, I'm trying to put out a cockpit fire.' "

"It reminds me of something that happened when I was flying the line," Janet said. "A passenger gave me a note for the captain and I sneaked a look at it on the way up. He had written, 'You have an oil leak in number 4.' I gave it to the captain and he gave me back a note for the passenger. I looked at this one too—it said, 'I know it and I'm just as worried as you are.' "

Dudney grew to admire and respect Silvanius as well as like him. At first she thought him a bit glib and overly smooth, even shallow, an opinion fortified by a pilot who had represented ALPA at the crash of a Trans-Coastal DC-6 at Seattle one foggy night a few years before.

"Shallow—and cold-blooded," the pilot had told Dudney. "I worked with Silvanius for about forty-eight hours after that accident and he wouldn't have batted an eye if his own mother had been on that plane. The sonofabitch must have frozen formaldehyde in his veins. I saw him give out stuff to reporters like he was handing out the starting line-ups in a baseball game. One of the stews killed was a bridesmaid at his wedding, but she was just another name to Silvanius. Hell, I watched him go into the FBI identification tent, identify the girl's body, and then come out and give reporters a briefing on the ILS procedures for the Seattle airport. He's a slick, unfeeling bastard, our vice president of public relations."

Dudney swallowed this appraisal without challenge, but the first time she had dinner at Jason's home she heard the sequel to the pilot's story—from Janet Silvanius. While Jason was mixing drinks in the kitchen, Janet got to talking about her husband and the kind of person he was.

"I remember when we lost a DC-6 at Seattle," Janet related. "One of my bridesmaids was a stewardess on the flight. Jason identified her body. When he got back from Seattle he walked in, poured himself a triple shot of bourbon, drank it in two swallows, put his head in my lap and cried for ten minutes."

Silvanius, Dudney learned, had been an aviation writer for a Midwestern newspaper where his propensity for objectivity and accuracy won the attention of Tom Berlin. The airline's starting salary was not much more than Jason was making at the paper, but Silvanius had by then acquired a large dose of respect for the airline industry—more than he had acquired for certain aspects of the newspaper business —and he willingly committed his future to Trans-Coastal.

Dudney also liked Jason's wife. Tall, slender and self-possessed, with classic, almost delicate features, Janet was the kind of woman who still would look beautiful at sixty because her beauty was merely a layer of pulchritude over her serenity. She was, to put it simply, so totally contented with her marriage that her inner glow seemed to seep through her skin. In a sense, it made Dudney uncomfortable and vaguely dissatisfied—a marital relationship so effortlessly happy had to reflect her own nomadic life as empty by comparison. She would not have traded places with Janet because she was intelligent enough to realize that what made Janet happy was not necessarily what would make her happy, which primarily was Jason. Thus her envy was sincere without being devouring or frustrating.

And Dudney was not unhappy, even though she was lonely on too many occasions. If she merely existed between trips, the latter offered more than adequate sublimation. She loved flying to new cities and the excitement of exploring for good restaurants and cozy bars. Of discovering that cities, like people, can have personalities. She warmed to the friendly small towns like Idaho Falls, or Great Falls, Montana, which reminded her of Alaska with its frontier atmosphere. She liked the clean beauty of Denver, the glamorous tinsel of Las Vegas, the brawling masculinity of Seattle. She relished the feeling of being part of a flight crew. The mass check-in at the layover hotel, the dash to their rooms so they could change for dinner; the easy, laughing informality of post-flight companionship when they swapped jokes, remembrances and occasional lies. She always had a room by herself, as did all pilots, an appreciated privacy because she had feared that Trans-Coastal might make her share layover quarters with a stewardess.

Dudney had never been east of the Rocky Mountain states, so one month she bid a horrendous schedule involving a Los Angeles–Minneapolis trip with intermediate stops at San Diego, Phoenix, Denver and Sioux Falls. The cockpit workload on a multi-stop trip was hectic and the day was long. The flight left Los Angeles at 7:00 A.M. and it was 4:00 P.M. local time before they touched down at

Minneapolis-St. Paul, but the layover was wonderful—the return flight didn't leave until noon the next day, which made drinking permissible.

The captain on her first Minneapolis trip was a gangling, red-haired beanpole named Bert Huntington, who endeared himself to Dudney by telling her at sign-in, "I've been looking forward to flying with you," which was a great improvement over the "Oh, God, I drew the dame" look most captains gave her on first meeting. Huntington had hands the size of boxing gloves, an infectious grin that reminded her of Ernie Crum, and a gold wedding band on his left hand which tentatively qualified him in Dudney's eyes as a Nice Guy—some pilots were known to remove their rings and don an air of silent, mysterious sadness if a stewardess asked about their marital status.

It was Huntington who on this trip introduced Dudney to a couple of Trans-Coastal institutions. The first was a Minneapolis culture center known as Dirty Daphne's—i.e., a bar, but a bar the likes of which Dudney had never seen, not even in the gamier areas of Alaska. The proprietress was Daphne O'Malley, who tended bar in decrepit bedroom slippers and boasted the most obscene vocabulary on either side of the Mississippi. She was built like a Japanese wrestler, and if she had ever used her normal voice outside her establishment, noise abatement procedures would have been required within a radius of three miles. A mutter from Dirty Daphne carried the equivalent decibels of a title-winning hog caller.

Her bar was just that—a bar and nothing else, without a table or chair in the place. Dirty Daphne's loyal clientele, which included every airline crew that flew into Minneapolis and a number who were based there, did their drinking standing up or they didn't drink. It was freely speculated that Daphne insisted on stand-up drinking because it was such a reliable thermometer of intoxication; if a customer couldn't stay on his feet, he didn't deserve another drink. Obviously it was no environment for the timid, stuffy or pious. Dirty Daphne's greatest love was to be challenged to a profanity contest, and in thirty-eight years she was unbeaten—a statistic which Huntington related proudly to Dudney and his two stewardesses en route to Daphne's.

"She must be something," Dudney marveled.

"She is. Sent three kids through college and right now she's supporting about five deadbeat relatives. By the way, one of you gals order a martini when we get there."

"I'd rather have scotch," Dudney protested mildly, and the two stewardesses nodded in support.

"No matter. I just want one of you to order something besides scotch or bourbon—that's all she serves."

Dudney shuddered. "No, thanks. I don't want to get killed. From your description, she's her own bouncer."

"You'll be safe. Just order a martini. It's an experience."

It was. Huntington ordered three scotches for himself and the two stewardesses and looked hopefully at Dudney.

"A martini, please," Dudney said in a quaver.

Dirty Daphne's eyes flew up to half-staff. "WELL, I'LL BE A ——," she roared. "THIS MUST BE THE FIRST TIME YOU'VE BEEN IN THIS —— JOINT, DEARIE. WE DON'T SERVE THOSE —— SISSY DRINKS. YOU WANNA SCOTCH OR BOURBON, DEARIE?"

"A scotch and water, please," Dudney quaked, retreating behind Huntington and whispering, "My God, I can see why she's never lost."

Dirty Daphne, she discovered, remembered every customer by face but it did little good for her public relations because she could not remember anyone's name. All men were called "HONEY" and all women "DEARIE." She had two bartenders helping her but they might as well have been part of the woodwork; Daphne was the one at whom the orders were hollered.

A Trans-Coastal 720 crew was there that night—the captain, copilot, flight engineer and three stewardesses—and they joined Huntington's 737 crew for dinner. On the way back to the hotel the 720 captain suggested playing "Jackass"—and this was the second Trans-Coastal institution Dudney encountered. They went to his room for instructions, which turned out to be slightly less complicated than ground school. Two of the 720 stews and the flight engineer begged off in favor of sleep, which left four Jackass veterans and three uninitiated novices—Dudney and the two 737 stews, both fresh-faced youngsters only three weeks out of stewardess school.

"I've heard about the game," one of them whispered to Dudney. "It's a kind of strip poker. We were warned about it in stew school."

Huntington overheard her. "It's nothing of the sort," he said reassuringly. "It's a game of skill, judgment and coordination, designed to keep your reflexes sharp and your mind alert."

"It's also a kind of strip poker," the other captain confessed. "We can play it two ways—the loser has to chug-a-lug his drink or take off an article of clothing. Tonight we'd better do the stripping penalty because our trip leaves at 0800 tomorrow and I've had enough to drink."

Dudney suspected that his libido rather than his sense of duty dictated the choice of penalty, but she went along dubiously. Jackass, it turned out, involved dealing four cards to each participant. Pennies equaling the total number of participants minus one were tossed into the pot—in this case, the center of the captain's bed. There were seven players this time, so six pennies were used. The rules, as the captain explained it, were simple: the dealer handed one of his four cards to the player next to him, that player handed one of his cards to the person next to him and so on around the circle. The first person to get four of a kind reached for one of the pennies. This was the signal for the others to grab a penny, and the tardy player who failed to come up with any penny was awarded one of the letters in the word "Jackass." For each letter earned, a piece of apparel had to come off.

"What happens to the one who finally gets the whole word?" Dudney asked.

"In theory, the grand loser has to sleep with one of the other contestants," Huntington said. "In practice, it never comes to that. I've been playing it for five years and nobody ever got all seven letters—the game takes too long to play. If the penalty per letter is a chug-a-lug, you're too bombed before anybody gets to be a full-fledged Jackass. Same thing with stripping—I have yet to see anyone reduced to complete nudity. Some of the older stews who've played it a long time are pretty cute. They'll wear four pairs of stockings to a Jackass game, or three sets of panties. It would take twelve hours before you could get all the clothes off them."

"It won't take twelve hours for me," one of the stewardesses complained. "I've got on only one set of panties and I'm not wearing a bra."

"Let's play," the 720 captain said eagerly.

Dudney's first game of Jackass was no model of polite decorum, but it wasn't the orgy she feared, either. The pilots and the more experienced 720 stew had a decided advantage at the start, Dudney losing both shoes and one of her stockings, while the bra-less stew tottered on a precipice of violated modesty—she lost both shoes, both stockings and her skirt. Saddled with J-A-C-K-A, she lost a sixth time and the three pilots leered and smirked expectantly—until with sudden inspiration she removed a pin from her hair.

"And I've got a garter belt in reserve," she confided to Dudney.

Actually, Dudney discovered, the game was fast and fun. She had to keep her eyes on her cards and the pile of pennies simultaneously, constantly alert for someone to draw four of a kind and make the first move. Arms and hands could get bruised and clothing torn in the laughing scuffle for the coins. But it was a relatively harmless pastime that had been played by Trans-Coastal crews on layovers since the days of the DC-3, and Dudney learned that a few senior stewardesses were more adept at it than pilots.

At any rate, games like Jackass, places like Dirty Daphne's, the companionship of flight crews and the constant challenge of the job itself, all made her life reasonably full. She did begin dating a little. Doug Worthington asked her to a dance and she accepted—demonstrating purely female illogic by vowing to kill him if he made a pass, and then being forlornly disappointed because he didn't. Jason Silvanius fixed her up with a novelist he knew—a clever, witty man, Dudney admitted, but one who spent the evening criticizing the airlines and making cracks about stewardess intelligence and morals. She was, perhaps, overly defensive on any aviation subject and she regretted calling the author a "bigoted, phony intellectual"—inasmuch as she called him this to his face, and knew it was their last date as well as their first. But she had acquired a large chunk of respect for the cabin attendants. As a group, they were loyal, adaptable, dedicated and generous. Their faults were the weaknesses of women as individuals, not stewardesses. Dudney could not help feeling slightly superior to them, but she was fair-minded enough to appreciate the importance of their job which, in some ways, was harder than her own. If the cockpit was a test pad for technical competence, it also

was an ivory tower refuge from the more mundane aspects of a trip
—such as irate, unreasonable passengers who took out their frustrations and fears on the nearest available target—the stewardess.
Somewhat to her surprise, passenger reaction to seeing a woman
pilot was confined mostly to curiosity; at least nobody ever walked
off her airplane.

She also realized it was hard for anyone outside the airline industry to appreciate or even remotely grasp its *esprit de corps*. Airline
humor, for example, was often like military humor—born of adversity,
mistakes and the ability to laugh at both. This was why Dudney loved
her Characters, with which any airline is well populated. There was
a Trans-Coastal captain named Rod Davenport, for example, whose
Achilles' heel was his mysterious inability to write up a mechanical
discrepancy in language that a mechanic could understand. This failing eventually led to a running feud between Captain Davenport and
Maintenance, the latter deeply resenting the former's vague phraseology.

Davenport noted in a 737 logbook one day that "something's loose
in tail." The next time he saw the logbook, a mechanic had recorded
the corrective action: "Something loose in tail has been tightened."

"Smart ass," Davenport grumbled to his grinning first officer. The
next time he found something mechanical to complain about, he wrote
it up as "Number 2 engine missing." He was advised a few days
later, "Number 2 engine found and put back."

His next discrepancy write-up was a masterpiece of clarity, detail
and technical accuracy. He reported that "trim tab adjustment stuck
50 miles out."

The logbook came back to him with the notation: "Adjusted trim
tab from 50 miles to one inch."

Davenport swore revenge and got it. He informed Maintenance
one day that the left wing on ship 334 seemed heavy. The corrective
write-up advised, "Centered trim tab."

The next day Davenport complained that "right wing seems heavy."

The subsequent logbook entry read: "Centered tab."

Davenport's third write-up informed Maintenance:

"Both wings heavy."

Ernie Crum told Dudney of an incident which reminded her of the story Robinson had related the last day of ground school. Ernie was flying copilot one day when the captain's vertical gyro stuck before they left the ramp. They had to wait until it came back to level and one of the stewardesses popped into the cockpit to ask why the delay.

"We're waiting for this damned thing to erect," the captain growled, pointing to the gyro instrument.

The stewardess thanked him and returned to the cabin where she picked up her PA and calmly intoned:

"Ladies and gentlemen, the captain has advised me he's waiting for an erection before we can take off."

Ninety-eight per cent of the women passengers looked shocked and seventy per cent of the men aboard were laughing. The second stewardess, more worldly, whispered a hasty and radically digested sex lecture to her colleague, who retreated to the Blue Room (lavatory) in complete confusion and tearful humiliation.

"It took the captain to calm her down before she could face the passengers," Ernie recounted gleefully.

There also was the sad case of Captain Marty Philbin, who could sleep almost indefinitely as long as his bedroom was dark. He made the mistake of confessing this to a few colleagues, one of whom was a pilot of dubious morality but devilish ingenuity. While Philbin was out to dinner on a layover, the pilot got into his room with a can of black paint and coated both windows. He then informed the hotel desk that Captain Philbin was not feeling well and was not to be awakened under any circumstances.

Philbin returned to the room and went to bed without noticing the window paint job. He awakened once to go to the bathroom, saw it was still dark outside (it was an hour past dawn) and went back to sleep. When he failed to sign in for his trip, the local crew scheduler called the hotel, which advised him that Captain Philbin was sick and had left orders not to be disturbed.

Crew sked was rightfully miffed that Philbin hadn't called in himself but swallowed the story, grabbed a qualified captain off another trip for Philbin's flight and requested Los Angeles to deadhead a replacement for the man taking Philbin's place. While all this was going on, Captain Philbin slept. And slept. And slept. Through the entire day and well into the evening when his stomach told him it needed nourishment. His watch read seven o'clock—fifteen minutes before his wake-up call—so he informed the desk he was already up, showered and shaved and went down to breakfast only to find it was dark outside.

Philbin never found out who did it to him. There were too many suspects and nobody was confessing, particularly when the hotel billed Trans-Coastal for the replacement of two windows and requested the airline to find another hotel for its crews.

There was the immortal line uttered by Captain Wilbur Kowarsky, who lost nine feet of his right wing in a collision with a Piper Apache, turned around and landed safely with the torn wing on fire. When the 727 stopped rolling and a convoy of fire trucks clustered around the burning wing, Kowarsky shook his head and wistfully said to his co-pilot: "It kinda makes you forget about sex for a while, doesn't it?"

There were times that Dudney wished she had flown back in the days of the pistons, when things were more informal and aircraft and people alike were not quite so sophisticated. This included passengers. Crusty loved to recall an elderly woman on her first flight, a DC-6 trip from Los Angeles to Las Vegas. She had gone into the Blue Room and emerged quickly to ask a stewardess if she had a safety pin. The girl located one and the old woman returned to the Blue Room where she remained for about fifteen minutes.

When the passenger was back in her seat the stewardess happened to open the Blue Room door, and reported a few seconds later to Captain Callahan that the passenger had used the pin to close the little curtains over the lavatory window. At sixteen thousand feet.

Life in the jet age was still interesting enough, however, as well as more demanding. Dudney joined ALPA as a probationary member, partially to ease Captain Callahan's conscience, and even attended several meetings, thus going beyond what many of the regular members ever did. But somehow she felt out of place at these gatherings —so predominantly male that she might as well have been a Unitarian trying to get along at a convention of priests. It was different on the flight deck where her contact with the male sex was antiseptically professional. It was different, also, in layover socializing when she definitely seemed closer to the stewardesses than the pilots. Once she took off her uniform and donned a dress for dinner, it was as if she had somehow divested herself of her first officer status and was relegated to the position of mere woman. She accepted this as just one more cross to bear in her peculiar middle-ground existence, and she did not even resent it because she was, in actuality, a woman who appreciated the niceties of male courtesy and attention. She might as well have been two persons and this, more than anything else, prevented any closer relationship with the younger captains and copilots. They were never sure which was the real Dudney Devlin: the businesslike, almost coldly efficient first officer, or the rather shy, winsome, affection-starved girl who was embarrassed when she found herself waiting for a captain to light her cigarette. Not being sure, they chose neither. It was the older, more tolerant captains who gave her the most aircraft handling time and—off duty—the warmest companionship and the deeper friendships.

As her experience and logged flight hours grew, she found herself more critical of the captains with whom she flew, the early awe of the fourth stripe dwindling to some extent as her own skills were sharpened and honed. She established no particular correlation between left-seat performance and seniority; by and large, the senior captains were damned good but there were younger ones who matched them. She knew she would rather be with a veteran in a real emergency, yet some of the more junior captains were superb pilots from whom she willingly learned and absorbed.

One of them was Mark Ashlock. She flew with him only once in her first six months and it was a lesson in fourth-stripe responsibility that went beyond flight duties. Ashlock was one of those captains who considered himself a part of the whole airline, not just a member of its flight crews. He was a loyal, very active ALPA member but he gave allegiance equally to Trans-Coastal. Dudney was surprised when he left the flight deck just before leaving the ramp on a Los Angeles–Las Vegas–Denver trip. Through the open cockpit door, she saw him walk down the cabin aisle, chatting with passengers, answering their questions and going so far as to bring a wide-eyed eight-year-old boy back to the cockpit for a few minutes during which he explained some of the controls and instruments.

After the Las Vegas and Denver landings, he stood in back of the stewardesses as they bade good-by to deplaning passengers, nodding his own farewells and stopping the eight-year-old to hand him a pair of junior captain's wings which he solemnly pinned on.

They had a quick turn-around at Denver and she had no chance to talk to him about his above-and-beyond-the-call-of-duty attitude. When she mentioned it to Crusty, he snorted, "Aw, Mark's a nice guy but he's too damned company-minded"—a typical Callahan non-sequitur judgment inasmuch as Dudney considered Crusty's own PAs models of good-humored information, even when occasionally salted with pro-ALPA propaganda. Callahan was like the majority of his brethren—he was violently critical of Trans-Coastal until he met a pilot from a competing airline, thereupon becoming violently protective of Trans-Coastal. Dudney knew a number of captains who were strongly anti-management, which surprised her because the average airline captain was the personification of a conservative capitalist. She asked Jason Silvanius once about this paradox.

"It would take a psychiatrist to figure out what makes pilots tick," Jason mused. "John Battles has a theory that most of them suffer from guilt complexes. That subconsciously they're uneasy about getting paid a hell of a lot of dough for doing relatively little work, so they compensate by exaggerating their problems and being overly belligerent toward management."

"Their 'relatively little work,'" Dudney bristled, "refers to time only. Five or six hours of flying a jet is the equivalent of three days' hard work in some ground job. They need more time off than the average person. I know I do, and I haven't got a captain's responsibilities and worries."

Silvanius smiled at her truculence. "You don't have to sell me on pilots, Dud. For one thing, I've never bought the argument that they're overpaid prima donnas. Prima donnas sometimes, maybe, but not overpaid. An airline captain's like a doctor. People think a senior four-striper's a fat cat, pulling down fifty grand a year for working seventy or eighty hours a month. But they forget how long it took him to climb that ladder—not to mention the training—just as I can't quite begrudge a doctor for trying to make some dough after all the hardships of being an intern and getting a practice started. As for their being anti-management, maybe it's partially management's fault. I never thought we've utilized our pilot force the way it should be used. There's a good collection of brains there . . . a hell of a lot of talent and personality that we stick in the cockpit and forget. Me, I think Battles has something in that theory of his. We make an executive out of a captain every time he steps foot in a plane. We entrust a multimillion-dollar piece of machinery to him and we put the lives of hundreds of passengers into his hands on every flight. We give him the same godlike authority that a shipping company gives a sea captain. In other words, he *is* management to the nth degree. But as soon as he steps out of that plane, management looks on him as nothing but a union member with a chip on his shoulder, and if he opens his mouth to suggest, criticize or advise, his motives are suspect. I suppose this is heresy to my fellow brass hats, but I wish we'd consult with our pilots more. I think that very visible chip they carry around might fall off of its own accord."

"But the night we graduated, Mr. Berlin said Trans-Coastal does listen to its pilots and—"

"I know what Mr. Berlin said. He says it every time he talks to a group of pilots, new or old. And he means it. The trouble is that, president or not, he's still just one man and the days of one-man airlines are over. He doesn't run Trans-Coastal all by himself, like he used to. He has to delegate authority and he puts that authority into the hands of labor relations experts and personnel experts and lawyers and financial geniuses and statistical wizards and even public relations smoothies like me. By and large, they're competent, hardworking guys, but they're not airline, not the way Tom Berlin is. They look at figures, not people, and an airline *is* people. An airline is history and tradition. An airline is corny sentiment. An airline is guts and drive and determination. An airline is achievement the hard way —progress made up of setbacks and shoestring operations and boners and sometimes even death. That's why I respect our captains, Dud— particularly the older ones. They're about the last link we have to the days when an airline was a family, not just a bunch of individuals and groups pulling in opposite directions, everyone out for themselves— and I include management in that, not just the unions. Hell, take our stewardesses. We turn them out of a mold like so many robot dolls. We teach them make-up and service and style and even how to smile. We teach them how to mix drinks and save lives. But I sometimes wonder if we teach them pride. Pride in their industry, in their airline, in their own profession. We're graduating another stew class tomorrow. How many of those kids know what it was like when Trans-Coastal took only three hours to train a cabin attendant—in the back room of an old hangar, using a four-page mimeographed manual? They had to fly a hundred hours a month to make a hundred and twenty-five bucks a month. They worked in airplanes that were ice-boxes in the winter and ovens in the summer and their chances of getting killed on the job were about three hundred times greater than they are today. They had only one thing to give a passenger and that was pride in what they were doing and whom they were working for. They were pros, Dud. We're not turning out many pros today, my young friend—not stewardesses and not even enough pilots. We educate them but we don't motivate them. They memorize a contract as fast as they do their manuals. So do mechanics and baggage handlers and reservation agents. You know why I admire a guy like Crusty Callahan? Because he's a pro. He's an evil-tempered, unreasonable sonofabitch but he's a pro. Put an airplane in his hands and if he doesn't get it down in one piece it's an act of God or somebody else's goof. He's a bastard but he's a dependable, completely honest bastard. He's more loyal to ALPA than he is to Trans-Coastal but somewhere along the line management let that happen and by God I wish I knew how we could get the Crusty Callahans back."

"Maybe," said Dudney, "he hasn't wandered as far away as you think. I've gotten the impression that Captain Callahan and Mr. Berlin have a great deal in common."

"Sure they do. Including mutual distrust of each other's motives. Which explains why we have labor-management troubles. Sorry, Janet. Dudney touched a tender spot. Let's have one more drink and eat. . . ."

Late in November she took her six-month check ride under an FAA inspector who threw everything at her but an actual crash—and at the end of the flight asked her for an autograph.

"I told my ten-year-old daughter this morning I was giving the famous Miss Devlin a check ride," he explained sheepishly. "I guess she has a severe case of heroine worship, if that's what you call it, and she made me promise I'd come back with your autograph." Feeling both embarrassed and flattered, Dudney gave him a slip of paper inscribed "To Marcia Dennis with the best wishes of Dudney Devlin." She wished she could have been more inspiring and original but autographing was a new experience.

The inspector thanked her and also imparted the verdict that it was one of the best check-ride performances he had ever observed—praise that somehow helped her through the holiday season when she had to fly on Thanksgiving, Christmas and New Year's Day. Actually, she was supposed to have Christmas off but Hank Mitchell asked her to fly his trip. She was a pushover for any copilot wanting to trade flights, and her altruism had a beneficial result: crew sked suddenly informed her she was illegal to fly again for ten days, which amounted to an unexpected mid-January vacation. Momentarily she thought about getting a pass and flying up to Alaska but somehow it smacked too much of a college student rushing home for a holiday. Except for the Macklins and one or two others, she had no close friends there. And ten days was sufficient time in which to go where she had always wanted to go—Europe. She was still too provincial, in some ways, to risk a country with a language barrier, so she decided on England at least as a starter. If Britain got too dull, she figured she could always go over to Paris or Rome.

She put in for a reduced-rate fare on a TWA polar flight from Los Angeles to London. As a Trans-Coastal employee, she was entitled to a fifty per cent interline discount and positive space—and the latter came in handy when she boarded. Despite the time of year, the coach section was jammed and TWA assigned her to a first-class seat. She boarded a little late and was climbing over the occupant in aisle seat 4C to get to a window seat 4A when she realized she knew the occupant of 4C.

It was Mark Ashlock.

CHAPTER TEN

The night Barbara died, Mark Ashlock cried for the first time since he was ten years old. But unlike many bereaved, he was crying not for himself, out of self-pity, but for his wife. She had feared death, she had clung pitifully to her ebbing life, and her last words to Mark were burned into his soul and brain forever—an unanswered prayer that seared and branded memory.

"Help me, Mark . . . please help me . . . don't let it happen. . . ."

The final squeeze of a hand so thin it was that of an old woman. The tired, angry, futile look on Dr. Hall Luther's face as he shook his head and murmured, "She's gone, Mark."

Sound. Touch. Sight. Remembering all three with pain that dulled more than it hurt. Remembering her ravaged features, her emaciated body, with ugly sharpness, while the beautiful girl he had married was a vague, indistinct and shadowy dream. Remembering the bitterness toward her murderer, insidious and relentlessly cruel—bitterness he left unspoken because he could not put it into words, but bitterness that exploded volubly from Doc Luther. . . .

". . . I'm sorry, Mark. Bloody sorry. We know so little. We're so damned ignorant, so fucking helpless!"

Somehow, the spontaneous profanity was inoffensive, because it was torn not from the tongue but the heart of a man of medicine infuriated at his own inadequacies.

"You did your best, Hall. I know you did." The mourner comforting the physician.

"You all right?"

"Yes. I guess so."

"I'll take care of what has to be done here tonight. You go on home. I'll meet you there in about an hour. Got any bourbon?"

"A couple of fifths, last time I looked."

"Good. Save one for me."

Much later, he found the captain sitting quietly in the Ashlock apartment, so beautifully decorated that it reminded Luther uncomfortably of the wife who had once shared it. He had known Barbara Ashlock when she was a stewardess and first dating Mark. She had breeding, taste, maturity and a self-assurance remarkable in a girl not yet twenty-three years old.

Mark was holding a framed photograph of Barbara, a picture taken when she was in stewardess uniform. The fifth of bourbon on the end table beside him was a third empty.

"I talked to Battles," the doctor said without preliminaries. "He wants you to take a couple of weeks off, compliments of Trans-Coastal. More if you need it. And I prescribe about four weeks—away from Los Angeles, flying, this apartment and maybe that picture you're clutching like it could bring her back. If you and Barbara had had any kids, they'd be part of the healing process but you're alone and that makes it rougher in some ways."

"No dice, Hall. After the funeral I'm going back to the line. If I loaf, I'll think. And remember. So I'll fly—and maybe it'll cut down the thinking and remembering."

"I could ground you, Mark. You know that. Emotionally unfit."

"But you won't. Because I'm not."

"Aren't you? Right now you may think you're not. You're numb. You're sitting there anaesthetized with grief and shock. And that whiskey is bourbon-flavored novocain. When it all wears off, you won't feel any more like flying an airplane than I do."

"Let's see how I feel when it wears off, then. I promise I won't lie to you. How about a drink?"

The doctor and the pilot finished the rest of the fifth, consumed fifty per cent of the second bottle and talked the rest of the night. Only once did Ashlock crack, but when he did it was a gaping crevice through which the pent-up sorrow poured in a flood of racking sobs. He had made the mistake of looking at the picture once too often. It was a friend and not a physician who could only pat his shoulder with the tenderness of silent understanding.

"It's the picture," Ashlock finally gulped. "It's like looking at a stranger. A ghost I can't recognize. All I can remember is how she looked when she died. God, Hall, she was so afraid. And there wasn't anything I could do."

He took only ten days off. In that time he sold all their furniture and moved into a smaller apartment. He gave away Barbara's clothing, distributed her jewelry among wives of fellow pilots plus a few stewardesses he liked and respected, and kept only the framed photograph and a second possession of hers. The picture was never in sight but hidden in a drawer from which he would occasionally take it when he felt he could look at it without the tears rushing unwelcomed and unwanted to his eyes.

The other item he retained was her stewardess wings.

Eventually, the pain diminished to an ache. He began dating; where some men try to forget through drink, he turned to women. Usually stewardesses, because he had something in common with them and because they understood his moodiness, his forced gaiety. No girl ever expected to fill the void, not even those he bedded, knowing he was grasping for a few hours of forgetfulness. Quite a few hoped to but abandoned any idea of permanence quickly, particularly after giving themselves to this man of quiet sadness. It was after he had made love that he was in his blackest mood, as if in desperation he had taken a powerful medicine to cure a deadly sickness and found it had no effect. He went through the motions of post-sexual assurances of affection and gratitude, despising that cruel male habit of discarding that which has given pleasure, but he didn't fool anyone with this sham of gallantry. Sex with Barbara had been sharing rather than possessing, where the prelude and the aftermath were as delicious as the consummation itself. Now, in the wake of satisfied desire, he had only a residue of renewed emptiness and even guilt, and those he slept with somehow knew it without resenting it.

He would have existed rather than lived had it not been for his job. The responsibilities of a captain were too great for him to use self-pity as an excuse for shirking, and he honestly loved flying. This provided the only real surcease from that gnawing void, that unerasable, imbedded memory of the night of death and its sight, sound and touch. It was John Battles who unwittingly—or perhaps with instinctive wisdom—gave him help from an unexpected source. He called Mark in one day and informed him, almost belligerently, he was to have Trans-Coastal's newest black pilot as a first officer for the Negro's initial flights.

"That's fine with me, John," Ashlock said with sincerity. "What's his name?"

"Hank Mitchell. Good record, good attitude. Sort of a black male version of that Devlin kid. Wants to be an airline pilot more than he wants to be an example of emancipated slavery."

"You seem a bit defensive. I've met Mitchell and I've flown with our blacks before—never had any trouble. You got any particular reason for letting me break this boy in?"

"Not especially. A few of the pilots resent our black brethren and some of the guys just tolerate them. From what I've heard, you're neither. But you've never drawn one for that first twenty-five hours of supervised flying, and it's a damned important twenty-five hours. So I figured you might like to try it. By the way, Mark, when the hell are you gonna let me make you a check captain?"

"Someday. Not right now."

"It's generally a nine-to-five proposition. Most nights free."

"That's exactly what I don't need. If Barbara were alive I'd think about it seriously. Ask me again in about a year."

"I will. Take care of our young Mr. Mitchell."

Ashlock liked the big Negro. He was diffident without a semblance of fawning, nervous but self-possessed. And a damned fine pilot, one who followed orders and worked with the smooth efficiency of a man who knows his job. Mark sensed a certain wariness that was more uncertainty than antagonism. It was not really a chip on the shoulder but rather a kind of cautious pessimism, as if Mitchell were waiting for the other shoe of prejudice to drop. Ashlock felt it strongly enough to bring the matter up on a layover, when they were having a drink in a bar by themselves.

From his pocket the captain took a piece of paper on which he had typed several paragraphs. "Copied something out of a book last night, Hank. Wanted to read it to you."

Mitchell waited curiously.

"Martin [Ashlock read] was perplexed by their first caller. He was a singularly handsome young Negro, quick-moving, intelligent of eye. Like most white Americans, Martin had talked a great deal about the inferiority of Negroes and had learned nothing whatsoever about them. He looked questioning as the young man observed:

" 'My name is Oliver Marchand.'

" 'Yes?'

" 'Dr. Marchand. I have my M.D. from Howard.'

" 'Oh.'

" 'May I venture to welcome you, Doctor? And may I ask before I hurry off—I have three cases from official families isolated at the bottom of the hill—oh yes, in this crisis they permit a Negro doctor to practice even among the whites! But—Dr. Stokes insists that D'Herelle and you are right in calling bacteriophage an organism. But what about Bordet's contention that it's an enzyme?'

"Then for half an hour did Dr. Arrowsmith and Dr. Marchand, forgetting the plague, forgetting the more cruel plague of race-fear, draw diagrams.

"Marchand sighed, 'I must go, Doctor. May I help you in any way I can? It is a great privilege to know you.'

"He saluted quietly and was gone, a beautiful young animal.

" 'I never thought a Negro doctor—I wish people wouldn't keep showing me how much I don't know,' said Martin."

Ashlock looked up. "It's from *Arrowsmith*, by Sinclair Lewis. I've always thought it was one of the finest novels ever written. And I've never forgotten the meaning of the lines I just read to you."

"I know what they mean to me, Captain. I'm wondering if they mean the same to you."

"They sum up my own views on prejudice. That it's as evil and unforgivable and deadly as the cancer that killed my wife two years ago. And that the business we're in, both of us, has something in common with medicine. Arrowsmith forgot the color of Oliver Marchand's skin because they had something binding them together—a desire to cure, to conquer sickness—which was a hell of a lot stronger than Martin Arrowsmith's preconceived ideas of black ignorance and servility. Likewise, Hank, we're bound together by what the wings on our uniform symbolize. Or, for that matter, the stripes on our sleeves. If our positions were reversed, I'd call you sir, or captain, and it would be with the homage and respect—and trust—I expect you to display toward me and every other four-striper. That applies to the captains who are racial or religious bigots. Out of the airplane, they deserve contempt. In the airplane, they warrant every ounce of allegiance you can give them. I'm not asking you to turn the other cheek. I am asking you to regard their professional status the same way you want me to regard yours. Those wings you wear tell me that you're a qualified airline pilot, period. I don't give a damn whether you're white, black, yellow or red; Jew, Christian, Muslim or atheist. I do give a damn that you're a first officer who's gone through the same training as everyone else—and *that,* my friend, governs my attitude toward you every second you're in that right seat with me or any other captain. Off duty, I'll judge you as a man—not a black man, but a fellow human being I may or may not like personally. It happens I like you. I hope the feeling is mutual."

"It's mutual," Mitchell smiled. "I'm curious to know why you felt it necessary to deliver the sermon."

Ashlock smiled back. "Let's just say I had a hunch you weren't sure how I felt about black pilots."

"You're right. I wasn't sure. You seemed okay but I figured it might go about as deep as the sweat on your skin. Too many white people patronize us because these days it's fashionable, not because they really believe in equality. Admitting prejudice is like being publicly in favor of sin."

"Reading that quote from Lewis seemed a good way to make my point."

"It was well made, Captain. I never read *Arrowsmith.* Seems I'll have to get acquainted with Sinclair Lewis."

"You don't have to read everything he wrote. *Arrowsmith, Main Street, Babbitt*—maybe *Dodsworth* and *Elmer Gantry.* They were his best. By the way, Hank, I'm about to exercise one of the prerogatives of the fourth stripe. I wish you'd start calling me Mark."

Mitchell nodded. "I've got a favor to ask you—Mark. You know Captain Simms?"

"Yes. The first one of you Trans-Coastal blacks to make captain. Very fine person. What's your—"

"He got me interested in going to the Watts area once a week.

Talking to some of the underprivileged black kids. He's been doing it for years—wears his uniform and gives them a little speech about not quitting school and maybe making it like he did. About not thinking that every white owes every black a living as reparation for past sins."

"So what's the favor?"

"I'd like you to go with me one of these nights."

"I think I'd like to. But I can't see what good a white pilot would do. Might even do some harm."

"Not if you tell those kids the same thing you just told me. Your ideas on prejudice. About how you look at the uniform and not the color of the pilot's skin."

Ashlock smiled wryly. "They'd probably also ask me if all white airline pilots share my enlightened philosophy. And I'd have to tell them no."

"Tell me something. Are there any pilots on Trans-Coastal who'd refuse to fly with a black?"

The captain thought that one over carefully before replying. "No, I don't think there are. I can think of a couple who'd resent you. Who might give you a rough time—until you proved you were as good as any white copilot. Most of them, Hank, just take some educating. I'll never forget our first Negro stew. One day she flew with a captain who was a native Southerner—a guy so biased he thought Abraham Lincoln was a communist. The other stews warned this black kid not to go into the cockpit but she told them politely to go to hell. The first time this captain rang for coffee, she insisted on taking it up. She opened the door, beamed at the bigoted old bastard and said, 'Good mornin', gentlemen—coffee, tea or watermelon?' So help me, the captain starts to glare, sees the copilot and flight engineer trying not to laugh, and he busts out laughing himself. He hasn't completely reformed but at least he treats our Negro stews with respect."

"I repeat, Mark, that's what I'd like you to tell those kids. That even racists can be made to accept blacks who prove themselves. You might even use Dudney Devlin as another analogy. She had the same prejudice mountain to climb as I did, maybe even a bigger mountain. I'll bet there are pilots who'd fly with me before they'd fly with her."

"Yeah," Ashlock agreed thoughtfully. "I met that Devlin girl in Operations yesterday. She had quite a run-in with her first captain."

He told Mitchell about Dudney's chewing out Callahan, and Hank in turn told him about the girl's training obstacles. It was four months later that Mark flew with her for the first and only time before deciding to visit London on a seven-day leave. Like Dudney, he had earned some extra time off by flying holidays either through deliberate bidding or trip-trading, because he knew that pilots with families hated to fly on such occasions as Christmas. It was his fourth trip to Britain; he loved the country and its people—"I think in some ways they're more civilized than we are," he told Hank Mitchell one night while they were returning from Watts. Captain Ashlock, it developed, had been a huge success with the black youngsters. He had that rare faculty of projecting sincerity—and he also possessed a more practical asset in the form of four season tickets to the Rams' football games. He and/or Hank took two or three Negro kids with them to every home game on Sunday when they didn't have to fly.

His association with the black first officer was not only rewarding but of immense aid in the forgetting process because he kept his off-duty hours fuller. Somehow, working with Hank in the ghetto gave him the feeling he was sanctifying Barbara's memory—doing something worthwhile, instead of sullying it with a succession of shallow affairs. Mark Ashlock was a most normal, healthy and virile male, however, and he was looking forward to a brief stay in London, which was an oasis for lonely males. He needed a change in scenery and people, if only to be with women who did not know of his loss and would not be pitying while they were being passionate.

He was mildly glad to see Dudney on the same plane, mostly because he welcomed companionship on the long polar flight. He had no idea of asking her to share his vacation and, in fact, for the first few hours he worried whether she might prove to be a liability. He gravely pondered the composition of a polite excuse if she expressed a desire to "tag along," as he figured she might phrase it. He decided he would invent some close friends with whom he'd be staying, if the problem came up. And he fully expected it would. Their initial conversation, naturally, dwelled on why they were going to England

—Dudney telling the truth about never having been there, and Mark being cautiously vague and noncommittal.

They talked about flying for the first hour and about themselves for the next two hours, each discovering that the other was easy to talk to. The big surprise for Ashlock was that he suddenly found himself telling Dudney about Barbara, something he had ducked since his wife's death because it hurt too much. He liked the way she was sympathetic without being maudlin, interested without being coy. Halfway to London, he impulsively asked her what he deliberately had been avoiding.

"Dud, where are you staying in London?"

"I don't know," she answered. "There wasn't time to make any advance reservations. At this time of the year, I figured I could call some hotel from the airport and get a room without much trouble. Del Fitzgerald gave me the names of a couple of places. She said they were reasonable and pleasant even if they weren't fancy."

A lot of women, Mark thought, would have asked him where *he* was staying with at least two ulterior motives—maybe a free meal or two, or even an offer to get them a room at his hotel. She not only didn't ask but seemed to change the subject intentionally as if she were trying not to put him on any spot. "I was over at Hank and Judy Mitchell's the other night—he thinks a lot of you."

"Vice versa," Ashlock said, pleased. "And I gather from a few of your classmates, Hank included, that you're quite a person."

"If it hadn't been for some of them," she said soberly, "I might never have made it through training. Who's flown with you?"

"Mitchell, mostly. Had a couple of trips with Ernie Crum and Bob Tarkington. Let's see, I think I flew once with a tall boy named Webster. Wasn't he in your class?"

"He was," she said, smiling to herself as she recalled her earlier opinion of Frank but refraining from asking Ashlock what he thought. "There was McCrae, Worthington, Dixie Miller—ever fly with him? I was closer to Dixie than anyone else in the class."

"Nope." Ashlock chuckled in recollection. "But I heard what happened the time he goofed with Crusty."

"Poor Dixie. It wasn't really his fault. He had just found out he was going to be a father. Crusty wasn't as mad at him as Dixie thought."

"Crusty seldom is. I've also heard you're getting along fine with him."

"Once you get to know Captain Callahan," she said seriously, "he does an extremely poor job of hiding the fact that he is a very great man."

"Heart of gold underneath a gruff exterior—he really makes that cliché come alive."

"That's what I've learned about the airline business," Dudney observed. "If you ever tried to put airline people into a book, they'd come out rather stereotyped—Crusty, for example. But the funny thing is that there really are a lot of pilots like him. Characters you couldn't believe until you get to know them. Mr. Berlin's a stereotype too."

Ashlock nodded. "Quite a guy, Berlin. He cut his teeth on the old Douglas M-2 mail plane and he used to fly Ford trimotors between L.A. and Denver—our first passenger route. I've heard him tell about the days when pilots were paid by the weight of the mail they carried, and Berlin had to stuff bricks at the bottom of the sack if he needed extra dough. Do you know that when he was flying for Trans-Coastal he and the other pilots threatened to strike when the company announced it was hiring female cabin attendants?"

"History," Dudney said grinning, "almost repeated itself. I guess Crusty was ready to lead a strike over me."

Mentioning Callahan prompted Mark to recount the loan incident, which led Dudney to volunteer a few of her own experiences with the irascible little captain—such as the time he bawled out a stewardess for stirring his coffee with a pencil. "It's —— unsanitary," Crusty had scolded in his usual subdued tones, i.e., in a bellow approximating a short-tempered bull. "I never again want to see those —— pencil marks at the bottom of a cup!"

She had brought him a second cup with suspicious politeness and a seeming lack of resentment. Crusty drained it and startled Dudney with another blast of fiery invectives, handing her the empty cup for inspection with the injured air of a man displaying proof that his wife had cheated. At the bottom of the plastic cup, was a very legible penciled message:

GO TO HELL

They exchanged airline stories for another hour, forgoing the movie in favor of sitting in the forward lounge where they could talk without disturbing other passengers. They also indulged in that favorite game of airline personnel riding a competing carrier—namely, criticizing the service while knowing perfectly well it was just as good as the service on their own airline.

"We're being hypocrites, you know," Ashlock chuckled, immediately after agreeing fervently with Dudney that TWA's hostesses were inefficient shrews compared to Trans-Coastal's gracious, far harder-working cabin attendants. "There's nothing really wrong with this service or the gals. I guess the most hypercritical passenger in the world is an airline employee."

"I'm even a back-seat driver," Dudney confessed. "I could swear whoever made the takeoff rotated too soon."

"You've just stumbled on one of aviation's aphorisms. Pilots make lousy passengers. They're more nervous than old women."

"Because they feel out of it," Dudney guessed.

"Like a football player watching a game from the stands. He swears everybody must be doing everything wrong."

Their conversation was natural, spontaneous, alternately light-hearted and serious. When the movie was over, fatigue and the accumulative effects of the first-class liquor service overcame Dudney. She reclined her seat and napped while Ashlock watched her. My first officer, he mused—one of the best young pilots with whom he had ever flown and right now she looked like a helpless, trusting little girl, long eyelashes forming a demure awning over the lids. He could not resist touching, ever so gently, her tousled brown hair and was surprised to find it as soft as fine silk. She sighed in her sleep and turned toward him, curling her long, shapely legs into the seat. Ashlock got a pillow down from the overhead rack and slipped it under her head—she was so sound asleep by now that it was like lifting an inanimate object. She wasn't beautiful, Mark Ashlock thought. She wasn't even really pretty—not if you itemized her features individually.

Nose too small, mouth too wide, hair too short, figure too slim. He wasn't sure about the figure, however. Some slender women were deceptive, so firmly proportioned they appeared to be flatter-chested than they actually were. She could be one of these—he had never seen her in anything other than her uniform until now, and the black suit she was wearing was cut so severely it merely accentuated her slimness. There was something sexy about her, though. That low, perfectly modulated voice. Her infectious little laugh, just a degree away from being a giggle. Her unaffected enthusiasm about anyone or anything aeronautical, from people to airplanes. Those superb legs. He theorized that she was the kind of woman who could be a colleague in the cockpit, a warm, affectionate companion in private, a lady in public, and—he suspected—an uninhibited harlot in a bedroom.

Why the hell was he indulging in this cataloguing, this analyzing? Dudney couldn't compare in pulchritude to Linda Littell, an English actress he figured on seeing when he got to London. A swinger, that Linda, according to a fellow Trans-Coastal pilot who had given him her phone number and shown him her picture. A knockout with long black hair and a forty-inch bust. And if she was busy, available girls in London were as plentiful as cars on a freeway at rush hour. Yet here he was feeling strangely, almost frighteningly close to this pug-nosed female pilot whose link to him was more professional than personal. There was something about her that reminded him of Barbara. God knows, not in looks. Barbara had been rather tiny, almost dainty and fragile, with perfectly chiseled features. They must have something in common to make him think about Barbara, but it was so elusive he could not put it into words; in fact, he could not even explain it. Maybe, he decided, the similarity was within himself rather than Dudney—his need for affection and companionship, his appreciation of mutual interests and intelligent communication, all of which he had derived from Barbara and all of which, in the space of a few hours, he had instinctively sought from Dudney. Her response must have been the blurred mirror image, the intangible parallelism. While the specifics of this chemistry still eluded him, he definitely was aware of its effects. He knew he did not want to say good-by to her when they landed. He was pushed by an urgency to share, to give. That it was not a sexual urge surprised him; the intensity of wanting to spend his vacation with her was in direct conflict with his motives for taking the trip. It was disturbing to realize that just being with her was preferable to the casual, no-strings assignations he had planned and anticipated.

She finally awoke and stretched, like a lean, tawny cat, contentedly drowsy but refreshed.

"Hi. I feel better."

"Good. Feel wide awake enough to discuss something?"

She sat up, rubbed her eyes and grinned at him. "Cleared for discussion, Captain."

"I'm staying at the London Hilton. Suppose I get you a room there, and then show you the town."

She shook her head. "The last part's great. But the London Hilton sounds too expensive. Why don't I make like a bargain hunter and call you at the Hilton when I've located a room?"

"Got your Trans-Coastal I.D. with you?" She nodded. "Well then, no trouble. I know the manager at the Hilton and he'll give you an airline rate—shouldn't be much more than what you'd pay at a smaller hotel. And you'll like the Hilton. It combines all the best features of American luxury and British atmosphere—maybe a little more of the former than the latter, but it's a damned fine hotel."

She was doubtful, not a little curious about the motives (if there were motives) behind his invitation, and yet wavering toward acceptance because, like virtually every American going abroad for the first time, she was apprehensive. To the normal fears of a rookie tourist was added the worst: the prospect of loneliness and boredom. Captain Ashlock represented an antidote, being not only male but an experienced visitor to England. She could not quite conquer her cynicism—the notion that he was being nice to her because out of gratitude she might become a companion by night as well as day.

"Let me think about it awhile," she said, but she could not keep the cynicism, the doubts, the wariness, out of her voice and Ashlock smiled.

"No strings, Dudney," he assured her. "But think about it and meanwhile I'll get some shut-eye."

This time it was the girl who studied the man as he slept and her thoughts moved down the same track he had followed, a path of introspection that sought to explain the attraction she felt. Certainly it was not entirely physical, for he had no imposing, soul-stirring male beauty. She did like his mouth—thin, strong lips over a square jaw —and his eyes. They still had that film of regret clouding them even when he smiled, as if the muscles that created a smile had somehow been disconnected from those that moved the eyes. Obviously his company was welcome—a breath of familiarity in the metal tube hurtling her toward a strange country. And she could not remember when she had enjoyed talking to anyone more. He had the knack of being informal without being condescending, amusing without trying to strain for an effect, impressive without any conscious effort to impress. She had been moved by his recollections of his wife and their marriage. His frankness had been a bid for mature understanding, not mawkish sympathy, and perhaps even a form of self-therapy. A trifle reluctant at first, he had opened up so verbosely that she had the idea he had not talked about his wife for a long time.

She wondered why he had suggested the London Hilton, knowing that it was tantamount to inviting a shared holiday. He had even mentioned showing her the town, which was a pretty good indication he was not going to dump her at their hotel and go about his own business. For that matter, what was his "own business"? He had been purposefully vague about his own trip and he did not seem like the type of unattached male who would go to London strictly for sightseeing purposes. Now she remembered what Crusty had said—about Mark Ashlock having been a faithful husband but something of a social playboy after his wife died. Looking for Barbara's twin, Crusty had added. She found it hard to believe Ashlock's interest in her was in the nature of wife-hunting. Maybe he was just lonely and preferred the company of someone he knew rather than women he would have to meet and court before attempting seduction. Yet he had just emphasized, no strings, and she believed him. On the single occasion she had been his copilot, he had impressed her with his thoughtfulness, his responsible approach to his job. He did not seem to be the seducing type—or perhaps that was his way of seducing. A formidable technique, she had to admit, and if true, a threat to her resolve, her instinctive repulse of any involvement with fellow pilots. She wanted badly to be with him in London, but not if it meant a meaningless affair of which he might brag to captains with whom she would be flying. On the other hand, it was entirely possible he merely was being decent and kind.

She closed her eyes and fell asleep again, undecided. It was a hostess who awoke them both. "We'll be serving breakfast before we land—in about ninety minutes."

"I'm going to freshen up," Dudney announced—grabbing at a chance to do some thinking in solitude. When she returned from the Blue Room she wasted no time in the usual man vs. woman sparring.

"Why do you want me to stay at the Hilton, Mark?" she asked. "It sounds like you wouldn't mind our spending this vacation together. Which is fine with me, except I want to be fair with you. I wouldn't blame you if you wanted some hanky-panky—I'd figure there was something wrong with me if you didn't—but I don't want you to expect any. If you're figuring on a sure thing, get yourself another girl and no hard feelings. And I mean it, Mark. If I were a man, I'd probably prefer a Miss Round-Heels to a Miss Treat-Me-Nice-But-No-Sex."

"Quite a speech," Ashlock said. "Wasn't there a question at the start of it?"

"There was. Why?"

"I'll be damned if I know, Dudney. And that's the only honest answer I can give you. I had intended to shack up, if possible, with a different girl every night I'm in London. I have no expectation of shacking up with you. Not that I wouldn't want to, but right now I just feel as if showing you a good time would be a hell of a lot more fun than casual sex. Maybe I need companionship more than I need sex—I don't know. I do know that I've enjoyed this flight because of you. That I've felt relaxed for the first time in two years. And that I don't want it to end—which is why, I guess, I promised no strings. And meant it."

"Offer accepted, Captain Ashlock. What are we going to do in London?"

"The usual sightseeing bit. Tower of London, Madame Tussaud's, Windsor Castle, Hampton Court, Westminster. We don't have the time to see everything worth seeing but we'll hit the high spots. We'll do some shopping on Regent Street, take in a couple of plays—the

British theater is good. And if you've been told that British cooking is lousy, forget it. There are some restaurants in London that compare with any in New York. For that matter, we don't have to leave the hotel to eat; the Hilton has three good places."

For once, Dudney's anticipation did not surpass the actual event. She fell in love with London and England, from the time they deplaned and Mark called the Hilton for her room, which proved to be luxurious without being ostentatious. They started out as soon as she unpacked and for the next three hours she shuddered at the clammy atmosphere of the Tower, marveled at the realism of the Tussaud wax figures and stood in awe at the magnificence of Westminster Abbey. They prowled up and down Regent and Oxford streets window-shopping, had tea in a quaint little restaurant on a side street that was right out of Dickens, introduced Dudney to London taxicabs—"the best in the world," Ashlock assured her—and stopped in a pub for a late afternoon drink.

They ate at the hotel, discussing the day's activities like two children recalling every scene of an exciting movie they had just seen.

"I think I could ride in those taxicabs forever," she enthused. "The drivers are so polite. What are they, Mark?"

"The drivers?"

"No, the funny little black cabs."

"Austins. They haven't changed the body style for years. I swear I'd love to own one. But I'm glad you flipped for London taxis. They're reasonable and I've never known a driver to cheat someone who didn't understand the British monetary system. If you tell them to take out a fair tip, that's all they will take—a fair amount. What would you like to do tomorrow?"

"Gosh, you're the tour guide. I would like to do some shopping if there's time."

"First thing in the morning. Then I thought we might take a bus trip out to Windsor Castle and Hampton Court. We'd be back in time for dinner and the theater. Sound okay?"

"Sounds great." She beamed at him, in lieu of kissing him publicly and not exactly platonically, and then worried momentarily over the impulse. She did not have time to think about it the rest of the evening. Ashlock took her to the Playboy Club a block from the Hilton, where she gambled a little and suffered the ignominy of feeling abnormally flat-chested amid the busty Bunnies. They had a nightcap at the hotel before Mark accompanied her to her room—one floor above his—and kissed her good night chastely on her cheek. She fell asleep the second her head hit the pillow.

They went shopping as soon as the stores opened at nine-thirty, Dudney picking out small gifts for Jason and Janet Silvanius, Dixie and Norma Jean, and the Mitchells. She also bought Captain Callahan a cashmere sweater and his wife a bone-china cake dish with matching bone-handled knife.

"Crusty will kill you," Ashlock warned. "I doubt whether anyone except his wife has given him a gift in the last ten years. And thanking you will be like passing a kidney stone."

"He'll say thanks," Dudney predicted placidly, "by going into an absolute tantrum. He'll call me an apple-polishing, brown-nosing bitch and he'll swear he wouldn't be caught dead wearing a sweater which doesn't fit him and whose color he hates. Then the next time I fly with him, he'll be wearing it under his uniform—complaining that Fat Albert's cockpit is too cold."

Mark wanted to visit Hamley's, a big toy store, so he could look for any new commercial airliner model kits. "Sort of a hobby," he explained. "I've been making them for years. Got about a hundred of them. Hamley's usually has two or three new ones every time I come over here."

"Is that all you're going to shop for?" Dudney asked. "You said you liked that sweater I got Crusty. Why don't you buy yourself one?"

"Too much bother. I'll pick up a new pipe before we leave. The English make great pipes. Let's go to Hamley's, Dud."

"I want to browse around a little more. Suppose I meet you in the toy store in about a half hour."

He gave her directions to Hamley's. After he left, she waited a few minutes and then walked down Regent until she found a pipe store where a bluff, tweedy salesman lectured her on the proper methods of selecting a pipe for a man.

"It has to fit his face, miss. Is your gentleman friend tall or short?"

"Medium," Dudney said.

"Does he have a full face—rather broad—or is it long, like mine?"

"Uh, medium, I guess," she said uncertainly.

"I see. Well, let me suggest this apple shape. Very popular. It fits almost any face. This Dunhill, for example—extremely light, beautiful grain, and yet a large enough bowl to satisfy him if he prefers a bigger pipe."

She bought the Dunhill, stuffing it in her handbag and walking briskly through the cold to Hamley's where she found Mark engrossed in an electric train display. He had picked up model kits of an Irish Airlines 707 and a BOAC 747 which he showed her with the enthusiasm of a philatelist who has just located and purchased two rare stamps.

"Best 747 kit I've seen," he chortled, "and I don't have any Irish Airlines aircraft. Say, look at these trains, Dud. Beautiful detail, isn't it? These passenger cars—you can see the little chairs. If I ever get a house, I'm gonna go in for this small-gauge stuff." His boyishness made her want to hug him. "You finished your shopping, Dud?"

"All finished. Were you going to look for a pipe before we catch the bus to Windsor?"

He consulted his wristwatch. "We've got about an hour before the bus leaves. I think there's a pipe shop around here somewhere. If you don't mind the expedition."

"Let's get some hot tea instead. Unless you want to exchange this." She opened her pocketbook and handed him the Dunhill. He looked disbelieving, then fondled the pipe expertly, first testing its weight in his hand and next getting the feel of it in his mouth. He was grateful but embarrassed.

"It's a beautiful pipe, Dud. Exactly what I would have picked out myself. But it wasn't necessary."

"I thought it was," she told him. As will most women pleased at the reception given a surprise gift, she recounted her dialogue with the salesman while they sipped hot tea. Before noon they were on a bus for Windsor, speculating in whispers about their fellow passengers, who seemed to be a typical cross-section of tourism. A young oriental couple—the man with a camera, at which Mark kept sneaking admiring glances—sat directly in front of them. Behind them were two middle-aged American women loudly discussing their low opinions of British traditions, customs, cooking, plumbing, beer, lack of ice in drinks, speech and the length of skirts on young women. Dudney took it as long as she could and then began loudly discussing her highly favorable opinion of British traditions, customs, cooking, plumbing, beer, lack of ice in drinks, speech and the length of skirts on young women. Captain Ashlock thought it was funny, although he squirmed a little.

Apparently she ignited a small war. The thick fumes of cigar smoke coiled slowly around her nose and she hated cigars.

"Somebody's smoking rubber," she complained to Mark, and the captain turned around in his seat to remonstrate mildly with whatever man was offending. He turned back to Dudney, chuckling.

"It's one of those women," he whispered.

"So tell her to put the damned thing out."

"I would if it was a man," he apologized. "But I'm a Caspar Milquetoast when it comes to raising an issue with a female."

"Light your pipe, then," she suggested. "If you're too chicken to open your mouth, you can at least counterattack." Ashlock complied, sending billowy puffs of fragrant but heavy pipe tobacco toward the rear. They heard an angry "Well!" from their opponents, followed by the opening of a window which blew cold air on Dudney's neck.

"Want to try an armistice?" Mark murmured.

"Let's just retreat," Dudney sighed. "We'll change seats."

She salvaged the satisfaction of glaring at the two women as they moved to different seats. But the incident was forgotten under the spell of Windsor itself—walking through the castle gates into a huge courtyard was like stepping out of a time machine and finding oneself in medieval England. Dudney had the same reaction when they reached Hampton Court—Henry VIII's country home—and wandered through the immense gardens, the long corridors lined with portraits of royalty dead for centuries, the faded but still beautiful tapestries, the glittering chandeliers and the period furniture so well preserved that she expected the castle's inhabitants to emerge any second and begin using it.

This was what she loved best about England—its pride in and respect for ancestral history without worshiping it blindly. She also liked every Britisher she met—even the rather haughty doormen at the Hilton, because they gave her the impression they turned their snootiness off and on depending on the attitude of the guest. She had heard the English were cold, but she found them exactly the opposite—warm, friendly and surprisingly happy considering the general economic state of the country. She remarked about this to Ashlock on the way back from Hampton Court.

"I think they're probably the bravest people in the world," Mark said. "I wonder sometimes if Americans could take the beatings Britain has—blitz, never ending austerity, murderous taxes, comparatively few luxuries, too many politicians as stupid as the ones we've got at home, a generally miserable climate, a shortage of everything from land to food to raw materials. Yet with all this they maintain a kind of dignity that seldom gets pompous. They have that wonderful dry sense of humor, they're rugged individualists and they're intensely democratic even while they're paying homage to their monarchy, which is quite a trick. They can be arrogant, stubborn, overbearing and self-righteous, but they're magnificently proud, sentimental and courageous."

"Crusty once told me Trans-Coastal should hire nothing but Britishers because they're so cool when everything gets hot."

"Crusty's stretching things a bit as only Crusty will—but in a sense he's right. I'd never have any qualms about flying with BOAC or BEA pilots, for example. They're as good as there are in the industry. Anyway, I'm glad you like the British because I've got a suggestion. If you buy it, fine. If you don't—you're making a mistake."

"That's a very objective way to make a suggestion," she laughed. "Okay, I'll buy it. What is it?"

"You say you like England and its people. Actually, all you've seen is London and its people. There's a little town only two hours away by train. Place called Broadway. It has an inn that's about four hundred years old, the Lyndon Arms. I've stayed there before and I've got a hunch you'll love it as much as I do."

She did. They stayed only one more night in London, taking in a British musical and leaving for Broadway by train the next morning —a supposedly prosaic mode of travel but one which excited Dudney, who had never been on a train in her life. Mark was amused at her reaction—she was as wide-eyed as a child when they boarded their first-class compartment, surprised at its bright, cheerful cleanliness and air of privacy, and totally enthralled at the trip itself. She commented on the presence of at least a small garden in the back yard of virtually every home they passed, sat transfixed at the beauty of the English countryside and was awe-struck when a steward brought sandwiches and drinks to their compartment.

"I didn't know trains were like this," she marveled. "When you said we were going by train, I had visions of a slum on wheels."

"That's the average American train. Trains are a way of life in Europe. We'll rent a car and driver in Broadway, though. I'd like to go back to London by way of Portsmouth—take a look at H.M.S. *Victory*, Nelson's flagship. And there's no direct train service from Broadway to Portsmouth."

"Model planes, model trains and now ships? You have a wide variety of interests, Captain Ashlock."

"Not just ships. The old galleons and frigates—the days of wooden ships and iron men, as they say. Ever read any of Sabatini's Captain Blood stories? Or Forester's Horatio Hornblower series?" She shook her head. "I've devoured every Hornblower book ever printed—not once but three or four times. Yet in all the times I've been to England, I've never seen the *Victory*. Always wanted to but Barbara was a nut on castles, English ghosts and antiques. So we never got down to Portsmouth."

"You and your wife have been here?" She shouldn't have been surprised but somehow she was. It was just that he did not seem the kind of man who would torture himself by revisiting scenes of potentially painful nostalgia.

"Once," Mark said, and his jaw muscles tightened inadvertently. "On our honeymoon."

She felt chilled, disturbed, even disappointed. She did not want to ask the next question but she had to. "This inn we're going to in the little village—did you stay there with with your wife?"

He nodded, looked directly into her troubled eyes and took both her hands in his. "That bothers you, Dud, doesn't it?"

"A little. I didn't figure you for the masochist type. What are you trying to prove, Mark? That you can stand torture? Or maybe you'd like to relive your honeymoon and I'm supposed to play the part of your wife."

"Knock it off, Dud." His voice was hard and stern, the first time he had ever raised it to her. Only the ever present glaze of hurt in his eyes diluted his anger, and those gray eyes now burned into her own, holding her as if he had impaled her on a spear. "I told you there were no strings. That still goes. You asked me a question that deserves an answer. The only trouble is that I don't have any answer. So help me God, Dud, I don't know why I wanted to take you to Broadway any more than I could explain why I asked you to be with me on this little vacation. I suggested the Lyndon Arms on impulse. I love that little inn and always will. I instinctively thought you'd love it too. That's about the only answer I can give you."

She was mollified, but only partially. "If I had known you took Barbara to England on your honeymoon, I don't think I would have been so willing to be with you."

"Does the fact that Barbara's dead mean I've been banned from every place we enjoyed together? I'm never to go back—with you or anyone else?"

"No," she answered in a low voice, "but I don't relish competing with a lot of memories. Maybe that's being selfish."

"It's being logical and very normal, Dud. But it's not being entirely fair either to me or yourself. You're not competing with memories. You're helping me save the ones I want to save and get rid of the ones that make me sad and bitter and even angry that someone like Barbara had to die before she was ready to die. Let me put it this way: if I hadn't met you on that plane, if I hadn't had fun with you in London, I wouldn't have come within a thousand miles of Broadway and the Lyndon Arms. Yes, I love that little town and that wonderful old inn—but I couldn't have faced them alone, with just memories to keep me company. I think I can face them now. Am I making sense?"

He still was holding her hands, and this time she squeezed his. "For a guy who didn't know how to answer why, you just gave me a pretty good why. Except I've got one more question before we drop the subject. What did you tell the inn when you made the reservations?"

"Tell them?"

"I mean about . . . about who you were bringing. Did they remember you and your wife? Did they . . . oh hell, Mark, I just don't want to blush when I sign the register."

He smiled. "They remembered me—and Barbara. I told them she had passed away two years ago. I also told them I was coming up with a good friend who worked for my airline, and that we needed separate rooms. You got any other questions?"

"Yes. Can we order another scotch?"

A car from the Lyndon Arms met them at Moreton-in-Marsh, the closest station to Broadway, which had no rail service. The driver, much to Dudney's surprise, was a comely English girl who either really did remember Mark or had been nicely briefed by the inn's management.

"Captain Ashlock," she said in that pleasant lilt of a British accent, "so nice to see you again. You may not remember me—I'm Valerie Ross, Ken's wife."

"I certainly do remember you, Valerie. And I'm looking forward to seeing Ken again. May I present Miss Dudney Devlin, a good friend and a colleague of mine on our airline, Valerie. One of our pilots, as a matter of fact." He continued, as the women shook hands and liked each other on sight. "Ken Ross, Dud, runs the local car rental agency in Broadway. He was very kind to Barbara and me when we were here."

"I was sorry to hear about your wife, Captain Ashlock," Valerie Ross said. Neatly, diplomatically and skillfully, she put Dudney at ease by turning to her in open admiration. "You're really an airline pilot? How exciting! You must be quite a celebrity in the States. I hope I get a chance to hear all about it while you're at the Lyndon Arms."

No snide, sniggling looks, Dudney thought. No half-disdainful raising of moralistic eyebrows. No sham of politeness so blatantly phony that she might as well have asked if Dudney and Mark were sharing the same room. She warmed to the British girl, and simultaneously realized that she hadn't even thought about her job until Valerie Ross expressed interest and, in fact, hadn't been thinking about it since landing in England. Captain Ashlock, you've achieved something of a miracle, she said to herself. You've made me feel like a woman without ever dropping me a level or two in status.

Even on a gray January day, the countryside was beautiful. Dudney's initial glimpse of Broadway was one of incredulity—she could not decide whether it reminded her of a toy village or an elaborate, carefully authenticated movie set. This was the heart of the Cotswold country, virtually every house built in that style of stone architecture combining antiquity with graceful permanence. What she had already seen from the train windows, from the car on the drive to Broadway, and now in the village itself, was a picturesque quaintness that somehow managed to give the equal impression of solid strength, of a people who had sifted traditions and customs through the strainer of modern needs and retained only that which was beautiful and inspiring and proud.

The Lyndon Arms fitted into the picture like the last piece of a jigsaw puzzle. Unimposing from the outside—it actually resembled an oversized pub—it was magnificent inside, the smoky fragrance of its fireplaces blending perfectly with the huge beamed ceilings. The inn *was* old, but it was a dowager kind of age, a place that had grown old gracefully like a lovely woman gradually metamorphosing into a stern but beloved matriarch, her beauty preserved by serenity.

Wisely, Mark had spurned the newer section of the inn and had chosen quarters in the much older, original main building. When the porter deposited Dudney's suitcase in her room, she almost clapped her hands in sheer childish glee at the enormous four-poster bed with its thick, heavy quilt. On the dresser was a glass of freshly poured sherry and a little card welcoming her to the inn. She had never particularly liked sherry, but this she sipped with relish, savoring its sweet, nutty flavor. She could not wait to unpack, dashing down the corridor to Mark's room and coaxing him to inspect the village immediately.

They peeked into china shops, tiny art galleries and antique dealers. They walked through the immense garden grounds of the Lyndon Arms, denuded of flowers but silently promising beauty in the future. They had tea and tasty, delicate sandwiches in an exquisite little establishment that was a combined gift shop and restaurant. They hiked to the outskirts of the village, responding to the friendly nods of every inhabitant who passed them. It was a two-hour expedition that exhausted Dudney, but she had bought numerous postcards and insisted on addressing and mailing them before Ashlock convinced her she could use a brief nap.

She dressed carefully for dinner, bringing out a dress she had bought just before leaving Los Angeles—a plain white shift with a smart black cape lined in white. Both the color and the lines set off her slim figure and she relished the startled look in Mark's eyes when he met her in the lobby.

"Captain to copilot," he said admiringly. "You're a damned pretty copilot."

"Compliment acknowledged," she laughed. "Request permission to have a quiet cocktail before dinner."

"Cleared for cocktails."

They had their pre-dinner drinks in the inn's lounge. Dudney, over a rare martini (she usually spurned them because she knew she couldn't handle more than two), industriously fished out the olive, munched it with a satisfying "Mmmm," and informed Ashlock, "I've got a question."

He grinned. "A question from you, First Officer Devlin, is an itch in a place you can't scratch. What's your question?"

"You may not like it."

"Ask it anyway. I'm broad-minded."

"We've had fun today."

"Yes, we have. I know I have. But you just gave me a fact, not a question."

"I'm stalling. Now I'm afraid to ask."

He was still smiling. "Now you've given me the itch, Dud."

"Okay." She felt as if she should take a deep breath first. "I . . . I was wondering if you thought about Barbara today."

His grin disappeared. She flushed and miserably wished she had never asked. But his answer was neither angry nor sad, but instead curiously detached, delivered in the same calm tone he would have used if she had asked him about a technical problem.

"Yes, I thought of her. Several times. Many times, in fact." His gentleness was more of a rebuke than if he had snapped at her.

"I'm sorry, Mark," Dudney said softly. "It's none of my business. I apologize for asking and I'll promise I won't bring it up again."

"Don't apologize. You have a way of being frank without being brutal. You say what's on your mind. Now I'll say what's on mine. I said I've had fun. I have. I said I've thought of Barbara and I have. The distance between those two remarks is two years of lonely hell. Up until now, I couldn't have covered that distance. I couldn't have had both simultaneously—memories *and* fun."

"Mark, I didn't—"

"Let me finish. Yes, I've been thinking of my wife. I think there's a vast difference between sadness and poignancy, and 'poignant' describes my thoughts, not 'sad.' I've been thinking of Barbara warmly and affectionately. I've had a rebirth of the great love I had for her. But not in any way that excluded you, Dud. You were part of those thoughts. Sometimes the things you said, the reaction you had to something you saw or enjoyed—it was like hearing them from Barbara all over again."

He paused, but something told Dudney not to interrupt.

"I guess it's time to tell you something about the memories I've had. They haven't been pleasant. I haven't been able to remember the girl I loved and married. All I've ever remembered is the frightened, sick caricature of a woman who pleaded with me to do the one thing I couldn't do—keep her from dying. Until today. Today I remembered my wife, not a sobbing, helpless child. Today, for the first time in two years, I had happy memories." He scrutinized Dudney and at this moment she realized the glaze of sadness no longer filmed his eyes; it was replaced by tenderness. "For this I've got you to thank, Dudney, and for this I am beholden to you."

Tears sprang to her eyes. "I'm a stupid, thoughtless bitch," she blurted. "I've been resentful of a ghost when I should have been helping you."

"You did help me, Dud. You sort of exorcised the ghost. Finish your drink, Copilot. I'm hungry."

They ate in the main dining hall of the Lyndon Arms. A handsome room that was a scaled-down replica of the great baronial dining halls she had seen in pictures of English castles. Service and cuisine were superb and Dudney, who loved wine with dinner, had enough to give her a warm, happy glow. They took a brief walk after dinner, holding hands in the brisk, clear cold, and played bridge with an elderly British couple in the inn's cocktail lounge. It was after midnight when the bridge game ended and Mark walked Dudney to her room.

"Tomorrow Ken Ross will drive us up to Warwick Castle and we'll stop at Stratford upon Avon, Shakespeare's town," he said.

"Sounds fine. When did you make all those arrangements?"

"While I was dummy on the second rubber. Incidentally, Copilot, you play pretty good bridge. Bid my trips next month and maybe we can scrounge up a few games on layovers."

"Affirmative, Captain. Mark, I've had a beautiful day."

"So have I, Dud. Get a good night's sleep."

She wanted him to kiss her so badly that she was trembling inside. Instead, he hugged her, pressed his cheek against hers and walked away. Except that, from the force of his hug, she had the idea he was running away.

Warwick, one of the few medieval castles in England that was still inhabited, was fascinating. Stratford upon Avon was a disappointment—too commercialized, Dudney thought, and Mark agreed. "It's Atlantic City with a British accent," he said after Dudney commented that every third building seemed to be a souvenir shop. The resortish atmosphere of Stratford, however, failed to dim their enjoyment of the day. Dudney like Ken Ross, a rosy-cheeked, black-haired man with the bluff heartiness of the English middle class. He had served in the British Navy for more than fifteen years and had started his car rental business with a secondhand Austin. Now he employed four other drivers, owned six English Fords and was about, he informed Dudney and Mark, to buy a new Jaguar sedan for special charter trips.

"For some of those rich American tourists who look down on these Fords," he explained unabashedly.

"Well," Ashlock chuckled, "how about driving us down to Portsmouth in a couple of days—and I'm not one of those rich American tourists."

"Portsmouth?" asked Ross. "Will you be seeing the *Victory?*"

"That's why we're going."

"My old ship," the driver beamed. "Anyone who wants to see

Nelson's flagship gets a special rate. I'll discuss the details in private with you, Captain Ashlock."

"If you served on the *Victory*," Dudney wondered, "when on earth were you in the Navy?"

"Lord love you, miss," Ross laughed. "The *Victory*'s still in commission. She's manned by Royal Navy personnel—your guides will be regular seamen. That's what I did when I served on her. Conducted the visitors around the ship, I did. And proud of her I was, too. You're going to see a splendid old girl, I promise you."

They ate again at the inn that night but their bridge companions were missing and they had the lounge to themselves for after-dinner drinks. For the first time since they had come to Broadway, their conversation gravitated to flying and their profession.

"What's your ambition, Dud," Ashlock asked, "to make captain someday?"

"Affirmative. Isn't that every first officer's ambition?"

"Normally, yes. But you're a rather unusual first officer. I can't quite picture you flying into the years of gray-haired seniority."

She was amused but a trifle miffed. "Neither can Captain Battles. He told me the day he hired me the sun would set in the east before he'd upgrade me to captain. I suppose you feel the same way about women airline captains."

"I'm not sure how I feel. I've never really thought about it. I'll admit it would be somewhat illogical to argue against your getting a fourth stripe if I've accepted you as a first officer."

"So don't argue against it. I could pass an ATR check tomorrow, Mark."

"Without a doubt. But is that all you want out of life—to be a captain? How about marriage and kids someday?"

"Is that all you want out of life—to be a captain?"

"I don't quite follow you."

"I mean, are you going to spend the rest of your life just flying airplanes—and remembering a happy marriage? Or do you want to get married again someday? Same question you asked me, Mark, in a sense."

"I asked you first."

"Okay, yes. Someday I'd like to get married and have children.

Two, preferably. Definitely more than one and definitely no more than three. Over to you, Captain."

He sipped his brandy thoughtfully. "I've thought seriously about never marrying again. Mostly because I'd be comparing the second marriage with the first, and I'd be afraid of being unfair to my second wife because Barbara was just about a perfect wife. I've dated a lot since she died. But dating different women was something of a shock after being married to Barbara. I found myself getting bored with every woman I've gone out with. So much so that taking them out was a waste of time unless we wound up in bed. And even sex wasn't enough. I discovered that if you can't get satisfaction out of just being with a woman, just talking to her, sooner or later you won't want to sleep with her either. And that, Copilot, is why I may never get married again. I've just described what's wrong with most marriages."

"What you've described, Captain, is what's wrong with Mark Ashlock. You're not afraid of a second marriage. You're afraid of marriage to the wrong person."

"Granted. But the events of the last two years have made me wonder about finding the right one. I've been with intelligent women, passionate women, kind women, generous women, thoughtful women and amusing women. I've known a few who combined several of the better qualities. But you know something, Dud? I've seldom gone out with the same girl two or three times in succession. I got bored."

"You have a very discouraging philosophy," Dudney observed with a twinkle. "You seem to lose interest the second or third time you unhook a bra."

"Sex," he acknowledged obliquely, "is usually like reading a book. Once you know the plot, it's a rare book that you'd want to read over and over again."

"Conversely, a good marriage is like a good book for the same reason. However, I'm glad you gave me that no-strings pledge. I'd probably wind up on the discard list as soon as I went to bed with you."

"You might." His voice was so low she could hardly hear him and for the first time he avoided looking at her, staring instead into his brandy glass. The silence hung between them like a gauze curtain.

"That pledge," he said eventually, "along with one other little item, has equipped you with a figurative chastity belt built by American Machine and Foundry out of chrome, steel and armor plate. Also figuratively speaking, I closed the lock myself and threw away the key."

"And what, may I ask, was the other little item?"

He waited longer to reply than he had a few minutes before. "Well, I . . . I guess I'm afraid of discovering I could get bored with you too."

"Why should you be afraid?"

"Because I don't want to find that out." His voice was still low, almost hoarse. "You've given me the first real happiness I've had since the night Barbara died. You don't look like her, you don't talk like her, you don't act like her. But dammit, there's something about you . . ." He did not finish and once more he refused to meet her eyes.

"My red-blooded, brave captain," she started to chide, teasing only because she was unsure of her own emotions.

"God damn you, Dud!" he suddenly barked. "Don't go figuring me for a holier-than-thou moralist. *You* happened to me . . . and you happened so bloody fast I can't figure it out."

"I don't figure you for a holier-than-thou moralist, Mark," she said gently. "I figure you for a very decent, wonderful guy. So before you get any more mixed up, let's have one more nightcap and we'll get some air before we turn in."

They got thoroughly chilled walking through the village again, thawed out in front of a fireplace with two final brandies and climbed the ancient stairs to her room, holding hands.

"What's on the agenda for tomorrow, Mark?" She was conscious that her voice seemed harsh and nervous.

"Thought we'd rent a car from Ken and just tour the countryside—show you a few villages. I supposed we can leave day after tomorrow and run down to Portsmouth, if you don't mind my playing Horatio Hornblower."

"I don't mind. I'll love it. Good night, Mark."

"Good night, Copilot."

Copilot. He had been calling her that with such increasing frequency that it had taken on the glow of an endearment. Their hands were still joined, and as she pressed his, she noticed they were trembling. He loosened his grip as if to pull away but she squeezed harder. Her mind was swirling and she felt drugged and dizzy.

"Dud, I . . ."

Whatever he was going to say was swallowed by her mouth seeking his, soft, warm, moist and then suddenly alive as she opened it, her tongue a twisting serpent. He felt fire and ice on his spine and he knew there was no turning back. Now they were inside her room and she slammed the door shut, turning to him, and he could swear her eyes were shining in the dark like a cat's.

It was cold in the morning and she snuggled up to him under the thick quilt, her warm, naked body pressing against his until he felt desire ignite again, stoked by affection and incredible gratitude for what she had given him. He looked into her eyes and saw hesitation, questioning, and yet trust.

"I love you, Dud," Mark Ashlock said.

CHAPTER ELEVEN

They flew home four days later, having spent an extra day at the inn and a single afternoon in Portsmouth for Ashlock's *Victory* pilgrimage before returning to London and a final two-night fling. On the long flight back to Los Angeles they talked of marriage without a specific decision—merely a vague kind of informal engagement.

"And, Mark, I'd just as soon nobody knew how we feel—for a while, at least," Dudney told him.

He grumbled at this. "I wasn't planning to put it on the front page of the Los Angeles *Times*," he remarked, "but I don't see anything wrong in telling a few of our friends."

"Telling a few friends will be like putting it on page one," she pointed out. "Keeping a romance secret on an airline is like trying to keep it secret in a women's dormitory. They'll know soon enough —just seeing us together a lot will have all the tongues flapping."

Wisely, he deduced the reasoning behind her reluctance. "It's something to do about your flying, isn't it, Dud? You're afraid John Battles will tell you that a female first officer in love makes a lousy first officer."

"Something like that," she admitted. "For one thing, what's the company policy on two crew members marrying?"

"The company's never faced the problem of two pilots marrying," he reminded her whimsically. "A pilot marrying a stewardess—well, the brass doesn't like it but there's no rule against it. I imagine that'll be the case with us."

Dudney heaved a sigh, one that seemed to blend happiness with bewilderment. "You're a problem, Captain Ashlock. One I didn't expect to face until I'd been flying the line for another three or four years. It hasn't been even a year yet and now love rears its head."

"What's the problem? We'll get married and let the flying business take care of itself."

"What does 'take care of itself' mean, precisely? That the marriage vows will be instantly followed by my letter of resignation?"

He paused before answering, sensing that they had reached a crisis stage already in their new relationship. "You don't want to quit, do you, Dud?"

"No, I don't. Not right away."

"And what, to paraphrase your own question, does 'not right away' mean precisely?"

She, too, hesitated, tiptoeing in her choice of words. "I can't give you a date, Mark. To start with, I'd like to wait a few months before we decide definitely on marriage. This has happened too fast, for both of us. Then, if we do get married, I'd ask you to let me keep flying until one of three things happened. First, pregnancy. Second, if my job interfered with a happy marriage. Third, if I got tired of flying the line."

He smiled wryly. "I'll lay odds that subconsciously you've got a fourth condition circling around in your pretty little head."

"And what would that be?"

"That you'd like to keep flying until you made captain—and God knows how long after that great event."

She had to smile herself, also wryly, because she knew there was some truth in his guess.

"You'd draw the line there, I suppose?" she asked, taking his hand.

"I honestly don't know, Dud. For that matter, I don't even know whether you'd make a good captain."

"Balderdash!" she bristled, withdrawing her hand as if it had touched a hot wire. "Mark Ashlock, you're the last pilot I'd expect to show ridiculous male prejudice. How in the name of—"

"Hold it, Copilot. I would have said that to any first officer with less than a year in the right seat. That fourth stripe is awarded for more than just ability to fly. There are other factors, such as ability to command. To work well with subordinates. To—"

"You sound like a tape recording of John Battles the day he interviewed me," she said sarcastically. "He gave me the same guff about women captains."

"Get off your suffrage soapbox, Dud. I'm talking about first officers becoming captains, not female first officers becoming captains. But if you persist in interjecting the male vs. female issue, use your own yardstick—judge performance, not sex. There are valid, logical and entirely unemotional arguments against a woman captain, based on the peculiar demands of the job itself."

"Name them," she challenged.

"Crew coordination would be one. For instance, lack of respect or even resentment on the part of male first officers and flight engineers. Cockpit discipline could be a very real problem. You wouldn't expect Trans-Coastal to upgrade a copilot who couldn't work with other crew members, who couldn't command their respect because they didn't quite trust the captain. That applies to some men and it would definitely apply to virtually every woman who tried to sit in that left seat."

"It would apply only temporarily," Dudney said. "It applied to me, Mark, until captains got to know me and accepted me as a pilot and not a woman. Likewise, a woman captain undoubtedly would have trouble at the start until her copilots realized she could cut the mustard as well as any man. I don't deny there'd be difficulties, just as I had difficulties. What you're saying is that the friction would last indefinitely, and I don't think it would."

"All women pilots are not Dudney Devlin," Ashlock said. "I'll admit you wouldn't have any trouble proving yourself as captain, both in the matter of proficiency and in crew relationships. But, Dud, I suspect you're an exception because you're an exceptional person."

"You're prejudiced," she chided. "Anyway, the whole discussion is moot. I'm about four or five years away from facing the question of upgrading."

"Which brings us back to the original question, Miss Devlin. Do I have to wait four or five years before you marry me?"

Her face, alive with the stimulation of their debate, sobered and softened. "Maybe four or five months, Captain. Give me a chance to get used to being in love. Let me make sure it's love. I've never even gone through an adolescent crush, Mark. Unless you could count Dixon."

"And who the hell was, or is, Dixon?"

"A pilot who flew for my father. I was fourteen at the time."

"How about that football player you told me about?"

She blushed and was mad at herself for doing so. "That was alcohol, not infatuation. Let's play gin rummy."

Officially, the exact status of their relationship was left unsettled. Unofficially, they became more dependent on one another with increasing intensity, not only in physical intimacy but in companionship. She partially surrendered to convention and reputation by refusing to bid his trips, knowing that they inevitably would wind up in the same hotel room. Not that they fooled anyone; they were seen together too often for the airline gossip mill not to function with devastating efficiency. It started, as a matter of fact, as soon as they got off the plane from London and bumped into Captain Angus McPherson. Angus casually mentioned to another pilot the next day that Ashlock and Devlin had been in London together. Within forty-eight hours, approximately eighty per cent of Trans-Coastal's flight crews had Ashlock and Devlin going steady, engaged or even secretly married.

Crusty's initial reaction was that of a father who has suddenly discovered that his fifteen-year-old daughter has started dating a fifty-year-old man.

"He's too old for you!" he decreed loudly to Dudney, totally forgetting that he had once recommended Ashlock as a fine prospect.

"Oh, for God's sake, Crusty," she retorted. "He's forty-two."

"May and December, that's what it is. May and December. It'll never work out."

"It's more like May and late August," Dudney said.

"It'll ruin your flying," Callahan complained, shifting from the illogical to the unlikely in desperation. "Besides, what the hell kind of cockpit discipline are you gonna have if the captain's nuts about the copilot and vice versa?"

"I'm not going to fly with him if I can help it," she explained patiently. "Damnation, Crusty, I thought you'd be happy about it.

You've been needling me for months about not living a normal life."

"I wouldn't have thought it of Ashlock," Callahan glowered. "Just like the rest of those pilot swingers. Always trying to get into some dame's pants."

"Crusty!"

"Aw hell, Dud, I'm thinking of your own good."

"I'm thinking you're an evil-minded, phony Puritan, so help me."

"Aw—!" denied Captain Callahan, once more retreating behind his fortress of profanity in lieu of admitting he could be wrong.

Eventually, of course, he not only came around but took full credit for playing Cupid, bragging that he had introduced them and swearing he had talked Dudney into dating Mark. Neither bothered to correct him, knowing that winking at occasional prevarication was one of the prices to be paid for having Crusty as a good friend. It was true they grimaced at how far Callahan could stretch the truth. They were in Operations one day and overheard the little man assuring a crew scheduler:

"If it hadn't been for me, they never would have gotten together. That Devlin listens to everything I tell her, believe me."

"I suppose he's like Goebbels," Ashlock sighed resignedly to Dudney. "He keeps telling the same lie over and over until he believes it himself."

The one thing she dreaded was the reaction of John Battles when the rumors and gossip reached the chief pilot. Her fears seemed to be justified when she came off a trip and found a note in her mailbox.

D. Devlin:

Please see me at your earliest convenience.

J. Battles

Her earliest convenience was immediately and she was quaking when she entered Battles' office, realizing it was the first time she had been there since the original and fateful interview and also recalling most vividly what had been said on the subject of falling in love.

"You wanted to see me, Captain Battles?" She kept the concern out of her voice—she hoped.

He was surprisingly cordial, rising to greet her and insisting he "just wanted to chat with you."

She waited, suddenly aware that Battles was as ill at ease as she. "Uh, is what I hear true?"

"What do you hear?" She figured she might as well play innocent.

"About you and Mark Ashlock."

"What have you heard?"

"Well, uh, that you've been dating pretty seriously."

"We have. Is that all you wanted to talk about?"

"How serious is it?"

"We're not engaged and we have no immediate plans for either betrothal or marriage. Or does our dating constitute grounds for my dismissal?"

She was hiding her nervousness under the thin armor of pugnaciousness and he chuckled; the armor was too transparent. "Relax, Dudney. Mark Ashlock is one of our best captains and a very fine guy to boot. I'm glad he found someone like you. Frankly, I hope it does turn out to be serious. It's the best thing that could happen to either of you."

"Matrimony for him, resignation for me, and a millstone removed from around your neck," she said, but without rancor.

He could be as direct as she for getting down to the nitty-gritty. "The thought had passed my mind. But I guess it'll have to cruise around a bit more before it passes by again."

"Correct. I have no intentions of an immediate marriage. I want to keep flying. If that's all you called me in for, your millstone has a date with your captain to play some golf. Am I excused?"

He laughed and rose to bid her good-by. "You're excused. Still figuring on making captain?"

"Affirmative."

"Well, I didn't expect anything else from you. But the day you quit to marry Mark Ashlock, I'll give you the finest wedding present in the world. I'll transfer him over to training and you can have him home with you almost every night."

"It is," she assured him with an ingratiating grin, "a tempting proposition. I'll hold it in abeyance. Except you forgot one thing."

"I did?"

"You did. I doubt if I'll quit even if we do get married."

"In that case," Battles said with a straight face, "I shall utter a nightly prayer for Captain Ashlock's fertility."

"Go to hell," Dudney said sweetly and Battles laughed. In fact, he not only was jovial but suggested that she and Mark have dinner with the Battles the next week. The date was arranged and somewhat to Dudney's amazement (she spent three days worrying about the event) she had a wonderful time. Mark was not surprised at how well the two couples hit it off, but he had been at the invitation itself.

"John doesn't socialize with crews much," he commented. "He figures it's too hard to fraternize with a pilot he might have to discipline. In fact, the only pilots he'll usually be seen with off duty are a few senior captains he's known for years—guys who are almost above criticism. That's only the second time I've had dinner with him since I came with Trans-Coastal. Did you have a good time?"

"Very. Battles reminds me of somebody."

"Who?"

"A younger Ralph Devlin. Or maybe an older Mark Ashlock."

"Don't ever put me in the father-image category, Copilot. By the way, better not tell Crusty you were out with the chief pilot and his wife. He'll accuse you of going over to the enemy."

"He already has. I told him before we went out. He said I was a female Benedict Arnold and that the only thing I was good for on an airplane was to move the center of gravity two and a half inches forward. He really sounded angry, Mark."

Ashlock laughed. "Boy, that Crusty. He and John bowl together every Friday night, they belong to the same Masonic lodge, and the Callahans play bridge with the Battles at least twice a month. Crusty is one of the few exceptions to Johnny's non-fraternization policy."

"Well," Dudney said ruefully, "I should have known better."

She observed her first anniversary with Trans-Coastal in May, going off probation and marking the occasion by tossing a kind of class reunion to which she invited Mark. She was a little apprehensive on the latter score, not because she did not want her classmates to see them together—most of them either already had or knew about Ashlock and Dudney—but because she had qualms about his fourthstripe status. She was afraid they would think her obvious close association with a lordly captain might be interpreted in the same way Webster had once resented her flaunting aeronautical knowledge. Dixie, of course, would not have lost his puppy-like informality if she had invited President Nixon, and Hank, she knew, was extremely close to Mark. But of the others she was not quite sure.

There was no need to worry, as she discovered quickly. Few captains donned mantles of supercilious superiority with first officers of a year's experience, and Mark Ashlock definitely was not one of them. Once a copilot proved himself, the distance between the left seat and the right seat narrowed magically in terms of protocol and friendships. Many captains were closer to certain first officers than fellow four-stripers, forming their circles of cronies on the basis of individuals rather than rank. The successful reunion party brought this home to Dudney, along with the belated realization that she had missed "my guys." Frank Webster, it developed, was on intimate terms with more captains than copilots and all of them talked about being particularly friendly with several captains.

It was after the party that she gradually fell into the flight crew habit of joining cliques, islands of friendships organized not from snobbery but mutual interests and compatible personalities. Hers was a happy little world centering first, of course, around Mark but also including Crusty, Jason, Dixie, Hank, Frank and Ernie and their wives—Crum had married Nancy a few weeks before the reunion shindig and, much to Dudney's delight, asked her to be a bridesmaid.

She even admitted a few females to her island, one of them Del Fitzgerald—the stewardess on her first line trip—and another stewardess who moved into the apartment next door shortly after she returned from England. Cathy Henderson was a registered nurse who had gotten fed up with bedpans, lecherous interns and nasty patients —trading all three unpleasant associations for the happier contacts with burp bags, lecherous pilots and nasty passengers. She was a short but busty brunette, possessing a vocabulary uncomfortably close to that of Dirty Daphne and Captain Callahan. She was, in fact, almost a female version of Crusty—bawdy, sharp-tongued, outwardly cynical and the most loyal and dependable of friends. She was going steady with a married but separated TWA captain when Dudney met her, waiting patiently (and fearfully, as she confessed to Dudney after a few drinks that dissolved into tearful doubts) for his divorce.

Del and Cathy filled Dudney's need for close friends of her own sex, her small but lively clique provided her with the off-duty interests she had once so sadly lacked, and from Captain Mark Ashlock she derived mature physical and emotional fulfillment. His competitor was flying; frequently her resolve not to marry immediately wavered and sagged as their love deepened, stiffened only by her reluctance to abandon her job. He offered no objections to combining the two careers, insisting there would be no serious conflict for the time being, but she sensed more of a potential conflict than he did.

Mark did not press the issue, giving Dudney her head as he would a spirited filly, and if he was frustrated in their sporadic contacts he at least was secure in the sureness of her growing love. That they could discuss the subject with no ill-feeling, with objectivity and even with humor was indicative of their maturity. He admitted—to himself—that he wanted an early marriage mainly to protect her from gossip, for he knew that if she continued to fly after marriage their existence would be changed relatively little from what it was then. They were together almost constantly when they were not on trips, and they would have shared the trips if Ashlock had had his way. It was Dudney who drew a firm line on that score, and not entirely for reasons of propriety.

"You're my guy and I'm your girl when we're off airplanes," she told him. "Which is exactly why I don't want to fly with you. You're a pro in that left seat, Mark, and I figure I'm a pro in the right seat, and if we get into the same cockpit there's too good a chance we'd stop being pros."

So the status quo continued through that spring, summer and well into the winter schedules. Her birthday rolled around in November and Mark conspired to surprise her. She was supposed to fly a Los Angeles–Salt Lake City turn-around with Bert Huntington, intending to have a late snack with Mark after the return flight. Without telling her, Ashlock swapped trips with Huntington and also talked Cathy

Henderson into trip-trading so she could help him make the flight a special occasion.

"There's a little bakery right around the corner from where you and Dud live," he told Cathy. "I've already ordered a birthday cake —the frosting will have a reasonable facsimile of Fat Albert, with the date and flight number—378—and a 'Happy Birthday to Copilot Devlin' underneath. Pick it up sometime in the afternoon before we leave and sneak it on the airplane before we board. Here's twenty bucks."

"All that on one cake?" Cathy asked. "For Christ's sake, it must be three feet wide."

"It's a big one, all right. I figured when we leave Salt Lake on the way back, you can tip off the passengers it's the copilot's birthday. Unless there's an FAA inspector on board, I'll open the cockpit door and maybe you can get everybody to sing 'Happy Birthday, dear Dudney.'"

"Dear Dudney," Miss Henderson predicted, "will castrate you."

"Don't forget to bring along a knife and about a hundred small paper plates—we can share the cake with the customers."

"I may use the knife to castrate you myself. Don't we have enough work back there without serving a hundred pieces of birthday cake?"

"We won't have a full load going back at that time of night. Shouldn't be more than forty aboard. Okay, Cathy?"

"Okay," she agreed, "but I wish to hell Dud had fallen for an un-sentimental creep."

She smuggled cake, knife and plates aboard before signing in for the trip and when Dudney reported to crew sked Cathy explained that "June Baxter had a hot date tonight and traded trips with me." Dudney swallowed this but knew something was up when she saw Mark's name on the trip sheet.

"You fink, you're planning something," she accused him when he showed up for sign-in.

"Just thought the best gift I could give you was a great captain for your birthday flight," he informed her gravely.

"If you really want to give me a birthday present, you'll let me make the takeoff."

"I'll have to think about it. Down deep, I don't believe women were really meant to fly airplanes. Besides, I hate feminists. Ever tell you about what happened after the *Titanic* sank?"

"No, you didn't and I'm not going to ask."

"I'll tell you anyway. A couple of women's rights outfits complained because women and children were allowed to get into the lifeboats first. They said this was discrimination."

"Fine. If we crash, I'll let you evacuate first."

"Thank you. By the way, checked the weather yet?"

"Yep. Salt Lake City's okay—snow and some fog but above minimums. We don't have much choice for alternates, Mark. Boise, Grand Junction and Pendleton are all down. That leaves Denver and Denver looks real good."

"Tell you what, Dud. If you'll get me some coffee while I go talk to Dispatch, I'll let you make the takeoff and maybe the landing too."

"Deal." She marched off happily to the crew lounge while Ashlock, watching her trim figure admiringly, finally forced himself to think about business and approached Dispatch.

"Hi, Robert," he addressed one of the six dispatchers on duty—a heavy-set man named Bob Compton whose perpetually worried expression belied a dry sense of humor, a cheerful disposition and an affinity for getting along with even temperamental captains.

"Captain Ashlock, I do declare. I just heard you switched with Huntington for 378—and you should go to a head shrinker. It's a lousy night for flying."

"It's Dud's birthday and she's on 378."

"Say no more. It's a beautiful night for flying. Wanna see what the computer has decreed for you?"

"Got a flight plan already? You're an efficient bastard, Compton. Let's take a look."

Like most major airlines, Trans-Coastal's flight planning was done by computer. Dispatch fed into the electronic brain such data as type of aircraft, weather, winds, planned speed, fuel and weight. Then, in effect, Dispatch asked, "Give us the safest, most comfortable and economical routing with the best chance of maintaining schedule." Compton this time had asked the computer figuratively, what was the best way for Flight 378 to get from Los Angeles to Salt Lake

City? The small white piece of paper Compton handed Captain Ashlock provided this answer:

```
01:29/01:30     90BO     60     70:DEN
  90  560NM  998/1000  908/980 RT:  1   778  220
RCA  134  33  73  -01  423  32030-011  412  21  37  183
POD  327  33  75  -01  434  31031-007  427  47  46  137
SLC   99                     29013-006       21   7  130
 29   999 01:26      91       91 X M78
 27  1002 01:24      94       94 X M78
 25  1004 01:23      96       96 X M78
 23  1008 01:23     100      100 X M78
TC 378 B737/A   0423 LAX P2330   330
LAX DAG TWO BLD J9 SLC
```

To Ashlock's practiced eye, these hieroglyphics simply told him,
among other things, that Flight 378's best routing appeared to be a
departure corridor named Dag Two out of Los Angeles until it in-
tersected with a jet airway labeled J9, after which Flight 378 was to
continue on J9 into Salt Lake City. Considering the weight of the
fuel, passengers, freight and mail aboard this Boeing 737, and taking
into account the winds aloft, the computer recommended that Flight
378 cruise at thirty-three thousand feet, an altitude it should reach
exactly one hundred and thirty-four miles out of Los Angeles. When
the instrument known as Distance Measuring Equipment showed
Captain Ashlock that he was three hundred and twenty-seven miles
from Los Angeles and ninety-nine miles out of Salt Lake City, he
could figure that he had reached his Point of Descent and should start
letting down—Air Traffic Control willing, of course. All this naturally
assumed that he started out with twenty-two thousand pounds of
kerosene fuel in his three tanks, duly assigned him by Dispatch, and
that if Captain Ashlock followed this recommended flight plan he
would burn nine thousand pounds of fuel on the five-hundred-and-
sixty-mile flight from Los Angeles to Salt Lake City, leaving him
thirteen thousand pounds just in case he found it necessary to divert
to Denver, his prescribed alternate.

"Looks good to me, Bob," Ashlock told the dispatcher as he

handed back the computer data. "Before I file, let's have that weather sequence you showed Dud."

He looked at one line first.

SLC W4X1/2 S-F 141/34/32/3004/993 R34L26V32

"Four-hundred-foot ceiling, half-mile visibility with obscuration in light snow and fog," Ashlock translated aloud. "Temperature 34 and dew point 32—nuts, that means the fog'll probably get worse with only a two-degree spread—wind three hundred degrees at four knots out of the northwest. RVR for Runway 34 Left twenty-six hundred feet variable to thirty-two hundred millibars. Hell, it could be worse."

"Provided it doesn't get much worse," the dispatcher added with inbred caution.

"Yeah. Let's see—Boise, Pendleton, Grand Junction—all heavy snow, socked in. But Denver's fine. Sixty-five-hundred-foot ceiling and fifteen miles visibility. Couldn't ask anything more for an alternate. Let's have a flight plan and dispatch release, Bob."

The dispatcher handed him the eleven-by-nine-inch form which Ashlock filled in swiftly. He looked up at the huge Dispatch board for the ship number. "Balls, 360. That's the Fat Albert with no CAT II equipment yet, isn't it?"

"That's the bird, Mark. She's due for an eight-thousand-hour overhaul in about a week. They'll be adding all the gizmos then—and you can land her when the birds are walking."

Ashlock and the dispatcher both signed the flight release under a printed announcement:

We agree that the weather analysis applicable to the above flight meets the requirements of Federal Aviation Regulations.

"Have a good trip, Mark," the dispatcher said.

Another computerized message tumbled out of a teletype several hundred feet away from Operations. A Trans-Coastal ticket agent scanned the message and looked up, pleased, at the thin, well-dressed man standing in front of his counter.

"We do have space available on 378, Mr. Hoffman—first class or coach?"

"First class is near the front of the plane, right?" His voice was pleasant enough but he seemed to breathe his words rather than speak them, so that they came out almost with a hissing sound.

"Then make it first class. That's what I want." He was smiling, in the way a chorus girl smiles—the grin painted on the mouth and totally detached from the eyes.

"First class it is, Mr. Hoffman," the agent said, pulling out a ticket form. "Round trip?"

Hoffman hesitated. "Uh, no, make it one way. I'm not sure when I'll be returning."

"Well, if you'd like a round trip we can leave the return part open and you can make your reservations in Salt Lake when—"

"I said one way." The passenger was still smiling, but without humor.

"Of course," the agent said politely. He filled out the ticket. "Credit card or cash?"

"I'll pay cash," the man said. "I don't trust credit cards."

"Sixty dollars, including tax."

The man took a wallet from an inside coat pocket and carefully counted out three twenty-dollar bills. The agent gave him the ticket.

"There you are, Mr. Hoffman. Gate 32. Be boarding about eight forty-five. Have a nice flight."

The smile broadened as if the agent had just said something hilariously ridiculous.

"Oh, I will, I will," he said, his head bobbing. "Jesus will be riding with me on the plane."

The agent looked at his departing figure. They sure get some nuts around here, he thought.

While his appraisal of Mr. Hoffman might have been hasty and unscientific, it was devastatingly accurate. Peter Hoffman was a nut. Or, to be psychologically correct, he was a schizophrenic, released only two months before from a mental institution in the custody of his sister, not as cured but in a state of regression that made him appear as normal as anyone else.

In the last few days he had shown symptoms of slipping back into that dark, ugly, warped world of unreality that seemed so real to him. His sister noticed it but said nothing and did nothing. When Peter Hoffman announced he would like to fly to Salt Lake City to visit some old friends, she even urged him to go. Of course, it was hard to blame his sister for wanting him out of the house, even for a brief time. It also was hard to blame her for not warning the airlines that a recently released mental patient might need watching. After all, this precaution never occurred to her and, besides, she had no way of knowing that in the right-hand coat pocket of Peter Hoffman's suit when he left for the airport was a snub-nosed, .38-caliber revolver.

Fully loaded, of course. Peter Hoffman had decided to murder Jesus.

Mark Ashlock decided only a few moments after takeoff that Dudney had been wrong about their not flying together. Aside from the implications that layovers might have involved, he had worried privately that she also could be too distracting. Strangely, she was not. In uniform, under the pressures of the cockpit duties and cockpit ritual, she was a curiously two-dimensional Dudney Devlin. Looking at her through the eyes of an airman and captain, rather than the eyes of a man in love, he found her a different person—a distorted mirror image of the girl he worshiped, lacking the depth of intimacy; an impersonal acquaintance who could have been any highly proficient first officer. If there was an undercurrent of distraction, it was more subconscious than apparent, a delicate and deliciously subtle knowledge that another Dudney Devlin was inside the façade of technical efficiency, her presence hinted only by the slight curve of her breasts under the uniform blouse and the faint aroma of her perfume.

This was only the second time they had flown a trip and he admired anew her unhurried smoothness on the controls, her easy confidence born of knowledge and competence, so laconic without ever hiding the fact that she also was blissfully contented. It was typical of her that she hand-flew the airplane while they climbed to thirty-three thousand, disdaining the autopilot until they leveled out at cruise altitude and relaxed into that watchful euphoria of a routine airline flight.

"You fly," he observed as she finally engaged the autopilot, "like you make love."

"Passionately?"

"Nope. Skillfully—and giving the impression that you're enjoying every minute of it."

"I do."

"Making love or flying?"

"Both."

It was their only non-professional dialogue of the flight. The fat-bodied Boeing sped effortlessly across the cold night sky, the invisible miles and mountains and fields and cities flashing by under wings that taunted the boiling storm clouds far below.

The skinny passenger in 1C bothered Cathy Henderson. Normally, she welcomed people who smiled during a flight—vastly preferable to those who bitched, griped, complained and frowned. She couldn't decide why she didn't like the way 1C smiled except that it gave him the appearance of an amiable gargoyle. The trouble was that he never stopped smiling; he wore it like he wore his shirt, tie, suit and shoes. There was something evil about its fixed intensity. He looks, she told herself, like a happy executioner.

Which, of course, Peter Hoffman was.

His sick mind had slipped completely and irreparably into the twisted blackness of schizophrenia. He was convinced Jesus was behind the tiny door at the front of the airplane, the door marked NO ADMITTANCE—FLIGHT PERSONNEL ONLY.

"Trans-Coastal 378, you're cleared to descend and maintain one-four-thousand. Report leaving one-six-thousand on this frequency, then contact Salt Lake Approach Control on one-two-oh-point-nine. Please squawk ident on zero-four-zero-zero."

"Roger, Salt Lake Center. Identing. Trans-Coastal 378, out. Okay, Dud, let's start down." Ashlock was consulting a Jeppesen airways chart. "We'll plan to cross Provo at fourteen thousand, so suppose we establish a descent rate of twenty-five hundred feet a minute."

"Down we go." Dudney disengaged the autopilot. "Gonna let me make the landing, Captain?"

"I'm still thinking about it. Maybe I'll be in a more generous mood if I have one more coffee." He lifted the intercom mike from its cradle and rang the intercom bell three times. "Cathy, any chance of a coffee if you're not too busy? Good. Want one, Dud? Just one for me, Cathy—black with sugar."

He glanced at the rate of descent indicator and nodded approvingly. Fat Albert bucked slightly in mild turbulence, as if the airplane was emerging from its relaxed state and was feeling the same heightened tenseness, the same sharpened alertness as its human crew.

Three taps on the cockpit door, and the click of Cathy Henderson's key as she opened it and brought in Ashlock's coffee.

"Thanks, Cathy," he said. "Everybody happy back there?"

"Reasonably so. We gonna get in on schedule?"

"Probably. I'll know more in about five minutes when I get the latest weather."

She glanced at Dudney and grinned wickedly. "She know how to fly this bucket?"

"She's an expert," Ashlock said. "I taught her to pull back for going up and forward for going down. Or is it the other way around?"

"How do you go sideways?" Dudney inquired.

"I think I'll go back to the galley and pray," Cathy said.

She opened the cockpit door to leave, considered having a cigarette with the flight crew before returning to the cabin, and then changed her mind. In that moment of indecision, the door was ajar and the man in 1C, the smile still frozen on his thin mouth, was peering into the cockpit from his aisle seat. He stared beyond the stewardess at Ashlock. The picture transmitted from a sick mind to his eyes was not that of an airline captain.

Although Dudney was flying, it was Ashlock who planned the approach and landing in accordance with his command prerogatives. They were now at fourteen thousand and letting down, thirty-five miles from the Salt Lake City airport, speed four hundred and fifty knots, rate of descent fifteen hundred feet per minute. Flight 378 was only six and a half minutes from touchdown and the captain's brain was a living, fleshed computer, calculating how much altitude they had to lose within a space of so much time and distance. He was planning the power reductions well in advance so they would lose altitude at a perfectly timed rate, hitting the Riverton fan marker at ten thousand feet with an indicated airspeed of not more than two hundred and fifty knots.

"I'll leave my nav receiver on the Salt Lake VOR, Dud, for a DME readout. I'll let you know when we're five miles from the outer marker."

"Roger."

Approach Control broke in, a loud metallic voice invading their concentration. "Trans-Coastal 378, you're cleared for an ILS approach Runway three-four-left. Current RVR for three-four-left is twenty-four hundred. Informatively, the RVR has been decreasing fairly rapidly."

Ashlock frowned. The Runway Visual Range reading, an electronic measurement of visibility, was down to twenty-four hundred feet and that was right on the marginal line for a legal landing.

"Nuts," he said. "We're flirting with minimums."

"No sweat if we had CAT II equipment," Dudney remarked.

"But we don't on this airplane," Ashlock said. "This is the only 737 in our fleet that doesn't." He picked up his radio mike. "Salt Lake Approach Control, this is Trans-Coastal 378. Appreciate your latest weather."

"Roger, 378. Snow mixed with fog, wind negligible, four knots, southeast. Braking action on Runway three-four-left good, RVR still twenty-four hundred. Altimeter two-nine-point-nine-one."

"Thank you," Ashlock acknowledged. "Three-seven-eight out."

He was considering taking over but he abandoned the impulse. She was perfectly capable of shooting a good ILS approach. Yet he wondered, momentarily, whether he would have assumed the controls if his copilot had been anyone but Dudney. No, he decided—any first officer with more than a year's line flying could be relied on. Too many captains were prone to trust only themselves.

They were at ten thousand feet, nine miles from the airport, slowed to less than two hundred and thirty knots.

"One degree flaps," Dudney requested.

Peter Hoffman touched the bulge of the gun in his pocket as if in reassurance and rang the stewardess call button. The young Marine sitting next to him in 1A glanced at him curiously. It was Cathy who answered the summons, a trifle impatient at this typical manifestation of passenger unreasonableness—demanding something when the FASTEN SEAT BELT sign had just gone on and they were about to land.

Hoffman was out of his seat and standing in the aisle when she came up.

"You'll have to take your seat, sir," she started to scold, and then stopped, paling.

The gun was out of his pocket, pointing at her chest. A hijacking, she thought crazily. A stupid hijacking—the damned fool probably wants to go to Cuba and in a 737 we couldn't even make it to Chicago.

"I have to talk to Jesus," the passenger said pleasantly enough.

"Jesus?" Cathy asked.

"Up there." He gestured toward the cockpit with the gun, then quickly aimed it at her again.

"Jesus isn't there," she said in what she hoped was a soothing tone. "Just the two pilots." Behind her, she heard the startled murmurs of passengers and one frightened woman sobbed once in choked hysteria.

"Jesus is one of the pilots," he said calmly. "I saw him. He's sitting on the left side."

"That's Captain Ashlock," she said quickly. "You must be mis—"

His voice rose, as if he had tired of discussing the obvious with a fool. "I know Jesus when I see him. If you don't let me in, I'll have to shoot you. It's important that I talk to him."

"The cockpit door is locked," she said desperately.

"You have a key. I saw you open it when you brought Jesus his coffee."

Don't argue with mental cases or would-be hijackers, the stewardess manual warned. Safety of the aircraft and passengers is primary. If a stewardess is unable to reason with a disturbed person, she should not try to resist.

"I'll have to let Captain Ashlock know you want to see him," she told Hoffman.

"I don't want to see this Ashlock person, miss. I have to see Jesus."

Ominously, he flicked off the safety lock on the gun.

"Come on," Cathy said. There was an intercom on the forward bulkhead, above the stewardess jump seats. She picked up the phone and rang the intercom bell four times.

The sound startled the two pilots, intent on the initial phase of the approach.

"For God's sake," Ashlock snapped, and picked up his own intercom. "What's wrong?"

Cathy tried hard to keep the panic out of her voice. There was a set, prescribed phraseology for reporting a hijacking attempt to the cockpit and she retained enough presence of mind to use it. "Captain, may I please come into the cockpit immediately?" Her enunciation was precise, yet a touch of panic penetrated the crispness.

Ashlock cupped his hand over the mike. "Hijacking," he told Dudney curtly. He picked up the mike again. "He got a gun on you, Cathy?"

The stewardess swallowed. The man standing behind her gestured with the gun once more. "Yes, sir," she said into the intercom, and her voice cracked slightly.

"Goddamned son of a bitch!" Ashlock swore. "Go ahead and open it, Cathy."

With trembling fingers she inserted the key and turned it. The woman passenger who had sobbed once was now crying loudly, but this was the only sound in a cabin frozen by fear.

There was one exception. The Marine in 1A unfastened his seat belt and very cautiously moved into the aisle.

Cathy Henderson pushed on the cockpit door. She felt Peter Hoffman's hand on her shoulder and nausea raced to her throat at the clammy touch. He pushed her aside.

"Thank you, miss," he said politely. "I see Jesus now."

Ashlock started to rise, turning as he did so and exposing his right shoulder and right chest to the bluish-black object in the intruder's hand.

"Hello, Jesus," Peter Hoffman said. "I've come to punish you for putting me in that terrible hospital."

He fired.

Ashlock, a look of stunned, unbelieving pain on his face, slumped back in his seat.

"Mark!" Dudney cried. She took her eyes off the instruments and saw the rivulets of blood forming paths down his white shirt. She could not speak another word. Through her mind ran the instantaneous conviction that it had to be a nightmare.

Hoffman pointed the gun at her.

Cathy started to scream but choked it off. Quietly, the Marine had moved past her. Peter Hoffman never saw the karate chop that broke his neck. Ashlock was groaning and the sound was a knife that simultaneously slashed cruelly into Dudney's heart but also severed her from her hazy mesmerism.

"Cathy," she barked. "See if there's a doctor on board. Quick!"

The stewardess was heading for the forward cabin PA before the word "quick" was out of the copilot's mouth. She muttered, "Thanks, pal," to the Marine who was standing over Hoffman's body and hissed, "Get back there and calm everyone down," to the younger stewardess who had rushed to the cockpit. She flicked on the mike and spoke as coolly as possible.

"Folks, please keep your seats. The emergency is over. Just stay calm. The captain has been wounded slightly and if there's a doctor on board we'd like him to come to the cockpit immediately. The rest of you stay seated."

She looked at the tube of faces, not entirely released from fear, and shook her head at the sight of the single hysterical passenger, still crying.

"Please," she repeated, "if there's a doctor on board, come forward."

There was no response. She remembered the time she had had to handle a passenger throwing an epileptic fit on an airplane. She had prevented him from swallowing his tongue by jamming a metal spoon wrapped in a cloth napkin into his mouth, after calling in vain for a doctor to help her. When the crisis was over another passenger had introduced himself as a doctor and asked if there was anything he could do. People just hated to get involved, she thought. She depressed the PA button for one final plea and then released it, wordlessly.

Now, she knew, it was up to her to take care of Mark Ashlock—and up to Dudney Devlin to get everyone down in one collective piece. She re-entered the cockpit, pausing only to ask the Marine if he could find something to bind the gunman.

"It won't be necessary," he gulped. "I think he's dead."

She studied his strong young face and saw shifting emotions of regret, defiance and pride. "Don't let it get you down," she said shortly. "If you hadn't cold-cocked him, we'd all be dead. Go back and ask the other stewardess for the first aid kit. Bring it up to me on the double."

She came into the cockpit just in time to hear Dudney talking to Salt Lake City Approach Control.

". . . repeat, I don't know how bad the captain was hit. Have an ambulance and doctor stand by."

"Roger, 378. You're released for an ILS approach to three-four-left. Descend to six-one-hundred and stay with us on this frequency. We'll turn you over to the tower four miles south of the outer marker. We know you've got your hands full so don't bother to read back. Just acknowledge if you read us okay."

"Three-seven-eight, roger."

She looked over at Mark just as Cathy arrived. "Find a doctor?"

"Negative. I'd settle for a dentist at this point. Mark, how is it?"

The captain grinned feebly. His face was white. "Dud," he whispered, "I think I'm hit bad. Bleeding inside. Can almost feel it. Get her down fast. I'm sorry—I can't help you. Feel weak."

"Everything under control, honey. We'll be landing in about five minutes. There's an ambulance waiting." In this moment of crisis, she did not realize she had said "honey."

The Marine chugged up carrying the first aid kit. Cathy opened it and swiftly wadded up a chunk of gauze bandage, pressing it directly above the wound where the bullet had entered. The Marine peeked over her shoulder and Cathy snapped, "Go back to your seat. I'll call you if I need you."

Dudney, eyes on instruments, asked, "How's he doing?"

"Not so good. I'm trying to stop this bleeding but it's still bad."

The girl in the right seat wanted to scream and cry and beg for someone to help the man next to her. The pilot in the right seat said, through taut lips, "We'll be on the ground soon." Her voice was firm but the instruments in front of her blurred momentarily through a film of tears.

"Uh, 378, we show you four miles south of the outer marker. Change to tower frequency one-one-eight-point-six. Over."

"Roger." To Dudney, her own voice was a stranger. "Have you got an ambulance standing by?"

The answering voice was one of desperate, helpless sympathy. "On the way, 378. FYI, the RVR reading on three-four-left is now eighteen hundred."

Eighteen hundred. Oh, God, below minimums. She couldn't land now. She glanced at Mark as if expecting him to make the decision, to give her guidance, to issue the right command. The captain's eyes were closed and his face, under the red night lights on the instrument panel, was ghostly. Dudney's eyes caught Cathy's and saw nothing but naked concern.

"Approach, 378. I'd like to reverse course and hold somewhere while we decide what to do."

The controller's response was so fast, his words seemed to be in the same sentence she had just uttered: "Okay, 378, reverse course. Make a left turn and you can hold south of Provo on the one-hundred-and-sixty-degree radial. Hold at twelve thousand. You're cleared to climb."

"Roger." She went into a climbing turn, heading back toward Provo. Now she was acting more like a pilot, her panic disintegrating. She was thinking clearly, logically, as she had been trained to do. She had no choice. Salt Lake City was closed as far as 378 was concerned. If her airplane had been equipped for Category II operations, with radio altimeters and all the rest of the electronic gear that made virtually blind landings possible, she could have landed with little difficulty. But this particular 737 was not and she had only one choice if that RVR reading didn't improve. Yet fog was tricky; it could swallow up a runway one second and roll away the next. Maybe, just maybe . . .

"Salt Lake Approach, 378. I'd like to reverse course again and try another approach."

"Roger, 378. What's your altitude?"

"Ten-zero and climbing."

"Okay, 378. Take a heading of three-four-oh. Radar shows you at the Riverton fan marker. When you get your new heading, descend to six-one-hundred."

"Three-seven-eight. What's that RVR now?"

"Fourteen hundred and deteriorating." The voice was matter-of-fact but with an undercurrent of grim warning.

"Stand by, Approach."

She picked up the Jeppesen approach chart for the Salt Lake City airport which she had taken from her brainbag when Ashlock told her she could make the landing. The airport was in a valley, almost completely surrounded by high terrain, and she could not trust to sheer memory. She had to make sure she was following all the rules and procedures and routes. Yet she could not ignore the basic task of flying the airplane. She remembered Dan Smith telling her on a training flight that too many pilots let themselves be carried away by an emergency to such an extent that solving the emergency took priority over flying itself. "I've known of guys doing a beautiful job of putting out an engine fire," he had lectured, "but while they were putting out the fire they let the plane fly into the ground."

Panic returned, chilling and relentless, freezing her common sense and judgment. There was so damned much to remember. So damned much to do in so little time. She glanced down at her localizer needle just in time to see it nudge the 340-degree mark. Hastily, she straightened out the aircraft. Now she was heading back toward Runway 34-L, with about sixty seconds left for decision.

"Approach, is that RVR still at fourteen hundred?"

"Negative, 378. RVR now shows eight hundred and deteriorating fast. Informatively, the tower advises visibility is almost nil."

The moment of truth. The moment for command decision.

"Okay, Approach. That does it. I'll maintain six-one-hundred and go up to the VOR and I'll take up the missed approach procedure from there if it's okay. Can you get me a clearance to Denver? That's the only alternate open."

"Roger, 378. What altitude to Denver?"

"Anything that's available. Two-nine-zero if you have it. We've got to go now—captain's in bad shape."

"Roger, 378. We understand. If you'll change over to Departure Control on one-two-five-point-seven, he'll handle everything for you. Give you radar vectors if you desire. Just continue with your missed approach and he'll pick you up north of the field. Good luck."

"Roger and thanks."

With her left hand, Dudney tuned up her VHF receiver to the new frequency but she did not even have to identify herself to Departure Control. Operating out of the same darkened radar room as Approach Control, it had been alerted to 378's emergency and was standing by for the handoff from Approach. Just before the handoff, the departure controller assigned to the flight discussed the situation briefly with the watch supervisor.

"That copilot sounds like he might be panicking," the controller observed. "Notice how high his voice is pitched? Almost like a woman's."

"It could be a woman," the supervisor guessed. "That's a Trans-Coastal two-holer and they've got a dame flying as a 737 copilot. Wonder if it's her?"

"I'm not gonna take the time to ask. He or she's got enough trouble. Okay, Departure, I've got 378." He inserted the slip of paper marked "TC 378" on his flight rack—the only aircraft he was working on this night of fog and limited operations. "Salt Lake Departure Control, 378. How do you read me?"

Damn, he thought, when the flight responded, it *is* that dame.

"Three-seven-eight reads you okay, Departure. Can you give me some help to expedite my missed approach?"

"Roger, 378. You are one and a half miles south of the Salt Lake VOR now. Turn left to a heading of two-five-zero and climb. What's your present altitude?"

"Maintaining sixty-one hundred."

"Okay, start climbing to flight level two-five-zero and—"

The pilot's voice came back sharp, challenging, impatient. "Departure, we asked for two-nine-zero, repeat two-nine-zero, if possible. The captain's wounded and we can make more speed at—"

"We know the situation, 378." The controller was patient as if he was reassuring a frightened child. "Two-nine-zero will conflict with over traffic at Meeker and two-five-zero's the best we can do. Start your climb to flight level two-five-zero. I'll give you a turn back over the VOR as soon as you report out of nine thousand."

"Roger, 378." The pilot's voice was still impatient, tense, but resigned.

The controller watched the white blip on the green radar scope—a tiny, scurrying bug that represented a four-million-dollar airplane and its cargo of threatened human lives.

"Okay, 378, turn observed. Are you ready to copy clearance?" That'll frost the poor gal, the controller thought. Trying to fly, navigate and copy clearances all at once.

"378, ready to copy." She must be quite a dame. That answer was prompt and no nonsense. But he read the clearance more slowly than usual.

"Trans-Coastal 378 is cleared to the Denver Airport via Jet five-six, repeat five-six, maintain flight level two-five-zero, cross the Salt Lake VORTAC eastbound at ten thousand feet or higher. Ah, in the event of loss of communication, 378, you can follow the Salt Lake Four Departure with Meeker transition. Did you copy okay? I can read—"

"Roger 378. Cleared to Denver, J five-six, maintain two-five-zero, cross the VOR at ten or above and okay on the communications failure procedure. We're leaving ten-five now and I'll start a turn back to the VOR. That's a right turn-around, okay?"

"You're cleared for a turn either way, 378. Your altitude looks good."

Dudney banked the 737.

"Turn observed, 378," Departure Control advised her. "Squawk ident zero-four hundred on transponder and contact the Salt Lake Center now on one-two-three-point-eight and, uh, give them your altitude leaving. Good luck."

She never had a chance to change frequency to the Center. Even as her hand reached for the tuning knob, Cathy Henderson—her hand on Ashlock's pulse—shook her head worriedly. "Dud, how long to Denver?"

She reached into the pocket of her uniform blouse and took out her worn computer, twirling the dial swiftly. "At twenty-five thousand feet with our gross, an hour and nine minutes."

"If you want this guy to live," the stewardess said grimly, "you'd better make it nine minutes."

Dudney's heart was pounding. "Cathy, I can't land at Salt Lake. We've got to go to the alternate."

"Take a look, Dud." Ashlock's face was white, perspiration pouring out in huge beads. "His skin's cold, he's breathing too rapidly and there's no pulse in his right arm. I'm a nurse, not a doctor, Dud, but I'd swear that bullet hit an artery on the right side. And if it did, he's bleeding to death."

Now Dudney was almost as pale as the stricken captain. "How much time do we have?"

"Twenty minutes at the most. I've got a pressure bandage over the wound and the bullet's still in there."

Twenty minutes.

Denver, one hour and nine minutes away.

Dudney Devlin, first officer, Trans-Coastal Airlines.

Dudney Devlin, woman, in love with a dying man.

"Salt Lake Departure, 378. Do you read me?"

The controller's voice came back surprised, not expecting to hear from the flight again. "Read you, 378. Any trouble?"

"I've got to land at Salt Lake. The captain won't last until Denver."

"RVR one hundred feet on three-four-left. Are you CAT II equipped?"

"Negative."

"Holy cow," the controller blurted unprofessionally. "What are your intentions?"

"To land. Can you vector us?"

"Roger, 378. Change back to Approach Control, frequency one-two-oh-point-nine. Are you still squawking zero-four-hundred?"

"Three-seven-eight, affirmative. Changing to Approach Control." She turned the frequency knob so fast that she never heard Departure Control whisper, "God help you."

The watch supervisor at Approach Control pursed his lips, frowned, mentally crossed himself and told the controller working 378:

"Give her all the help she needs—and she'll need plenty."

"Right. Uh, 378, what's your altitude?"

"I stopped climbing at thirteen thousand and I'm maintaining thirteen."

"Roger, 378. Our radar has you just about over the Salt Lake VOR eastbound. Take up a heading of one-seven-zero and descend to ten thousand. We'll be giving you radar vectors to the final approach course and we'll follow you as close as we can with ASR."

ASR, she thought blindly. What the hell is ASR? Memory rushed to the rescue of panic. Air Surveillance Radar. Not as good as Precision Approach Radar, decommissioned at Salt Lake City and too many other airports because pilots didn't trust a ground-controlled approach unless the man handling PAR was exceptionally skilled. PAR could monitor an approach, though, correcting altitude as well as direction and the glide angle of an aircraft employing the Instrument Landing System. On the ILS the localizer—directional—beam and the glide slope beam—glide angle—were accurate only down to the last two hundred feet. CAT II equipment automatically would keep localizer and glide slope perfectly centered through the last two hundred feet, even providing the final pitch-up before the wheels touched, but she was reminded again that she didn't have CAT II.

She flipped the course "bug"—a tiny white arrow—on her Course Indicator to 170 degrees, then rolled into a right turn until the steering needle centered on 170.

"Ah, 378, we'll take you down to Riverton for a one-eighty turn and we'll tell you when to slow down."

Good man, that controller, she thought appreciatively. He knew she'd be pushing the throttle all the way to the Riverton fan marker, even with a two-hundred-and-fifty-knot speed limit below ten thousand feet. If she slipped only a few feet under that altitude and went that fast, she'd be violating the FARs but the controller, in effect, had told her nobody was going to be a rules stickler about speed. Let's see, at ten thousand feet with 378's gross load she'd be doing around three hundred and fifty knots before the barber pole showed up—those striped lines on her airspeed indicator which warn when excessive speed has been reached.

She looked at Cathy, still applying the pressure bandage. "How's Mark doing?"

The stewardess was feeling the captain's skin. It was cool, clammy and coated with sweat. Ashlock's eyes were open but glazed and he was mumbling incoherently.

"Not good," Cathy said, her own forehead glistening with sweat. "His pulse is a hundred and thirty and his breathing rate is forty—which means, if I remember my medical books, he's going into shock. We haven't got much time, Dud."

Dudney Devlin's jaw tightened. Once again, her eyes filmed as they stared at the panel—whether from strain and concentration or from grief over Mark, she could not tell. They were indicating three hundred and forty-eight knots when Approach Control broke in.

"Uh, 378, we show you four miles north of Riverton. What's your altitude?"

"Leveling at ten."

"Okay, 378, start slowing down to approach speeds so you won't go too far south of Riverton."

She eased back on the throttles, her hands firmer than her swirling thoughts.

"Fine, 378, you're just about at Riverton and crossing the localizer. Turn right, heading two-one-zero for thirty seconds, then turn left heading zero-three-zero and intercept the localizer. We'll follow you on radar. You should be okay on terrain clearance."

"Roger, 378," she acknowledged gratefully. She realized that Approach was handling her with special care—it was far from routine for a controller to tell an airline flight it didn't have to worry about terrain; that was the pilot's responsibility and ATC had a right to assume a crew had studied its approach charts, aware of all minimum altitude restrictions.

She rolled gently left, keeping her eyes on the instrument clock until thirty seconds ticked, and then banking right toward the localizer intercept heading of 030 degrees. Instinct, natural ability and the relentless training she had gone through dropped a curtain in her mind, a barrier between her concern for the man in the left seat and what she had to accomplish. Now the seeds that had been planted in the hours of simulator flying, in the ruthlessness of training flights, sprouted and blossomed.

Okay, gotta go to auto-approach mode on the flight director. Auto-

approach on. Here come the yellow fly-bars dropping down toward the little orange airplane. All I have to do is get those bars down to where they form a V and keep the airplane nestled smack in the center of that V cradle. My course bug is set to 030. Where are the amber lights for the localizer and glide slope—to show me the flight director is armed and ready to capture the ILS glide slope and localizer beams? I've got an amber VOR-LOC light but no amber on the glide slope. Something's wrong. What did I . . . oh, Christ, I forgot to tune the localizer to the Salt Lake frequency. There. Thank God, amber on both . . .

"Three-seven-eight, you should be getting a localizer intercept shortly. How does that check with your instruments?"

I should be over the Riverton fan marker now. There's the intercept light—oh boy, what a beautiful light! And the signal . . .

Beeeep-beep. Beeeep-beep. Beeeep-beep.

"Approach, 378. I'm over Riverton."

"Okay, 378, crossing Riverton inbound. Descend to six-one-hundred."

Her mind was clicking like a machine and her hands moving with instinctive precision. Programing flap settings, correlating them with airspeed. Flaps down one degree at two hundred and thirty knots. Ease back on the power. Flaps five degrees at two hundred and twenty-five knots. Fifteen degrees at one hundred and ninety-five knots. Still back on the throttles. Twenty-five degrees flaps at one hundred and eighty-five knots. How many times had she done this in simulators, in training, check and line flights?

Flap and power settings perfectly coordinated. A stabilized approach, Art Prentice had called it the first time she flew a simulator. Plan ahead so you'll have thirty degrees of flaps with an airspeed of not more than one hundred and eighty knots just about four miles from the outer marker—that electronic signpost indicating a specific distance from the runway threshold. Keep your eyes on that IVSI—Instantaneous Vertical Speed Indicator—and make sure that rate of descent doesn't get away from you. Eight hundred feet per minute—almost perfect. A little on the high side but don't worry about it until you hit the outer marker.

A blue light flashed on the instrument panel. The pulsating sound of beep-beep, beep-beep, beep-beep. Over the outer marker. On course. Keep those fly-bars in that cradle and you should touch down about eight hundred feet from the threshold.

Airspeed bled off to one hundred and seventy knots. Gear down. Gear lights green—gear down and locked. No time for a checklist. Can't fly and read. Maybe Cathy could help and . . . no, she's trying to keep Mark alive. She couldn't help. Please, God, let him live. Please. Help me get this bird down okay. No time to think about Mark. Remember when Dave Robinson talked about the three-man crew on Fat Albert. . . . I'd settle for the luxury of just one guy to help me. Maybe the other stewardess . . . Oh hell, I forgot the passengers. I can't keep them in the blind. We could splatter over two miles of airport real estate. Gotta get them ready just in case something goes wrong . . .

"Cathy! Can you leave Mark and set up the cabin for a planned emergency?"

"Right. Only thing that'll help him now is a doctor. I'm on the way."

"Wait a sec." The stewardess paused, hand on the cockpit door handle. "Better tell 'em what's happening. I haven't time to use the PA. Just say—oh hell, use your own judgment."

"Good luck, Dud." The stewardess was gone and the cockpit was like a lonely prison cell. Over the muffled whine of the turbines, Dudney heard Mark Ashlock's labored, tortured breathing. Then the curtain dropped again.

Pressure and fluid okay. Gear down and locked. Here comes the glide slope needle. Gotta get that nose down. Flaps thirty. Keep this bird at approach speed. Glide slope mark is green. Localizer green. I've intercepted the beam. Approach speed—dammit, I forgot to set the speed bug. Let's see—fuel just under eleven thousand pounds so I'm grossing ninety thousand. That gives me reference speed of . . . of . . . one hundred and twenty-three knots. Gotta keep it on the bug. Keep that little orange plane in the V cradle . . . keep it center and I'm on course . . . maintain a glide slope of three degrees and that should stabilize rate of descent at seven hundred.

"Three-seven-eight, this is Salt Lake Approach. Stay with me on this frequency—never mind going over to the tower. You're cleared to land and emergency equipment is standing by—fire trucks and ambulance. RVR on three-four-left is indicating zero . . ."

The controller hesitated. Every nerve, every fiber, every emotion he possessed was riding in that white blip on his scope. He might as well have been in the cockpit himself. Sure, it was the pilot's decision, the pilot's responsibility. He had given that first officer all the legal, prescribed information—including the final RVR reading which in so many words told him that the Salt Lake City airport was closed to Flight 378. But he had to try once more.

". . . repeat, 378, RVR on three-four-left is indicating zero. Over."

The response he got was clipped, terse, positive and final.

"Three-seven-eight, landing."

The controller made the sign of the cross.

Dudney Devlin said a prayer. She flicked on the NO SMOKING and FASTEN SEAT BELTS signs and hoped Cathy and the other stewardess had prepared the passengers—bracing positions, all loose objects out of pockets . . .

Full flaps, forty degrees.

Oh, God, where are the runway lights? Where in God's name are those lights . . . ?"

Her hands were sweating. Rate of descent one thousand feet per minute. Much too fast. No wonder. The yellow fly-bars had slipped below the orange airplane representing the horizon. Get the nose up. Bleed off that airspeed. Not too much. Don't want to stall. Easy now. Where were the approach lights? . . .

Altitude, three hundred feet.

She turned on her landing lights but the beams rammed helplessly against the dancing snow and fog. Fog so thick it was like smoke from burning oil.

Altitude two hundred and fifty feet.

Two hundred feet.

Mark Ashlock groaned. An inadvertent moan propelled by pain from his bleeding insides.

Dudney's hands tightened on the control yoke. She peered ahead. Nothing. Nothing but the opaqueness of the fog and smoke. She had the crazy feeling she was back in the simulator with its coated windshield.

Ashlock groaned again, this time louder.

"Dud. God, it hurts."

Even as he spoke, in pure instinct as involuntary as a sneeze, she took her eyes off the instruments to look at him worriedly.

In that moment, as the 737 swept toward the unseen runway, she was still looking hopelessly at Mark while the fly-bars dipped un-noticed below the little orange airplane and the IVSI crawled rapidly over the two-thousand-feet-per-minute mark.

She never saw that IVSI, nor the last of the blue approach lights flash by, their reflection agonizingly dim, nor the fly-bars skidding even lower. All she did see, in a single horrified glance like the blinking of an eye, was the altimeter winding down to zero.

She pulled the nose up and was reaching for the throttles to add more power when the gear touched down with terrible force in mud fifty feet short of the runway, held for a split second, and then collapsed as metal surrendered to stress.

The mud cushioned the impact so that Dudney heard the sound of rending, tearing metal more than she felt the jolt. They were sliding on the runway now but decelerating as the speed brakes automatically flipped up. Her actions were pure instinct, the subconscious product of countless simulated emergencies. Air conditioning packs off. Fuel pump switches off. Start levers off. Engine fire warning switches pulled and rotated. APU fire switches pulled and rotated.

Flight 378 skidded to an ignominious but safe stop, and the wail of screaming sirens filled the cold night air.

In the cockpit, Dudney thanked God that there was no fire. She was limp, empty and ten years older. With an effort that was like lifting a hundred-pound weight, she reached for the battery switch and turned it off.

Only dimly did she hear the sound of the fast but orderly evacuation in the cabin behind her. When Cathy Henderson opened the cockpit door, she found Dudney with her arms around Mark Ashlock, sobbing softly, fresh blood from the captain's wound staining her own white shirt.

Many minutes later a passenger agent going through the battered but intact cabin for passengers' personal effects found a crushed object that had fallen out of the galley.

"I think it's a birthday cake," he said to another agent. "Look, you can read some of the letters. I can't make out the rest of it. Somebody went to a lot of trouble. It's got the flight number and date on the frosting."

"Lousy way to celebrate a birthday," the other agent said. "Should we take it off the airplane?"

"Naw. Whoever it was for wouldn't want the damned thing now. Leave it on and let the salvage crew worry about it."

He tossed the cake back on the galley where it teetered precariously, the marred frosting illuminated by the blood-red light from a rescue truck outside.

HAP   BIRT   TO C   DEVL
FLIGHT 378
NOVE BER 8, 1971

Below the date there was just a suggestion of a tiny, twin-engine jet airplane, most of it mashed into the soggy cake.

CHAPTER TWELVE

The letter Dudney received ten days later from the Regional Office of the Federal Aviation Administration was brutally explicit, even though couched in that archaic, coldly legalistic litany of a governmental missive. It also was what she expected.

> Miss Dudney Devlin
> 6016 Maple Avenue
> El Segundo, Calif. 90245
>
> Dear Miss Devlin:
>
> Take notice that upon consideration of the report of investigation, it appears that you violated the Federal Aviation Regulations hereinafter specified by reason of the following circumstances:
>
> 1) At all times hereinafter mentioned you were and presently are holder of Airline Transport Pilot Certificate Number 9646383.
>
> 2) On November 8, 1971, you served as first officer on Trans-Coastal Flight 378, a Boeing 737, operating in scheduled air transportation on a flight from Los Angeles, California, to Salt Lake City, Utah. On this aforementioned flight, you were manipulating the controls.
>
> 3) On arriving in the vicinity of Salt Lake City, the captain was incapacitated by reason of a gunshot wound and you assumed command of the flight.
>
> 4) After being cleared to land at the Salt Lake City Airport, you were advised by Air Traffic Control that the Runway Visual Range reading for Runway 34-L, the only available

ILS runway for your use under existing weather conditions, was below the prescribed minimums as established by the operating manual of Trans-Coastal Airlines.

5) The initial below-minimums reported to you was an RVR reading of 1,800 feet. In subsequent communications between you and ATC, gradually worsening readings were reported to you of 1,400 feet, 800 feet, 100 feet and finally a zero reading.

6) You elected to continue your approach and landing, advising ATC to cancel your clearance to your established alternate which was Stapleton International Airport, Denver, and after you replied negatively to an ATC inquiry as to whether your aircraft was Category II equipped.

7) You permitted the aircraft not only to be operated in violation of the procedures prescribed in your company's manual, but in the course of this violation you allowed the aircraft to contact the ground short of the runway with an impact force exceeding the design limits of the landing gear, thereby causing extensive damage to the aircraft and endangering the lives of 91 passengers and your three fellow crew members.

8) You implied, in your communications with ATC preceding the landing attempt, that your decision was based primarily on the serious condition of the captain. In subsequent conversations with investigative personnel from this agency and the National Transportation Safety Board's Bureau of Aviation Safety, you stated that your judgment of the captain's condition was derived from an opinion expressed by a stewardess who was providing the captain with emergency medical treatment.

9) The aforementioned stewardess, while a registered nurse, was not a qualified practicing physician.

By reason of the foregoing facts and circumstances, you violated the following sections of the Federal Aviation Regulations:

(a) Section 121.651 (a) in that you executed an instrument approach and landing under IFR at an airport when the latest U. S. Weather Bureau report or a source approved by the Weather Bureau indicated that the visibility was less than that prescribed by the Administrator and/or the company rules under which your flight was being operated.

(b) Section 91.9, in that you operated said aircraft in a careless manner so as to endanger the lives and property of others, by reason of the foregoing facts and circumstances.

By reason of all the foregoing facts and circumstances, you demonstrated that you do not possess the degree of care, judgment and responsibility required of the holder of an Airline Transport Pilot Certificate operating in air transportation. Therefore, taking into consideration all of the circumstances of this case, we propose, pursuant to the authority vested in the Administrator by Section 609 of the Federal Aviation Act of 1958, as amended, to revoke your Airline Transport Pilot Certificate.

An order for such revocation will be issued unless, prior to November 28, 1971, you elect to appeal this revocation notice, in which case you may proceed in accordance with the proper appeal machinery.

Very truly yours,

John Sharkley
Chief Regional Enforcement
Officer
Federal Aviation Administration
Los Angeles, California

The fact that it was no surprise had no effect on her reactions. In successive order she was angered, frightened and then prone to rationalize—all three reactions sending her inevitably to ALPA for help. Before the revocation notice came, she couldn't care less what happened to her; she felt singularly unlike a heroine, although she knew she had saved Mark Ashlock's life. But once Mark was out of danger, Dudney had her own ordeal to face.

Ordeal it was, starting with the traumatic experience every pilot dreads—the knowledge that she had wrecked an airplane. She dreamed of the abortive landing nightly, and in waking hours she thought about it—reliving with stark clarity every moment, from the time the crazed gunman fired the single shot to the sickening scream of tortured metal giving way under impact. Painfully aware of what had gone wrong and then rationalizing, excusing, justifying every time she faced up to the terrible truth: she had violated regulations and then closed her only escape route by messing up the landing. The crash itself did more than destroy the main gear—it also destroyed her alibi, compounding her sin by emphasizing the danger to which she had exposed passengers and crew. Only luck had saved them. If fire had resulted, there could have been fatalities, for she knew only too well the thin margin of survivability in a post-impact fire.

It did not help much to have Mark thank her. She saw him in a Salt Lake City hospital the day after he underwent emergency surgery, sitting by his bed and holding his hand with unspoken love and gratitude that he was alive. Before she was admitted to his room, he was told of the crash and he realized the depth of her devotion, the terrible finality of the decision she had made, how rawly vulnerable she now was to punishment.

At first she did not want to talk about it, putting on a front of bravado for his benefit and insisting she wasn't worried. But he saw fear in her eyes as well as relief that he would recover.

"Have you talked to Battles yet?" he asked.

"On the phone, right after the . . . landing. He said not to worry and that he'd talk to me when I got back to L.A. I'm going to see Crusty as soon as I get back. He'll—"

"Don't be afraid of Johnny. He'll be on your side as much as he can. Tell him everything that happened."

"As much as he can," she repeated, bitterness creeping into her voice. "That won't be very much, will it?"

"Maybe more than you think. If the chief pilot defends you, it'll carry more weight than ALPA. There *were* extenuating circumstances, Dud. I know that more than anyone else. I know why you did it. I'm grateful, darling."

Tears flooded her eyes. "They'll throw the book at me, won't they, Mark?"

"Possibly. Just tell the truth. Hell, honey, *I'm* the extenuating circumstances, and if it had been you who caught that bullet I probably would have done exactly what you did."

"With one difference," she said with a faint, feeble touch of her old humor. "You wouldn't have wiped out that gear."

"Maybe. Without knowing all the details, I'd say it would have been luck if anyone, including myself, had gotten her down in one piece, and it was just plain bad luck that you didn't. Fifty-fifty."

"Fifty-fifty are pretty bad odds for an airline pilot's decision," she said soberly.

"I'm thinking of the other odds."

"What other odds?"

"The odds I had if you had gone on to Denver."

The interview with Battles was not as painful as she feared, but neither was it very encouraging. At best, he was gentle—so gentle that she almost wished he would revert to his old harshness. His sympathy was that of a doctor trying to reassure a patient he knows is doomed, and lacking the courage to break the news. As best she could, she recounted the events of Flight 378—not hiding her own culpability.

"Everything was fine down to the last two hundred feet," she told him candidly. "I had everything locked in for a coupled approach. The localizer and glide slope looked good—a little low on the glide slope but I was correcting. Then . . . then . . ."

He waited patiently.

"Then, I heard Mark groan. He said something. Like how much it hurt. I took my eyes off the instrument panel to see if he was all right—it was pure reflex. When I looked back at my instruments, all I saw was the altimeter. I don't know what my glide slope showed, or the IVSI, but I knew I had run out of altitude. I was going to apply power—I had a feeling, a sixth sense, that my sink rate had gotten away from me. Then we hit, and it was too late."

"I'm afraid," Battles said glumly, "those few seconds of distraction add up to pilot error. Dudney, why didn't you have one of the stews sit in the left seat and call out your altitudes? Or even one of the passengers? You might have found one with some flying experience."

"There wasn't time. Mark was bleeding to death and we were

afraid to move him out of the seat. Besides, I sent Cathy back to the cabin just before we landed. I knew the landing'd be hairy, and if we busted up, her place was with the passengers, not me. I figured the same thing applied to the other stew."

He searched her tense, strained face, compassion showing in his own.

"I suppose there'll have to be a hearing," she ventured.

"There will. I'll be there to testify if needed as to your qualifications, your over-all record and so forth. Whether I'll defend you to the hilt, I honestly can't tell you right now. I do know there were extenuating circumstances, plus the fact that nobody got a scratch in spite of that fouled-up landing."

The same words Mark had used, she thought. Extenuating circumstances. The cornerstone of her defense.

"If . . . if they decide I was wrong, what will they do?" she asked. "Ground me for thirty or sixty or ninety days? Or the full book—revoke my license?"

He decided he had to be blunt. "They've already revoked your certificate—for thirty days. An emergency revocation, it's called. To make sure you don't fly again until your case is settled. FAA just notified me about an hour ago."

She was jolted, and from her expression of misery and shame, he knew he might as well have slapped her in the face.

"An emergency revocation was inevitable, Dudney," he said, not unkindly. "After all, you did prang that airplane. I'd slap a two-week grounding on you myself, as company punishment, for letting yourself get distracted. Mind if I give you some advice?"

"No, sir."

"Go talk to Crusty. He'll line up some legal aid from ALPA. If and when you get notice of a hearing, you'll need all the help you can get. Don't try to be your own attorney. Don't try to run your own defense. Meanwhile"—the look on his own features matched hers in unhappiness—"you're grounded until further notice. I'm sorry, Dudney, but I can't fight an emergency revocation. Don't take it too hard. You might beat the rap, and besides, I wouldn't let you go back on the line right away even if the FAA hadn't suspended you. It's best you rest for a couple of weeks. Line up your ducks with

ALPA, I'll rush through a positive space pass for Salt Lake City any time you wanna see Mark, and keep your chin up."

She did run to Crusty. He impractically cursed the FAA as a bunch of Gestapo-trained, bureaucratic bunglers obviously re-enacting the Spanish Inquisition. In a far more practical way, he introduced her to Tom Culbertson, an ALPA attorney whose youthful face belied his shock of unruly white hair, making him resemble a youngish Everett Dirksen. Wearily, she retold the story of the flight while he took copious notes, his expression never varying from one of interested concern. He had to ask her what Battles didn't because the chief pilot already knew.

"Your, uh, relationship with Captain Ashlock, Dudney," he said haltingly. "It, ah, might very well be brought up by the FAA, if their enforcement people have done a thorough job of investigating. The question is whether we should bring it up ourselves, as part of our defense."

"Extenuating circumstances," Dudney said, managing a hollow smile.

"Exactly. On the other hand, it might be bad strategy to hang our hats on this aspect."

She mulled this over before replying. "Let's wait and play it by ear. If the FAA brings it up, I'll tell the truth."

He looked doubtful, started to argue, but changed his mind. A few days later, when she received the permanent revocation threat, Culbertson didn't waste time with false reassurances.

"I'm a little surprised," he admitted. "If you had been a captain, I would have expected something this drastic. But not a copilot— you've only had about a year's experience and the FAA knows you were in one hell of a spot. Ninety-nine out of a hundred first officers might have made the same decision you did. I won't promise you we can protect you from any punitive action, Dudney, but we're not going to let them hang you."

"I'll take any justified punishment," she said dully. "But permanent revocation is the same as a death sentence. I don't think I deserve that."

"Neither do I. We'll do our best."

The hearing was set for the day before her emergency revocation expired. She was glad to discover that it was closed to the press, even though the press had clamored—both through Jason Silvanius and the FAA public affairs officer in Los Angeles—for an open hearing. Jason also had done much to keep the press off her back after the first few hectic hours following the crash. She visited his office a week later and he saw her wince when she looked at some headlines from the clips on his desk.

WOMAN AIRLINE PILOT INVOLVED IN COCKPIT SHOOTING AND
    CRASH

NATION'S FIRST LADY AIRLINE PILOT IN NEAR-FATAL ACCIDENT

GUNMAN SHOOTS PILOT; AIRLINER CRASHES WITH WOMAN AT
    CONTROLS

WOMAN AIRLINE PILOT CRASHES AFTER GUNMAN SHOOTS CAPTAIN

"If the FAA's as unfair as those stories," she told Silvanius, "I'm dead."

"The stories themselves aren't too bad, Dud," he said. "The headlines are misleading, but you can't blame reporters for what's put over their copy."

"I'm not going to read them, Jason, but I would like to know what they said about . . . about Mark and me."

"Nothing, Dud. They don't know and I'm not going to tell them. Even though it's an angle they'd devour like a starved tiger. I'm not even sure the FAA knows or whether it'll be brought out at the hearing."

The FAA did know. And it was brought out.

Dudney had imagined a hearing in a kind of small courtroom. It turned out to be more like the Trans-Coastal Board of Directors room, albeit on a much smaller scale and, in comparison to the Board's plush quarters, possessing all the aesthetic appeal of an operating room.

Its chief feature was a long rectangular table encircled by leather-padded chairs in the center of the room. John Sharkley, FAA's chief regional enforcement officer, sat at one end and rose politely when

Dudney entered. Culbertson and Ashlock were with her and she saw Battles sitting in a chair placed against the wall.

"Miss Devlin, I believe," Sharkley said with a thin smile. He was small, dapper and wore a bow tie that fitted his rather prim personality as medals fit a general's demeanor.

"Yes, sir."

"And Tom, good to see you again. Tom, have you met Mr. Feldman, our deputy administrator for the West Coast region? Mr. Feldman, this is Tom Culbertson of ALPA and Miss Devlin of Trans-Coastal."

Dan Feldman was a tall, rather slender man with laughing eyes and a quizzical mouth turned down at the corners as if he were always ready to express doubts. He acknowledged Sharkley's introductions, shaking hands vigorously with Culbertson and bowing slightly to Dudney. Sharkley looked at Mark Ashlock questioningly.

"I don't believe I've had the . . ."

"Captain Ashlock, Trans-Coastal."

"Oh yes, Captain Ashlock. Congratulations on your recovery, Captain. Must have been a harrowing experience." Sharkley was speaking stiffly, formally, almost giving the impression he was ill at ease.

"Very," Ashlock said laconically. "I'm only here thanks to my first officer."

Sharkley frowned, as if Ashlock had opened fire prematurely. "Captain Ashlock, this is Mr. Feldman." As the two men shook hands, Sharkley added, "We might as well take our seats and we'll start the proceeding."

Dudney sat between Mark and Culbertson, to Sharkley's left. Battles moved to a seat next to Ashlock and Feldman was at the enforcement chief's right. The only other occupant was a bespectacled little man with a shiny bald dome who was parked unobtrusively in a corner behind Sharkley, adjusting the paper on a stenographic machine. The noise reminded Sharkley of his presence and he mentioned that "Mr. Gerber is our official stenographer."

"Just a minute," Culbertson said. "Are you acting as the hearing examiner, John?"

"In view of the, uh, unusual aspects of this case, I thought it proper if I assumed the role of hearing examiner," Sharkley replied, implying surprise that the ALPA attorney had raised the issue. "I assumed you'd have no objections."

"You assumed incorrectly," Culbertson growled. "In a proceeding involving the loss of an airline pilot's right to fly, I would expect the FAA to observe every legal amenity."

"There's nothing in the rules that says an enforcement officer can't conduct a certificate revocation hearing, Tom," Sharkley said in the tone of an adult soft-soaping a recalcitrant child.

"Maybe not, but it's damned unusual—"

"I said this was an unusual case."

"—so unusual that I must protest. It's like having the prosecution sitting as the judge."

"Your protest is duly noted," Sharkley said mildly but firmly. "I assure you, Tom, and you, Miss Devlin, that, acting as hearing examiner, I have no preconceived notions about this matter and—"

"The hell you don't!" Culbertson snarled. "You signed a notice of permanent revocation after issuing a thirty-day emergency revocation. If that's not a preconceived attitude, you might as well call a hanging judge impartial."

"I'm not here to hang anyone," Sharkley said, his face reddening and his voice rising. "I'm here to ascertain facts and make a judgment accordingly. May I remind you, Tom, that the burden of proof is on the pilot at this stage. He has . . . I mean *she* has already been found in violation of the FARs. This hearing is at her own request, part of the appeals procedure. If she can present evidence to warrant our lifting or modifying the revocation order, I'll sign it willingly and gladly. Is that understood?"

"I would still prefer to have this hearing conducted by a regular examiner," Culbertson said coldly.

"As I said before, your protest has been duly noted. Let's get on with it." Sharkley lifted a bulging, rather dilapidated briefcase to the table and removed a thick file from which he took several sheets of paper. He tapped on them, then handed the sheaf to Culbertson. "These, Tom, are the various depositions taken in the course of the investigation. I sent you the carbons a week ago. The transcripts of ATC communications, eyewitness accounts, testimony of passengers and crew—everything pertinent to this case. Plus First Officer Devlin's training and line flying record. If you'll glance at them, I think you'll find they're exactly what I supplied you."

Culbertson examined them briefly. "Okay, I'll agree this is a complete record as of up to now. I have my own copies for reference." He took these out of his briefcase.

"Then, if you have no objection, I suggest we accept as factual this record of Flight 378 on the eighth of November last, and the events preceding and subsequent to the flight."

"Agreed," the ALPA attorney said. "In the interest of time, we accept this record as a factual account."

"Good," Sharkley said. His face tightened into a semblance of a frown bordering on a look of accusation as he faced Dudney. "Miss Devlin, it is the contention of the FAA that you violated in fact FAR Section 121.651 (a) relative to landing below prescribed minimums, and that you violated both in spirit and in fact Section 91.9 relative to your exercising the care, judgment and responsibility expected of a pilot holding an ATR. By appealing our notice of revocation, you in effect denied these two allegations. Am I correct?"

"No, sir," Dudney replied.

"You do not deny them? Then what, may I ask, is the—"

"I do not deny that I landed below minimums, knowingly and with premeditation. That's on the record. I do deny I failed to exercise care, judgment and responsibility."

Culbertson broke in. "And on those grounds, Mr. Sharkley, ALPA considers the punitive action taken by FAA as arbitrary, unjust and excessive."

"If this action is unfair, Miss Devlin," Sharkley said ponderously, "I will be happy to make amends. Both the FAA and ALPA have agreed there is no point in reviewing the events of that unfortunate night, except as they relate to the specific charges against First Officer Devlin. Now, inasmuch as Miss Devlin has stipulated that the first charge is valid, we can concentrate on the finding which she has denied. Captain Ashlock, are you strong enough to answer a few questions?"

Ashlock straightened up in his chair and Dudney, with the inopportune illogic of a woman, thought he had never looked handsomer despite his paleness and loss of weight.

"I'd be glad to, Mr. Sharkley."

"Good, Captain. If you feel any fatigue or would like a brief break, just let me know." Ashlock nodded. "Now then, I gather from the previous interrogations of you conducted by the NTSB, subsequent to the accident, you at no time issued orders to First Officer Devlin regarding the conduct of the flight, from the time your wound was inflicted. Is that correct?"

"No, sir, it's not entirely correct."

"No?" The one word was an expletive of accusation and disbelief. "In what way, may I ask?"

"I recall telling D . . . Miss Devlin after I was shot to 'get her down fast.' Or words to that effect. I told her I thought I was bleeding to death. Which, I learned later, was the truth."

"I see. Did you, as captain of Flight 378, regard this as an order?"

"I certainly did," Mark said grimly, glancing at Dudney.

"Tell me, Captain Ashlock, at the time you issued this 'order,' as you phrase it, what information did you possess as to the weather conditions at the Salt Lake City airport?"

"The last RVR reading we had for our assigned runway was twenty-four hundred feet, with indications of deterioration."

"But the last reading provided the flight, preceding the shooting, was twenty-four hundred feet, which was the minimum RVR for a legal landing in an aircraft not equipped for CAT II operations."

"And a deteriorating RVR," Ashlock prompted.

"I find no mention of the RVR deteriorating in the ATC transcript," Sharkley said sharply. "Nor in the transcript from the cockpit voice recorder."

Culbertson interrupted, his finger speared on a page in one of the transcripts. "Page nine, Transcript One," he pointed out to Sharkley. "Towards the bottom. It says, and I quote: 'Trans-Coastal 378, you are cleared for an ILS approach runway three-four-left. Current RVR for three-four-left is twenty-four hundred. Informatively, the RVR has been decreasing fairly rapidly.' Find it, John?"

The enforcement officer scowled. "I found it. But I still can't see where there's any mention of the RVR's being likely to continue a previous decrease. The reference is to past deterioration, not future. Is it your contention, Captain Ashlock, that this advisory showed you already were encountering or were about to encounter below-minimums, and that you ordered First Officer Devlin to land regardless?"

Mark hesitated, choosing his words carefully. "It is my contention that the information provided us at the time I ordered Miss Devlin to land indicated every possibility we were below minimums or about to go below."

Sharkley's eyes narrowed to near slits. "Frankly, Captain, I fail to see how you could interpret that advisory as a below-limits warning."

"I'm sorry you can't," Ashlock said blandly, "because that's exactly how I did interpret it."

"I see. Captain Ashlock, let me ask you this. If no shooting had occurred, would you have continued your approach on the basis of this advisory?"

Again Mark paused. "Yes and no," he finally replied.

"What do you mean—yes and no?"

"I would have continued the approach pending a further weather advisory. The RVR was on the margin. If it had dropped further, I would have had to abandon the approach. But I have to point out, Mr.—"

"One moment, Captain. You say if the RVR had deteriorated further you would not have attempted a landing?"

"Of course not." Ashlock's voice was brittle. "But as I was saying, that decision would have been predicated on normal circumstances, uh, routine conditions. The situation facing my copilot was far from routine or normal."

"I see." Dudney thought that if Sharkley said, "I see," once more, in that tone implying unvarnished doubt, she'd hit him. The enforcement chief was looking at Feldman with a glance that might as well have been a shrug of hopelessness.

"Captain Ashlock," Sharkley resumed, "was your alleged 'order' to First Officer—"

"I said I told her to land," Ashlock snapped. "There was nothing alleged about it."

"I beg your pardon. Was your order to First Officer Devlin the last time you exercised command authority?"

"To the best of my knowledge, yes."

"You said nothing further to her, nothing that in any way could be described or interpreted as a command?"

"I don't remember much after that. Everything was pretty hazy. Like a bad dream. In a sense, I suppose my condition was something of a command."

"I'm not sure I follow you, Captain."

"Well, I mean that the last thing I said to First Officer Devlin was to get the hell down as fast as possible. From then on, all she had to go on was the fact that my condition was steadily worsening. She knew I was in bad shape when I gave her the order. When she saw that I was dying, the order took on more urgency."

"I see. Captain, you said that under normal circumstances you would have abandoned your approach if the RVR had continued to decrease. Suppose your position was reversed. Suppose First Officer Devlin had been gravely wounded. Would you have attempted to land at Salt Lake City, assuming the same weather conditions that confronted your copilot?"

"I would," Ashlock said promptly.

Sharkley sniffed suspiciously. "Captain Ashlock, you are an experienced command pilot with a spotless record, an excellent reputation and—from everything I've heard about you—possessing judgment and a sense of responsibility far above average. Do you mean to sit there and tell me you would have jeopardized the lives of nearly one hundred persons because you *thought* your copilot *might* be dying? You would have traded off one life for more than ninety lives?"

"I'd say there was a damned good chance I would have done just that."

"You say 'a chance.' I'd appreciate your elaborating on that."

"Naturally I would have weighed all factors. Including my experience, which would have been an overriding factor." The minute the words were out of his mouth, he cursed himself for saying them. Sharkley lunged at him with the alacrity of a duelist who has spotted an opening.

"In other words, only an experienced pilot should make the kind of decision that First Officer Devlin made," Sharkley said quickly.

Ashlock tried to pick up the fumble. "Such a decision would be a calculated risk regardless of a pilot's experience."

"But a greater risk for a relatively inexperienced pilot."

"Not necessarily. Under the conditions we had that night, a senior captain might have crashed as easily as a pea-green rookie. It was literally zero-zero and a landing under those circumstances is extremely difficult for any pilot. Completing it successfully would be as much a matter of luck as skill."

"But," Sharkley pressed, "you said if you had been faced with the same set of circumstances confronting your copilot experience would have been an overriding factor in your final decision."

"Mr. Sharkley," Ashlock said with a trace of impatience, "I don't think anyone in this room including yourself or even Captain Battles could sit here in the cloistered safety of this room and honestly say what he would have done given the same emergency facing my copilot. The decision had to be made instantly, under terrible stress. Anyone who claimed he definitely would not have acted as she did is at best guilty of hindsight, or at worst a damned liar. I swear to you, sir, I don't really know what *I* would have done."

"You don't, eh?" The enforcement officer's tone was saturated with scorn.

"No, sir, I don't."

"Captain Battles," Sharkley said, shifting his attack like a gunnery officer switching targets, "I think it would not be amiss to ask you if you agree with Captain Ashlock."

Battles, his big hands cupped under his chin, stirred uncomfortably. "I agree with Captain Ashlock that no pilot—whether he had twenty thousand hours logged or two thousand hours—could say before the fact or after the fact whether he would have made the same decision as Miss Devlin. I'm inclined to think, Mr. Sharkley, that in this particular case there has been too much hindsight and Monday morning quarterbacking. If an airplane hadn't been washed out, First Officer Devlin's decision would seem far less critical to us. Certainly less erroneous. After all, she didn't expect to crash. She admittedly took a calculated risk but I'd venture to say she regarded the odds as being in her favor."

"I see. Miss Devlin, did you consider the odds in your favor?"

"Yes, sir, I did."

Sharkley picked up the file, waved it twice and laid it down again. "The deposition from the senior stewardess, Miss Henderson, which I can read aloud if you like, mentions that just prior to landing you told her to prepare the cabin for a planned emergency. In other words, for a possible crash. Do you recollect doing so?"

"Yes, sir."

"Then how does that square with your claim that you thought the odds were in your favor?"

Dudney started to answer but Culbertson slammed his fist on the table. "Just a minute, John! If she hadn't issued those orders to the stewardesses you would have stuck her with another charge—failing to prepare for a possible crash. What the hell are you trying to pull?"

"Calm down, Tom," Sharkley said placidly. "You're right. If she hadn't told the cabin attendants to institute planned emergency procedures, there would have been a third charge made against her. I commend her for being prudent. Nevertheless, the fact that she *did* issue such orders indicates that she was not entirely confident of completing the landing. Isn't that the case, Miss Devlin?"

"I didn't expect to crash, if that's what you're implying," Dudney replied sullenly.

"Of course you didn't," Sharkley said with sarcasm. "But there had to be an element of uncertainty in your mind."

Battles growled, "I'd hang any pilot of mine who didn't make the necessary precautionary preparations for emergency evacuation in a zero-zero landing. For Christ's sake, Sharkley, are you telling us she didn't have an emergency? I'd hate like hell to have been in her boots."

"So would I, Captain Battles, so would I," Sharkley said hastily. "The FAA is not denying that First Officer Devlin was under extreme tension, and that a real emergency situation existed. As the revocation notice stated, however, her reaction to that emergency was totally unwise, undeniably imprudent and completely lacking in the responsibility expected of an airline pilot. Now, Miss Devlin, inasmuch as you have chosen to challenge this verdict, I would be happy to hear you justify your actions. As I said earlier, I'm not interested in hanging anybody. I am merely doing my duty to protect the public from flying with potentially dangerous pilots."

"I resent that!" Ashlock slashed. "She's about as potentially dangerous as Santa Claus. You're trying to ruin the career of a professional airline pilot on the basis of one forgivable mistake, forged under the most incredible stress imaginable."

Sharkley fingered his bow tie. "We'll see, Captain Ashlock, we'll see." His voice was ominous, nastily confident, and Dudney shuddered inwardly. She had an idea of what was coming.

"Miss Devlin," the enforcement officer said with deceptive politeness, "if you have a legitimate defense for the actions you took, I'd be very glad to hear it. And, I might add, consider it in determining whether to lessen the drastic punitive measures we've taken against you."

"I believe," Dudney said slowly, "that the phrase 'extenuating circumstances' would be the crux of my defense."

"'Extenuating circumstances,'" Sharkley repeated. "I see. Tell me, what would these extenuating circumstances be?"

"You know damned well what—" Culbertson started to say.

"Let her answer," Sharkley interrupted.

Dudney cleared her throat. "I would say, Mr. Sharkley, the knowledge that the captain would bleed to death in another twenty minutes if I didn't get that aircraft down would constitute extenuating circumstances."

"Twenty minutes, you say. From where did this prognosis come?"

"Miss Henderson, the senior stewardess. She was in the cockpit trying to help Captain Ashlock. When I told her we were going to our alternate, Denver, she asked me how long the flight would take. I said a little over an hour and that's when she told me we had twenty minutes at the most. Before Mar—the captain would bleed to death."

"I see. You based your decision on the medical knowledge of a former nurse?"

"There was no other knowledge available," Dudney snapped, anger flashing from her brown eyes. "Cathy advised me there was no doctor on board. I had to take her word on the captain's condition. How serious it was. After all, she *had* been a nurse."

"It was later determined, Mr. Sharkley," Culbertson interposed, "that Miss Henderson's diagnosis was only too correct. The doctors who operated on Captain Ashlock in Salt Lake City were of the opinion that twenty minutes was just about all the time he had left. His life was on the line."

"The FAA does not argue with the fact that First Officer Devlin saved Captain Ashlock's life," Sharkley said dryly. "But the FAA does contend that, in doing so, First Officer Devlin put the lives of ninety-one passengers on an equally precarious line."

He looked at Dudney with the expectant air of a man about to drop a bomb. "And the FAA further contends that First Officer Devlin made her decision on purely emotional grounds, unbecoming an airline pilot and providing us with unfortunate but undeniable proof that the revocation order was both justified and wise."

The room was so silent, Dudney could swear she could hear breathing. It was Culbertson who broke the spell.

"Are you saying that First Officer Devlin is emotionally unfit to be an airline pilot?"

"I am saying," Sharkley replied with deadly emphasis, "that she endangered ninety-one lives with a decision stemming from emotionalism, not professionalism."

Culbertson looked first at Dudney, then at Ashlock, as if seeking permission to open the Pandora's box. The captain's face was grim. Dudney's was pleading. Sharkley, sensing the ALPA attorney's dilemma, said with syrupy smoothness, "Do you have a question, Tom?"

"I'd like to know what you mean by emotionalism," Culbertson replied with obvious unhappiness.

"I mean the decision was the product of an emotional conflict, ignoring the far more vital issue of the flight's safety." Sharkley was milking the moment of truth dry, sucking on the insinuation as one would drain through a straw the last drops of a savory beverage.

There was silence again.

"I think," Dudney said curtly, "you'd better say what's really on your mind."

"Very well, Miss Devlin. Let's get to the heart of the matter. It has been brought to our attention that your relationship to Captain Ashlock is a romantic one. Is that true?"

"It is," she answered, her voice powder-puff soft.

"Captain Ashlock, I regret the necessity of invading what normally would be an extremely personal province, but I find it essential to ask you the same question. Is your relationship to Miss Devlin something other than that of a captain to a first officer?"

"Yes," Mark Ashlock said.

"Mr. Sharkley, I'd like to say something if I may." It was John Battles, and the enforcement chief nodded. "As the immediate supervisor of both Captain Ashlock and First Officer Devlin, I must point out that I have been aware of this relationship for some time. If I thought for one minute that it was affecting Miss Devlin's performance as a line pilot I would have grounded her immediately. As a matter of fact, it was Captain Ashlock who informed me that Miss Devlin preferred not to fly as his copilot because she thought their mutual personal feelings might have an effect on cockpit discipline."

"Then why was she flying with him on this—"

"I'm coming to that. It was Captain Ashlock's idea. He traded trips so he could be on 378, which was Miss Devlin's regularly assigned flight. It was her birthday and he wanted to surprise her. She had no idea Ashlock would be the captain until she signed in with crew sked an hour before departure. In other words, Mr. Sharkley, her attitude has consistently been one of admirable professionalism. I might add that in all the years I've been both a line pilot and chief pilot I've never known a more skilled, dedicated and responsible first officer than Miss Devlin. Speaking as Trans-Coastal's chief pilot, and for Trans-Coastal's management, I am authorized to tell you, sir, that the company regards permanent certificate revocation as far too severe and unjust. The company is prepared to levy its own punishment— grounding without pay for two weeks."

Dudney looked at him with something akin to pure, unadulterated worship. Sharkley looked at him with something akin to patronization.

"Thank you, Captain Battles," the presiding officer said. "I must compliment Miss Devlin on having earned the loyalty and support of her superiors. But, Captain Battles, you have by implication raised a very interesting issue. In your spirited defense of First Officer Devlin you described her as—let's make sure I remember the exact terminology—as skilled, dedicated and responsible. Were those your words?"

"They were."

"Then, Captain Battles, would you—as Miss Devlin's chief pilot —describe her decision of the night of November 8 as representative of a skilled, dedicated and responsible pilot?"

Battles mentally thrashed in the trap he had sprung on himself.

"I would describe that decision as questionable, but one that must be understood in the context of the circumstances under which it was made," he replied cautiously.

"The circumstances being great emotional stress?"

"Any pilot faced with that decision would be under great emotional stress," Battles insisted. "On one side of the coin, it's certain death for the guy you're flying with. On the other side of the coin is the somewhat better chance that you can get your bird down safely."

"But wouldn't you say that because of this, uh, romantic attachment existing between Captain Ashlock and Miss Devlin her emotional stress was far greater than what other pilots would encounter?"

"Possibly. To a degree, but who's to say how much of a degree? Let me put it this way, Mr. Sharkley. Nine out of ten pilots would have been tempted to try that landing."

"Oh, tempted, you say. I agree, Captain Battles. Tempted, to be sure. But would nine out of ten pilots actually follow temptation?"

Battles snorted. "I've already told you it's too hard to say what anyone would have done—and I don't exempt myself."

As if tiring of Battles, the enforcement chief turned back to Dudney.

"Miss Devlin, the ATC communications transcript shows that Departure Control, in advising you that the RVR was down to virtually zero, asked you if your aircraft was CAT II equipped. Is that correct?"

"Yes, sir."

"And your answer was negative?"

"Yes, sir."

"Is it fair to say that at this crucial point, knowing you lacked the electronic aids essential for a blind landing and that the visibility was as bad as it possibly could be, you were aware that the chances for a successful landing were lessened drastically?"

"I wasn't aware of much except Captain Ashlock's condition," she answered.

"Oh, come now, Miss Devlin. The thought didn't flash through your mind that things were about as bad as they could get? That you weren't aware of the danger? Are you trying to tell me you regarded that landing as routine?"

"Of course not. I . . . I weighed the difficulties against the possibility that Mark might die. There wasn't any time for self-debate, Mr. Sharkley. I had to act quickly. I suppose I acknowledged the hazards subconsciously, even while I was concentrating on the more real hazard facing Captain Ashlock."

"I appreciate the time element, Miss Devlin. I realize this wasn't a matter of mentally listing the pros and cons of landing versus the pros and cons of proceeding to Denver. Am I accurately describing your mental state at the time?"

"Yes, sir."

He seemed to be gathering himself for one final, killing stab into her vitals. His lips tightened, he put both hands on the table and he leaned forward.

"Let's quit pussyfooting around, Miss Devlin. Are you in love with Captain Ashlock?"

"Yes, sir." Defiantly, proudly.

"Then tell me, Miss Devlin—if the wounded man bleeding to death in that left seat had been anyone but Captain Mark Ashlock, would you still have attempted to land at Salt Lake City?"

He leaned back in his chair before she answered, triumphant, waiting.

"I don't know. I . . . I think so."

"The truth now, Miss Devlin."

"I don't know what the truth is."

"You're the nation's first woman airline pilot, Miss Devlin. You have achieved that status against great odds, overcoming prejudice and God knows how many other obstacles. Your record to date, as Captain Battles testified, has been one of highest merit. I find it hard— no, impossible—impossible to believe you would have flaunted safety, forgotten all your training and abandoned every tradition of an airline pilot's responsibility to his passengers unless your sole motivation was emotional. I am giving you, Miss Devlin, the answer which you're so reluctant to provide yourself—that you would *not* have landed that aircraft illegally if the captain had not been Mark Ashlock. I'm telling you and everyone else in this room that your feelings toward

Captain Ashlock dictated your decision. The revocation notice accused you of failing to possess the degree of care, judgment and responsibility required of a holder of the Airline Transport Pilot certificate. I'm saying you abdicated care, judgment and responsibility. Now let me ask you again. I want to hear it from your own mouth. Would you have tried to land at Salt Lake City, or would you have proceeded to Denver, if another captain was in that left seat—helpless, critically wounded and pleading with you before unconsciousness overtook him to get that airplane down on the ground as quickly as possible?"

Her face was as ashen as Mark's.

"I don't know," she repeated. "As God is my witness, I don't know."

"I think you do, Miss Devlin," he said quietly, not without pity. "I think you do."

Again, the hearing room was snow-silent.

Dan Feldman took a fat, curved pipe out of his pocket, filled it with tobacco and touched a match to the brown flakes. The smoke curled around his head and drifted lazily toward the ceiling.

"It seems to me, John," he said to Sharkley, "what you're trying to say is that First Officer Devlin responded to this emergency like a woman instead of an airline pilot."

"Well . . ." Sharkley began uncertainly.

"I'm wondering if we're trying to hang her solely as a woman, rather than punish her as an airline pilot," Feldman pressed. "I think, John, we should make every effort to be fair."

Both Dudney and Culbertson glanced at the FAA official with surprised gratitude. Sharkley frowned.

"I assure you, Dan, we're not being anti-feminine. Nevertheless, it's only too apparent that her motivation was purely emotional and if that's not being feminine at the wrong time in the wrong place—well, if the shoe fits, as the saying goes. I must point out, furthermore, that we should not lose sight of the crash itself. The fact that there were no injuries, nor any fatalities, does not lessen the seriousness of her offense. She landed short of the runway at an impact force which the flight recorder showed exceeded twenty-one hundred feet a minute. The gear is stressed to withstand somewhat higher impact forces, but in this case the first impact was on rather muddy ground, imposing severe lateral forces as well. Disregarding all other aspects of the case, this alone would warrant major punitive action. May I remind you that First Officer Devlin herself has already admitted to investigators that just prior to contacting the ground she was distracted by hearing Captain Ashlock groan, that during this momentary distraction she failed to monitor essential instruments, that she allowed her sink rate to increase excessively, and that she failed to halt the sink rate by applying power because there wasn't time. I repeat —there wasn't time! Not only her decision to land illegally but the very commission of pilot error was the product of what we might term the factor of female emotionalism. Now I don't blame Miss Devlin for trying to save her career and I don't fault Tom Culbertson here for trying to defend an ALPA member. But I am surprised, Captain Battles, that a responsible representative of airline management would tell the FAA—in the face of all this evidence—that this girl possesses the temperament, stability and skill of a qualified airline pilot."

Battles turned red.

"That's a bunch of crap, Sharkley!" he exploded. "You might as well question my own integrity and that of Trans-Coastal's training department. May I remind you, sir, that this girl was far above average throughout training and line flying. I rode shotgun myself on her rating flight. One of your own inspectors rated her superior after her six-month check ride. If all that adds up to a bum pilot, you might as well indict me, our instructors and the FAA's check-ride procedures. Miss Devlin's performance on the line has been exemplary. Exemplary, hell—it's been damned near perfect! So don't sit there, you desk-flying sonofabitch, and tell me this kid can't fly an airplane as well as ninety-nine per cent of our pilots. You're crucifying her for one lousy mistake committed during a one-in-ten-million set of circumstances, and under conditions that would have made some senior captains come apart at the seams!"

"A man with your experience, Captain Battles," Sharkley fired back, "should know perfectly well that pilots who come apart at the seams during an emergency have no business in the cockpit. It is your so-called one-in-ten-million set of circumstances that separates the men from the boys."

"Or the girls from the boys," Battles retorted savagely. "I think Mr. Feldman called it right—would you have taken such drastic action against a man?"

"I certainly would. Except that I doubt whether a man would have ever gotten involved the way Miss Devlin did. A man wouldn't have let emotionalism paint him into a corner."

"The hell he wouldn't. If a copilot was flying with a captain who was his best friend and he had the same choice Dudney had, he would have gotten that airplane down as fast as possible and damn the FARs!"

"And in that case," Sharkley said smugly, "we would have filed revocation notice. Particularly if he cracked up the airplane trying to save one man at the risk of losing everyone's life, because he got distracted at a critical moment. However, I question whether your hypothetical male hero would have crashed. It is my belief that this accident occurred largely because First Officer Devlin's, uh, personal involvement with Captain Ashlock undermined her flying ability. I don't think this would have happened to a man."

"Dammit, Sharkley, I just got through telling you she can fly as well or better than any man."

"Except under conditions of extreme stress."

"She's had every kind of emergency tossed at her except loss of a wing and you can't simulate major structural failure. She has met every test with professional skill."

"She flunked this test—the real thing."

"So would most pilots. No CAT II equipment. An RVR reading of zero. A totally incapacitated captain who inadvertently distracted the person flying the airplane alone. How many captains, let alone copilots, could have passed *that* test?"

"How many, Captain Battles, would have gotten themselves into Miss Devlin's bind in the first place?"

"I don't know, Mr. Sharkley. And neither do you, nor anyone else except God himself."

"I'll say to you what I said to First Officer Devlin, Captain Battles.

I think I do know. The answer is damned few—and those few would be facing the same charges as Dudney Devlin."

Sharkley turned to Dudney. "Miss Devlin, I am not trying to crucify you, as Captain Battles accused me, because you're a woman. I want you to realize I have not only profound sympathy for you but a great deal of personal admiration. Both as a pilot—and as a woman. Particularly the latter. You demonstrated great courage and, more important as far as Captain Ashlock is concerned, great love. You have placed me in the awkward position of wanting to pin a medal on you while I'm simultaneously throwing the proverbial book at you. I could award that medal to a woman, Miss Devlin, and gladly. But I can't give you a medal as a pilot. When you demonstrated your love, you unfortunately gave this finest of human emotions priority over the lives of those passengers who trusted you. It is for this reason, primarily, that the Federal Aviation Administration has judged you so harshly. If you have anything further to say in your defense, any information or argument you'd care to present, any justification other than the one already presented for the decision you made, please do so at this time."

She remained silent, looking not at Sharkley but first at Battles and then at Mark, in a kind of pathetic and helpless pride that fell too far short of defiance.

"Mr. Sharkley," Ashlock said in a hoarse voice, "I'd like to say she deserves a medal not only as a woman—but as a pilot. Among the lives you say she risked was her own."

The enforcement chief, his own emotion spent, looked unhappy. "I concede that, Captain Ashlock. Does anyone else have anything to add?"

"The only thing I have to add is that she can fly for me any time, anywhere," Battles rumbled. "I think she's getting a bum rap."

"For once," Culbertson said, "ALPA agrees with management."

Feldman sighed audibly and relit his pipe. "Captain Battles, may I ask you a question before we close these proceedings?"

"Yes, sir."

"As her chief pilot, you have stated with great clarity and emphasis that you regard Miss Devlin as a highly proficient first officer, one with whom you would fly any time, anywhere, as you put it so vividly.

I'd like to ask you if you would qualify that statement. Would you fly with her any time, anywhere if you were occupying the right seat and she were in the left seat—the sacred position of command? Knowing, Captain Battles, that in this first critical test of command authority she let personal feelings override duty?"

The chief pilot's homely face clouded. He was thinking of what had been said to an eager girl, alive with hope and ambition and enthusiasm, a long, long time ago. When he had bluntly told her:

"*. . . I would not mind riding with you if I were in the left seat. I would be very much afraid to ride with you if* YOU *were in the left seat. I'd be worried about how you'd react to an emergency . . . simply because women are creatures of emotion and emotionalism has no place in a cockpit, not when the chips are down.*"

Yes, he remembered, uncomfortably, saying that. He remembered saying other things when she had asked him to define a good airline pilot. . . .

"*Simple. A good airline pilot is one who'll make a good airline captain someday. . . . Miss Devlin, we don't hire copilots. We hire prospective captains. That eliminates you—or any other woman.*"

"*I think, Captain Battles, that judgment requires some justification.*"

"*Very well. Suppose we took you on. Let's assume you sail through ground school and flight training. You're a qualified first officer. For all I know, you may even be a damned fine first officer. So good, in fact, that sooner or later you'll be eligible for that fourth stripe. And the sun will set in the east before I upgrade a woman to captain. . . .*"

Then, conviction had wrestled with admiration. Now, conscience was struggling with compassion. His mouth opened just a sliver before Dudney's voice gagged it.

"Just a minute, Captain Battles, you don't have to answer. Mr. Sharkley, I would like to say something." She hesitated, feeling five pairs of eyes searching her face, pale but as if frozen in icy composure. "First, I'd like to thank Captain Battles for his faith in me, and his defense of my actions. I want to say to him publicly that flying for Trans-Coastal this past year and a half has been the happiest time of my life. I am truly, desperately sorry that I let him down. I want you to know, Mr. Sharkley, and you, too, Mr. Feldman, that whatever mistakes were committed on Flight 378 stemmed from the weaknesses of an individual pilot, not through any failings of the instructors and the many captains who taught me not only airline flying but a way of life. I let them down too.

"I have heard much today concerning weaknesses to which I referred. Those weaknesses have been described as purely feminine, including the final error that caused the crash. That error I don't condone, Mr. Sharkley, although I humbly submit that a fair-sized minority of pilots might have been as easily distracted as I. This mistake was the product of unfavorable odds and my own inexperience. I cannot blame the FAA for wanting to punish me because I made this mistake. It is obvious, however, that the revocation action was directed not so much to my failures in flying proficiency as to the decision which made those failures almost inevitable. And in fairness to my airline, to the FAA, to my superiors and to my fellow pilots, including Captain Ashlock, I must plead guilty—"

"Just a minute, Dudney," Culbertson started to protest.

"No," Dudney ruled. "I'd like to finish. Please. I think I have weighed the evidence more objectively, more coherently than even Mr. Sharkley could. I agree I did not act with the sense of responsibility, judgment and care expected of an airline pilot. I think it is only too obvious that I almost killed more than ninety human beings to save the life of one human being." She looked at Mark as she said this, and tears filled her eyes. "As I understand it, Mr. Sharkley, even if you deny this appeal, I still have the right to appeal further to the National Transportation Safety Board. Am I correct?"

Sharkley nodded, unable to connect his tongue with his brain.

"Then I'd like to advise you, sir, I have no intention of proceeding with any more appeals. I'll simply ask you for understanding, fairness and perhaps a little bit of pity for one to whom flying has been her whole life."

"This, Miss Devlin," Sharkley said in a low, choked voice, "you already have earned in enormous measure."

"Thank you. No, Tom, there's nothing more you can say which will accomplish anything except dragged-out torture for me. I would like to tell all of you—my allies as well as my opponents, so to speak—why I do not wish to offer any further defense. This decision may appear impulsive, as the one I made on Flight 378 was impulsive. It is not, however. I am merely confessing out loud what I have been confessing to myself for many days. I *am* unworthy of that priceless certificate, Mr. Sharkley. Because I know that if I were faced with exactly the same circumstances again I would do exactly the same thing. In simplest terms, I would give priority to saving one life, that single life so precious to me, at the possible expense of all others. So long as I admit this to myself and to you, there can be no question that I am unqualified to be an airline pilot.

"But let me add this very important point. I said *I* am unqualified. Not in the sense that I cannot fly as competently as anyone else. Not even in the sense that I could not continue to fly for Trans-Coastal as a first officer. I could. Captain Battles knows it and so, I suspect, does Mr. Sharkley. But Mr. Feldman put his finger on the real reason for disqualification—my ability to command. No one should continue flying for an airline as a copilot if he does not expect—no, desire as well as expect—to become a captain. I am disqualifying myself in this respect for the reason I've given. I *was* captain of Flight 378. As a captain, I made the wrong decision. Yet it is the same decision I would make if I had to do it all over again.

"Captain Battles, Mr. Sharkley—I said before that this was and is my vital weakness. Feminine, yes. But a weakness of one individual woman, not necessarily all women. I have set a precedent as the country's first woman airline pilot. I implore you not to regard the events of November 8 as another kind of precedent, one that automatically stamps *all* women as untrustworthy airline pilots, as poor prospects for the fourth stripe. You found *me* wanting. Don't assume that you would find every woman pilot vulnerable enough to make the same choice I did. Give each of them the same break you gave me—for which I will always be eternally grateful. And not a little ashamed. Not for what I did, because I'd do it again. But for failing as a pilot even as I succeeded as a woman."

She stopped, drained of all resistance, resentment and emotion. With a feeling of immense weariness, she surveyed the solemn, tense faces of the five men. On them she saw etched admiration, awe and the pity she knew could not help her.

She turned over her page of triumph and tragedy.

"Let's go home, Mark," Dudney Devlin said.

Mr. Horace Studebaker entered his office on another Monday morning, whistling the University of Southern California fight song with martial fervor if slightly off tune.

"Good morning, good morning," he beamed in the direction of the secretarial desks.

Miss Martinez took advantage of his obvious good humor to exercise her prerogative of satisfying female curiosity—and womanly respect for romance.

"How was the wedding Saturday, Mr. Studebaker?" she inquired.

"A most happy occasion," he enthused. "Dudney made a beautiful bride. Captain Callahan gave her away—I think it was the first time in his life he went more than an hour without using one cuss word. Cathy Henderson and Del Fitzgerald were the bridesmaids and Janet Silvanius was the matron of honor. They all looked splendid, Mary, absolutely splendid. But Dudney was the most beautiful of them all. I really think she's happy."

"Was it a big wedding?" Miss Martinez wanted to know. "Who else was there?"

"Oh, Mr. Berlin. Mr. Silvanius, of course. Lord knows how many pilots—Dudney's whole class, among others. John Battles. I honestly don't know how we operated the airline Saturday. The church looked like our terminal on a Friday night."

The next question from his secretary was inevitable. "Where are they going on their honeymoon?"

"England, I believe. And Captain Battles' wedding gift was quite original. Very original. Not his real gift, of course. More of a little surprise. He told Dudney that when she and Captain Ashlock get back from the honeymoon she's going to go to work for Art Prentice in Simulator Training. A very happy ending, Miss Martinez. *Very* happy."

"That's nice," Miss Martinez said wistfully, but Studebaker didn't hear her. He had just opened the first letter in the morning mail, and his secretary heard him gurgle in dismay.

The letter he was examining was an application blank from an exceptionally well qualified pilot applicant. It was signed (Miss) Tracy Welling.

"Oh hell," said Mr. Studebaker, "Mary, get me Jason Silvanius."

ACKNOWLEDGMENTS

I want to express my thanks to Ray Silvius, Vice President-Public Relations of Western Air Lines, and the entire Training Department of this carrier for affording me the privilege of attending Boeing 737 ground and flight school as part of the research for this novel. While in some ways Western resembles Trans-Coastal for reasons of establishing authenticity, I offer to Ray; Western's instructors; Captains Mark Johnson and Smitty Dent, and the members of "my class," not only gratitude but assurances that the characters portrayed herein are products of a writer's imagination.

My deep appreciation to Captain Sam Huntington of United Air Lines for his patient assistance in helping me tell the story of Dudney Devlin's last flight. Any technical errors are to be blamed on the author, not this cockpit professional and treasured friend. The same accolade belongs to Doctors W. Luther Hall and Philip Philbin and to Dennis Feldman of the FAA, whose aid is gratefully acknowledged.

My appreciation, also, to Patricia Gray for the long hours spent on manuscript typing; to Walter Bradbury of Doubleday for his understanding support and editing skill; to countless airline friends for supplying so much invaluable background; and, finally, to Priscilla Arone Serling for proving once more that airline stewardesses make wonderful wives.

Robert J. Serling
Bethesda, Maryland